THE CURSE

Breath of Yesterday

The Curse

Breath of Yesterday

Emily Bold

Translated by Katja Bell

The Curse: Breath of Yesterday was first published in 2012 by Emily Bold as *The Curse – Im Schatten der Schwestern*. Translated from German by Katja Bell. Published in English by Skyscape in 2014.

Published by Skyscape, New York

www.apub.com

ISBN-13: 9781477847145
ISBN-10: 1477847146

Library of Congress Cataloging-in-Publication Data available upon request.

Printed in the United States of America

For my family who makes me strong,
even when I feel weak.

Prologue

Scotland, February 1740

Everyone at Castle Galthair was in high spirits. Clan Stuart had gathered to celebrate Imbolc, the festival of rebirth and the return of the light. The tables in the Great Hall were decked with heather, celandine, and laurel branches, whose earthy scents fused with the aroma of freshly baked bannock bread. Even the maids attended to their tasks with smiles today—for the festivities also signaled the day that the laird traditionally paid them for the past year's work.

Nathaira Stuart didn't share in her servants' joyful anticipation. After all, she was the one tasked with watching over the preparations and getting the guest chambers ready. Not a moment ago one of the kitchen hands had inconvenienced her by hurting his arm on the bread oven. As if she had nothing better to do than to look after clumsy little butterfingers! Fortunately, the boy was now patched up and installed in the kitchen with a soothing cup of milk, finally allowing Nathaira a precious moment to herself. She swung back the shiny black braid that reached all the way to her hips; then she smoothed her emerald-colored dress. Silver embroidery on the front of her dress emphasized her small waist, but that remained hidden under an apron while she was on duty. She now took off the apron and handed it to one of the kitchen maids.

"I wish no more trouble from here on. You all know what is expected of you. If you want your pay, you had better not disappoint my father."

The girls curtsied deeply as Nathaira gracefully disappeared from the servants' realm and slipped back into her own world.

The stress and the heat had gotten to her, so she stepped into the castle yard and raised her face up toward the sun. While the wind dried her sweat, she enjoyed the feeling of leaving winter behind. Just the day before—as though the sky itself wanted to join the festivities—it had stopped snowing, and the heavy cloud cover that had weighed on them for two full months had finally opened up. The castle courtyard was still blanketed in snow, and the first rays of sunshine made it sparkle and glitter as if made of countless diamonds. Icicles hung like thin crystal blades from the beams supporting the parapet wall.

The startled cries of several men prompted Nathaira to look up. She couldn't help but smile when she noticed a snow avalanche tumbling from the top of the tower, almost burying the handful of warriors beneath it. She stretched her neck to better see the men who had now burst into laughter.

Sean McLean was brushing snow off his boots, and he—by all appearances—had been the intended victim of the little prank. Nathaira recognized her brother Cathal among the men. His best friend, Blair McLean, was there, too, enjoying a laugh with Sean, his younger brother. But Nathaira didn't pay much notice to them.

Instead, she fixed her gaze on the last man within the group—a blond giant whose size alone sent pleasant shivers down her spine. His unruly flaxen hair blew in the wind, and his muscular upper arms were naked under a vest of leather and fur. The bone-chilling cold didn't seem to bother him, as he was laughing—a sound that made it hard for Nathaira to breathe. As if feeling Nathaira's presence, he turned around and looked her straight in the eye. He tilted his head in a silent greeting and elbowed Sean. The men stuck their heads together and talked. Upon separating, they both drew their swords.

Nathaira squinted, blinded by both the sun's reflection on the snow and the glistening sword blades. What were those two up to?

Muscles and tendons tensed as they took combat positions. Then a whole band of men came running, and the stable boy used his cap to collect the first bets on the fight's outcome. Sean and the blond giant circled each other like beasts of prey, sounding out each other's strengths and weaknesses before the fight even started. Even the guards on the parapet wall stuck out their heads and cheered them on.

In Sean he faced a skilled fighter and master swordsman, yet the stranger with undeniably Nordic ancestry smiled calmly. Cathal stepped between the two men, talking, but the giant barely seemed to listen as he gazed unblinkingly at Nathaira. When Cathal left the circle, Sean widened his stance and thrust his blade upward. The Nordic stranger still didn't look but instead raised his eyebrows and winked at her before nonchalantly fending off the downthrust of the attacking blade. He then went on the offense, and it seemed clear who would emerge the winner. His blows came quickly, with great precision and a strength that kept driving Sean farther and farther back even as he skillfully dodged the attacks. It was pure pleasure just to watch this unknown warrior. Like a dancer he elegantly pursued his opponent, warding off his attacks with a slight turn to the side before immediately proceeding to the next blow. Snow crunched under boots; metal blades clunked together.

Nathaira shivered from the cold but couldn't bring herself to turn her back on the performance. The Norseman mesmerized her. Just at that moment, the castle wall cut off Sean's retreat, but he managed to clear space for himself underneath the sword from above with a swift sweep from below. He threw himself under the next oncoming blow and slid on icy ground underneath his opponent's grasp and over to the other side. He leapt to his feet behind the giant's back and suddenly was at a clear advantage.

The stranger, seeing the blade aimed at his throat, turned and lifted his head to give Nathaira a triumphant smile—as if he had just won the fight. Slowly he lifted his weapon, slid it back into the leather sheath on his back, and raised his hands in resignation.

Sean laughed, moved in closer, and lowered his blade. Then his seemingly defeated opponent kicked a load of snow into his face. This moment of inattention was Sean's downfall. The blond giant leapt up and grabbed a parapet beam, swinging himself forward and up enough to kick Sean's sword out of his hands before landing on his knees on top of the parapet. In one fluid move he pulled his sword from its sheath and threw himself at a startled Sean, whose skull he could easily have split in two with one blow. He crashed into Sean's chest, landed, and drove his blade into a pile of snow.

Nathaira held her breath as the stranger's eyes met hers, offering his triumph as a gift. It was as though in that moment he'd sworn an oath to honor her with all his strength if only she'd let him.

The crimson in her cheeks no longer stemmed from the heat in the kitchen but from the fire this man had stirred in her.

She blinked, and the magic moment was gone. The stranger rose, pulled Sean to his feet, and went to collect his bets. Amid the cheering crowd of onlookers, Nathaira managed to escape undetected back into the Great Hall.

Her heart was pounding, and she kneaded her trembling hands. Who was this man? Maybe the new liegeman Cathal had told her about? Alasdair Buchanan, the Viking outlaw who had left his home and joined Grant's men? The Nordic ancestry of the stranger was undeniable, and Nathaira wondered what he must have done to be made an outlaw.

Chapter 1

Delaware, Present-Day October

One look into his eyes and I understood.

I gave him a conspiratorial wink and, completely spellbound, watched how he casually strolled past the dancing partygoers, past the torches illuminating the path along the lakeshore, and up to the patio door—only to disappear inside with an auspicious smile.

Luckily I wasn't drinking hard liquor, because the heat rising inside me could have ignited the alcohol in my glass. As my excitement grew, all I could do was force myself to a laugh with the chatty, cheerful group of friends by my side. And although I tried my hardest to seem casual and relaxed, my best friend, Kim Fryer, noticed that I was preoccupied.

"Hey, Sam, you okay?" she asked, gently pulling away from the arms of her boyfriend, Justin Summers.

I felt like she had just caught me red-handed. Hard to believe that Kim knew me so well that not even the smallest of my emotions escaped her attention, not even at a party.

"Sure! I just wanted to go inside for a bit. Put some more bottles on ice and such," I said, pointing back at the house.

"Jeez, it's your birthday! You don't have to do any of that stuff. You stay here—I'll take care of it," she offered.

"No, no, that's all right. I need a breather anyway. Pretty cool party, huh?"

In truth, I was actually surprised that so many people had made their way to the lake to celebrate my eighteenth birthday.

My popularity seemed to have increased significantly since that thing that happened at South Dupont Boulevard.

Ryan Baker and Justin Summers had of course told everyone what had happened there. And every time the story was retold, someone exaggerated and added to it. Except . . . the truth itself was missing from their story, because nobody would have believed it.

Nathaira Stuart, a Scottish witch, had tried to kill me. *That* sure was something nobody knew, because who'd have guessed that I would fall in love during a student-exchange trip to Scotland? And with a boy whose entire family had been living under a 270-year-old curse that damned them all to an eternal life without feelings or emotions.

Who'd have guessed that I—of all people—carried the power to break this curse, just because the blood of the Camerons runs through my veins? Clan Cameron was not supposed to have survived, because Payton McLean's clan had tried its best to murder every single one of my ancestors. It was only thanks to Vanora, another witch, that the plan had failed. And surely nobody would have thought it possible that, in the end, Nathaira Stuart would break Vanora's curse by making Payton choose love and want to give his life for me.

All of this seemed so unbelievable that Ryan's and Justin's exaggerations didn't even come close to what had really happened.

Still, the shoot-out at the motel, which concluded this blood-soaked drama, had been the number-one topic over the past few weeks, and, in my schoolmates' eyes, I had become as cool as Lara Croft. Since that day, even Lisa and her gang of cheerleaders had vied for my friendship and had gone so far as to organize a birthday party for me. Not too long ago this would have made me incredibly happy, but right now I was only interested in one person, and he was waiting for me in the house.

With an armful of empty bottles and plastic cups, I finally managed to escape inside. I gave the door a gentle push, and fear washed over me in the sudden silence. I put down the cups and bottles, and with palms sweaty from excitement, I wiped my hands on my pants. In this kid-free zone you could barely hear the cheerful partygoers and music. I nervously pushed my hair behind my ears and tugged on my shirt.

Then I took a deep breath and whispered with quivering lips, "Payton?"

"And I was worried you had stood me up."

He was leaning in the doorway, arms casually folded across his chest. In the weak glow of the party lights, all I could make out was his outline—and the sparkle in his eyes that were full of affection and anticipation. Magic seemed to draw me to him, and when his arms closed around me and he enchanted me with a gentle kiss, I knew: This night would be our night.

~

Somehow we were suddenly in my bedroom. I leaned against the door, my lips swollen from Payton's passionate kisses. He came at me strong and pantherlike, putting his hands against the door on either side of me and leaning in for another kiss. Then he withdrew his mouth and looked me deep in the eyes as he slowly turned the door key with a small grating sound—locking out the rest of the world.

I was scared. I had waited for him for so long, had wanted this to happen forever, but now all I could do was tremble with nervous excitement. I gave him a bashful smile but quickly closed my eyes so he wouldn't notice my insecurities.

"Sam?" Payton whispered into my ear. "Relax, *mo luaidh.*"

He knew how much I liked this Gaelic term of endearment, and I started feeling calmer. There was no need to be scared. Nothing bad would ever happen to me when I was in Payton's arms, of that I was sure.

"Tha gràdh agam ort," I said, confessing my love to him. That was about the extent of my Gaelic, so I wrapped my arms around his back and pulled him closer. I enjoyed the feel of his strong, muscular body snuggling against mine. After all, it was Vanora's curse that had prevented us from being close to each other without him suffering excruciating pain. Payton's hands trembled, too, as he slowly explored the skin under my shirt. I giggled.

"What is it?" he asked, stopping to caress my waist.

"Hmm, nothing. Your hands are shaking."

"So are yours," he whispered into my neck, only to follow up with a flood of kisses all the way down to my collarbone.

I closed my eyes and enjoyed that delicious feeling slowly awakening inside me.

"Yes, I know, but that's different. You . . . I mean . . ." Oh God, it was embarrassing enough to talk about it—how was I ever going to actually *do* it?

"Shhh," he said, taking a step back to unbutton his shirt. "Don't forget that I was only sixteen years old at the time," he explained, throwing his shirt over the back of a chair. I couldn't help but admire his athletic figure, even though I found the small white bandage under his heart distracting.

"But you've done it before—and I haven't!" I managed to squeeze out.

"*Mo luaidh,* that was a long time ago. Long before I lost all feeling under Vanora's curse. So you see, it doesn't count at all anymore," he said, laughing and pulling me back into his arms.

And it was true: It didn't matter at all after our next kiss. Nothing mattered but him and me—and our night full of love.

Chapter 2

Dr. Lippert, please report to the laboratory. Dr. Lippert, please report to the laboratory," yelled the hospital loudspeaker. The physician, who was about to wrap up his forty-eight-hour shift, snorted as the call echoed through the hallway. Exhausted, he rubbed his red-rimmed eyes. Before he could allow himself a good night's sleep, he needed to finish one final operation report. And now this. Gnashing his teeth, he slipped the ballpoint pen back into the breast pocket of his hospital lab coat and made his way to the basement.

~

"Hey, Frank, you called?" he said as he entered Dr. Frank Tillman's laboratory. The automatic sliding door closed behind him—something that made him feel a little claustrophobic. He always hated coming down here. But the concerned look on Tillman's face—clearly noticeable despite the hairnet and mouth guard—demanded his full attention.

"Right. Thanks for coming right away."

Tillman pointed to a cardboard box beside the sink and prompted Lippert to put on a mouth guard himself.

Rubbing sanitizer into his hands, Lippert stepped over to his colleague's side and peered at the test tubes and petri dishes Frank was working on.

"So. What is it?"

"No idea. That's just it. I was hoping to get your opinion."

And with that, Frank thrust a printout with test results into Lippert's hands and pushed the test tube rack and one of the petri dishes over to him.

With just one look at the numbers on the printout, Lippert frowned.

"Did you double-check these?" he asked, lifting the rack and holding it up to the fluorescent lights overhead. He pulled out one of the narrow test tubes and shook it to stir up the dark, flaky deposit.

"Twice even. What *is* that stuff?" Tillman asked.

"No idea. Never seen it before. Is it possible that the blood sample got contaminated?" Lippert offered.

"With what, though? What would cause such changes to a cell?"

"Hmm. I don't know."

Lippert, who didn't feel like adding extra overtime to his already long and arduous shift, looked at his watch. He then closed the patient file, glanced at the name, and made a suggestion. "Listen, you check these numbers one last time. If the results are confirmed, I'll call the patient back in, just in case. If the numbers are right—which I think is impossible—I'd be surprised he hasn't come back in himself."

Tillman nodded and walked over to the refrigerator where the blood samples were stored. "If the numbers are right, then he's beyond help anyway," he quipped.

"Probably, but I still can't think of an explanation. If I recall correctly, he was in perfect shape when he was discharged two weeks ago."

"Is it possible that he got an infection from the stab wound that you guys treated?"

Lippert was already washing and disinfecting his hands. He was off duty now and couldn't get out of there fast enough. Let Frank check the numbers once more. In his own expert opinion—and after all, he was an experienced physician—the problem had to do with the laboratory and not the patient himself.

"It's possible, but I doubt it. Such damage to cells caused by an infection . . . is unlikely. Look, I have to go. Send the results up to my office when you have them. Then we'll talk again."

With a quick good-bye, Lippert left the lab, first for his op report and then for the well-deserved end of his shift.

By the time he sped away in his Camaro an hour later, his tired mind had banned any thoughts about patient McLean's strange blood work.

Chapter 3

I opened my eyes.

The molded ceiling in my bedroom looked like it had since my childhood, but I had changed. I was no longer that little girl who admired the pretty roses on her bed and imagined what it would be like to marry a prince.

I was eighteen years old. I had lived through indescribable things during my visit to Scotland. And I had to come to terms with the fact that for centuries my own family's history was inextricably linked to Payton's.

Fate had brought us together to right a past wrong and to finally allow love to claim victory over hatred.

Vanora's curse caused Payton McLean to suffer terrible pain every time we were together. Although he realized that I carried within me the blood of the Camerons—the blood of his enemies—he fell in love, and his feelings for me softened the curse and brought him back to life. His love for me was strong enough to defy even death. He would have died for me—and he almost had died from a stab wound to the heart.

And now he was lying beside me. His breathing was regular, so I knew he was still asleep. I gently caressed the bandage. I could feel his heartbeat. Once during the weeks in the hospital, I had seen the wound that Nathaira had inflicted. She had wanted to stab *me* with her dagger. She had wanted me dead, but she lost, and her hatred and anger died with her.

I could barely believe my luck. The coolest boy in the world with a small crescent-shaped scar on his chin and the most intense look in his eyes, a look strong enough to turn my legs into Jell-O: That boy was my best friend and boyfriend all rolled into one.

I was still staring at him when Payton woke up with a start, grabbing his head and groaning.

"Good morning," I whispered, fully in love—but I didn't get a reply.

Payton swung his legs around and sat upright on the edge of the bed. He held his head and mumbled something in Gaelic.

I clambered up next to him, caressing his back.

"Payton, are you okay? Is the wound hurting?"

"*Ifrinn!* No. Don't worry, everything's all right."

"You're crazy! I can see you're not well. What's the matter?"

It made me angry that he thought he needed to play the bulletproof Highlander in front of me. His smile seemed forced.

"Hmm, maybe last night was a bit much. I had no idea how insatiable you could be, my sweet little Sam."

I knew that he was only trying to change the subject, but I still blushed at his words.

"As if!" I protested. "Don't blame me if you're not feeling too hot."

He seemed to be feeling better already, because he got up and started picking up his clothes. That was a sensible thing to do since it was almost eight o'clock. In an hour, Kim would descend on the house with her "party evidence removal team" to clear away as much of the mess as possible before my parents returned. Especially given the most recent events—most of which they luckily knew only little about—I thought it was cool on their part to leave me the house for my birthday party. But in return they had requested that everything be back in its place by noon. Which was what we needed to focus on right now.

~

I was loading the rest of the glasses into the dishwasher when Sean dropped in through the back door. Content to see that his help was no longer needed, he slumped into an armchair.

"You guys have been busy this morning." He nodded approvingly.

"Well, you could have come a bit earlier and helped us pick up." I couldn't help giving a snap reply when it was obviously on purpose that he only turned up now. "Kim and the others have already left. We're as good as done."

"Sure, sure, I could have, but then I didn't want to," he quipped, giving me a mischievous wink that charmed a smile out of me.

"Where's the little guy?" he asked jokingly. Even though Payton was a few years younger than Sean, the brothers were both of considerable height.

I used my elbow to point at the stairway while I continued cleaning the big chili pot.

"Upstairs. He's taking the fairy lights up to the attic and should be back in a minute."

"Good, because now that he's feeling better, I wanted to drive up to Ashley Bennett's for a couple of days."

"Really? I had no idea you guys were getting serious."

Sean shrugged. "Yeah, well, I thought it was only this strange situation that had brought us closer together, but we're getting along really well. We call each other every day. To be honest, I miss her."

I couldn't really relate to someone missing Cousin Ashley. After all, her annual visit during the summer holidays was one of the main reasons I'd wanted to go on that student-exchange trip to Scotland in the first place. I didn't like having to share my bedroom every single summer.

But by now Ashley and I were getting on pretty well. It was all my fault that she'd been dragged into this crazy story with the curse. Payton's friends, who were all under the curse, had kidnapped Ashley because they thought that the blood of the Camerons was running through her veins, too, which wasn't true. Sean had managed to avert the worst from happening. When he met Ashley, the curse in him had already weakened, and in my mind that was why he was blinded by her beauty. After all those years he had spent without feelings or emotions, any woman probably could have won his heart.

But maybe I was wrong, because Sean seemed to truly mean what he said.

"Don't worry, I'll look after Payton. The wound seems to be healing well."

For a split second I thought I saw Sean's eyes darken as if he were hiding something from me, but a moment later I was sure I had only imagined it.

Footsteps coming down the stairway announced Payton's return from the attic, and immediately my heart beat faster. After last night I longed for him even more than during the whole time we were separated because of the curse. A few words of swearing in Gaelic followed by a loud rumble jolted me from my daydream.

Before I could even react, Sean had jumped up and rushed into the hallway. I let the big chili pot slide back into the sink and hurried after him.

Payton lay motionless at the foot of the stairwell. His brother knelt beside him, tearing open his shirt and checking his wound.

I froze in helpless shock while Sean carefully lifted the bandage on Payton's chest. I noticed his worried face as he gingerly traced the length of the stitches, and I saw his relief when he realized that the stab wound hadn't reopened.

"*Daingead!* How handy it was to be invulnerable," he cursed, then added with a whisper and a hint of regret, "And immortal."

Cautiously, I knelt beside my love and caressed his forehead. He was pale, his face distorted with pain. Slowly his eyelids started fluttering, and he opened them with a groan. I firmly pressed him down with the flat of my hand.

"Payton, stay still, *mo luaidh.*"

Sean stood up in obvious relief at the sight of his little brother moving. He shook his head in mock outrage.

"Brother, my brother. Seems to me you can't hold your liquor anymore. How much exactly did you have to drink last night? You're staggering around like a drunk person."

"He wasn't drinking at all last night," I explained. The fact that Payton wasn't even trying to get up had me worried again. He really was in a bad way.

"Could you try to lie on the couch? Maybe we should get you to the hospital. You've been feeling miserable since this morning."

"No, no, I'm all right," dismissed Payton, struggling to his feet. I could feel Sean's skeptical eyes on my back as I dragged Payton to the couch.

"Ciod tha uait?" Sean asked.

I gave him a puzzled look. Why would he speak Gaelic? Was he trying to hide something from me? I didn't have time to dwell on it. Payton asked for a glass of water, and I hurried into the kitchen, glad to be of use and forget about my worries.

When I returned, the brothers were engaged in a heated debate. I understood very little Gaelic, and what I heard just sounded like two dogs barking at each other. Still, I could tell that for once they weren't in complete agreement.

"What's the matter? What are you talking about?" I inquired. But both of them ignored me.

They flashed their eyes at each other angrily, until Payton held out his hand and dragged me down to the couch with him. He quickly kissed me on the lips and gave his brother a warning stare. Sean turned away sullenly.

My mood started to sour. Did these two really think they could get away with jerking me around? Something was up—I was sure of it—and with all the authority I could muster, I demanded they tell me what it was.

"You two are going to tell me right now what's going on! Why are you being so secretive?" I asked.

Sean completely ignored me, inspecting the tips of his shoes instead. Payton remained doggedly silent, too. If there was anything I had learned from these pigheaded Scots during the past couple of weeks, it was that I would never emerge the winner in an argument. Furiously, I jumped up and slammed the kitchen door behind me. This helped soothe my anger. Probably, I admitted to myself, I was only irritated because I was so very worried about Payton when in fact he seemed perfectly all right. At least that was what I thought when I heard a heated curse in Gaelic coming from the living room, where he continued arguing with Sean. Feeling mellower already, I took out the rest of my anger on the stupid chili pot.

~

Payton stared angry holes into the door that had just slammed shut behind Sam. Sean didn't say a word but fixed his gaze on his brother.

Finally, Payton rubbed his hands over his face as if to wash away the horror that had taken ahold of him.

"Are you sure?" he asked in quiet disbelief.

"No, I'm not. But I know what I've heard."

"How is it possible that she has the power to do this?" Payton said.

"Don't forget who Nathaira was! Maybe she carried her mother's strength inside her. And remember that her mother was powerful enough to put all of us under a curse for two hundred and seventy years!"

"How come you never told me this?"

Sean couldn't take Payton's accusing eyes any longer, and he sank into the armchair.

"I didn't want to believe it at first. When she died, I thought the curse had died with her. After all, you survived her attack and the surgery, too. And you seemed to be getting better every day."

"Oh, so that's when you thought it wasn't worth mentioning that this cursed witch Nathaira—the one who killed our brother Kyle, the one who tried to kill Sam, and the one who didn't even shy away from driving her *sgian dhu* into my chest—that she tried to curse me with her dying breath?" Payton's voice was now a scream. "Is that what you thought, Sean? That it wasn't important enough to mention?"

"Listen, you'd been stabbed, I didn't want to upset you, and . . ." Sean shrugged helplessly, but Payton wasn't looking for an explanation.

"And now? What do I do now? What's going to happen to me?"

"I don't know, Brother, but I swear I'm not going to let you die," Sean reassured him, knitting his brow as he frantically worked on a solution.

"She spoke the curse. I didn't understand every single word of it, but she said something about it being a mistake to let Sam go and that—because you were prepared to die for her—you must die for her now."

"Let Sam go? What did she mean by that?"

"That's just it. I thought she was babbling, which is why I didn't really take it seriously. I guess I underestimated how full of hatred and resentment she was."

Payton saw that remembering the events at South Dupont Boulevard made Sean's skin crawl. Nathaira had tried to stop the curse from being further weakened by Sam, but the moment she felt cornered, she had admitted to murdering their little brother Kyle *and* her own stepmother. He'd rather forget the excruciating pain that her confessions had caused, forget everything that had happened there—even though his selfless act of standing up for Samantha had ended the curse that had weighed on them all for almost three centuries.

"If I have to die for saving Sam's life, then I don't regret what I did. If that was what Nathaira wanted to achieve, she shouldn't have bothered. I would do it all over again, knowing what I know about her curse—except, this time around I would first cut her throat!"

"I'm sure that was exactly her intention. Can you imagine how much guilt and blame that would put on Sam? You were to die because she survived. . . . You think Sam can handle it?"

Payton shook his head. He hadn't even thought that far ahead. Sam would blame herself, and it would surely destroy her life.

"We can never tell her. She must never know!" he implored.

"And how do you imagine we do that? Do you want to stick it out and wait for Nathaira's curse to come true?" Sean inquired. "I told you all of this because there must be a way to save you!"

"Save me?"

What could possibly save him? That would be like winning the lottery twice in a row.

"I don't know, but up until recently, we didn't even think it possible to break Vanora's curse, remember? I mean, we have to try."

"But how?" Payton asked, the anxiety visibly sapping his energy. He felt wobbly and weak. And he was afraid. He didn't want to die or for Nathaira to win from beyond the grave. He buried his face in his hands and took a deep breath. Whatever Sean would suggest they do, Payton would agree to it. He would put up another fight this time around. Only this time he didn't know where his strength would come from.

"I thought maybe we could find something in Nathaira's papers. After all, she was always preoccupied with this sort of stuff," Sean suggested.

"Hmm, or maybe this Roy Leary guy might help me," Payton said, thinking out loud.

"Roy who?"

"You don't know him. I don't know all that much about him, either, but he seemed to know a hell of a lot about Vanora and us. It can't hurt to ask him."

"Very well. Either way, we had better get back to Scotland as quickly as possible. I'll go pack our bags. You wrap things up here and then follow me to the motel so we can leave."

"Wrap things up? What exactly do you want me to tell Sam without her blaming herself?"

"Tell her nothing. If she finds out that you're not doing well, she won't let you return to Scotland by yourself. But if she comes with us, she'll either see you die or interfere with our investigations. Unless we want her to find out what role she actually plays in this. . . .”

“But I can’t just leave her!”

“Do whatever you think is right. But for someone her age, I think it’s easier to get over someone who leaves you than to blame yourself forever for the death of someone you love.” With that, Sean turned around and left the way he had come, out the back door.

For a good while afterward, Payton sat motionless. Then, one last time, he went upstairs to the bedroom where he had made love to his beloved Sam for the first time.

~

Washing the dishes really did have a soothing effect on me. Brothers sometimes had their secrets, and I tried to convince myself that this was completely normal. After all, I would never share any of Kim’s personal stuff with the boys, and so Payton was surely entitled to a bit of privacy, too.

I was so sympathetic and tried to spread a cheerful mood for the next hour or so, but Payton still seemed dejected and crestfallen. Somehow he was miles away from me.

“What’s wrong? You didn’t hurt yourself when you fell down the stairs, did you?” I probed.

“Hmm? Did you say something?”

“Payton, what are you thinking about right now?”

He pulled me into his lap and wrapped his arms around my hips. And with his velvety voice—which had enthralled me ever since our first meeting at the Glenfinnan Monument—he whispered into my ear. “*Mo luaidh,* all I think about is you—every minute of every day.”

"Aw, you're cute. Maybe I'll keep you," I jested before quickly getting up and glancing at my watch. My parents would be back soon. They weren't against my relationship with Payton, but they weren't exactly overjoyed, either. After all, I had gotten mixed up in a shoot-out and had almost fallen to my death from the fourth floor of a motel. Up to a point, I could even understand their skepticism, although none of it was Payton's fault, of course.

Anyway, they would probably arrive any minute now. I wanted to avoid a confrontation, so I pulled him with me to the front door.

"This is very hard for me, you wicked, wicked Scotsman, but I'm afraid you have to leave."

I couldn't entirely read his expression. He was as closed off now as he was when Vanora's immortality curse ruled his life. Yet I detected an unspeakable sadness as he pulled me close and looked deep into my eyes.

"You're right," he said. "It's time for me to leave."

Why did this give me the shivers? Why did I suddenly feel so funny? I withdrew from his arms and gave him a long, questioning look. But his eyes were as deep and bottomless as the depths of a Scottish loch.

I got up on tiptoes to kiss him good-bye, but he pushed me away as if wanting to memorize my face.

"Sam, I . . . I have to go. *Tha gràdh agam ort,*" he whispered against my lips, and every single word was like a caress.

"I love you, too," I told him.

He walked along the garden path but stopped after only a few yards. He came back, his face contorted with pain.

"Sam, I can't leave without kissing you one last time."

It sounded almost like an apology, but I wouldn't have complained if he'd wanted to kiss me good-bye a thousand more times. Who would have thought that being kissed could feel so amazing?

His kiss was soft and tender. I felt his deep, endless love, which left me floating on cloud nine long after he was gone.

Chapter 4

Scotland, November 1740

Vanora had done her deed. The curse was spoken. One final, blazing lightning flash streaked across the dark night sky. A moment later the winds died down, and the clouds disappeared as quickly as they had gathered. Motionless, the old woman stood atop the mountain peak and looked down at the castle.

She knew about her fate. She knew about her approaching death—a death her own daughter would cause—and yet she felt no fear. After all these years, she would finally see her daughter, Nathaira—the child that Grant Stuart had so cruelly taken away from her.

The men on horseback bore down on her, getting ever closer. A sense of tranquility descended upon Vanora. She had saved the baby: Muireall Cameron was alive. And so tonight the Stuarts' coldhearted plan to kill all of the Camerons had failed.

Vanora had little time left in this world, but for one last moment she turned away from her relentlessly approaching fate and scanned the dark hills behind her for the young woman who would be the beginning and the end of this story, the young woman whose destiny was to forever change the history of the two enemy clans, the young woman who was without guilt, yet guilty nevertheless.

Vanora now sensed that very girl standing behind her. A horrified scream escaped her throat but was carried away by the wind, unheard. She did not belong here. But nobody escapes his destiny.

That thought comforted Vanora, and with peace in her heart she welcomed her daughter's death-bringing dagger.

She barely felt the pain in her chest as she reached for the dark-haired girl's blood-soaked hands. With a mother's pride, she recognized the similarities she shared with her beautiful murderess: the bright, ethereal skin of the Fair witches; the high cheekbones; and the natural force they carried within themselves. Vanora smiled at the thought of how Grant must fear his own daughter, just as he had feared her. For even though he had forced himself on her for so many nights, she had always felt that he was afraid of her powers.

"Sguir, mo nighean. Mo gràdh ort."

Her words were barely more than a whisper. She kissed her daughter's hands in forgiveness. Then her spirit left her body and Vanora was gone.

Chapter 5

Castle Burragh, Scotland; Present-Day October

I had surely lost my mind. It was only now, watching the taxi that had brought me here drive away, that the thought occurred to me.

During my long transatlantic flight I'd started having doubts about this crazy endeavor. But now that I was standing here on the side of some road in rural Scotland, with nothing more than a suitcase in my hand—just like I had a year ago—I had to allow for the possibility that I was suffering from a medical condition that seriously impaired my cognitive abilities. There was no other reasonable explanation for my coming here.

I tried to focus on all the right reasons for this trip as I approached the gray stronghold, Castle Burragh. Chills ran down my spine at the sight of the dark, forbidding stone walls towering above me. I could almost see the heavily armed guards behind tiny arrow loops that would have defended the castle hundreds of years ago. Even though there was not a single cloud in the bright blue sky, I felt a cold wind blow across the flat, treeless mountaintop.

I pulled the zipper up higher on my Windbreaker. Was I really in the right place?

Unfortunately, it was a little late for doubts, as the taxi had long since returned to civilization. I didn't even dare to check whether I had cell phone coverage out here. Suddenly, I felt pretty dumb. To stop myself from getting even more worked up, I knocked on the arched door beside the massive portcullis as loudly as I thought I could get away with and still be considered polite.

My sweaty palms betrayed my fear of not being welcome. Ever more nervously, I wiped them on my jeans. My fear seemed entirely warranted since nobody was opening the door. I knocked again—and this time as hard as I could—even though my knuckles really hurt.

Then I leaned back and glanced up at the tall castle wall. Nothing. Not a peep.

"Dammit!"

And again I tried to fight the feeling of being *utterly alone* in this godforsaken place and at the mercy of all kinds of danger—maybe even a psychopathic killer.

"Hello? Anyone there?" I called out, hoping to hit upon better companionship than my own voice. But no reply came, just as I'd feared.

I had always tended to take charge of my own destiny instead of waiting for something to happen, so I dropped my suitcase and walked a few yards back down the graveled road. Here, a narrow, overgrown path led around the periphery of the castle. All right, I would try my luck at the back of the castle.

Deep down I cursed myself for being so naive. When Payton had told me that he and Sean lived in a castle, I'd immediately thought of one of those lovingly restored castles I'd visited during my big sightseeing tour. This one couldn't be farther from that image. Nobody in his right mind would pay a single buck to visit this derelict ruin. It was in complete disrepair and far from any human settlement.

I tromped through a thicket of Scotch thistles and felt glad that sunset was still a long way off.

I kept calling Payton's name but never got a reply. And when I finally twisted my ankle walking along that overgrown path, I was sure that I had nothing in common with tough girl Lara Croft after all. I was more of an awkward Indiana Jones type, anyway. I limped over to a protrusion on the wall, sat down, and massaged my throbbing ankle. There really was no one around.

~

What was I to do now? Wait until somebody showed up? Or somehow try to get back to the city? A quick glance at my cell phone confirmed that there was no network coverage, but I thought I'd spotted a red telephone box a few miles back. I wondered whether the phone box would actually work, or whether it was just a nostalgic reminder of the good old days.

I slouched and cautiously stretched out my sore foot. All of this was my fault, of course. Why couldn't I just have stayed home? He was the one who left me! Broke up with me, to be precise—just like that, without saying a single word. *Except for that stupid breakup letter on my pillow.* I could almost feel that overwhelming pain again.

~

It had taken several minutes before I was able to gather my thoughts. I sat there, numb, staring at the ink on the page. How could he do this to me? Only a few hours ago we had been so close, and now I was sitting here crying my eyes out. Was this supposed to be it? Had he maybe been using me? Or had he not enjoyed our night together? After calming down, I needed answers. I kept trying his cell phone, but he didn't pick up. My pain flipped to anger. I had risked so much for him, trusted him, opened up to him. Surely it wasn't too much to ask for him to give me a reason we couldn't see each other anymore—and why I should forget about him.

Forget about him? Did he have any idea what he was asking me to do? I could never forget Payton McLean, and I didn't want to! Finally, I'd even tried calling Sean, but the sobering result was exactly the same: no answer. My fury about this outrageous, unacceptable behavior managed to ease my heartbreak—well, almost. But when I returned to the motel to confront Payton later that evening, all I found in his room was a cleaning lady buzzing about. And she told me in a disimpassioned voice that all the guests had already checked out. That was when I could no longer hold back my tears. I cried and cried and cried, using my sleeves instead of a tissue.

I saw myself running. The town around me seemed to have changed forever. The glaring billboards and blinding headlights of passing cars made my head spin. Sirens and all the other traffic noise followed me as I left Route 113 and turned onto the much quieter Kings Highway. It was impossible for me to go home now, back to my room where I had been so happy with Payton such a short time ago. So I ran all the way to Silverlake and sat down in the tall reeds.

Summer was over, so the cold, damp earth soaked through my jeans to my butt. Still, I pulled off my shoes and socks, rolled up my pant legs, and stuck my feet into the water.

The piercing cold helped me think clearly again, and I recalled the day when Payton and I had gone for our very first walk at Glenfinnan Monument and waded barefoot through the ice-cold river.

That day during my student-exchange trip to Scotland had been indescribably beautiful. It marked the beginning of something special.

Which was why I couldn't believe that Payton would throw it all away with just one letter. There had to be more to it. After all, he had been acting very strange all day, and after Sean left, he had been deep in thought.

Eventually, I pulled my feet out of the water, and I actually felt a little better. I didn't want to believe that Payton no longer loved me. There had to be a logical explanation—and I would find out what it was.

With a heavy heart but with renewed optimism, I returned home and dialed the number of perhaps the only person left to help: my cousin Ashley.

~

I took a deep breath, wove my long, dark hair into a loose braid, and then carefully tried to move my ankle. Luckily it almost didn't hurt anymore. I walked back, treading more carefully this time. In a way, Ashley had brought me here.

So if this was a truly dumb idea, then it was at least partially her fault. Because my heartache and anger alone would certainly not have made me book that flight to Scotland.

But when Ashley told me that Sean had canceled his visit to her because "Payton needed him desperately" and because "he had to return to Scotland for now," I felt that my suspicions had been confirmed: Our so-called breakup was just pretense.

I was very concerned about him, because he had been in such a bad way the last time I saw him. These worries had prompted me—impulsive little me who never wasted a thought on possible consequences—to come here. In the end I'd told myself that I would find the two brothers here, that all would be revealed, and that Payton and I would get back together.

But now all I could do was sneak around an obviously abandoned castle, and my two handsome Scotsmen were nowhere to be seen.

I was just turning a corner when I heard engine noise. Knowing my luck, I was sure this would be the psychopathic killers I had fantasized about earlier. But I chose to ignore that thought and run to the gate.

My relief in seeing that it was in fact Payton approaching in his white SUV quickly turned to unease. What if he really *didn't* love me anymore? What if he really didn't want to see me, despite all my hopes for a happy ending? Maybe he was already in the process of getting over me, like he had advised me to do.

Fighting a sense of turmoil, I stopped to face the brothers.

~

The driver's door opened, and I found it impossible to turn away. How did this Scottish guy get under my skin so much? It had been only a few days since I'd seen him, but still my heart pounded like mad at the sight of him. And I could have sworn that, in addition to his clear surprise at seeing me, I also noticed a glimmer of joy rush over his face.

But not much joy was left as he marched up to me. On the contrary, he looked really angry. Before he could intimidate me with his powerful masculine presence, I squeezed out a feeble "Hi, Payton."

Sean had also gotten out of the car and was leaning against the passenger-side door.

"*Daingead,* Sam! What are you doing here?" Payton demanded, pulling me farther away from the car. He shot his brother a quick glance and backed away from me.

I wanted nothing more than to wrap my arms around him, but he seemed so distant that I wished I had never boarded that flight.

"What am I doing here? What do you think? You just ran away from me without saying a word!" I shouted. This was not how I had imagined our reunion.

"I wrote you a letter," Payton said flatly, but he couldn't even look me straight in the eye.

"Oh, right, the letter! You mean those three meaningless lines you wrote?" I snapped, trying my best to stab him to death with my eyes. His glacial brush-off had hurt me more deeply than I cared to admit, so I tried to coat my pain in as much anger as I could.

"Sam, listen, it really would be best for you to go home. That thing that happened between us . . . it's over, and I'm over it."

No, that was not what I wanted to hear. Not at all. I shook my head to try to unhear it. Hot tears streaked down my cheeks, and my voice shook. I wanted to feel him, feel his strong arms around me. I was willing to renounce everything—everything but his love.

"No!" I said defiantly. "You're lying! You told me you loved me, you risked your own damn life to protect me! Do you think I'm so stupid that you can trick me with a Post-it note full of lies? That's not you, Payton, and you know it!"

I ripped the crumpled breakup letter from my bag and hurled it at his face. All I got in response was embarrassed silence. How could he stay this calm when I had never fought harder for anything in my entire life!

"Payton!" I screamed. "Goddammit, you stupid man! That's not how this is supposed to end!"

I didn't know what else to do. I shook my head and watched him from behind a curtain of tears. I scanned his face for those feelings I had always seen reflected on it.

"Sam, please . . . ," he whispered.

"No, Payton. I love you—that's why I'm here. You want me to go? You don't love me? Then convince me. Look me in the eye and tell me!"

I stepped up to him and grabbed his hand.

"Say it, Payton. Just say it, and I swear you'll never see me again."

I braced myself for his reaction. Payton lifted his gaze and our eyes met.

"Sam . . ." He took a deep breath. "Sam, I . . . *Ifrinn!*"

With that, he yanked me into his arms and kissed me. My ribs almost cracked in his grip.

I could hear myself sobbing. My chest heaved with relief, and when we kissed, I tasted both our tears. Yes, our tears, because Payton seemed overwhelmed by his own feelings. He couldn't stop kissing me and muttering sweet Gaelic nothings into my ear. I practically levitated with joy. I only noticed Sean again when he angrily pulled us apart.

"Payton! *Bas maillaichte!* What the heck? We talked about this!" he yelled.

"Screw you! I need Sam, and I won't make the same mistake again to let her go. I've been to hell and back these last few days! Now that she's here, I feel so much better. Don't you get it? If I can make it through this somehow, then it will be with her by my side!"

I didn't understand a single word of *any* of this. Of course it was nice to hear that I hadn't come all this way for nothing, but the rest of it made absolutely no sense to me. The furious silence between the two brothers was charged with tension, but Sean finally gave in and shrugged.

"You know what? It is your cursed life, not mine. Do whatever the hell you want." And with that, he left Payton flat and reached for my suitcase. As he disappeared inside the castle, he said, "Milady, how lovely to see you. Maybe we should talk it out inside." And I took this to mean that I was invited to stay.

Turning his attention back to me, Payton sighed, saying, "Ah, *mo luaidh.* I've missed you. I didn't mean to cause you any pain."

Again he pulled me into his arms, and I snuggled up to him. He gently rested his head on top of mine, and I could feel his heartbeat under my cheek.

"So, what's going on? Why did you leave?"

I felt safe and snug in his arms, even though I knew that much loomed unsaid between us. His sweater smelled so comforting and familiar. I breathed in the scent of the man I loved and savored the feeling of his hands running up and down my back.

"Come on in, I'll tell you everything. But I had better warn you—it's not a very nice story."

Chapter 6

I was exhausted. What a stressful day this had been. First there had been the long flight, the constant worries, and the uncertainty of what waited for me on the other end. Then there was the emotional roller coaster. Payton and I had quietly agreed that we would not get together again until we had talked everything out, until we had spoken about the events that led up to us finding ourselves on a different continent. Meanwhile, I had taken a hot shower, put on my nightgown, and wrapped myself in a big fluffy blanket.

I guess it was almost impossible to sufficiently heat this huge hall where all the castle dwellers of old had dined and probably sometimes slept. But close to the fire, it was surprisingly warm and cozy. The brick wall and woodwork behind the ginormous fireplace—which back in the old days might have been used to roast the occasional whole ox—were black with the soot of years past. The logs on the fire crackled, and every now and then sparks flew up, hissing and popping when a drop of resin exploded in the flame.

As stark and forbidding as the castle seemed from the outside, it was just as cold and sparse on the inside. The McLean brothers had wasted little thought on furnishings or decoration. And, thanks to Vanora's curse, almost three hundred years without emotions had made them completely indifferent to their environment.

Nevertheless, the leather armchairs in front of the fireplace were extremely comfortable. Sean had made *mince and tatties* for us. This traditional dish was absolutely delicious, even though the main ingredients were only humble ground beef and potatoes.

A feeling of blissful comfort came over me just as Payton heaved a big sigh into our lovely after-dinner silence. I knew what would come next: He wanted to get it over with and let me in on his deep, dark secret.

I was afraid to find out what was really going on. But it had to be important, because by now I knew that Payton would never have left me without good reason.

Silently I listened to his account. He sat opposite me, holding my hand, and every now and then he caressed the back of my hand with his thumb. I had no idea who that gentle touch was meant to reassure—him or me—but it certainly wasn't working on me.

This "talk" seemed like a bad dream. One where you know right away that it's not real but you can't seem to wake up and escape back to reality. A dream that haunts you afterward with its vivid images—even in daylight. All I wanted was to wake up from this nightmare. To open my eyes and realize that I was lying in my own bed in Milford, Delaware—where everything was all right and Payton was right there beside me.

But I was still deep inside this dream as Payton ended his story and scrutinized my face for a reaction.

"I . . . I . . . ," I stammered, searching for the right words. What do you say when the person you love announces that he's going to die?

"I . . . Payton, I mean . . . I don't understand. Die? You're going to die? But how, I mean . . . and when?"

Bewildered, I stared at the strained faces in front of me.

"We don't know. Sean couldn't hear every word Nathaira said, but something is happening to me. Every day I feel worse than the day before."

"This can't be true, Payton. You can't die!" I howled.

"He won't! Not if we can find a way to stop it," Sean reassured me. "We came here for good reason. We hope to find a solution in Nathaira's papers. After all, we managed to break a curse once before. We won't give up, I promise!"

Sean was right. We had to save Payton. And not only because *I* was the reason for Nathaira's curse. We had to save him because a world without Payton was lonely and lost, because my life without him wouldn't be worth living. With newfound resolve I jumped up.

"All right then, let's go—let's not waste any time. What can I do? Where do we start?"

With a smile, Payton pulled me into his armchair.

"Keep your cool, *mo luaidh.* We haven't been idle. We've pored over a good number of her old books, searched every last corner in her study, and brought here all the papers we thought might be relevant. As you can imagine, we did not want to spend a moment longer than necessary in that awful Castle Galthair. Evil seems to lurk in every corner of that place."

Even Sean shuddered at the thought of it.

"Yeah, it was strange to walk into Castle Galthair even though we've spent so much more time there than here over the past few years."

To fight my unease, I tried to focus on what was essential.

"So? Did you find anything? What do we need to do?" I asked.

"I'm afraid it's not as simple as you think," Payton explained with a level voice. "There's no old book that says, 'In the event of a curse, kill ye a toad during a full moon, paint ye yourself with pig's blood, and spin ye around three times, and thus the curse shall be broken.'"

"Oh really, you don't say!"

His cool composure infuriated me. How could he stay so calm? He was going to *die*. Didn't he get that?

"Yeah, really." He winked at me and stole a quick kiss before I could continue griping.

"Well, what are you hoping to find?" I asked.

Sean put another few logs on the fire and poked them with a fire iron.

"Oh, there are a good few notes. Many stories that we know as legends nowadays have some truth to them. Except, it's all about filtering out their truth content. Unfortunately, we don't know where to look."

Sean was in the shadows as he turned toward us, and the fire iron in his hands looked like a weapon.

Even though Sean was friendly and kind, even though his impish smile and natural charm made him a very handsome man—he was the only one of the three brothers in whom I could see the wild and dangerous warrior he must have been at one time. I'd noticed it the night Nathaira died. He was a merciless Scottish warrior ready to kill to protect himself and his family. And even though there was no tangible opponent this time around, I knew that he would fight with all that he had to save his brother.

That was why I loved him. He wouldn't give up on Payton, and neither would I.

"We were hoping that maybe Roy Leary might give us a hint. He seems to possess a lot of the old wisdom. And he once offered to help us," Payton continued.

"That's a good idea," I agreed. "He knows all about Scotland's myths and legends. I think he talked about having ancestors on Fair Isle. If anybody knows anything, he does!"

~

We threw around strategies for quite some time. But as much as we tried to convince ourselves that all would end well, we started losing hope. Desperation descended like a dark and sinister blanket, threatening to suffocate us all.

Finally, when none of us was able to come up with more viable ideas, Sean yawned and stretched.

"Kids, it's time for bed. We've got a long day ahead of us, so we should all go and get some rest."

And with that, he left us by the fire that had burned down to smoldering embers. His footsteps on the bare stone floors faded away, and Payton gently pushed me from his lap without letting go of my hands.

"Come on," he said, leading me out of the Great Hall, up the stairs, and into his bedroom.

It was cold up here, but the large, ebony bed with dark brown velvet curtains looked inviting. In fact, his bedroom looked so much cozier than the hall. The bare stone walls were covered in old, green tapestries embroidered with dramatic hunting scenes from right around the time when Payton, no longer a child, must have moved into this room. Clearly, the clothes trunk, bookshelf by the door, and table with its artfully carved legs all stemmed from the same era. The dark woods and heavy green and brown fabrics took me back in time.

Payton leaned against the door, patiently waiting for me to take it all in. I sat down on the bed, plopped over backward, and felt warm and safe under the velvet canopy, just like the lady of the castle waiting for her husband—a fierce Scottish Highlander, no less—on her wedding night. It was with this same excitement that I now awaited Payton. This would be our second night together. I didn't know how many nights we had left, and I didn't want to waste a single one of them.

"You coming? It's cold here without you," I said, crawling under the covers.

"Let me savor this moment for a little while."

"What are you trying to savor? That I'm freezing my toes off?"

Payton batted his eyelashes. "No. I want to soak up this image of you, love of my life, lying here in my bed. To know that, no matter what happens, no one can ever take this away from us. You have no idea how happy you make me, *mo luaidh.*"

Tears welled up in my eyes, and I had trouble swallowing.

"You know how I could make you even happier? If you would bother to swing that cute Scottish butt of yours into bed!" I tried to play down my overwhelming emotions by acting all cool and funny. And, although I was awfully cold, I folded back the comforter and tapped the mattress beside me. A wide grin brightened Payton's face, and he undressed with breathtaking speed.

As he lay down beside me, he cursed when one of my ice-cold feet touched his lower leg.

"Good God, Sam! You're freezing! Am I forever condemned to suffer in pain whenever I'm near you?" he called out in a theatrical voice. I snickered, and he crawled on top of me, covering my shivering body entirely with his. I was no longer cold. Certain parts of my body were on fire, in fact.

"Mmm, much better," I purred while caressing his back. "Do you think we . . . ?" I asked, embarrassed and suddenly at a loss for words.

"Huh? If you think I'm going to pass up this opportunity, then you, my dear, are mistaken."

And with that, he sealed my lips with a long, gentle kiss.

Chapter 7

The next afternoon we all sat together like old friends in the Learys' tiny home. Alison and Roy, who had been my host parents during last summer's student-exchange trip, were happy about the unexpected visit. Before we could even explain why we'd dropped in unannounced, we found ourselves sitting at a nicely decorated table with a steaming pot of tea and slices of a delicious fruitcake called *black bun.* The beautiful china cups and delicately embroidered linen napkins looked lovely and very old, and when Alison noticed my admiring looks, she explained full of pride, "Family heirlooms. At first I didn't want to use them, but then I thought what a waste it would be to let it all gather dust in the cabinet."

Payton was way too restless to participate in our discussion of fine china and fancy napkins. After all, we had come here hoping that Roy knew something that would help us. Sean had stayed back at the castle to dig deeper into Nathaira's books.

Roy, a red-haired mountain of a man with a skeptical look on his face, sat opposite Payton and turned his head to this side and then that, while Alison went to get an extra chair from another room.

"Well, don't you seem to attract bad luck, aye?" Roy turned to Payton once we had laid out our request as best we could.

I frowned but didn't respond.

Payton, who seemed to be drained of all energy today—because of the curse?—gave him a cynical grin.

"So, can you help me? You knew things before that nobody else could have known. I really don't care how you come to know all this stuff. But please, just tell me if there's any hope for me."

All of a sudden I felt queasy. When I arrived yesterday, Payton wasn't showing any weakness at all. But the hopelessness I heard in his voice right now hit me like a slap in the face. I didn't understand why destiny was so cruel to us.

Payton and Roy ignored the world around them, staring at each other. There was a strange kind of tension between them. Alison sipped her tea as though not having noticed how extraordinary that moment was. And I tried to make sense of the few words spoken between the men—some in Gaelic, some in English.

Finally, Roy reached for a piece of fruitcake, and I wondered whether I had just been imagining the whole thing.

"Aye, very well, who'd have thought that Vanora's daughter would be capable of that. Nathaira is what you said, right? Did you know that *Nathaira* is an old Celtic name meaning 'snake'? It's as if they'd known since her birth that she'd possess evil powers," he reflected.

"So what now?" I asked impatiently. "Can you help us, or what?"

Roy leaned back in his chair and shrugged apologetically.

"No, I won't be able to help you. All I can do is tell you what I've heard and what I know. Whether or not you will find a way to change Payton's fate . . . well, that's not up to me. And, to be honest, I can't imagine that you will find a way."

Payton's body seized up.

"All right, then, let's hear it. We have no time to lose. Just tell us everything you know, Roy," he begged.

Roy nodded, wiped his fingers on his napkin, and closed his eyes. He seemed to be sorting through memories, digging up the required information. Then he spoke in a calm and quiet voice.

"The power of the Fair Witches is transmitted from generation to generation. This is the only reason Nathaira was able to speak the curse in the first place—because a witch's supernatural powers runs through her veins. But Nathaira's blood is not pure. She lacks the purity of heart that the men of Fair Isle possess, and that is passed on only from father to daughter. Nathaira would never have been able to achieve Vanora's strength without this purity of heart. Which is why she turned to evil. She did not have the control and guidance of a loving mother who could have taught her how to use her gift for good.

"Having said that, it is lucky for you that she's missing this important other half of her powers. I don't know if you're able to use this to your advantage, but I'm sure she was not as powerful as her mother. She carried within her Vanora's blood mixed with Grant's blood, and so she had the power to speak the curse. Vanora's blood mixed with *Payton's* blood—now that would probably be strong enough to lift the curse. Yes, I suspect that only Vanora's blood can save Payton's life," said Roy, concluding his odd monologue.

In the stillness that followed, all I could hear was the hiss of the teakettle Alison had put on again.

"There's no hope at all, then," I established at last, because neither Payton nor Roy seemed to want to state the obvious.

"I told you I didn't know whether this would help, aye?" Roy admitted.

"Vanora is dead. Her blood was spilled centuries ago," Payton muttered flatly.

~

This couldn't be the end of it! There had to be a solution! Why would destiny bring Payton and me together if we weren't allowed to live happily ever after? Or was there a way to save him, and we just couldn't see it?

Buried in thought, I stared at the colorful embroidery on the old-fashioned linen napkins. I couldn't make sense of the play of colors. It looked like flowers that had been lovingly hand-stitched on the fabric. I carefully touched the fine needlework and followed one of the threads with my finger. It was the most conspicuous—a vibrant red and the highlight of the entire image, outshining the prettiest of all the flowers with its intensity. And then I noticed it—a faulty stitch, a rough, black thread overlying the delicate red one. It seemed to be jealous of its beauty and covered it almost entirely.

Driven by an impulse I couldn't comprehend, I traced the thread to the end. A small knot held it together. Gingerly, probingly, I pulled on it and—little by little—I loosened a faulty stitch. Then another one, and another one. I saw how the brilliant red unfolded its beauty. When the whole thread finally came away and disappeared inside my palm, it was as if the sun itself had offered the flower her radiance, as if the color red had never been so perfect before. It was a true *blood*red.

~

My head started spinning and my ears started ringing. The length of thread slipped from my hand as I closed my eyes and barely noticed how I slid from my chair into the darkness.

~

Pain spread like wildfire through my arm all the way to my fingertips, which were completely numb. I gasped for air. The smell of copper filled my nose and mouth, making me sick to my stomach. Then slowly, as feeling returned to my fingers, I opened my eyes and stared down at my hands. Blood, hot and slimy, gushed onto the dagger—and onto me. I clutched the knife in my hand. I had thrust it in so deep that my fist touched the man's lifeless chest, and I could tell that the heart beneath my fingers had stopped beating. A single word flashed through my addled brain: betrayal.

~

With a panicked cry, I came to. I found myself lying on the floor with my head in Payton's lap. My heart was thumping, and I was sweating all over.

I had to blink several times to get rid of the powerful images in my head. I didn't understand what had just happened or why I was so queasy. Somehow my arm still hurt, and I tried to massage away the pain.

"*Mo luaidh*, are you all right? You passed out."

I swallowed hard. *Was* I all right? I had no idea. What I really wanted to do was cry. All eyes were fixed on me, with Alison holding out a glass of water. Because I still felt unable to get up, I took a sip. My hand around the glass was shaking, and Roy wore a worried frown.

"Should we call a doctor?" Alison said.

A doctor? Oh God, no. It was hard enough to recall the images that had been so vivid only a moment ago. They had faded as quickly as they had come, and a second later all I was left with was a nervous tightness in my chest. I clenched my teeth and scrambled to my feet. Payton held my arm and wouldn't let go, even after I assured him that I felt much better, thank you very much.

~

After the good fright I had given everyone, we all seemed almost glad to turn to something as morbid as a curse. At least nobody found himself in immediate danger anymore, so we allowed Alison to pour us another cup of her delicious Earl Grey tea.

Roy kept his eyes glued on me, and his worried, wrinkled forehead did not bode well.

"Are you sure you're all right?" he asked.

I gave him a reassuring smile because I really was feeling much better. The images I'd seen when I fainted were still there, hidden deep inside the recesses of my mind, but I couldn't seem to grab and hold on to them. Oh, I was fine all right. Only my nerves were acting up. All that talk about blood, curses, and dying would give anyone nightmares. I wanted Roy to concentrate all of his energy on Payton instead.

"Don't worry, Roy, I'm okay. But where were we? Did I miss anything?"

"No, you didn't miss anything," he replied. "There is no solution. Vanora is dead, and all hope of saving your boyfriend has died with her."

I saw the pain on Payton's face—that sense of hopelessness and dread he'd been hiding so well.

"Roy? Is that true?" I asked, my gaze fixed on the great scholar.

But it was Alison who spoke. "I think you're giving up too quickly. Vanora has been dead for a long time. And Payton should have died long ago, too—or am I wrong?"

"What exactly do you mean?"

"Well, I might not be familiar with Roy's mysteries, but I have ears. People from the Highlands have been telling one another legends for as long as I can remember. And this young Scot right here who looks like he's in his early twenties—when exactly was he born?" With her eyebrows raised and finger extended, she demanded full disclosure.

"In 1721," Payton replied with a glimmer of hope in his eyes.

"So there you have it. That's the stuff legends are made of. There are gaps in the fabric of time, ken? Roy, how many legends talk about creatures from another time traveling to visit the human realm?"

"Well, there are a few." Roy nodded, only to object right away. "But those are old stories without any tangible proof."

"Ha! That's where you're wrong! When I was a child, my mother always warned me to never play too far away from the house. Otherwise the fairies would come and get me—just like they had this American lady who disappeared without a trace by Craigh na Dun. Three years later, dressed in rags, she turned up at the exact same spot where she had disappeared. It caused a real sensation and was all over the papers at the time."

"Still, that's no proof at all."

"All right," Sam said, "let's pretend for a second that Alison is right and that there exist tears or openings in the fabric of time. How would we go about finding them? And how would we *operate* them? How could we possibly find answers to these questions?"

I couldn't believe that we might waste our energy on something as silly as that, especially with Payton's life on the line. On the other hand, a Scottish boy, damned to eternal life, was enough for me to look at outrageous things like time travel and witches as something within the *bounds of possibility*. As I had experienced firsthand, more things existed between heaven and hell than we could possibly imagine. Something like time travel almost seemed trivial in that regard.

"None of us has any knowledge of such things, but we can try to find out if there is a chance," Roy declared.

"Maybe we'll get lucky and uncover something, but even then there's no guarantee that it's true and that Payton can in fact be saved. But it's worth a try, so let's get to work."

~

Two hours later back at the castle, Payton and I sat with Sean in the Great Hall. Old books and scrolls were piled high on the big banquet table in front of us.

Since we now had a starting point, we all felt much better and had quietly decided not to give up. A freshly delivered pizza was to feed us for the next few hours so that we could put all our focus on our research.

"Time travel?" Sean pondered. "That seems a bit unrealistic, even to me. Are you sure we're not wasting our time here?"

By now Payton had lost all color in his face, and he frequently needed to stop for a break. His fever ran high, and the medication didn't seem to work at all. We had to hurry.

I pulled the next big tome close to me and flipped open the heavy leather binding. The first page was beautifully written in quill by an artful hand, but I couldn't decipher any of it. Those Gaelic or Celtic words, written in narrow letters and spread across the entire page, made me groan. I wasn't of much help, given that I didn't speak any of the old tongues.

"Anyway, what are we going to do if we really do find a tear in the fabric of time?" I asked, grabbing a slice of pizza.

Sean looked up from the book in front of him and, in turn, snatched a slice of pizza from the box. Payton, who was soaked in sweat, walked around the table and sat down beside me. I thrust my half-eaten pizza slice into his hands and took a fresh one from the box.

"I would of course try to get Vanora's blood somehow," he said out loud.

"How do you imagine that?" I asked. "Do you want to walk up to her and tell her you've come from the future and that her blood is your only hope? Makes no sense! Besides, what would you then do with her blood? Drink it? Eww!"

Payton shrugged. "I don't know."

Sean was already on his second slice and pointed the floppy end of it at his brother. "That's not how it would work. Right now you're in no condition to pull off something like that. Travel back in time? I mean, look at yourself! You need to conserve your energy, and there's no way you'd be able to face any of the dangers that we used to experience back in the day. No way."

"But I have to at least try. I have no other choice!"

I pressed Payton's hand in encouragement. If we got to a point where we found a way, he would be capable of doing whatever was necessary. I was sure of it.

We kept working for a while without any real results. Then Sean suddenly stopped.

"Did you find something?" I asked, jumping from my seat. Even Payton looked up anxiously from his papers.

"No, unfortunately not. But I was just thinking what would happen if one of us really were to travel back in time. Imagine if we could save Kyle's life! Maybe even stop the attack on the Camerons. Wouldn't that be fantastic?"

"Fantastic . . . sure, but maybe also disastrous, wouldn't you think? I mean, who knows what might happen if someone were to change history," I reminded them.

"I'm not sure. What do you think might happen? Could we perhaps undo the terrible harm we did that night?" he reflected.

"Yes, but then what about me, for example? I'm a descendant of Muireall Cameron. She married an American after she escaped. If she doesn't escape, if she never makes it to America, will I even be born? And what about my parents and grandparents? Will I meet you guys? Or, I should rephrase my question: Would I even have met you last summer? You two wouldn't be alive today if the massacre had never happened and Vanora had never spoken her curse. I think it's very risky!" I pointed out, slowly getting angry. Because, seriously, all I needed now was a sudden end to my existence thanks to a change in the historical timeline.

"Sam's right," Payton agreed. "If we do find a way to accomplish the *unimaginable,* we will also need to think about the personal responsibility that goes along with it."

I suddenly remembered something else that lacked any scientific evidence whatsoever but seemed logical all the same.

"Um, I'm not sure, but I remember that in *Back to the Future,* Marty McFly was not supposed to meet himself. What do you think about that? Shouldn't we be extra careful, too?"

Payton smirked. "Oh yeah, sure—there it is: definitive proof that time travel is possible. After all, Michael J. Fox did it several times!"

Even Sean burst out laughing before burying his nose again in the book on his lap.

"You guys are idiots!" I shouted. But I couldn't stop myself from laughing, either. "Seriously, though, we have to try to not leave any footprints."

Payton stared at me in disbelief.

"What do you mean 'we'?" he called out. He'd raised his eyebrows so high that they almost met his hairline. "You don't seriously think that I would agree to your doing something this crazy and highly dangerous? Let me be very clear about this, Sam, *mo luaidh.* I am in this . . . let's call it a *regrettable* circumstance that will soon lead to my demise . . . because I saved *your* life. And now you think that I would agree to your carelessly risking your life for *me*? No, my dear Sam. If necessary, I will personally lock you up in the dungeon that—yes—does exist in this castle. I will do that if it's the only way to stop you from doing something stupid. Am I being clear?"

He stood with his hands on his hips, glaring at me furiously.

Sean's barely restrained laughter from behind a discolored parchment scroll destroyed the poor illusion of Payton uttering a threat, and I gave him an amused wink.

"All right, all right. Calm down already. But do you think you and Sean could maybe try not to reinvent life on this planet by way of some history-changing, space-time-bending maneuver?"

Sean peered at us over the edge of his document and decreed, "I will lock both of you in the dungeon, because I'll be going alone. And yes, I'll make sure your cute little butt doesn't dissolve into stardust."

With that, he turned his attention back to his parchment.

"What do you mean you're going alone? Are you nuts? Did you forget that I'm the one who needs this blood?" Payton exclaimed. He walked around the table and reached for the document Sean was hiding behind, when Sean suddenly stood up and shrunk back.

"Wait, wait! I've got something!" he called out, wiping several papers off the table to make some room.

"Here, take a look at that! Maybe it's something!"

We immediately stuck our heads together to examine his find. The old document might help us save Payton. My palms began to sweat from the excitement. That inner Indiana Jones of mine was sick of dusty old books. He was ready to pull out his bullwhip and fight. Payton and I looked at each other over Sean's head. I took his hand, and his smile made me incredibly happy.

"Come on, you guys, look!" Sean demanded, pointing at several words he deemed important.

"What does this mean?" I asked.

Payton was fully immersed in the content, silently mouthing the words he read on the parchment.

Without looking up, he explained, "It's an old legend. The legend of the five sisters of Kintail."

"A legend about what?"

I silently cursed my ignorance. What the heck was written in that text? It was like pulling teeth with these guys! Payton had already advanced by a few pages, and when he reached the end, he smiled at his big brother.

"Yep, there could be something to it," he admitted.

"For crying out loud, will you tell me already!" I demanded. "What secret are these five sisters guarding?"

~

Talking about the old legend in detail made time fly for the three of us. It was deep into the night when we finally parted, tired but full of newfound hope.

Payton and I crawled into his warm, cozy bed and cuddled up to each other. We were unable to find sleep despite our exhaustion.

"Tell me again," I asked, afraid of missing anything significant. Besides, the legend was so extraordinarily beautiful that I'd almost cried when Sean had translated it for us.

I caressed Payton's chest, touching the scar under his heart. It was still fresh and pink. His chest trembled as he started to talk.

~

"The legend of the five sisters talks about a long-ago man who lived near Kintail with his five daughters. People said that he was a druid. He was also said to be so protective of his daughters that they grew up full of innocence—but also very unaware and ignorant. All of them were said to be exceptionally beautiful. So beautiful that no man from around there would ever dare to talk to these girls. Men were also very afraid of the girls' father.

"One day, the man sent his daughters to the loch to catch some fish. That day was to become the tragic day of their doom, because evil awaited them in the shape of two handsome men. The two oldest sisters had stayed behind on the shore and, when the men approached and introduced themselves, the girls immediately fell for their flattering words and good looks. Because they had never seen the face of evil, they were unable to recognize it. It was easy for these warriors from a faraway place to deceive the beautiful girls and steal their hearts with false promises.

"Several days later, the sisters again went fishing. The youngest sisters rowed into the lake, while the two oldest again stayed behind on the shore. Every single day thereafter, the men returned and continued to gain the girls' trust. Not only did they steal the fair maidens' innocent hearts, but they finally took their bodies, too. In their virtue and purity, these girls trusted the warriors' whispered words. They mistook the warriors' advances for true love. And so the two men made these lovely, naive girls their brides in a traditional handfasting ceremony.

"When the sisters returned the next day, the handsome warriors were gone. The girls realized their mistake, and their broken hearts screamed in so much agony that it almost killed them. Bound by their intense love for one another, all five sisters felt the betrayal equally—and all of their hearts seemed lost forever. They didn't know what else to do except confide in their father. The father blamed himself for his beloved daughters' misfortune. He could not bear to see them in pain. Their pure hearts were unable to cope with the wicked betrayal, so he did the only thing any loving father would do to relieve his children's misery. He saved their hearts and released them from their suffering.

"He turned his daughters to stone to keep them safe from harm for eternity. As unique and beautiful as his daughters had been, he sculpted the mountains to honor each one of them. And when the time came that they felt as strong as the rocks surrounding them, they would only have to raise their golden voices to turn themselves back into the happy, carefree maidens they had been before looking evil in the eye. Then they'd be able to follow the rose-lined *path* that he would hold open *for all time* so they could return and forgive him for carrying the terrible guilt of their pain and sorrow. For as long as the roses will bloom in the shade of the mountain sisters, their path back to life and youth and their father's loving arms shall always remain open."

~

As Payton finished, my tears fell onto his chest.

"Isn't this the most wonderful story?"

I found it hard to make my voice sound even and strong. That was how deeply the sisters' fate had touched me.

"So it is, *mo luaidh*."

We lay in silence, and our hearts beat as one. Silvery moonlight fell through the window, shining on our bed, and I saw the five mountain peaks before me—five souls, safely locked away from the world within hard, eternal rock.

I thought about the path that the father had vowed to keep open for them. Could it truly exist?

"How would we go about finding it?" I whispered, saying my thoughts out loud.

"I have an idea of where we might start," Payton replied sleepily. A moment later, his regular breathing told me that he had fallen asleep. I lay awake for a long time, watching over him and praying for a future with this wonderful man by my side. Because there was nobody in my life who could turn me into stone and take my hurt away, if it came to that, I would have to suffer through the pain.

CHAPTER 8

It was a damp and foggy morning. The cold clamminess of it soaked right through my skin and made me shiver. Longingly, I glanced back at Payton's car, whose heated seats had kept me warm until a moment ago.

I found it impossible to keep up with my two Scots on this uneven terrain. The brothers had already reached the small cemetery by Auld a´chruinn on the Road to the Isles. Right behind it I could see the majestic mountain range of Kintail with its five peaks—the Five Sisters.

I wasn't sure if I felt chilly because of the weather or because the legend was still reverberating in my brain. But I did feel unsettled when I left the narrow dirt road and entered the cemetery by way of its crumbling gate.

An eerie silence welcomed me. It might have felt peaceful and serene on a less murky day, but the quiet only increased my uneasiness on this day in which my nerves were all over the place. As I continued, a bird scattered up and escaped, screeching, into the tree canopies. The haze rising from the lakeshore reminded me of a horror movie, and the sheer remoteness of this long-forgotten place seemed to fit that creepy picture as well.

I rubbed my arms to warm myself up, and I called Payton's name. I'd feel much better once I was near him again.

"Right here," he hollered. He stepped out from behind the former chapel at the center of this old decrepit boneyard.

I moved carefully so as not to stumble over one of the sunken gravestones. The more graves I passed, the more relaxed I felt. Luscious green grass had taken over the reins of the once carefully landscaped paths. Several of the headstones had submitted to the elements, and they now leaned to the side or had even broken in half. Silvery cobwebs stretched across the barely recognizable paths. I was glad when Payton put his arms around my shoulders and gently kissed me on the forehead.

"What do you think? Could this be the right place?" I asked.

"Take a look around! This is a place where legends are forged, don't you think?"

"Sure, but how can you know if there really is a tear in the fabric of time somewhere around here? Or this *path through all time* mentioned in the story?"

"I can't say, but the location looks about right. We're at the foot of the Five Sisters—in their shade—which might also indicate protection. At Loch Duich in front of us, the girls must have met their fate. And over there on the hill, do you see the big memorial stone? They call that the Druid Father."

I swallowed hard. Was it possible that all of this was a coincidence? But before I could reply, Sean trotted over to us. He had walked the length and breadth of the entire cemetery and seemed a little lost.

"I've found nothing," he said angrily, running his fingers through his short blond hair. "Maybe we were wrong. Just because cemeteries have played a prominent role in so many other legends or are supposed to possess a lot of power doesn't mean it's true for us."

"But I had a good feeling about this place. Somehow it seems *right,*" Payton said, looking around as if searching for something.

"What if we tried our luck with the Druid Father stone? Maybe it marks the spot or contains a hint of some sort," I suggested.

The brothers agreed, so we made our way up the short, steep slope of the hill. I was pretty hot from all the exercise and opened my jacket. Up here the air was clear, and with every step we took, the view of the sparkling lake—nestled between the gentle foothills of the Five Sisters—became more beautiful.

"I've been thinking," Sean started. "I was serious yesterday. Payton, I don't think you are strong enough for this kind of journey. Remember how hard life was back then? The trip from here to Burragh alone will take several days."

We had reached the Druid Father stone. Just the short hike up the hill had drained Payton of his strength, and he had to sit down by the foot of the stone to get some rest. I slipped out of my jacket and sat down, using it as a cushion so I wouldn't get my pants dirty. One last time, Sean let his eyes wander over the lake below. To him it seemed almost ghostly in this pale early-morning light. Then he looked at his brother.

"I really have no idea how I would manage, but we haven't found the path through time yet . . . if it even exists," Payton muttered, dejected.

Sean wasn't ready to give in just yet.

"But once we find it, we can't afford to waste any more time. So we may as well think about it now. I will go in your stead and bring you Vanora's blood. And you will do your goddamn best to hold on, stay alive, and wait for my return. Aye?"

Payton looked at his brother for a long time before holding out his hand. Sean shook it with great relief.

"Brother, I swear to you that I won't let you die," Sean pledged.

I turned away, feeling like a third wheel eavesdropping on an intimate moment between siblings. At the same time, I was glad that Payton wouldn't be putting himself at risk. I trusted Sean unquestionably, as he had become like a brother to me. If anyone had the strength and ability to master this challenge, it was this brave young Scot in front of me. After all, he was already familiar with the time period and wouldn't have any trouble finding his way around.

"Mending it. Right, Sam?" a voice rang into my thoughts.

"Huh? Were you talking to me?"

"Sean wants to know if you could mend his old plaid. If we really find a way, then we need to start preparing. Sean will need to look as inconspicuous as possible. His old plaid would be perfect! In addition to his dagger, he'll also need his broadsword. And he should take along some food, because supermarkets were few and far between back in the day," Payton said, clowning around.

I had to laugh even though I was in no mood for jokes. These two were crazy just thinking about all of this.

"Do you really think you can take all that stuff with you?" I voiced my doubts. "Just like that, like you're on vacation or something? Maybe fill your little Louis Vuitton duffel bag with ramen noodles? And don't forget your smartphone so you can bring back unforgettable pictures and videos from the eighteenth century to show to your friends. Oh, and remember to pack a Tupperware container for Vanora's blood."

Still, it was a relief to be making plans, even if we were as far away from saving Payton as we had been yesterday. It just felt better. We had hope—and something of a plan. We cracked a few more jokes before we started working on the marker stone.

We examined every nook and cranny, every line chiseled into it. We walked around it clockwise and counterclockwise, and followed every inch of its surface with our fingers. The brothers even lifted me up so I could get a look on the top of it. There wasn't a trace of a hint on the entire goddamn stone.

"Maybe we weren't that far off back at the cemetery. There's nothing here, that's for sure."

Although I knew we wouldn't come across neon signs flashing messages like *"Return to the past"* or *"This way to the tear in the fabric of time,"* I had hoped we'd have more luck. Hadn't movies and novels proven that there were always mysterious signs to be found glistening in the sunlight—like a thick layer of cobwebs hiding some secret passageway? On the other hand, if a portal to the past was so easy to find, there'd probably be a thriving tourism business exploiting it.

The hike uphill had been easy enough for me, but the hike back down proved almost impossible. Wearing nothing but simple sandals, I kept slipping on the dewy grass, and the seat of my pants was smeared with muck after only a few yards. I was irritated, knowing that the steepest part of the journey down was still in front of me.

The boys laughed at my ineptitude, and Sean handed me his *sgian dhu.*

"What am I going to do with this thing? Do you think it's easier to fall into a knife than into the mud?"

"When you're climbing down this next part, just ram it into the earth and use the handle to hold on. Oh, and try *not* to stumble into the blade, aye?"

Sean grinned up at me before taking a sure-footed jump down the slope. It looked so easy. Full of doubt, I glanced at the small knife in my palm and then at the downward slope. Luckily, a grinning Payton offered me his hand. I carefully slipped the dagger sideways into my belt and slid down into Payton's arms.

Once we finally made our way down the hill, we hurried to follow Sean back to the cemetery. But before we passed through the gate, Payton grabbed me. He shot a quick glance over the cemetery wall before ducking behind it and pulling me down with him. Before I could complain about being back in the damp grass, he closed my mouth with a kiss. His hand reached behind my neck and pulled me even closer to him. Almost without a will of my own, I submitted to his hungry kiss, returning it with the same ferocious passion.

"I am sorry, *mo luaidh,* but I had to feel you close to me. I am worried that I don't have much time left."

I caressed his cheek with my fingertips, touched his lips, and lingered on the little scar on his chin. Of course he was afraid. I myself was barely able to breathe because I worried about him so much. I didn't want to think about all these terrible things. Didn't want to imagine what it would be like to lose him. Didn't want to allow this fear to germinate and take root.

"How did you get this?" I changed the subject, kissing him very gently on his chin.

"The scar? Oh, I've had it for ages. I can't even remember when I got it. When I was young, Kyle and I would earn our daily share of scrapes and bruises. This is probably one of those."

"Kyle? That's your little brother? The one Nathaira mentioned?"

Payton didn't respond, but his eyes grew darker.

"Why did you get so many cuts and bruises? Did you get into a lot of fights?"

There it was, a smile. "No, during that time, Sean and Blair tried to share their broadsword skills with us, their little brothers. They were both excellent warriors but very bad teachers. Not a day went by that we didn't lose some blood."

"Well, my theory is that your brothers realized that you were the handsomest of them all, and so they tried to put things right," I teased.

"Oh yeah? You think? Honestly, Kyle was the handsomest of us all. He was pretty cute even as a baby, and he just got better looking with every year. All the girls were crazy for him! They got into fights and used love potions just to get his attention."

"It's true!" Sean interjected, swinging his legs over the top of the cemetery wall. He scowled. "And just so you know, if Blair or I had really wanted to cut Payton down to size, then your hunky boyfriend here would barely reach the tip of your nose today. Besides, I am shocked that you think *he's* better looking than I am!"

"How long have you been listening?" Payton cut in. He didn't seem to appreciate how Sean was talking about him.

"I'm not eavesdropping. I've been sitting over here on the other side of the wall because I wanted to show you something. But then you decided to have a make-out session right here on the heath, and I didn't want to intrude."

"Thank you for being so considerate," I said, "but we were *not* making out!" I could feel my cheeks burning.

"All right, then. What is it that you wanted to show us?" Payton cut through our bickering.

Sean pointed at a line of graves on his side of the wall. Behind the gravestones was a gray obelisk rising up into the sky.

"Since we don't know what we're looking for, searching every square inch of this place could take days. I've been thinking this whole time that there must be some small hint or some kind of mechanism hidden around here. When I saw this crow land on top of the obelisk, something occurred to me about time. Obelisks symbolize rays of sunshine that have turned to stone, and they're supposed to connect the heavens and the earth. So it wouldn't be entirely unusual to see a gravestone in the shape of one. But that one over there is not on a grave. It's completely freestanding, nowhere near a grave. Back in the day, people measured the passage of time using the shadow cast by such an obelisk. I know it's not much, but it's better than nothing. So, what do you say? Should we take apart that obelisk and find your damn portal?"

Actually, Sean's explanations sounded logical—so with newfound courage and a lot of enthusiasm, we set about examining that long stone pillar in great detail.

Sean and Payton were completely engrossed in inspecting the old, withered letters on a moss-covered inscription.

That was my chance. Since the moment I'd sat down on that cold, damp ground I'd had to pee. I had tried in vain to suppress it, but the need was getting urgent. So I took advantage of the guys being distracted and disappeared behind what was left of the decrepit chapel. The decaying walls were still high enough to offer protection from unwanted attention. Since I really wanted to avoid defiling one of the old graves, I hurried over to the cemetery wall where there were only a few headstones, and I relieved myself behind one of them. Fortunately, the brothers were nowhere in sight.

When I stepped out from behind the gravestone, Sean's dagger slipped out of my belt. As I bent down to reach for it, I noticed an inscription on the stone.

Mo còig nighean
Mora, Fia, Gillian, Robena, Alba,
Gabh mo leisgeul
Tha gabh mi gradhaich a thu

I couldn't make it all out because a rosebush covered parts of it, but I felt I'd discovered something significant. I picked up the *sgian dhu,* put it back in my belt, and knelt on the ground. Carefully, I pushed away the branches and examined the inscription in more detail. I didn't know many words in Gaelic, but I knew *nighean*. It meant "daughter." And *còig* was easy. "Five." My heart thumped inside my chest. This wasn't a headstone! Trembling, I pushed a strand of hair from my eyes and wiped the moss off the next line.

"Ouch!" I'd caught my hand on some thorns.

I flinched and saw a big drop of blood squirt from my finger. It was as red as the flowers on the rosebush. I quickly put my finger in my mouth, but the taste of copper on my tongue made me queasy.

I opened my eyes and stared down at my hands. Blood, hot and slimy, gushed onto the dagger—and onto me.

I took a few deep breaths, trying to shake the strange feeling of having a flashback to my fainting episode at Roy and Alison's house. All right, back to the inscription.

"Mora, Fia, Gillian, Robena, and Alba," I muttered.

I felt sick to my stomach, and I held on to the stone to keep from keeling over. A drop of blood fell onto the stone, seeped into it, fused with it—and with the intensely bright appearance of an all-consuming blaze, my world ceased to exist.

Light.

Pain.

Nothing else.

I seemed to fall without moving, without actually falling, without even existing. There was nothing. My body and mind had come apart, and they were carried away on burning wings while simultaneously being torn to shreds by an icy fist.

"Payton," I wanted to scream—but I had no voice or even air to breathe, no consciousness that could have made any of this possible. And still it was as if I were slowing down in my fall into this bottomless, bright abyss. I could no longer even control my thoughts.

Everything was bright, so bright. I myself seemed to be made of only light. All my senses were superimposed with this painfully intense luminosity. My lungs were filled with liquid gold, and my blood was a white-hot liquid coursing through my veins. The light expanded, trying to break out of me like a baby bird hatching from its shell. If I had been able to think straight, then this is what I would have thought:

I'm dying.

A while later, I became aware of coldness around me.

And a long time after that, dampness.

Eventually sounds became audible again to my brain, and in a daze I opened my eyes and sighed a breath of relief. It was almost dark. I could not have taken seeing that intense brightness again. But what had happened? Every one of my bones hurt as if they were all broken, and it took an enormous amount of effort just to blink.

Had I passed out again as I had at Roy and Alison's house? I sat up slowly, moaning in pain, and the world around me blurred. Blink, blink. Finally, my surroundings shifted into focus. Where were Payton and Sam? How long had I been out? Judging by the fading daylight, it had to be late in the evening, and the two of them must have noticed by now that I was missing.

"Payton? Sean?" I called, flinching at the sound of my own voice. I definitely felt like I had suffered a concussion. Still, I strained my neck to look for them. No reply came, and I was terrified. I shook my head. Pain throbbed in my temples, and I tried to suppress my rising panic.

Panic. Obviously my subconscious self was already aware of what had happened. It had been something seemingly impossible—but it had happened nevertheless.

No, no, no.

I squinted and touched my head. *I have a concussion, that is all.*

There had to be a logical explanation for Payton and Sean leaving me behind. They went to get help. Went to call an ambulance or something. They'd be back any minute now and would laugh if they knew about the crazy thoughts trying to take over my mind. All I had to do was keep calm and sit still. That thought managed to calm me down for a moment or two. But then I opened my eyes again, and I seemed to be seeing my surroundings for the very first time.

That was when I knew.

I was in a crap ton of trouble.

In complete hysterics, I struggled to my feet, ignoring the stabbing pain. Standing on wobbly legs, I threw up all over my shoes. My mind fought against everything it was being forced to realize. It fought tooth and nail against the truth that lay right there in front of me.

Shaking, I bent over and spat out the rest of the bile in my mouth. Then I sank back into the grass, wrapped my arms around my knees, and waited for the panic to subside. I shook and shivered uncontrollably while crying for what seemed like an eternity.

Meanwhile, the world around me had gone pitch-black into the night. But instead of feeling frightened, I found comfort in knowing that the truth lay hidden beneath a cloak of darkness. That was when my mind was at long last able to grasp what had happened. Slowly, I comprehended that I had not only found an important marker to the portal through time, but that I had in fact traveled the entire length of the goddamn journey.

As soon as I allowed this thought, I felt calm again. I breathed in the air that was essentially old and part of history, but I soon realized that it filled my lungs and enriched my blood with oxygen, just like the air back in my own world. Which somehow seemed comforting.

And so, under the cover of darkness, I tried to familiarize myself with my state of affairs. I knew where I was—but not *when*. I hoped that this portal would not prove to be a one-way street—that I'd be able to take the road back to from where I'd come. But would I have enough courage? I couldn't remember the horrors I'd already lived through without feeling scared to the core. Still, I was determined to get back to where I belonged as quickly as possible. And then I would tell Sean how he could save Payton.

All I had to do was return.

Although my body had just released its largest-ever dose of adrenaline, I suddenly felt excessively tired. Comforted by the possibility of a way out, I relaxed enough for sleep to take over and heal my broken body and my exhausted mind. As I gave in, I hoped to wake up and find out all this had just been a dream.

Chapter 9

The screech of the wiper blades broke through the silence in the car. Payton and Sean stared into the night through the fogged-up windshield. Their soaking-wet clothes clung to their bodies and left wet patches on the car seats. The rain was relentless. Hours ago the clouds had opened the floodgates and transformed the small cemetery into a muddy boneyard.

Once the brothers had noticed Samantha's disappearance, they immediately started looking for her, combing every square inch of the place but to no avail. She had disappeared into the fog like a ghost, leaving no trace. They didn't give up, even in the heavy rain. When night fell, they finally admitted that their search had been unsuccessful. Still, they couldn't bring themselves to return to the castle—they wanted to be *here* in case Sam reappeared.

With every passing hour, Payton grew more desperate. What if she was dead? Neither of them wanted to voice that thought. Was it even possible that Sam had found the portal of time and had traveled somewhere into the past? It seemed much more likely that the druid's magic spell had killed her, and that neither Payton nor Sean would ever see her again.

"What are we going to do now?" Sean finally spoke.

Payton's expressionless face was his reply.

Sean wasn't surprised that Payton would once again blame himself for everything. Payton was obviously cursing himself for not having protected Sam. His younger brother had not uttered a single word since noticing her disappearance. But Sean also discerned that Payton had given his all and could take no more. Nathaira's curse was stronger than Sean had thought.

When Payton showed no reaction even as his cell phone vibrated with an incoming call, Sean grabbed it and answered.

"Hello?"

"Yes, this is Payton McLean," he lied, and listened to the caller.

"Uh-huh . . . yes, I see. That is impossible. I'm afraid I'm no longer in the States. . . . I understand. Thank you for calling. Yes, I hope you're wrong about that. Thank you."

Feeling utterly defeated, Sean hung up and stared at the rain running down the windshield.

"Who was that?"

Sean was glad they were side-by-side in the car. He didn't think he could give his brother the bad news while looking him in the eyes.

"That was Dr. Lippert from the hospital in Milford, Delaware."

"So? What did he want?"

Sean fidgeted in his seat.

"He wanted to examine you. Double-check some numbers. Said there was something wrong with your blood work."

"*Pog mo thon!* I'm not going anywhere. Plus, nobody needs to tell me there's something wrong with me. I know that already!"

Sean finally turned to his brother, and when their eyes met he couldn't keep the truth from him any longer.

"He gives you a month. At most."

Payton blinked. Then he nodded and opened the driver's door. Before Sean could say anything, Payton had exited the car.

Sean knew immediately where Payton would want to spend the next few weeks. Sean also knew he wouldn't be able to stop Payton from spending his final days in the presence of his beloved Sam.

Sean flinched when the phone rang again. He was relieved to hear Blair's voice on the other end.

"It's a good thing you called. I'm afraid we need you here. Payton is in really bad shape. I just talked with the doctor, and he confirmed our worst fears. It seems Payton is suffering from a mystery illness that nobody's ever seen before."

"*A Dhia, thois cpbhair!* I can't believe it! I'll be glad to be with you again. How is Payton taking it?" the eldest brother asked anxiously.

"He seems to have accepted his fate, but something else is killing him right now," Sean explained.

"What could be worse than that?"

Sean took a deep breath. He couldn't tell Blair over the phone what had happened to Sam. Sam's fate was hard enough to accept even if you had experienced it firsthand. So he tried to be vague.

"I'll tell you when you get here. When are you coming?"

"The sentencing hearing was yesterday. Neither Cathal nor Alasdair has to go to prison for kidnapping Ashley. But they've been sentenced to leaving the country right away. That's why I'm calling. We'll be on the plane in an hour. I'm taking Cathal to Galthair, and then I'll come meet you as quickly as I can."

"I don't understand how you can stick with him," Sean replied, stunned. "He's the reason that Nathaira murdered our brother!"

"Cathal has been my good friend since we were little. He has not gotten over his own sister being a cold-blooded killer. And I have forgiven Nathaira with all of my heart. After everything she told us at the motel, it's a miracle she managed to hide her hatred and insanity for so long. At the mercy of a stepmother as a child, only to find out that her real mother was a witch. As for her father . . . a brutal tyrant." Blair paused for a moment. "It hasn't always been easy for us, Sean, but I would not want to trade places with her. She's a victim, too."

Sean snorted with contempt.

"Bah! Even if there was a grain of truth to any of this, I'd advise you not to talk to Payton this way. Maybe she was a victim, maybe she wasn't—but the fact is that *her* hatred is killing him slowly and in the most painful way."

There was silence on the other end of the line. Sean knew that Blair was stuck in an emotional quandary. He had always adored Nathaira.

"She made us all suffer. The fact that she blamed Cathal for everything, that she did it all for him, is too much for him. Of course he wanted to lead the clan. After all, he was the firstborn and destined to do it. But he would never have approved for one of us to die just so he could be clan chief," Blair said quietly.

Sean shook his head at Blair's ignorance, but he didn't feel like engaging in a long, complicated discussion right now.

"Listen, I have to get to the gate. I know where you are. I'll join you as quickly as I can. In the meantime, please look after our little brother, aye?"

"Sure."

Sean hung up the phone and stared at the display for a long time.

Soon Blair, Cathal, and Alasdair would be back in Scotland. But none of them would really be going home. Because everything had changed. *They* had changed.

Chapter 10

Scotland, by the shore of Loch Duich; October 1740

The fog billowed, gray and sinister over the hills. It was so dense that you couldn't even see your hands before your eyes. The panicked mooing of cattle mingled with the angry barks of dogs. They sounded like dark, diabolical characters that had entered a dank and murky underworld and were stomping through the black smoke of a fiery inferno. The only thing missing from this hellfire was the smell of sulfur and brimstone.

"Come on! This way, you damn cows," Duncan Stuart said, his voice thundering through the fog.

If all of this seemed like a hellish depiction of Plato's cave, then Duncan Stuart was the inevitable demon. He was tall and dark, with eyes black as a moonless night. And this demon was in excellent company, for Dougal Stuart's appearance was in no way inferior to that of his twin brother. He was a giant man, too, and possessed just as much physical strength. His black hair was shorter than his brother's, his chin covered in dark stubble, and his jawline even more pronounced and strong.

"Every cow accounted for? Then close it."

After closing the gate behind their cattle, Dougal scraped some cow dung from his boot and cursed.

"All right, all done."

Duncan nodded approvingly. One of the dogs came up to them and started sniffing at Duncan's boot. This earned him a good kick in the side that sent him scampering back to his pack with his tail between his legs.

"Ross, call back your damn dogs already. I'm warning you," Duncan hollered.

One blow of the whistle, and the entire pack disappeared into the fog. Duncan raised his eyebrows in disdain. The dogs would surely knock skinny Ross to the ground again as soon as they jumped up on him.

"Come on, we have to get a move on. I don't think these cowards of the Cameron clan dare attack us if they value their lives at all, but I'll still be glad to be back on my own land," he grumbled.

Dougal pushed himself off the gate and adjusted the plaid around his shoulders.

"All right, then. We'll get our things from the cabin and be on our way. We have a good distance to cover before we meet up with the others. I don't think they'd be overjoyed that we are missing some cows again!"

With a sullen expression, Duncan followed his brother in the direction of the horses. Ross Galbraith was already waiting, reins in hand, and with a whole lot of dogs by his side. They hadn't really wanted to take their useless half brother along, but without his dogs, it would have been hard to round up the cattle in this kind of weather.

It was impossible to tell that Ross was related to them. He was scrawny and angular, with bright red hair and pale skin. And despite being seventeen years old, he still lacked the raw, masculine strength of his two brothers. He was like a puppy with long legs and a head far too big for his small body.

Dougal yanked the reins from Ross's hands and swung himself onto his horse. Not a moment later, Duncan followed suit and drove his boots deep into his horse's side to urge it on. Over his shoulder he called:

"Ross, if those flea-infested dogs of yours can't keep up, I will leave them behind. You hear me? We need to make haste."

Quickly, so as to not further annoy his brothers, Ross mounted his horse and whistled for his beloved dogs. The journey to come would be long. He hoped it wasn't too long for his furry, four-legged friends.

To him, they were much more than simple herding dogs. They were the only friends he had in the world.

The cold had seeped into my skin and made me shiver. I massaged my arms and struggled to get up from the cold, damp ground.

"Dammit!"

My pants were cold and wet, too, and they clung to my legs. Wishing I still had that rain jacket, I wiped clumps of earth from my butt and took a good look around. I couldn't make out much in this thick fog, but one thing was for sure: The old cemetery was gone.

Dense bushes of Scotch broom spread as far as my eyes could see, but the chapel, cemetery wall, and gravestones were nowhere in sight. The only thing still around was the rough-hewn memorial stone of the five sisters right in the middle of not much. Absolutely nothing else reminded me of the place I'd left in a swirl of magic. God only knew where I had landed.

I tried to get a sense of direction, but after taking only a few steps I was forced to admit to myself that I had no idea where I had even started out. The fog was so dense that I could be walking in circles. I couldn't even see the big stone anymore because I'd focused on handling the uneven terrain instead of on where I was going.

My stomach grumbled, and I realized that I hadn't eaten in ages. Just as a new panic attack tried to grab me with its angry claws, I spotted the outline of a building. I quickly ducked under the next shrub of Scotch broom.

Would I be able to get help here? I had to find out where and, most important, *when* I was. And I really needed some food. But, if I had really landed in the past, I couldn't just walk up to that lonely old stone cottage and knock on the door. The people here had most certainly never heard of the Black Eyed Peas, whose funky faces were printed on my tank top—and my jeans would probably even raise more questions than I'd like under the circumstances.

Dammit! When we'd planned to send Sean into the past, we wanted to dress him in period-appropriate clothes and equip him well before he started a dangerous journey into the unknown. But me? I sat here wearing nothing but a thin, faded tank top, a pair of blue jeans, and a dagger that I would sooner cut myself on than be able to use for defense. Still, I found the weight of it on my belt comforting. Anyway, I wouldn't stay here long and with any luck I wouldn't get myself into a situation where I would have to defend myself. I just had to find something to eat and practice a little patience until the fog lifted. Then I could find my way back to the cemetery and to my own century. I didn't just need to go back for my own sake, but also for Payton's. Sean urgently needed to know that there really was a way.

I crawled closer to the stone cottage. It looked abandoned. Nothing stirred, and no sound came from it at all. I pulled myself together and tiptoed to the side of the structure, but even from here I couldn't see or hear anything. I walked all the way around the humble building that leaned, crookedly, to the side. I looked around surreptitiously—but when everything stayed peaceful and still, necessity won over caution.

I pulled open the door of a wooden shed attached to the cottage. I peered into the darkness. A startled mouse darted between my feet, and the quiet rustle in a corner hinted at yet more unpleasant company. Cobwebs hung from the ceiling, and everything smelled of dust. Initially having held my breath, I finally dared to breathe out and enter the shed.

My worries were unfounded. Nobody had lived in this place for a long time. The barrels in front of me were filthy, and thick dust covered every available surface. Mice seemed to have chewed through some of the boxes over in the corner, the elusive content of which had spilled out and over the floor. Very faintly I was able to make out the aromatic scent of herbs, and a dried bunch of some kind of plant hung from the low ceiling. When the top of my head accidentally touched it, the bone-dry leaves crumbled and rained down on me.

Swiftly, I went farther in. It didn't look like there was anything edible around here. Whatever may have been stored in the barrels at some point, it was surely spoiled by now. My stomach protested loudly against this sad realization. Maybe I'd have more luck inside the cottage proper.

Just as I wanted to step back outside using the narrow doorway, the sound of loud barking made me come to a terrified stop.

"Shit!" I gasped.

Under no circumstances did I want to get caught here. Not only was I afraid of being mistaken for a thief, but the way I was dressed was probably enough for me to be burned alive at the stake. I pulled the door closed and was happy to have what little light came through the cracks and gaps in the wooden planks.

The sounds kept getting nearer. By now I could hear horses' hoofbeats as well. My mind went into overdrive. I couldn't hide in here. If anyone were to open the door, they would see me and I'd be doomed. They would take me for a witch, because how else would I explain my strange clothes, my surely anachronistic language, and my complete lack of knowledge about the customs and traditions of this place and era?

Hoping to hide behind one of the wooden boxes, I pushed it away from the wall, and its rotten lid broke off. I spied some coarsely woven fabric and quickly pulled away the rest of the wooden slats.

Male voices were now very close by.

"Fuck!"

Frantically, I dug through the box, trying not to make a sound. My hands were shaking. I grabbed piece of cloth by piece of cloth, until at long last I found something. It was some kind of a housedress, extremely simple and shapeless, but probably perfectly suitable for everyday life and work in the eighteenth century.

I pulled the scratchy fabric over my head, glad that I didn't have to wear it directly on my skin. I hurriedly smoothed down the skirt part of it over my pants and all the way down to my feet. But unfortunately that didn't work. My pants were clearly visible under the dress. Even though everything inside me struggled against taking them off, I really had no choice. Some kind of ribbon or belt around the waist would have given this sackcloth a little more shape, but if there was one thing I wanted to avoid, it was showing these men that I actually had a waist.

And so I tied a very loose knot and hoped that the wide, loose-fitting cut would look as unflattering as possible, while at the same time hiding the dagger that I'd tied to my upper thigh with my belt.

I gave a terrified start when I suddenly heard angry barking right outside the door. I could hear the dogs scratching up against the wood. I ducked behind a barrel and tried to make myself as small and inconspicuous as possible.

"What is it, girl? What did you find? Is there a big juicy rat in there?"

The whining and scratching continued, and the man laughed.

"All right, then, if you insist. Go get it!"

The door ripped open and, because my eyes had grown accustomed to the dark, I was blinded for a moment. Then I saw the man. I looked him square in the eye just as the giant dog pushed me to the ground and stood over me, snarling and baring its teeth. Thick saliva dripped from its mouth right onto my cheek, and I screamed. Screamed for my life.

The angry, slobbering beast was pushed aside, and I saw that pale, freckled face again. I felt nauseated, numb, and paralyzed. As I screamed, I couldn't even manage to lift my arms to block the fist I saw coming in for a blow.

Darkness swallowed me whole, but it wasn't kind. Haunting images flooded my mind, brought to life by the throbbing pain in my temple.

I was holding the knife tightly clutched in my hand. I had thrust it in so deep that my fist touched the lifeless chest of the man, and I could feel that the heart underneath my fingers had stopped beating. A single word flashed through my addled brain: betrayal.

I lifted my head and looked into his eyes. A tear, burning hot like melting metal, burned its way down my cheek and fell, unhindered, onto the blood-soaked earth.

Chapter 11

The dogs barked insanely as Ross stepped from the wooden shed, dragging a lifeless body behind him. That finally drew his half brothers' interest and, suddenly intrigued, they stepped closer.

"Who's that?" Duncan asked, resting his gaze on the young woman whose hair was dragging in the mud and whose cheek was visibly swollen.

Ross shrugged and pushed away the shaggy dog that had started licking the woman's face.

"I don't know. Barra was barking. I thought she had smelled a rat or something—and she had. This woman was hiding in the shed."

Dougal knelt beside the woman's slack body and turned her face to him.

"She's a Cameron!"

In disgust, he pulled away his hand and wiped it on his plaid.

"Interesting. That explains why you decided to pummel her half to death rather than ask what she was doing in there." He got up and slapped an unprepared Ross right across the face. The dogs immediately started defending their owner, growling and baring their teeth.

"Fool! We must find out who she is and what business she has here. Thanks to your rough welcome, it may now take hours before we can get an answer out of her—only we don't have hours!"

Ross pushed out his lower lip in anger. He could never do anything right by his brothers. This time, though, they should be grateful. They would never have noticed this enemy without Barra, his trusted dog.

"She's only a Cameron wench. We should just finish her off. Who knows what she's doing here in this godforsaken place. It's certainly not a coincidence that she was hiding here." Ross struggled to defend himself.

"Right, it's not a coincidence!" Dougal snapped. "Which is exactly why we need to find out who's behind this. We also need to get away from here as quickly as possible. In all likelihood, this wench was not on her own. Send out your dogs and see if they can find anyone else. I don't want any more Camerons hiding in the bushes. As for her"—he pointed at the woman on the floor—"we will take her with us, just in case."

Duncan knitted his brow. He could feel that this woman meant trouble, and he didn't like the idea of dragging her along with them. Taking a Cameron clan member prisoner could have serious consequences. But, even though she had the typical facial features of a Cameron, she was dressed in rags. The dress was barely good enough for a maidservant. Perhaps she was the result of an extramarital enjoyment between the great laird and some peasant woman? At any rate, her presence raised a few questions, and he supposed it couldn't hurt to have a bargaining chip. Which was why Duncan finally agreed with Dougal's plan.

Nerves strained, Duncan watched as Ross heaved the unconscious woman onto Dougal's horse and tied her up. Then he spat on the floor and entered the cottage through the main door. It was a perfect hiding place. The locals tended to avoid this old stone cottage because legend had it that the spirit of an old druid lurked here, waiting for forgiveness—the forgiveness he was never granted during his lifetime.

Duncan didn't care about such old wives' tales. He had learned early on to fight for everything and to be tough and strong. Which was why he had taught himself never to show weakness. The only things of importance to him were those he could touch and hold in his hands. He pinned the Stuart clan's brooch to his plaid and gently stroked its shiny silver surface. Then he took his broadsword and pushed it into the leather sheath on his back. Scanning the otherwise empty room one last time, he lifted his saddlebag off the floor. The silver pieces in it would at long last help him put his plan into action.

He hurried to untie his horse, fasten the saddlebags, and get on.

"Let's go!" he bellowed, galloping off and leaving his two brothers in a hail of flung-up dirt and mud.

The shallow hills seemed to fly away under his horse's hooves. He enjoyed leading with his brothers riding so far behind. It was only when he reached the crest of the first hill, after galloping through the gurgling source of a stream, that he pulled in the reins so his horse would slow down and allow his brothers to catch up.

In silence, they rode southward through the fog that was slowly dissolving. Their path took them deeper into the hillside, until mountains rose almost menacingly around them. A number of small torrents washed over the trail in front of them, carrying with them loose rubble. Their horses struggled to find a foothold in some places.

The uneven terrain and extra weight of the woman took their toll on Dougal's horse. By noon they had made only half the journey to their arranged meeting point. The horses had slowed down, and the last climb had made them foam at the mouth. They urgently needed a break.

Last night's rain had turned a trickle into a torrential stream a few miles farther up, and they took that as a good opportunity to stop and rest. Duncan and Dougal lay spread-eagled in the grass, broadswords within arm's reach, while Ross led the exhausted horses to the river. Even the dogs came running—panting, and lapping at the fresh, cold water. When one of them leapt into the stream, water spewed up. The horses got skittish, whinnying and nervously treading on the spot.

The unknown woman groaned in a haze, and Ross hurried to lift her from the back of the horse before she could startle the nervous animals even further with some careless movement.

I landed on the ground with a thud. The back of my head banged against the big rock someone had propped me against. I felt slack and awful, and the complete lack of control over my body terrified me. Only now could I get a good look at the man standing before me. Lightning flashed before my inner eye, but too briefly for me to make sense of it. It was the echo of a dream, or a faded memory. I ran my hands over my face and touched my cracked lips with my tongue. I was terribly thirsty. Maybe that was why I was unable to think straight.

The guy had longish red hair and looked at me with suspicion, as if expecting me to grow a second head or something. I felt like I'd been abducted by aliens, so the idea of a second head didn't seem too far-fetched. I grabbed my throat and desperately stared at the river a little ways away from me. At this point I didn't even care that these filthy dogs were frolicking *in my drinking water,* stirring up mud. All I wanted was to quench this goddamn thirst! The urge to drink was stronger than my fear of the stranger.

"Please," I begged with a scratchy voice. "May I please go drink some water?"

He glanced from the riverbank and back to me, before deeming it low-risk enough and nodded for me to move.

"Aye, but no funny business," he answered firmly, while also helping me to my feet and steering me toward the river.

I had no idea what kind of "funny business" I could possibly get up to, what with my hands tied and in the presence of these angry, snarling wolfhounds. But since my thirst trumped all my other thoughts, I limited myself to greedily shoveling fresh, precious water into my mouth.

God, I had never tasted anything so delicious. I could almost detect the minerals that the water had flushed out of the mountains on its way to the river. It was icy cold, but what a pleasure for my parched throat!

"Not too much at once," the boy warned. "Take smaller sips—otherwise you'll get sick."

Slowly, I lowered my hands and dipped them into the stream. I enjoyed the feeling of the cold, swirling water on my skin before taking a final scoop to wash my face. As I dried my face on my sleeve, the rough material of my dress scratched it. I took my time so I could gather my thoughts. I fought back fear, refusing to allow it to paralyze me. I needed to keep a clear mind, no matter how hard it was. I turned around and smiled at the redheaded boy, trying to seem genuine.

"Thank you."

He blushed unexpectedly and then quickly made an effort to look grouchy.

"It's all right," he grumbled. "Go sit back down, and don't even think about trying to run. The dogs would easily track and find you, and that would not be an enjoyable experience for you."

I nodded and did exactly as I was told. He seemed satisfied and turned away to tend to the horses again, strapping bags of oats over their mouths.

I had to find out what this guy wanted from me, and where I was.

Only now that I discreetly looked around did I notice the other two men lying in the grass. They were of much greater physical stature than my handler. Even though they were taking in the sun with their eyes closed, they looked big and strong and terrifying.

It dawned on me that the boy and his dogs were the least of my problems. I really had to try not to mess with those other two. Their giant swords sparkled in the sunlight, and I couldn't help but wonder how many lives they must have taken with them. Up until now I wasn't a hundred percent convinced that I had traveled back in time, but here I saw living proof.

The two men looked like brothers and true Scottish warriors. They wore boots, thick woolen socks, and dark-tartan plaids draped around their hips in pleats and held in place by a belt. The plaids extended up to their roughly woven shirts and were draped over their shoulders, held there by a silver brooch.

Still, even though their high-quality weaponry suggested that they belonged to a noble clan, they did not match the glorified, romantic image of a Highlander that I had created in my mind. They were filthy with uncombed, matted hair. Plus, even from where I was sitting, I could see the dirt under my handler's fingernails.

I averted my eyes when the dogs shook the water from their coats. The boy cursed, chasing the dogs away and wiping the water from his face. Glancing over at me, he sat down on a piece of rock a few yards away and rummaged through the fur pouch hanging from his belt. It took him a while to find the small piece of wood he was looking for; then he pulled a small knife from his sock and started carving. The dogs lay down at his feet and took a snooze.

This seemingly ordinary activity made my eyes well up. I suddenly felt extremely homesick. I didn't belong here. This was not my world. I couldn't allow these men, whoever they were, to keep taking me farther and farther away from the portal of time. I had to go back! After all, I didn't know where I was or where they were taking me—much less why they were doing this.

Seriously, dude! I had to pull myself the hell together if I wanted to get out of this alive!

I tore at the bindings on my hands and feet, but the knots were foolproof. The rope wouldn't give a single inch.

If only I could reach Sean's knife—which, lucky for me, they hadn't noticed. I knew I wouldn't be able to use it unobserved. But that fact raised my spirits and spurred me on. I had to act. The time for being a passive observer was over, that was for sure. Once before I had submitted to my destiny and given myself to fate—just as Vanora had predicted in one of my visions. If fate was now putting me to the test, then I would be strong enough to face it.

I would fight!

But how could I fight if I didn't even know how to talk to that guy? It seemed sensible to do as little talking as possible. Maybe then I'd have a chance to hide that I wasn't from this era.

I got my handler's attention by quietly clearing my throat. When he raised a puzzled eyebrow, I started talking.

"Who are you? And where are you taking me?"

The young Scot stopped but avoided looking at me. So I continued.

"I would like to know . . . ," I began, but his alarmed look and the almost imperceptible shaking of his head made me shut up. I raised my head inquisitively, trying to figure out his strange behavior.

"Don't! Stay where you are!" he hissed through gritted teeth.

He continued carving the piece of wood, all the while discreetly scanning his surroundings. I pushed myself closer against the rock behind me. He pretended to stretch out his legs and then touched his dogs with the tips of his boots as if by accident. The dogs immediately pricked their ears and lifted their noses into the wind. When their deep, sonorant growls confirmed his suspicions, he gently petted the closest dog and reassured it. *"Sguir, mo charaid."*

The wolfhounds twitched but obediently kept their position.

I nonchalantly looked at the other two men lying in the grass. Their eyes were still closed, but their swords had disappeared under their plaids, as had their sword hands—which probably already clutched the weapons.

Suddenly, my mouth felt very dry. I sensed that they were expecting an attack, and when the skinny, red-haired guy got up to seemingly put another bag of oats around a horse's mouth, he casually reached for his sword dangling from its leather sheath by the saddle. He pulled it out in one fluid movement and hid it in the pleats of his kilt. Then he pushed one of his dogs in my direction and bent down to pet the animal.

"Stay here! Don't move, and you'll be safe. Barra will protect you."

And just as he sat back down on his rock, all hell broke loose.

Five men, armed with axes and swords, stormed from the underbrush with the intention of clobbering to death the two "sleeping" dark-haired, dangerous-looking men before turning to the weaker-seeming teenager as their easiest victim. After that, nothing would stop them from stealing the saddlebags and precious horses.

But the first attacker died before even registering that their victims were already wide-awake and battle ready. His axe cut through air as his now-lifeless body slumped to the ground. One of the dark-haired warriors yanked his sword from the dead body with one strong, powerful move. Then he hurried over to the younger one who was in the process of fighting three of the bandits.

I crouched into the rock as much as I could. I made myself look as small as possible and was thankful for the tall, snarling dog by my side. It seemed that the attackers had not yet noticed me, because nobody made a move in my direction. Of the original five bandits, there were now only three left after my captors had rid themselves of another one with a well-aimed blow as the dogs brought the man down. Once the remaining three attackers realized that they couldn't possibly win, they beat a hasty retreat. Followed by the growls and barks of the hounds, they fled into the woods and disappeared in the underbrush.

"*Bas maillaichte!* Ross! You should have warned us. Those flea-ridden bandits almost killed us in our sleep!" one of the dark-haired hunks hollered while simultaneously wiping his blade on the clothes of a dead man. The one he'd called Ross—my handler—shrugged and walked over to me.

"I saw that you noticed them the same moment I did. They weren't particularly quiet about it, and, besides, the sun reflected off their weapons. Probably peasants who thought it'd be easy enough to mug some harmless, unarmed travelers. Had they succeeded in stabbing you in your sleep, Dougal, then that's exactly what you would have deserved."

He stepped up to me and held out his hand.

"Are you well?"

I only noticed that I was shaking all over when I tried to get up and my legs refused to work.

Was I well? Hell, no! And things weren't looking too well, either! Two dead bodies lay just a few yards away—killed before my eyes by dirty savages using broadswords! And as if that weren't enough, those same murderers had kidnapped me. What were they going to do to me? I was very close to passing out. Ross's friendly face—at least I knew his name now—was splattered with blood, and I found it hard to concentrate on anything but those shiny red specks of deadly violence.

"Woman, do you hear me? Get up, we have to leave." He pulled me up and steadied me when I tripped.

"No, sir! Leave me be!" I snapped at him while trying to break free.

I couldn't allow these savages to take me any farther away from the memorial stone of the five sisters. I didn't want to spend another second in their presence. They were cold-blooded killers!

"Please, sir, let me go! What do you want from me?"

Meanwhile, the other two came closer.

"Sir?" one of them mimicked my pleading tone before bursting out laughing.

The other one, the one Ross had addressed as Dougal, smirked and sank to his knees in a grand theatrical gesture.

"Please, *sir* . . ." He chuckled, pulling me up by my hair. "This lass seems to think she is at court with the Sassenach king. Just look at her hair! It's like she brushes it every day just to make it shine," he called out, and held up a strand of my brown hair. Even Ross, who had been nothing but friendly since I woke up, gave an embarrassed grin.

I had no idea what was going on. Why were these creeps laughing at me? Had I said something wrong?

"Stop it!" Ross said, trying to calm his dark-haired companions. But those two enjoyed pushing me around.

"Yes, maybe we're wrong, and this is in fact the queen of England!" Dougal suggested.

Doubling over with laughter and slapping his muscular thighs, the other brother—they were twins, for sure—joined in the game. "You might be right, sir! Just look at her soft skin, and her teeth! Very royal."

Ross pulled me away from them. He pushed me toward his horse, and even though I hadn't wanted to come with him a moment ago, he now seemed like my only option and savior.

"Leave her alone, Duncan! She was just trying to be friendly," he defended me.

"If she wants to be friendly, all she has to do is spread her—"

"We need to get out of here already!" Ross cut off the much bigger man and lifted me onto the back of his horse. "Or do you want to wait and see if the bandits decide to return with a few more of their peasant friends?"

After some hesitation, the twins each shrugged and turned to their own horses. They didn't even waste another thought on the peasants they had just killed.

"*Ifrinn!* I should never have opened that shed," Ross said as he mounted his horse and sat down in the saddle behind me.

For the next few miles, the men kept a watchful eye. We rode through a deep, dense forest, and I expected an attacker behind every little branch.

Never in my life had I been so afraid. I didn't know how to behave, or what dangers lay ahead of me now that I'd been kidnapped and taken into the unknown. I felt sick to my stomach and was breaking out in a cold, shaking sweat. It was hard to say which was the greater threat: traveling with these warriors or trying to make my way back to the memorial stone of the five sisters on my own. At least Ross didn't seem to pose any danger to me—not after he'd punched me that first time, anyway. So I was glad for the support his chest gave me.

After riding for a good long while, the shock from the attack subsided, and I finally stopped trembling and dared to rest my head against my Scottish handler.

"Better?" he asked with concern in his voice.

I simply nodded. I was afraid of saying the wrong thing again.

Ross had noticed that I kept stealing worried glances at the two men in front of us.

"Try to get used to it. They're always like that."

"What did I do to them?"

"Nothing. You don't need to do anything to set them off. Maybe it's because you are different from the other women we usually meet. And then the way you were pretending to be all courtly and whatnot . . . maybe they thought you were trying to make fun of them."

I couldn't believe it. I had been *too polite*? My parents would be so proud!

"I just wanted—"

"I know. Just stop with all the pretense and tell me your name. Otherwise, I might start to believe you are the queen of England."

I tried to figure out my safest bet. Should I tell him my real name, or should I make one up?

"Nothing? Should I call you 'Cameron lass,' then?"

I flinched. Cameron? They thought I was a Cameron? I shook my head. I remember Payton and his brothers being amazed at my close resemblance to my ancestors, but I always thought they were exaggerating. Was it good or bad to be taken for a Cameron? Was this the reason they had kidnapped me? Were these men mistaking me for someone else?

Because I didn't give an answer, Ross stiffened behind me.

"All right, fine! You can go to hell for all I care. You're nothing but trouble anyway."

He spurred on his horse to catch up to the others. I imagined that the twin warriors probably wouldn't appreciate our conversation. So I came to a decision.

"My name is Samantha. Samantha Cameron."

My heart beat wildly, and I was anxious to see if he would realize that I'd lied. The strange thing was, it didn't feel like a lie at all. And so I repeated it with more confidence—and also in order to convince myself, a little louder this time.

"I am Samantha Cameron, and who are you, sir—uh, I mean, what's your name?" I remembered that I had to stop with the *pretense*, which I had taken to be the polite way of talking to people in this era. Ross was right. I mean, we were riding through the Scottish Highlands all dusty and sweaty, and the men's hands were covered in blood, and they were unwashed and uncombed. Why should they worry about politeness? At least Ross didn't seem to mind that I no longer addressed him as "sir."

"Ross Galbraith." He pointed ahead of us. "And those two gentlemen in front of us are my brothers, Duncan and Dougal. Twins, they are."

I was glad that couldn't see my surprise. His *brothers*? I had never seen siblings that showed so little resemblance. I wanted to seize the moment to learn more, so I asked, "Why were you attacked?"

He shook with laughter behind me, then replied in an amused tone, "Why do you attack someone? Because we were there, and they were there. Couldn't you tell from their shabby clothes that they were peasants? They may as well have attacked us with pitchforks. They weren't even wearing their clan colors. Men like that toil for their laird all their lives. They pay their tenth and at the end of the month don't have enough left to feed their starving children. Winter is coming, and those poor sods have nothing to bite on. Desperation drove them to attack us."

"But if you knew that, then why would you kill them? Why didn't you just scare them off?"

I was shocked at how indifferent this guy seemed to the fates of those poor peasant men and their families. How were the women supposed to feed their children without the help of their husbands and sons?

"No, we couldn't have. If we had shown them mercy, they would have run away, hidden in the woods, and ambushed us somewhere else along the way. And next time they might be more successful. I'm surprised you don't know this. In fact, you seem to know very little about the ways of men. Didn't your parents warn you? Or are all the women where you come from like that?"

I didn't want to think about my parents now—it was just too painful. Instead, I focused on the horse's steady movements. My back hurt from riding so long, and my butt was getting sore. "So, where are we going?" I asked.

"You don't need to know that," he said. He whistled for his dogs and quickly caught up to his brothers. That was his way of letting me know that our talk was over. And for the rest of our long journey, he made it a point to ignore me.

I couldn't say how many hours had passed, but my whole body ached and I was doubling over with hunger pangs. It was almost dusk when we reached a clearing by the edge of the forest. Duncan stood up in his stirrups and scanned the vast plains that lay before us.

The scene was amazingly beautiful. No picture postcard could ever convey a better sense of the Highlands than this three-dimensional panorama. And despite my precarious situation, Scotland's wilderness and rugged beauty took my breath away. I drew strength and encouragement from the breathtaking view as Duncan motioned for his brothers to dismount. The dogs scattered, trotting through the grass with their noses close to the ground and marking the saplings by the edge of the woods.

My butt was completely numb by the time Ross lifted me off his horse.

"All right? Are you able to stand?" he asked, raising his eyebrows skeptically.

Dougal slapped him hard on the shoulder and doubled over with laughter.

"Ross, you're an idiot. Why are you courting her? If you want her, then just take her already! But for God's sake, stop pretending you care about her well-being."

Ross blushed to the roots of his hair and pushed out his chin as he glared at his much bigger brother.

"Shut up and leave the girl alone!" he defended me.

Dougal snorted and poked me in the shoulder. I inched closer to Ross, hoping for protection. The dark-haired giant raised his hands defensively and gave me a contemptuous look. Ross glowered.

"Calm down, little boy, I'm not getting involved. But if you are so desperate that you would actually do *her,* then maybe you should try to use your own hands. Did you not get a good look at her? Nothing about her body could please a real man."

I knew what Dougal was trying to do. He wanted to humiliate me—and humiliate Ross—to show us who was in charge. And even though I was glad he didn't find me the least bit attractive, I was hurt by his crude remarks.

"Dougal, I'm warning you." Ross took a step forward and raised a fist.

Not a moment later, he went down with a moan, blood welling from his lip. His brother looked over him menacingly.

"I would think twice about your actions, lad. One more try and I will throw your bloodless carcass to the dogs. Now, go and get some firewood!"

With that, he turned on his heel and kicked one of the dogs that was growling to defend its master. This made the dog submit and crawl up to Ross with its tail between its legs.

I bent down and petted the dog's head in empathy. Ross, on the other hand, refused my hand and got up without help. Angrily, he ran his sleeve over his lip and spat in the grass. Then he reached into his *sporran*—that fur pouch attached to the front of his belt—and fed a brown lump to his dog.

"What's that?" I asked, so dizzyingly hungry that I was jealous of the dog.

"Dried pig's ear. Come on, now. We'll need what little daylight is left to gather firewood." And he turned around and disappeared into the fir trees.

I trotted after him, and we quickly found what we needed. A storm must have uprooted a tree some time ago. It was so dry and sapless that Ross easily broke off a few branches for us to drag back to the clearing. With my bound hands and feet, I wasn't much help, but there was no negotiating with him when I asked him to untie me.

We got a good campfire going, and Dougal and Duncan returned with several freshly killed rabbits. After skinning and gutting them, they hung them over the fire on sticks. My mouth watered as I took in the delicious smell of cooking meat. But it remained to be seen whether I would get any of it. Right after his return, Duncan had grabbed me by the arm and tied me up to a tree a few yards away. I noticed a long cut beside the sleeve of his shirt, and that it was covered in dried blood. Had he been hurt during the attack? Despite my experiences in the past two days, the level of brutality people routinely used with one another in this time period still seemed surreal.

So now, tied to a tree, I had to sit and watch the men gorge themselves on freshly grilled rabbit. I greedily watched a drop of meat juice run along Duncan's finger and fall to the ground. The steaming-hot rabbit leg looked juicy, and I wished my teeth were tearing the tender meat off the bone. I swallowed hard. Duncan threw his clean-picked leg bone to the dogs, and they of course voraciously pounced on it.

I reached a point where I would have fought even dogs for the leftovers. I was just about to ask for some food when something stirred. The dogs pricked their ears and, yapping, tore into the forest that formed a protective barrier behind our backs. The men got up, too, reaching for their weapons. But compared to this morning's attack, they seemed relaxed.

I panicked at seeing the horde of horsemen emerging from the woods. Their horses were just as magnificent as Duncan and Dougal's, and some of the men wore the colors I'd seen on Ross and his brothers. The men greeted one another with booming laughter and shoulder slaps.

I tried to make myself invisible. Maybe this commotion would offer an opportunity for me to get at my *sgian dhu* and cut through my ties. Then I could escape and return to Payton. I had memorized every rock formation, valley, and stream on our path today—just so I could find my way back.

Suddenly I heard even louder and wilder cheers. Intrigued, I tried to catch sight of what all the fuss was about through the campfire's dancing flames.

The men had come closer. Over the back of one of their horses a big leather wineskin hung from one side. A large ham and several loaves of bread in a string bag hung from the other. An expectant grin slowly spread across my face.

Meanwhile, everyone had dismounted and taken care of their horses, and they now approached the warm and cozy campfire.

The night promised to be cold, and I desperately hoped someone would offer me something to eat. The newcomers had joined my captors by the fire and broken the bread into rough chunks to be passed around. Thick slices of cured ham also made the rounds. The mood was cheerful, and the wineskin was emptied quickly.

Finally, Ross pulled out a simple, hand-carved flute from his saddlebags and struck up a song. After the first stanza, he glanced at me over the fire, winking ever so slightly while continuing to play with happy enthusiasm. One of the new guys noticed and turned to see who was on the receiving end of Ross's wink.

Golden sparks from the embers burned up on their way into the night sky. And the smoke from the fire rose up high enough to invite the stars to dance to Ross's heart-wrenching music.

Our eyes met, and I let out a triumphant cry. I wanted to jump to my feet, but my ties kept me down. The rough rope chafed against my skin as I tore at it. Even though I sat outside the circle of light, my face must have given away my overwhelming joy at seeing the man rise and walk toward me.

With blood rushing through my veins, sweat trickling down my spine, and a sudden dryness in my mouth, I watched him approach.

Chapter 12

He looked so different. So unfamiliar. Like a . . . savage. I racked my brain about what I should say and do. But it seemed to have shut down completely. I couldn't take my eyes off him as he came closer.

Finally, he stopped within inches of me and studied me with a bewildered look.

"Well, well, well, who do we have here?" he said. The sound of his voice gave me goose bumps. It really was him!

Even though my mouth was open, not a sound came out of it.

He crouched down and wrinkled his forehead. Then he pulled on my ties.

"Oh, my sweet," he whispered, "whatever did you do that they had to tie you up? What a shame! I would have enjoyed your gracious company by the fire."

I couldn't believe what was happening and didn't notice Duncan approaching until his voice startled me out of my paralysis.

"Sean!" he called out. "Don't dirty your hands on that one. Don't you see that she's a Cameron?"

Sean, who was still holding my gaze, gave me a mischievous smirk.

"Duncan, you know very well that most fun things are also dirty."

Could it be true? The way he had greeted me made me doubt my own sanity. Was all this a dream? Or could this really be Sean, the charming smooth talker I'd met back in Scotland? Was that already the man in there that he was going to be? Was it possible that all these years really didn't change him at all?

My relief was so great that a tear ran down my cheek. I had no idea how I was going to explain things to him, but at least I was no longer surrounded by only strangers.

He held up my hands and turned to Duncan. "What's all this? Is this wee lass really such a wildcat that three strong lads such as yourselves can only keep her in check by tying her to a tree?"

"She's our prisoner—not our guest," Duncan grumbled.

Sean got up, smoothed his plaid, and gave me a final sympathetic look.

"So to what minor offense does she owe her involuntary presence?"

The dark-haired Highlander gave me a warning glare.

"We were following the tracks of our stolen cattle when she suddenly appeared out of nowhere and rammed a dagger into my arm. She heckled me like a crazy person. She tried to cut my throat, Sean! She's not all there, if you know what I mean. Or, maybe she has something to do with the cows that went missing. In which case I will find a way to make her talk. I can promise you that. Either way, she's coming with us to Castle Galthair."

"What?" I called out. "That's not true! I have—"

"Shut your trap!" Duncan barked. Little droplets of his spit landed on my face, and I was afraid that he'd hit me. I raised my arms to protect my face.

"Oh, if you don't shut your lying mouth, I'm going to shut it for you!" he growled.

I hoped for help from Sean, but he didn't seem to care.

"I would give her some food and water instead. If she dies from starvation, you'll be hard-pressed to get anything meaningful out of her anyway," he said flatly. "The lass is looking the worse for wear already."

With that, Sean turned away and reclaimed his seat by the campfire without another look in my direction.

In his stead, the dark-haired giant bent down to talk to me. I forced myself to look him square in his ink-black eyes.

"I'm not done with you yet. We'll talk tomorrow."

After the men turned in, I trembled with fear in the cold dark of the night. The fire's heat no longer reached me, so I tried to warm myself by curling up in the fetal position.

Although Sean slept just a few yards away, I had no chance of talking to him. How could he help me if he didn't even know what was going on? Exhausted and in despair, I closed my eyes and hoped sleep would soon take me away into the realm of dreams.

I woke with a start when something cold and wet touched my ankle. It was Barra the dog, who then lifted her nose and curled up across my legs into a soft, warm, hairy ball. Ross quietly giggled and sat down beside me. He opened his *sporran* and took out a small package wrapped in cloth.

"Here, for you. Enjoy."

Hungrily, I reached for the packet as best I could with my tied-up hands. I marveled at its contents: a cold rabbit leg, a thick slice of bread, and a big juicy piece of ham. I gave him a grateful smile before digging into his delicious gift. He giggled again, and Barra rested her head on my hips. Like a great warm comforter, she warmed me with her body.

After I gobbled up everything down to the last crumb, Ross handed me the wineskin. It had been filled with fresh, clear water instead. I gulped the delicious water so fast that I almost choked on it—twice. Still, I felt brand-spanking new. I wiped the water from my chin and returned the wineskin to Ross.

Ross gave me a sympathetic smile as he stood up.

"Sleep now."

Before he could turn away, I reached for his hand.

"Thank you, Ross. I—"

"It's all right." He looked me in the eyes. "And no funny business during the night, because I won't be here to help you."

"Where are you going?"

"Duncan has assigned me to guard duty."

I watched him walk past the died-down campfire, climb over the sleeping men, and leap onto his horse. He called his other dogs with a quick whistle and rode away across the plain. Barra lifted her head to listen for a moment before laying her head back down on my old housedress. I sat for a few minutes, gently petting the wolfhound's shaggy coat and staring up at the clear night sky.

Sean McLean was only a stone's throw from me.

A single question had been racing through my head ever since I'd seen Sean's face in the glow of the fire—and I wanted to scream it: "Payton McLean, where the hell are you?"

Chapter 13

A thair!"

His brother's horrified cry rang in his ears, and it took all his strength to disarm the opponent in front of him with another blow of his mighty broadsword. The enemy sword clanked to the ground, and the opposing warrior faltered. Payton McLean took advantage of the moment and held his blade to his opponent's throat. This fight was not over yet, but he had to find out what had happened to his brother.

A quick glance over his shoulder, and his blood froze. It wasn't his brother Kyle, but his father, Fingal, who was lying badly wounded on the ground.

Payton turned to the man in rags he had just beaten. He pressed his blade against the other man's skin, causing a thick drop of blood to ooze from the cut.

"Get out! Don't ever come back here! Make sure you ride fast, because if he dies, I will come and find you! And you'll regret the day that you came to steal our cattle."

Payton pulled back his blade, whirled it around his head in a wide arc, and delivered a hard blow to the man's head with the handle of his sword. The man first staggered away and then broke into a run.

With one move of his free hand, Payton motioned for his little brother to do the same with the two opponents he'd been keeping in check. Kyle stepped aside, and the two men hurried on after their pal. A pile of weapons they had taken off the bloodthirsty trio lay at Kyle's feet: a broadsword, a *sgian dhu,* an axe—and an archery bow.

The latter was the reason Fingal McLean was lying wounded on the ground. The shaft of an arrow protruded from his chest, blood trickling from the wound. The two brothers hurried over to him as soon as the cattle thieves were out of sight. With grave concern, they knelt beside their father, and Kyle pushed the graying hair from the fallen man's face.

"Father, we're right here," Kyle whispered.

Fingal's eyes darted back and forth, unable to focus, and then closed.

"Stay awake! *Ifrinn!* Look at me!" Kyle called, slapping him across the cheek. Fingal's eyelids fluttered open, and a painful moan escaped his lips. But in the next moment, he lost consciousness again.

Payton quickly cut away his father's shirt and now stared, terrified, at the old man's chest.

"The arrow is in deep, but it's not bleeding much. Pulling the arrow out might hurt him even more. What should we do?" he asked.

Kyle, whose eyes were narrow from hiding his tears, shook his head in resignation.

"I don't know. We need help, and quickly!"

"We have to take him away from here. It's too dangerous to stay. It's probably best if we take him to McRae's cottage."

Kyle nodded. His hands shook as he gently wiped the beads of sweat from Fingal's forehead. "Stay with us, Father, stay with us," he implored.

"Give me a hand. I will break off the arrow so that we can at least provisionally bandage the wound before carrying him away," Payton said.

Kyle gritted his teeth and grabbed the arrow just above the entry wound. Payton tried to break off the shaft directly above it, but without pushing it in deeper or tearing open the wound any further. The arrow broke with a quiet snap. Both brothers exhaled with relief. The arrow shaft now only protruded about two fingers' breadth from their father's chest. Payton cut off a wide strip of cloth from his plaid, and together they managed to wrap it around Fingal's chest like a bandage.

To put Fingal up on a horse in such poor condition proved a real challenge, but they eventually succeeded in lifting him into the saddle in front of Kyle. Kyle was only sixteen, but it was clear from his strong build that he would grow into a man of great strength and stature, just like his father and brothers. Still, he struggled to hold up and support the wounded man in front of him.

"Go now. McRae will help you carry him into the cottage. Lay him down and make sure he drinks a little water regularly. I will fetch the others, and then we will take Father home."

Kyle nodded and held on tight to the reins so that his horse remained still. He was worried that any small movement might drive the arrow deeper into his father's chest.

"Payton?" he whispered in a shaky voice. "Payton, wha . . . what if he dies?" This time he couldn't hide his tears any longer.

Payton looked Kyle firmly in the eye, and pledged: "He won't die! Not at the hand of a petty cattle thief, that much I swear! And now go—don't waste any more time. We will meet up at McRae's."

Kyle's horse broke into a trot, then into a gallop, and Payton silently begged forgiveness for having made a promise that he himself found hard to believe. He lifted the weapons from the ground and looked over at the handful of sheep standing and bleating quietly with their front legs tied. He had originally planned to return them to McRae, but now they would have to find their own way back. Quickly, he cut through their ties and pushed them in the right direction.

Next, he set off in the direction of where all three territories met: to the north, the sweeping plains of the Camerons; to the east, his father's land—the land of the McLeans; and to the west, the rolling hills and white shores of the Stuart clan. The other two parties would be waiting for them there, likewise searching the borderlands for bandits and cattle thieves.

The patrols were born out of necessity to fight the raids and thefts that had been taking place over these past few months. Cathal Stuart had asked the McLeans for help. Fingal was unable to deny this request because they were allies—even though his clan hadn't yet been affected by the attacks.

Still, the safety and security of the borderlands was in everyone's interest. If they didn't want war between the clans, then the raids had to be stopped. The wounds that long ago were torn by an old blood feud between the Stuarts and the Camerons would never heal, with or without stolen cattle. And Cathal was not yet clan chief, not by a long stretch. He urgently needed to prove that he was able to lead his men into battle, that he was capable of protecting his clan and, if need be, to defend it.

The recent attacks had caused a rise in the voices of those who'd imagined men other than Cathal should be clan leader. After all, there were alternatives should Cathal not hold up well. The old laird had legitimized his two bastard sons—a disservice to Cathal, his lawful son and heir.

Payton urged on his horse and tore across the green hills in a full gallop. He saw the majestic mountains of the Highlands rise to his right, and he prayed that his father would survive the journey there. He would take him to Burragh. He would not allow Fingal to die for Cathal's cause.

He bent closer over his horse's mane to help it fly ever faster across the plains, driven by the desperate hope that he would find his father still alive upon his return.

Payton headed toward the men, exhausted from his long trip. He noticed their questioning eyes as they searched the wide plains behind him for any companions. With his horse still moving, he leapt from the saddle and threw his reins to Kenzie, the youngest member of the Stuart clan. Everyone guessed right away what must have happened. The men came running, calling for Sean and Blair.

"Payton, what is it? Where is everyone?" Duncan asked upon reaching him.

"Father is injured. I came as fast as I could. We have to take him home, but Kyle and I can't do it on our own. We need a cart!" Payton called without stopping for courtesies.

In the meantime, his brothers had also reached his side. They exchanged worried looks.

"What happened? Tell us everything," Blair demanded. Blair, Fingal's oldest son, had a voice that was used to giving orders. One day he would become laird of the McLeans, and he had been preparing to assume that command all of his life. This often meant that he adopted the opinion of his best friend, Cathal Stuart. The Stuarts and McLeans had been friends and allies for a long time.

Payton looked into many a shocked face. These men were either family members or longtime friends and allies. Every single one of them was close to Fingal, and the worry about his health and well-being was clearly written on their faces.

"We passed by McRae's at dawn, and he told us that some of his sheep had been stolen during the night. We asked how he knew that his sheep weren't just having a snooze out on the heath, but then he showed us his best herd dog—dead from an arrow to the heart. Father became angry and promised the shepherd that we would find and bring back his sheep. Not long after, we found the thieves' tracks and confronted them a few miles farther up. They had all the missing sheep. I was fighting one of the thieves. I don't know what was going on behind me, but . . ."

The shame about his failure to help—a terrible shortcoming—made him pause.

"When I turned around, Father was lying on the ground with an arrow through his chest. I had to let the thieves go because I could not keep three men in check and help Father at the same time."

"How is Father? Is he well?" Sean pressed.

"No. When I left him, he was no longer conscious. Kyle is taking him to McRae's cottage. We have to get him to Castle Burragh quickly so Nanny MacMillan can take care of him."

The brothers' trust in the old wet nurse's healing powers knew no bounds. She had been part of the family ever since they were born. They had overcome many of their wounds and illnesses thanks to her skills as a healer. Even strong, grown men followed the wise woman's advice when it came to any kind of injury. If anyone could save Fingal's life, it would be Nanny MacMillan.

Without hesitation, Blair began dispatching orders.

"Very well. Let's not waste any time. Cathal, we will ride with Payton. Father needs us now."

Cathal nodded and looked into the ranks of men still gathered around them. There was his youngest brother, Kenzie, still holding the reins of Payton's horse. There were Dougal and Duncan, and Ross, their half brother. There was also Alasdair Buchanan, a man he could always rely on to do some dirty work. He'd be able to manage without Blair, Sean, and Payton McLean when it came to patrolling the outer sector of the borderlands.

"*Mo charaid,* I will also send Ross with you," Cathal agreed. "Payton mentioned you needed an oxcart, and it can't hurt to have an extra set of hands."

Relief came over Payton, because for a brief moment he was able to allow someone else to take charge. He was certain that Blair would do everything in his power to ensure their father's speedy recovery.

Ross looked up with a start before glancing at the tree where the girl was still curled up in a ball, quietly awaiting the fate his brothers intended for her.

"Why don't you give them Kenzie," he suggested sheepishly. "I can be of better service here with the dogs. And besides, one of us has to watch the prisoner while you're taking care of more important things."

Cathal's face darkened, and his voice took on a threatening tone.

"*You* will go with them! Don't ever dare question my orders again and recommend my brother for a peasant's work, you illegitimate bastard son! As for the prisoner . . ." He now directed his anger toward Duncan and Dougal. "You know full well how shaky the peace is between the Cameron clan and ours. Surely, it is not in our interest to abduct their women! We will discuss this further once we're back at Galthair. In the meantime, this woman will be under my protection."

Ross was relieved. Yes, he was furious at being put in his place by the clan leader. But then again, he was used to being yelled at. He had been treated this way all his life. In reality, he wasn't the illegitimate son—Duncan and Dougal were illegitimate. But the twin brothers bore the Stuart name, which was sufficient to make the questionable circumstance of their conception irrelevant. At least, now, Cathal would ensure Samantha's safety.

"But, Cathal, that girl has nothing to do with you!" Duncan disagreed vehemently.

"*Fan sàmhach!* I am the laird! My word is the law. Or did you forget that you swore an oath of blood?"

Duncan, pressed, stayed silent as Cathal continued. "Blair, you will take the woman with you. I have no use for womenfolk here, but maybe she can help with Fingal. Women seem to be more skilled at that sort of thing."

With his eyebrows raised provocatively, he awaited a reaction. But when Duncan nodded for Ross to pack his things and fetch the prisoner, a satisfied smile crossed Cathal's face.

In the meantime, Payton had turned away and put a bag of oats over his horse's mouth. His mind was preoccupied with the journey back. Having to wait for his brothers and everyone else made his patience wear thin. Annoyed, he turned around.

CHAPTER 14

A fly kept circling my head, and I just couldn't get rid of it. I worried that my not-too-pleasant smell had attracted it. I'd frankly had enough of *that* myself. It had been days since I'd been able to wash myself. On top of that had been the physical strain and a night spent in close embrace with Barra—neither of which had exactly made me smell of roses.

As the fly came at me again, I started thrashing as far as my tied-up hands would allow.

I thought the men had completely forgotten about me, because nobody had paid me any mind since Dougal had thrown a piece of bread my way in the morning. Nobody spoke to me. And Duncan—who had threatened me only yesterday—was nowhere to be seen.

Something was obviously happening, though, because all the men were standing close together, looking irritated and gesticulating. The wind carried only bits and pieces of their words over to me. Plus, I could only make out very little because the boy who had arrived here yesterday with Sean's group was holding the reins of a horse that blocked my field of vision.

Just when I spotted Ross's red shock of hair in the crowd, he was already making his way back to me. He crossed the campsite, lifting a few things here and there to stow in his horse's saddlebags. He then strapped his sword to his back and tied back his long hair with a leather band.

It was truly fascinating how *normal* all of this seemed after such a short time. These men didn't seem to miss running water or a warm bed. They just covered themselves with their thin plaids and inched up closer to the fire at night. Even I had slept fairly well, despite the rock-hard ground and the cold night air. Barra had not left my side all night, so I'd stayed snug and comfortably warm.

The dog now jumped up and happily scampered toward her master. But he pushed her off when she excitedly placed her front paws on his chest and licked his neck with her wet, sloppy tongue.

"*Sguir,* Barra! Stop it!"

Ross looked down at me.

"Get up so I can untie you."

He wasn't in the best of moods, so I did my best to quickly follow his orders.

"What's going on?" I asked.

"Do you seriously think these gentlemen deem it necessary to share their high-and-mighty plans with me?" he griped. "You and I are just chess pieces in this game of kings—we are pawns, if you will. Good enough to put our necks on the line, or clean up after them!"

He kept muttering while pulling at the ties around my waist. He was in such a foul mood that even Barra lowered her tail and hung her head.

Once he'd untethered me from the tree, I held out my still-tied hands. But he shook his head no.

"Those you will keep. What do you think would become of me if I *lost* you? You should be glad that we're in a hurry, because Dougal told me yesterday that he wouldn't ride another horse into the ground on account of your comfort, and that as of today you would have to walk."

Appalled, I pulled back my hands and did my best to fight back the urge to try to turn around and run.

Ross must have felt that, because he grabbed my arm and pulled me with him.

"As I said, we're in a hurry, so don't give me any trouble. Let's get moving. You don't have to be afraid of Dougal for now."

I felt pins and needles in my legs, so I awkwardly stumbled after him as he led me to the horses. There I noticed Sean. He had his back to me, but it gave me fresh hope that I'd be able to talk to him in private—*if* he were to come with us. Then everything could finally be made right again.

As we reached the small group of men by the horses, Ross suddenly stopped—which made me slam into him.

"Ifrinn!" he cussed, slapping his forehead. "I left something back there. You help this woman onto the horse, and I'll be right back."

He thrust the reins into the hands of a young Scot standing there, and he disappeared in the direction from which we had just come. I looked after him, irritated. But then I felt a tug on my hands, and I lifted my eyes.

For the duration of a heartbeat I looked into his face. Then the world stopped. Time and space ceased to exist.

Endorphins flooded my brain, blinding me like a supernova, and everything was ablaze with an almost painfully bright light.

Payton!

Before that heartbeat ended, the light retreated and I realized that even though I had found Payton McLean, the man I would love more than life itself sometime in the distant future, there was no spark of recognition in his eyes.

That knowledge felt like a punch in the gut. I staggered backward, wanting to tear away and escape back to the world where Payton's hands had touched me with loving tenderness. But his grip was merciless. His face was completely void of emotion as he yanked me back.

"What do you think you're doing? Stay here, woman!" he snarled.

I could not take my eyes off his face. There was irritation in his brown eyes as he looked me over.

His hair was a bit longer than in his modern-day edition. And the color was lighter, which made me think he must be spending a lot of time outdoors. He seemed so familiar, and yet so completely alien. I couldn't help but feel drawn to him; my body tingled all over in anticipation of his touch. At the same time, I shook like a leaf because my feelings for this stranger frightened me to the core. I wanted to brush that stray strand of hair from his face and to trace his lips with my fingers.

I blinked when I noticed that he didn't have that little scar on his chin.

"Are you deaf? Get on!" he snapped. He held out his interlocked hands to help me climb onto the horse. I shook my head to get rid of this confused chaos inside my mind.

But Payton was running low on patience. And with a mumbled curse I didn't understand, he grabbed me by the waist and lifted me onto the horse in one forceful move. My skin under the old housedress tingled as though his hands had burned through the coarse fabric, and a muffled sigh escaped my lips.

The expression on his face was gruff and distant, and his eyes all but warned me not to cause any trouble. Then Ross returned, and before I could gather my thoughts, the redheaded Scot sat up behind me and drove his horse away from the man who held my heart in his hands.

He held it without even knowing me. And I knew he'd be willing to give his life for me someday in the distant future. But right now he was walking away without even turning around.

I watched him hurry over to a better, more handsome horse. He jumped on it with great ease and swiftly pulled past us. It hurt so much that he didn't *see* me—that he didn't realize somewhere deep inside who I was, and didn't immediately fall in love with me all over again.

On the other hand, I wondered whether my feelings for him were wrong. Was I deceiving the Payton who waited for me in the present because I felt drawn to his former self? Could modern-day Payton, the one I loved so much, already be inside this rougher former version of him?

One thing was for sure. His presence completely threw me. The similarities between this Payton and *my* Payton were so strong that they evidently tricked my senses. I swore I could still detect his warm, familiar scent even as he rode well ahead of us. And I knew I could still feel his hand around my waist.

Time passed, and all I could do was stare at the strong back in front of me. Several times I tried to make Payton turn around by sheer willpower, but he stubbornly kept his eyes on the road ahead.

By now I was very familiar with every little movement of the muscles underneath his shirt, and I wished Ross would ride closer so I could see the tiny beads of sweat on the back of his neck. I could just imagine what it would be like to run my hands through his sweaty hair and pull him to me for a kiss.

A sigh escaped my chest, and Ross shifted nervously in the saddle behind me.

"Are you okay? Saddle sore?" he asked.

"Hmm? Saddle sore? No . . . I mean . . . I'll be okay. But why are we falling so far behind?"

Ross clicked his tongue. He leaned over to examine his horse's back hoof.

"Do you see the difference between my horse and theirs?" he said, pointing ahead with his hand holding the reins.

I nodded. Even I could tell that our horse was older and in worse shape than Payton's or Sean's.

"What does that mean?"

"Twice the weight is getting to him. He didn't get much of a break because I was up all night with him, making sure the area around our campsite was safe. Dougal knows that my horse struggles enough with just my weight, and that was why he took you on his horse yesterday. But we have only a few more miles to go now. We're already on McRae's sheep pastures. Which is why it is no problem for us to go a bit easier on the horse."

In actuality, the others had now disappeared from sight, and Ross was letting his horse go even slower than before.

Amid all this calm and quiet, I suddenly felt an urgent nature call, and I nervously drummed my fingers on my thighs. A few more miles, he'd said. How long would it take to travel *a few miles*? And would there even be a restroom there? Or just a few more Scotsmen who could watch me disappear behind a bush?

I swallowed my pride and squeezed out my concern: "Ross . . . I'm really sorry. I know we don't have time, but I really have to go. . . ."

"Have to go where?" he asked, still deeply absorbed in observing his horse's hind leg.

"Jesus, I have to go *pee*!" I snapped. I couldn't believe it didn't seem to occur to him that I maybe had to use the restroom once a day or so.

He sat up in his saddle, stiff as a poker, and looked at me suspiciously.

"Now?" he asked skeptically.

"Now?" I gave a testy reply, mimicking him. "No, if you must know, I've been needing to go for, like, *ever*, but now I can't hold it any longer!"

Ross stopped his horse but didn't show the slightest inclination of letting me get off.

"Listen, Samantha, I really don't want to hurt you, but I will if you try to trick me. For the first time in my life I'm on the right track—and I won't make the mistake of letting you escape. Go relieve yourself. But if you're not back in an instant, I will send the dogs after you. Do you understand?"

Did I understand? Oh yes, I understood all too well! This guy was insane! I was stuck in the goddamn past with a crazy person threatening to set his rabid dogs on me.

"I'll be right back, I promise! If you want, I can keep talking to you for the entire time. Just please keep your dogs at bay."

Although I wasn't necessarily afraid of the dogs, I didn't like the idea of them sinking their sharp fangs into my butt just because Ross didn't feel like waiting anymore.

He dismounted in silence, helped me down, and nodded toward a cluster of ash trees.

"Go already! I'm really not too keen to still be here in the woods when darkness falls. Ye ken?"

I hurriedly fought my way through the underbrush and ducked behind the thick foliage. The leaves were already fading in the vanishing daylight, and I rushed to finish my business. Carefully I peeked through the branches and saw that Ross was still standing with his horse. He pulled up its hind leg and frowned with concern.

As quickly as I could, I tugged my dress into place and returned to Ross. Running my hands through my hair, I plucked out a few loose leaves that my little trip into the underbrush had yielded. They were yellow. Which month might this be if it got dark in the middle of the day and the leaves had already changed color? And what year was this, anyway?

I racked my brain for any hints. Payton looked different, yes, but not really younger. If the curse had already been spoken, then he would have felt pain when near me—just like he did in the present day. But his earlier indifference helped me exclude that possibility. This meant that the Cameron massacre had not yet happened.

"We can't continue on horseback. The horse stepped in something, and I don't want to risk laming it," Ross explained, jolting me from my thoughts.

"What? What do we do now?"

Ross laughed. "What do we do now?" he mimicked. "Now we walk."

And with that, he bowed before me and let me pass by the horse before he took his place beside me. The dogs came running and kept pushing their noses up against his palm until he finally opened his *sporran.* Every dog got a little something; they all ate their treat right out of his hand. Ross gently scratched their giant heads as he apologetically shook the fur pouch.

"Get lost, there's nothing left!"

I had to giggle as I saw him struggle against the dogs that were constantly in his way, running between his legs and begging for more treats.

"Away with ye!" He shooed them while wiping his slobber-covered hand on his tartan plaid.

"Pig's ears?" I asked.

Ross nodded. "Aye, they love them."

I giggled as I tried to imagine where someone might go to get a dozen or so pig's ears. And I had to laugh even harder when I pictured Ross leaving his house in the morning and grabbing dried pig's ears for his provisions.

"What's so funny?" he demanded before finding it hard to stop himself from laughing, too.

"Nothing. But I'm so hungry that I wouldn't mind eating a pig's ear myself." I chuckled.

Ross gave a wide grin, then stepped over to a saddlebag to grab a chunk of bread for each of us.

"I'm afraid I'm all out of pig's ears, but I hope this will do."

I nodded gratefully, tearing off a small piece and putting it in my mouth. It was hard and dry, but my stomach grumbled happily.

We walked side by side at a pleasant pace, making good progress. And for the first time since leaving the cemetery by Kintail, I felt like I could breathe.

I looked at this skinny, redheaded guy next to me and knew that I had nothing to fear from him. He was a nice person, even though it wasn't up to him to decide what was to happen to me. But right now I didn't want to worry about that. As soon as I caught sight of Payton again, I would have to find a way to talk to him about everything that had happened to me. I had to make him believe me. Plus—since time was running out for the Payton waiting for me in the present, I had to somehow get him to help me get Vanora's blood. I didn't know how, but I had to find a way.

I chewed on my last morsel of bread and decided that it was the best plan anyone in my situation could possibly come up with. And even though my feet hurt, my butt was sore from the long ride, and the skin around my wrists was chafed—I actually felt pretty good.

A good while later—it was dark already—we reached shepherd McRae's small cottage. In a pen next to it, I could make out the rest of the horses. They stood together, nibbling on the tall grass. Ross made straight for the fence.

Our arrival had not gone unnoticed. The cottage door opened, and Sean stepped outside in a narrow glimmer of light.

"What took you so long?" He sounded annoyed.

"We had problems with the horse. But we got here."

Ross turned away and loosened the saddle before starting to rub down his horse with straw. He didn't say another word.

I stood between the two of them, unsure of what to do. It was pretty obvious that Ross no longer considered me one of his responsibilities, yet Sean didn't seem to know what to do about me, either. My eyes wandered between them while I waited for further instructions. Sean raised his head as if he'd had an idea; then he told me to stay where I was as he disappeared inside the little cottage.

When the door opened again, Payton stepped out. Obviously exhausted, he ran his hands over his face and came toward me. His gait was sluggish, and it seemed as though he barely had enough strength to lift his feet off the ground. I watched him expectantly, hoping this time to detect a glimmer of recognition in his eyes. With one swift move of his knife, he cut the rope off my wrists.

"Follow me," he said, continuing on without even checking that I was really following him. I looked back toward Ross, but he was busy. I couldn't hear any sound coming from the cottage, either.

I tried my best to hurry on after Payton, gathering my skirts and running after him into the darkness. I slowed down once I caught up and was only a few steps behind him. I didn't know what to expect. If he thought of me as a prisoner, how then could I talk to him? After my experience with the twin brothers, I was afraid that I wouldn't be able to pass for *normal.*

A thorny blackberry vine caught on my leg and tore open my shin.

"Ouch! Goddammit!" I cussed, continuing to run while lifting my hemline to inspect the bloody scratch. But Payton had stopped, and I accidentally stepped on his heels. I probably would have landed in the bushes behind me if he hadn't grabbed me. Suddenly, I found myself dangerously close to his chest. I tilted my head back so I could look him in the eyes. His lips were so close, and I could feel the blood rushing into my cheeks. A barely perceptible smile twitched around his mouth.

"Be careful, lassie," he cautioned. "There are men out there who wouldn't pass up a situation like this."

And just so I understood what he meant by that, he held on to me just a moment longer. Oh, gosh, how embarrassing! Surely he didn't think that I wanted to come on to him! Truth be told, of course, I wanted nothing more than for him to take me in his arms and kiss me. But he seemed immune to such yearnings of the flesh. He gently pushed me away and motioned toward a body of water visible between the tree line in front of us.

"You may go and wash yourself. I'll wait here by this rock and keep watch."

The most beautiful sight opened up in front of me. The lake lay still like a polished mirror. It almost looked like a crater framed by the dark, looming mountains. A silvery streak of moonlight danced on its sparkling surface, and it looked as though every single star had come down from the sky just to bathe in it.

Still, I gave Payton a quizzical look.

"Wash myself? You led me here so I could wash myself?"

He gave a deep, throaty laugh. "You *stink!* All right, to be honest we both stink. But because I want to protect your modesty, I will abstain from jumping into the lake with you. Instead, I will wait until you are done. I brought you here because I wanted a bath, and I thought you might appreciate one, too."

I was glad that the dark of the night concealed my shivering body from him, and I folded my arms across my chest. I was embarrassed about my BO, and I really wished Payton hadn't noticed. I wanted nothing more than to get rid of this awful dress and take a nice, hot bath; to massage silky shampoo into my hair; and then to put on my favorite yoga pants. But the night was cold, the water was probably freezing, and my favorite shampoo was nowhere in sight. Which was why I hesitated.

Payton sat down and leaned against the rock, pulling his knees up to his chest. "Take your time. I'm in no rush to return to the cottage."

I stared down at his broad shoulders. "Why not?"

"Because I can't bear to see my father like that. He's sleeping now, but I worry that he might not make it through the night."

He rested his elbows on his knees and buried his head in his hands.

"Wouldn't you rather be with him in case he really . . . ?" I couldn't bring myself to finish the sentence, because Payton seemed gloomy enough as it was.

"No. I've been feeling so terribly helpless all day. The cottage is tiny, and it's my brother Blair's place to take

Father's side. He's the oldest, and he will be our new laird should it come to the worst."

"I wish I could help you," I whispered.

"Oh, you will. As soon as the sun rises, we'll have to remove the arrow from his chest and dress the wound properly. You will help us. You womenfolk seem to be better at that sort of thing," he explained. "But first I would really prefer—only for Father's sake, of course—that you wash yourself."

There it was again. Maybe the smile didn't quite reach his eyes, but he did give me an amused wink. Strangely, I didn't find it at all odd that someone would want to remove an arrow from someone's chest without any medical training whatsoever. Not even when that someone was supposed to be *me.* What if he died during my botched attempt? Wouldn't the new laird have me beheaded right then and there?

"How about it, lassie, don't you want to go bathe?" Payton followed up in an almost-tender tone.

"Sam. My name is Sam . . . not Lassie."

I swallowed hard, wiping a tear from my eye. I wanted to shake him and yell, "Don't you recognize me, Payton? Doesn't your heart recognize me?"

But of course I didn't.

"*Lassie* means 'girl.' I called you that because I didn't know your name. I'm Payton. Payton McLean. So, Sam, what are you waiting for? Are you afraid of me? I swear on my honor that I am not going to hurt you. I will not even look."

I shook my head. No, he wouldn't hurt me, because whoever *this* Payton was, I could trust him.

So I turned around and walked down to the lakeshore. It was only a few yards, and I could feel his eyes following me. I glanced back at him over my shoulder, hesitating, and when our eyes met, he turned around so that I could undress in private.

I slid under a bush and loosened the belt with the dagger in it. I then tried to cover it up with some pebbles. I wanted to place the housedress on top of it, hoping that Payton wouldn't notice. Until I could convince him of my story, I really wanted to hold on to that knife. My hands shook as I pulled the horrible fabric over my head. I wondered what he'd think if he ever saw my Black Eyed Peas tank top, underwire bra, and black panties with the lace trim. A man of this era would never expect to see undergarments like mine on a peasant woman.

When I'd donned the dress for the first time, it didn't even occur to me that I would be forced to live among Highlanders for a while. Going forward, I needed to be more careful. The world wasn't ready for hip-hop, and I was deeply sorry when I took off my top, scrunched up the Peas, and fled with it into the water.

I held my breath, and my heart skipped a beat as the ice-cold water sloshed around my hips. I must have made a startled sound, because Payton turned around. I cursed, quickly submerging myself up to my chin so that he couldn't see my anachronistic underwear.

The freezing water stung me like a thousand needles, and my breathing turned into irregular gasps as my lungs tried to work against my cramping muscles.

"Everything all right?" he asked through the darkness.

"Go away!" I managed with chattering teeth.

"What? Are you well? You're not drowning, are you?"

Because he was already knee-deep in the lake, I raised my hands and screeched: "No! Go away! Everything's perfect!"

In the moonlight I could see his doubts very clearly, but he obeyed, took a couple steps back, and sat down on the lakeshore.

"I'll stay here, just in case. But don't worry, I've got my eyes closed," he called out.

I wasn't as cold anymore, probably because I was treading water and flailing my arms. Or perhaps the oxygen supply to my brain was affected and made me immune. Either way, I couldn't stay in the water a second longer without contracting pneumonia, so I took a deep breath and submerged myself fully. I had felt a big rock under my feet, and I now tried to lift it by one of the corners.

Jesus, it was so cold! My eyes seemed to turn into ice cubes, and my scalp burned from the freezing water. With stiff fingers I finally managed to push the tank top under the rock before letting go so that it snapped into place. I came up for air, gasping for breath. With my last ounce of strength, I dragged myself back to the shore, waded through the water on shivering legs, and squatted behind my bush. That was when I heard Payton giggle.

"What's so funny?" I asked, irritated. I peered at him through the branches while pulling my awful dress back on.

I saw him keel over and hold his stomach with laughter.

"Sam, you look . . . light as a kitten, all small and delicate. But when I close my eyes, you sound like a big old wheezing cow trying to climb out of a boggy swamp."

I could barely make out the last few words through his chuckles. But I could certainly guess what he was trying to say. Furiously, I grabbed a handful of pebbles and hurled them in his direction. And when I heard him yelp and jump to his feet, I couldn't help but chortle myself. The crunch of his steps drew closer, stopping when he reached my shrub.

"If you don't mind, I will go and quickly wash myself before we walk back."

He didn't wait for my approval but instead stepped up to the water and loosened first the brooch on his shoulder and then the belt around his hips. The length of material that covered him sank to the ground. His pearly white butt beamed at me in the moonlight, and I swallowed hard as he also ditched his shirt.

There he was, in all his glory and without any false sense of modesty, walking into the water as if completely immune to the cold. Elegantly, he dove in.

Fortunately it was dark, because even though I had wanted to use this moment to hide the dagger in my dress, I just sat there admiring this man. The moonlight turned the water drops on his skin into tiny diamonds, and I discovered muscles on this body that I knew he didn't have in the present day.

His body looked stronger, more athletic. Presumably it had been hardened by these living conditions. I finally managed to turn my attention back to my task, and I tried to focus on the belt on my upper thigh. Repeatedly, I glanced over the lake surface to watch Payton, whose magnificence I just couldn't let go of.

I heard him wading back to shore while I was still working on my dagger. I had just pulled down my skirt when he suddenly appeared in front of me again. The plaid was draped around his hips in perfect pleats, but his shirt was still unbuttoned. I really was tempted to reach out and wipe the remaining water droplets off his chest.

He looked me up and down, and a wide grin spread over his face.

"Well, well, who'd have thought that a little water could make such a difference."

And with that, he turned and walked away. I scowled and stared after him as he disappeared into the woods on the same narrow path we had come from.

Chapter 15

Cemetery by Auld a´chruinn, Present-Day October

The earth under Sean's feet turned to mud as he made his way toward the cemetery. All he'd been able to do for days was to keep Payton company here in this rain. His brother flat-out refused to leave his position by the Five Sisters stone. Because even though they had now found the memorial stone that they blamed for Sam's disappearance, they couldn't figure out a way of following her.

Whether the legend had killed Sam or it had just ripped her from this place and time, they did not know. He had tried to convince Payton to take it easy on himself, preserve his energy, and sit and wait for updates in the nearby village—but Payton wouldn't hear of it. No, his pigheaded brother insisted on using the last bit of his strength, exposing himself to the elements, and holding out to his dying breath. Sean knew that this was also Payton's form of self-flagellation. He wanted to punish himself for bringing this situation on Sam in the first place.

Sean didn't know how often in the last few days he had thought how easy it would be if Vanora's curse were still in effect, having robbed them of all their feelings. But her curse had been broken since last summer. Their feelings were back, along with all their pain and remorse. He couldn't stand to see his brother suffering.

Sean stepped through the cemetery gate. His eyes went first to the mighty obelisk that had distracted them from noticing Sam's disappearance until it was too late. Then he turned his attention to the cemetery wall—and stopped. Eyebrows raised, he approached Payton in bewilderment.

"Are you all right? Or have you completely lost your mind?" he asked.

Payton looked like the epitome of misery: wet, dirty, and with his skin drawn and pale. Still, he was laughing so hard that tears streamed down his face.

"Payton?" Sean insisted as his brother ignored him, holding his stomach with laughter.

Despite the muddy ground, Sean sat down and patiently waited for an explanation. As Payton came up for air, he struggled to keep his attention on Sean. With beaming eyes, he grinned from ear to ear.

"Oh yes, you are definitely crazy!" Sean confirmed.

"*Pog mo thon!* You don't know anything!" Payton defended himself.

"Because you won't speak up, goddammit! Tell me, what is it that you find so amusing?"

Payton smiled. "I have found her, Sean." He tapped his forehead with his finger. "In here. She made it! She's alive!"

Sean stared at him and raised his arms in disbelief.

"What the hell are you talking about? What did you find?"

"Why—Samantha, of course! I remember her. It's only a scrap of a memory, but it is as vivid as if it happened yesterday! I'm telling you: Sam has traveled back through time! And she's found me!"

Sean frowned. That he had serious doubts about Payton's sanity was clearly written on his face.

"What kind of a memory? I don't understand."

"I don't understand it myself, Sean! I was just sitting here hoping she's still alive, praying for her return, engulfed by feelings of guilt and remorse. But then this image flashed through my mind!"

Payton had jumped to his feet. He flailed his arms excitedly as he continued.

"So then, all of a sudden, I saw her before me—you know, like a memory. She was wearing a dress like one of those poor peasant women at Castle Burragh. I saw her stumbling, and I caught her. Also, she had terrible BO!"

Payton burst out laughing again, and tears streamed down his face. "It was the night when Father lay wounded in McRae's cottage. Don't you remember? You *must* have seen her, too!"

Sean tried to recall that night. Many of his memories had paled over the course of the centuries. The curse having robbed them of all feelings, memories had also become secondary, unimportant, because there was no joy or happiness in them. Still, it sounded impossible that he would have met Sam way back then.

"No, Payton—I'm sorry. I can vaguely remember that time, but not Sam . . . no . . . I don't remember her at all. Are you sure? Maybe your mind is playing tricks on you? Some kind of wishful thinking?"

Furiously, Payton kicked a rock. "Of course I am sure! How could I have forgotten about that? I remember how I had to laugh when she came up panting and wheezing from the lake!"

Payton closed his eyes as he recalled the scene.

"I was so confused when I saw her standing before me all clean and with her hair all wet. And because I couldn't place my feelings, I just left her there. I just walked away."

Shaking his head, Payton sat down on the wall. "Thinking back to that moment now, I think I fell for her right then," he said.

"Well, for the life of me I cannot remember ever having seen Sam before. So you think she is alive and that she's found us—but what now? Do you remember her telling you that she came from the future? Don't you think she would have mentioned a minor detail like that?"

Payton put his hands on his head. That was exactly the point. He remembered nothing but that one moment by the lakeshore.

"I don't know, Jesus!" he barked. "Until about an hour ago I couldn't remember that evening at all!"

Payton was frustrated that Sean didn't act too happy about his newfound memories. Sean didn't seem to understand that, whatever happened next, Samantha had at least made it safely through her journey through time. And she had found them. That was all that mattered right now.

Suddenly Sean came up with a start and slapped his thighs. "That's it!" he exclaimed. "She is rewriting your memories! You remembered it so suddenly because you are living through that moment right now—I mean you *have* lived through that moment . . . if you know what I mean! Sam is changing your memories."

He broke a twig from the brush by the cemetery wall and crouched to draw something on the ground.

"Look here. If this"—he drew a long, straight line—"is time—our life from *then* until *now*—then all we really have are our memories of the things we see and the people we meet during that time. But here"—he drew an arc from the point he had called *now* back to the center point on the straight line—"is when the change starts. Sam comes into our, um, already lived life, and changes it. Because of this, we now also remember this new path through life as seen through that particular point." He drew a second straight line, parallel to the first one, which ended in another endpoint called *now*. "So, I think you are right. She made it!"

"In that case, I hope we don't start having memories of her getting her pretty head cut off," Payton whispered, feeling exhausted. He sent a quick prayer up to heaven.

Chapter 16

The muffled voices of the men bending over the sickbed plus the poor lighting in the tiny cottage only increased the notion of sickness and death. I stood in a corner, stiffening up and wishing I were somewhere else—or, more precisely, somewhere else in time.

"Have to do something. He's running a fever and hasn't been responsive since last night."

There were animated gestures all around.

"Which is why we brought this woman here. She won't dare let any harm come to Fingal—not if she values her own life," Blair thundered, dragging me from my corner. The dark-headed Scot looked tired. His long hair covered his back in a limp, matted mess, and there were deep shadows around his eyes. "Now, go attend to him!" he commanded, shoving me toward the narrow, low-lying bed on which Fingal rested.

So this was Payton's dad. He was big and strong with thinning white hair framing his face. His white beard lent his face something powerful and extraordinary, and it was easy to imagine him as the clan leader.

For how much longer, though? His skin had yellowed, and thick beads of sweat covered his forehead and upper lip. His closed eyelids twitched as though he were having a bad dream. A wide, blood-soaked strip of fabric covered the wound on his chest. The rest of his body lay hidden under a rough blanket.

"Well, what are you waiting for? Tell me what you need, and get to work!"

Blair looked at me expectantly, as if I could heal his dad by the sheer power of my thoughts alone. Yet I wasn't even sure that he could be saved in a modern hospital. The dirt in and around the wound alone would probably cause an infection. Still, I had no choice but to tend to him. By the looks of it, I was the best chance he had right now. Poor guy.

I could feel the men's eyes boring holes into my back, but I tried to direct all of my attention to Fingal. "Can we take him outside?" I asked. "If you want me to help him, I will need more light." I swatted away a fly that kept landing on the blood-soaked bandage, and I wrinkled my nose at the sight of the rags full of dried blood covering the floor. "Besides, it would be best to clean his bedstead. He'll never get well with all these bugs around," I added, while Sean and Blair quickly set about getting the old man ready to be moved.

The bed was nothing more than a few planks of wood nailed together and attached to the wall. So the men simply first carried the kitchen table outside, and then Fingal, gently placing him on the tabletop.

Full of doubt, I stepped up to the table and looked into the faces of the men around me. I stopped on Payton's face. To see the pain on it was terrible. He held his dad's frail hand and nodded for me to get started.

"I need hot water. We need to wash out the wound."

Ross immediately lit a fire and hung a kettle of water over it.

Nothing here reminded me of my favorite hospital drama, *Grey's Anatomy,* and Ross didn't exactly look like Dr. Avery, either. Regardless, here at this table I would have to summon all of the knowledge I'd acquired watching that show. Unfortunately, I really was Fingal's best bet.

My fingers shook as I slowly lifted the blood-soaked strip of fabric, and I sure was glad that my patient was unconscious. With every inch that I lifted the bandage, I tore open the scab and reopened the wound. Biting my lip, I tried to focus and keep the damage to a minimum.

When I had finally removed the cloth, I was drenched in sweat. The arrow shaft protruding out at me made me feel sick to the stomach. The flesh around the point of entry was inflamed and oozing. I had to force myself not to turn away—and *not* to throw up. The arrow needed to be removed, that much was certain.

"How far in did the arrow go?" I asked, trying to ignore my queasy stomach. I thought maybe I should fess up now that I had passed out in biology class when we had to dissect a frog.

"Quite far in," Sean said. "It would be easier to take out if it had gone clean through, but this way . . ."

"All right, do you have any alcohol? I have to disinfect the wound," I said, trying to focus on the task. Shit, I was about to hurl—and I hadn't even started.

The brothers stared at me as though I'd just asked for a drink.

Oh gosh! Of course they had never heard of germs and bacteria, and they'd probably never disinfected anything in their lives. I needed to keep it simple. "Do you have any whiskey?"

Immediately everyone's face lit up, and Sean disappeared inside the cottage, emerging a moment later with a cup of the stuff.

I poured some of it into the wound, and Fingal winced. He was still unconscious. He thrashed around, groaning with pain, but didn't come to.

"Hold on to him, or else he will fall off!" I yelled while trying to keep Fingal from falling. The strain had caused my hair to fall into my face, and I blew it out of my eyes. I could tell that Sean and Payton felt the tension, too, but they motioned for me to continue.

"What are you waiting for? Get started already!" Blair barked.

"I am starting, but I can't promise that I won't cause him any more harm."

Blair grabbed me by the shoulders, and I flinched under his iron grip.

"Don't you dare!" he hissed, tightening his hold as I resisted.

"Ow! You're crazy! Let go!" I shrieked.

A moment later my head exploded in pain, and all the air was squeezed from my lungs as I hit the ground. I tasted blood, and my cheek burned like hell. Feeling woozy, I patted down my face and made a pathetic attempt at sitting up. A kilt was swinging right in front of my nose, and a pair of muscular calves blocked my field of vision.

"*Seas!* Leave her alone, Blair! Touch her one more time, and—" Payton descended angrily on his brother. He had protectively planted himself in front of me with his fists on his hips.

"And what, Payton? If this peasant woman thinks she can get out of helping us, then she is mistaken," the oldest said in a dark and threatening voice.

"Look at the girl, Blair. She *will* help us."

The adrenaline coursing through my veins gave me the strength to get up and face this god-awful task.

"I will, of course, do my best, but I can't work miracles. If I could, I certainly wouldn't be here right now. The arrow has to come out—otherwise the wound will get infected. But maybe it's sealing a damaged blood vessel, in which case Fingal could bleed to death if I pull it out."

I couldn't say for sure if that was a real risk, but I had seen that situation on TV. Too bad for Fingal that his life depended on me. Me, who had acquired all of her medical knowledge from a television series.

I scrambled back to my feet. All eyes were on me. My lower jaw still stung from the mighty slap I had received. Dammit, it really hurt! I still couldn't see clearly. Luckily, Payton reached out a hand to help me up. Nobody had ever hit me like that before in my life—all right, maybe Ross when he punched me that first day. The longer I thought about it, the less I wanted to know what lay ahead of me in the coming days.

With all the dignity I could muster, I tried to block out Blair's hostile presence. Not that long ago this imposing Scotsman had fought right by my side. Was it wrong to refer to something that would happen in the very distant future as having happened not that long ago? All this dwelling on our highly unusual circumstance wasn't getting me anywhere, though. In the here and now, Blair and I weren't exactly the best of friends. And the burning handprint on my cheek only strengthened that impression. I wasn't sure whether Payton's hand on my back was there to support and protect me or whether he wanted to direct me back to the patient. Whichever it was, his touch was comforting.

I finally pushed my confusing thoughts aside, gathered all of my courage, grabbed ahold of the arrow, and tried to pull it out of Fingal's chest at a right angle—as carefully and evenly as possible.

Shit, it was in deep! I'd never have thought that someone with such a long piece of wood sticking out of his chest could even survive for that long. Dried blood covered the arrow shaft, and I was woozy again. I felt a droplet of sweat run down my cheek, and with every beat of my heart there seemed to be ever more blood spurting from Fingal's chest. My stomach tightened.

I had pulled a good bit of the shaft out already, but still I couldn't see the arrowhead. More and more blood ran over my trembling fingers and oozed onto the table. Sweat seeped into my eyes, and I tried to blink.

"You're doing great. Take your time," somebody mumbled beside me. I hadn't noticed him before because I was so absorbed in my work.

I briefly glanced at the newcomer and swallowed hard. Right away I recognized who it was.

"Honestly, Kyle was the handsomest of us all. He was pretty cute even as a baby, and he just got better looking with every year."

Payton's words from a different era echoed inside my head

as I looked into his younger brother's face. Kyle McLean. The sixteen-year-old who would pay for Nathaira Stuart's plan with his life. He resembled Payton, but his features were softer, smoother. He was truly beautiful, and he would become an even more beautiful man once he lost those final traces of childhood.

But that would never happen. He would not grow up to be a man. It was his destiny to die by Nathaira's hand. Soon.

"Keep going, woman! Get it done already!" Blair's angry voice pulled me back into the present. *This* present. I smiled at Kyle, thanking him for his encouragement, and focused all of my attention back on Fingal.

Finally, I spotted the metal tip and slowly, carefully removed it from the wound. The men around the table inhaled deeply as I handed over the sharp, metallic culprit. Again I poured whiskey into the wound canal, and this time it took the strength of several men to hold Fingal down on the table. The alcohol had to burn terribly inside the deep wound, but I had no choice. Luckily, no artery seemed to have been damaged, because the blood flow started slowing down. I imagined that Fingal would have died already had one of his vital organs been hurt, and so I assumed that the biggest threat right now was an infection.

"I want to keep the wound as clean as possible," I explained. "We'll need clean rags."

Immediately someone handed me assorted rags and strips of fabric, but none of them seemed suitable.

"No, I need to boil them first. Is the water hot enough?"

Following Payton's nod, I took the cleanest-looking pieces of cloth and tore them into wide strips. Then I remembered something my mother had told me when I'd handed her a bunch of yellow yarrow during one of our camping trips. She'd said:

"Back in the old days, they used to make an infusion of ferns and yarrow to wash out wounds. Can you imagine?" Then she had told me to lick my fingers, and when I did and pulled a disgusted face, she had laughed. Those were the bitter compounds, she explained, to which yarrow owed its anti-inflammatory and healing properties.

I probably would have forgotten all about it if I hadn't been reminded of that unpleasant bitter taste every time I spotted the little yellow flowers by the side of the road.

"If we could find some ferns or yarrow, I think it would be good to boil them together with the rags," I thought aloud while adding the makeshift bandages to the boiling kettle.

"Medicinal plants? That's no problem. We can send McRae out later to collect some. He knows every single blade of grass out here on his pastures. You'll have to change the bandages regularly anyway, right?"

"Right. I'll make an herbal infusion later, then. In the meantime, I will clean his wound as best I can."

While unrolling the piping-hot strips of fabric and pressing them into the wound canal, I burned my fingers pretty badly. Carefully, I cleaned around the edge of the wound and dabbed off the dried, caked blood. Payton stood opposite me, passing me the boiled, sterile rags and observing my every move. Kyle, standing beside me, took the bloodied, dirty pieces of cloth I handed to him.

I had done my best. It wasn't much, but I didn't know what else I could do for Fingal. Relieved, I took a step back and put my hands on my hips.

"Done. Now to bandage him up. His body will have to do the rest."

Together Payton and Kyle lifted Fingal's upper body so that I could wrap the long fabric strips around his chest. This turned out to be harder than I expected, because the strips were wet and kept slipping through my fingers. After what felt like an eternity, I finally managed to tie it all up in a knot. I looked at what I had accomplished and felt satisfied.

My mother, a nurse at Milford Hospital, would throw up her hands in horror at seeing this, but I was pretty proud of myself. At least my patient was still breathing.

I felt a hand on my shoulder and looked up. It was Kyle, and he was smiling at me.

"Aye, you've done well."

His honest, open smile made me light up, and my fingers finally stopped shaking.

"Thank you. I—"

He cut me off by thrusting a silver flask into my hands.

"There! Drink—you deserve it."

I sniffed the opening of the bottle and was met by the overpowering fumes of alcohol. Carefully, I took a small sip. The whiskey burned its way down my throat. My eyes welled up, but the alcohol immediately kindled a warm and comforting fire in my belly. With Kyle smiling his encouragement, I took another sip. After all the stress of the past few hours, I enjoyed suddenly feeling pleasantly light-headed. I breathed in the clear, crisp air and closed my eyes for just a moment before being rudely jostled back to reality.

I clumsily stumbled to the side. I was apparently invisible to Blair, who had bumped into me while he and Sean carried Fingal back into the stuffy little cottage. The responsibility that these Scots had bestowed upon me left me no choice but to follow them inside. I checked the bandage to make sure it was holding firmly. Then I felt Fingal's forehead.

The arrow had been stuck in him for too long, contaminating the wound. Payton's dad was already running a fever, and I prayed that his body temperature wouldn't rise any further.

"My father is a warrior. He cannot be killed by some coward or cattle thief. You, on the other hand, look exhausted," Payton determined. He stood right next to me and touched my arm. "Come on, follow me."

Chapter 17

The clouds drifted leisurely across the sky and piled up in a huddle. I'd been lying on my back, watching. A pebble was pressing into my right shoulder blade, but I was too tired to flick it away. The small clearing not too far from the cottage was exactly what my soul needed right now. Payton sat nearby. He had led me here.

This was the moment I had been waiting for—the moment when we found ourselves alone and undisturbed, and when I finally wanted to tell him the truth. When I could at long last try to make my way home.

But suddenly this didn't seem so easy. This whole time, I'd been thinking about myself and my miserable situation. I had wanted to tell Payton everything—knowing then that he would make all the right decisions. After all, this ordeal was all about saving him. He was the one waiting for help in the very distant future.

But Kyle McLean had changed all that.

I wished I had never met that boy with the beautiful face. It had put me in a terrible, terrible bind. To be aware of the imminent death of a person you don't even know is hard enough. But Kyle's friendly nature and his winning smile had made it impossible for me to accept what the

Fates had in store for him. At the same time, I knew that his death would only be the start of a series of events that I was not allowed to change. My own life depended on everything happening exactly the way that destiny had intended.

If *I* found it impossible to see Kyle die, then how could I possibly expect Payton to be prepared to lead his own brother "to slaughter"? On the other hand . . . wouldn't I almost be guilty of Kyle's murder if I stood by and watched disaster take its course?

And it wasn't just Kyle's fate in my hands. There was also the fate of the Camerons. Before long, they would all fall for Nathaira's malice and deceit and be brutally murdered. Could I allow that to happen? But what would be the consequences if I decided to change the course of things? Would I even have the power to change the past? Because that was what I would be doing. I'd be rewriting clan history!

This was too risky. I couldn't get mixed up in these things. I was an intruder in this era, and I had to try my hardest to leave as few traces as possible. But how could I explain my situation to Payton without burdening him with all this responsibility? What right did I have to demand that he accept and allow his brother's death? To condemn himself to Vanora's curse for two hundred and seventy years? How could I be so selfish as to even consider this?

No, as long as I couldn't be sure that I wasn't doing any harm, I couldn't reveal the truth to him.

"You are a strange girl." Payton shook his head and knitted his brow as if studying an unusual bug.

"What?" I rolled to my side, propping my head on my arm so I could face him.

He plucked a blade of grass from his kilt and stuck it between his teeth before he started to explain. "All right: You talk strange. You move strange, and you even look a little strange. I've never seen a girl like you before. Don't you think *that's* strange?"

I nervously racked my brain about what I could possibly say in return. Luckily, I had come up with an explanation for my unusual behavior after my experience with the twin brothers: "I talk funny? Maybe it seems like that to you because I've spent most of my life living outside the Scottish borders. But I don't think that I move funny—much less look funny!" I tried to brush off my rising unease.

Payton laughed, and the sound of it touched my innermost self. He sounded less jaded, less burdened in this era than I knew him to be in my era.

"You look so clumsy when you're stumbling through the woods, and the way you sit on a horse—I mean, it's truly astonishing. You have the natural elegance of a Highland cow."

"Great, just great! Yesterday I was just a plain old cow—extremely flattering. And today I've been upgraded to a sturdy Highland cow. Got any more of those?"

It hurt that he seemed to think so little of me even though in my eyes he was still the coolest guy I had ever met.

Payton winked and twisted the blade of grass between his fingers.

"Oh, I could think of lots more," he said, fixing his gaze on me.

Our eyes locked, and I suddenly felt very hot under the collar. But before I could stammer anything stupid, he changed the subject.

"I am much obliged to you for helping my father. You've done us a great service."

I found it hard to concentrate on what he was saying. There would be butterflies between us, but then a moment later he'd withdraw back into his shell. I tried my best to keep my cool. I didn't want him to know he had such a strong effect on me.

"Thank you. I hope he'll get well soon. Where did his injury come from? I mean, who shot him?"

Payton tossed away the blade of grass he'd been playing with. He stretched out his long legs and wiggled his toes. His leather boots lay carelessly discarded beside him.

"That's a good question. Something's not right about that. We were tracking cattle thieves. And we caught them, too."

He stared at me with an intensity that made it clear he wanted to take in every little bit of my reaction to what he was about to say.

"They were wearing Cameron colors."

I sat up. Cameron colors? Was this whole story just now getting started? Was history actually happening?

I must have passed his scrutiny test, because Payton started sounding less tense.

"If the thieves hadn't shot at us, there would be no doubt in my mind that your clan was guilty of the attack. However, the arrow that they left in my father's chest really makes me wonder."

Cattle thieves, enemy clans, blood feuds—all of this seemed painfully familiar to me, and it didn't take much for me to remember that, in another time, Payton had already told me the story of how everything started:

"The year was 1740. One night, a band of young Scots who trusted their brother—for one, because they loved him; for another, because an oath of allegiance bound them to him—set out to lead a revenge attack against a group of cattle thieves. Back then, that sort of thing was very common. The Highland clans had been fighting one another for ages. Those were different times. Boys of sixteen were considered men. They worked, went into battle, and sometimes died in combat. Stealing cattle was common—especially when a neighboring clan was in trouble.

The Stuart clan at that time had been weakened. Their clan chief had recently passed away, and the identity of his successor was in question. Let me explain: The oldest son did not automatically make the best leader. So sometimes even siblings would fight bitter wars over the issue.

As for the Stuarts, the oldest son—Cathal—had been elected clan chief after his father's passing, and his men had sworn an oath of allegiance to him. But Cathal wasn't the only son. He had brothers, and if he were to show himself incapable of protecting his clan, then this could very well lead to violent conflict inside his own castle walls.

During that time, many cattle raids happened in the Stuarts' borderlands. That could very easily cause a rift among Cathal's followers. This was something he could not, would not allow. And so it came to pass that one night he gathered about twenty of his men to pay visit to his neighboring enemy clan. But the endeavor was ill-fated from the beginning. It would have been better for Cathal not to act in such haste."

"If it wasn't the Camerons, then who was it?" My pulse had quickened. I sensed a mystery that was just waiting to be solved—and I knew that a happy resolution was not necessarily guaranteed.

"Aye, lassie, that's the same question that's been floating around in my head. But, you know, I've caught many a cattle thief. And not a single one of them ever carried arrows with a reinforced metal tip. Someone who needs to steal cattle for a living certainly cannot afford that kind of a weapon."

I remembered noticing Fingal's sons taking in a sharp breath as I removed the arrowhead. But I had thought nothing of it at the time; I thought they all simply felt relieved.

"Why? What else would you use such arrows for?"

"If you're hunting rabbits or birds, all you need are regular wooden arrows with a sharp tip. Any peasant carries such arrows with him. But the penetrating power of a metal tip? That's something you'd only need against an armored opponent." He pushed his plaid aside and pointed to his chest. "Such as when you're trying to cut through a warrior's leather chest piece."

"So why would they have such arrows?"

"That's what I'm going to find out."

Payton got up, dusted himself off, and grabbed his boots with one hand while helping me up with the other. He looked down at me and lifted my chin with the tip of his finger.

"Sam? *An e 'n fhirinn a th' aquad?*" Payton asked, holding his breath in anticipation. He didn't even know why her reply to this question was so important to him. He should never have told her that he doubted her clan's involvement. Not only was she a girl, but she was one of them! A Cameron! But his heart didn't see her as the enemy—which made this all the more difficult for him.

Sam looked at him with big, innocent eyes, but she did not reply to his question.

Ifrinn, didn't she know how important this was for him—and also for her?

He grabbed her shoulders, making it impossible for her to dodge his question any longer.

"The truth, Sam. Tell me the truth. Do you know something about this?"

I got lost in his eyes. He wasn't hiding anything from me—contrary to the Payton that I knew. I could see all the way to the bottom of his soul. I saw fear and uncertainty, but I also saw resolve and courage. This man would fight for what he loved. Right now he was fighting for his family and considered me the enemy. And I didn't think I could say anything to change that.

"No, Payton. I swear to God, I know nothing."

It took all of my strength to fight back my tears. Why couldn't he see the truth? I didn't want him to hate or distrust me! I wanted him to open his heart and feel how much I loved him.

He looked at me for a long time with no reaction. When he finally let go of my shoulders, he weakly confessed, "How, oh how, can I believe you?"

~

Payton turned away so he wouldn't have to face her tears. He wished so much for her to speak the truth, but he didn't dare trust her. He'd be a fool to trust anything coming from her lips. But when he was this close to her, he found it impossible to think straight.

"Why not, Payton?" she cried.

"You're a Cameron. Your beauty cannot hide the fact that you're my enemy."

He had to get away from her. Otherwise, he would throw all caution to the wind and take her in his arms like a wounded doe—because that was exactly what she looked like with her big brown eyes. She was in terrible agony. Agony *he* had inflicted upon her. Despising himself, he walked away.

As if the sky itself felt my pain, the heavenly floodgates opened to wash away my tears. I lifted my face into the rain and finally felt nothing but the cold water on my skin.

Without giving me another look, Payton had walked back to the cottage.

So I was the enemy. How could I forget. His love for me had been put to the test before—when, after we first met during my student-exchange trip, he'd realized that I was a Cameron. Back then, love had triumphed over his hatred for my clan. But things were different then, and the blood feud had long since been forgotten. Now, though, the worst was yet to come, and his rage against the Cameron clan hadn't yet reached its heights. I couldn't bear the thought of his hating me.

But I couldn't confide in him or make him believe me. He would never love me—all because I was the enemy.

I had to get out of here, and quickly. I had to get back to the cottage where Ross had found me, and then find the rock that would take me back to my real life in the twenty-first century. Back to my Future Payton—the one who truly loved me.

Chapter 18

Without giving it another thought, I started running. I didn't look to the left or the right—I just raced into the woods. I wasn't aiming for McRae's cottage. Instead, I was trying to get as far away from it as possible. If I tripped over a root or something, I simply scrambled back to my feet and kept rushing along. Rain tarnished my vision and seeped through my clothes. I ran as fast as I could over this uneven terrain. Meanwhile, I kept glancing over my shoulder, relieved to see that nobody was following me.

Trees, shrubs, and bushes blurred into a tunnel of greens, reds, and browns—a tunnel with no light at the end of it. My lungs were on fire, and my sides hurt terribly. Still, I didn't dare stop. I would orient myself later. For now, all that mattered was to put as much distance as possible between myself and Payton, the Scots, and this nightmare.

Thorny brambles snapped into my face, and I winced, stopping briefly to take a deep breath and wipe the rain from my face. My fingers were bleeding, and the scratches on my skin burned from my salty sweat. The rough housedress clung to my body. It was getting in the way.

A snapping sound to my right made me freeze in place. I listened nervously, but all I could hear was the thumping of my heart and the rain pelting the tree canopy, taking the colorful fall leaves with it.

I did a 360-degree scan of the woods around me. Nothing. My nerves were playing tricks on me. Still, I lifted up my skirts and reached for Sean's *sgian dhu.* I heard rustling leaves and spun around. Gripping the dagger, I screamed when a blackbird not three feet in front of me stretched its wings and flew away. My heart raced, my legs turned to jelly, and my knees buckled.

"Goddamn bird!" I hissed.

I lowered my arm and breathed a sigh of relief. I looked around. Where to now? The forest extended deep, dark, and cold in all directions. I was soaked through to my bones, and it didn't look like the weather was going to turn any time soon. Whatever I did next, I had to keep going. I wasn't yet far enough from McRae's cottage to evade the excellent noses of Ross's dogs. I was actually surprised that I couldn't hear them bark yet. I held my painful side and hurried on.

The forest was denser here, and I had to duck under tree branches dripping with rain. The tree trunks were tightly packed, and every single one seemed to hide an unseen enemy.

Again I heard a rustling sound, a twig snapping. It was closer this time. I didn't dare turn around and so started running again. Wheezing and panting, I tore through the foliage. I heard steps behind me. A tree branch hit my face and made my eyes tear up. Leaves crunched under my feet. *Just don't trip,* I thought. I paused as I came to a downward slope. As I hurriedly tried to climb down it, I slipped and then glided the rest of the way down on my butt. That was when someone tackled me from behind and flung himself on top of me. As he turned me onto my back, I threw my hands up defensively. In the struggle, the dagger landed on a soft target—and with some nasty Gaelic cursing, my assailant pressed my hands over my head while pinning me to the ground with the full weight of his body.

I looked into Payton's angry face. Blood dripped from his chin and onto my dress.

"*Ifrinn!* You little witch!" It was way too easy for him to keep me in check with just one hand, while touching his chin with the other. "You're going to regret this!"

With one swift move he wrested the dagger from my now-numb fingers and put it in his belt.

"Get off me! Let me go!" I screamed, squirming under him with all my might.

"The hell I will. What were you thinking? How far did you think you could make it on your own? Would you rather be defiled and killed by a bunch of bandits than to come with us to Castle Burragh and be under our protection?"

"Your protection? Bah! Didn't you just tell me that I was the enemy? What kind of protection can I expect as an enemy of yours?"

I tried to ram my knee between his legs, but all that did was make my dress ride up. Payton's body pressed me down unrelentingly, and his breath came in fits and bursts. I was at his mercy. Yet just a moment ago I had wanted to never see his face again. To never look into his eyes that were now so full of expression that they stripped me of my own will.

He tried to calm me with a soft, almost tender voice.

"You don't have to be scared. I don't need to use force to find out what you know." His face came closer. "In fact, I don't need to use force to get anything I want."

His lips almost touched mine, and his breath caressed my skin. I got lost in the depths of his eyes, which burned with desire. I felt hot. Our bare legs were entwined, and we were so close. . . .

I swallowed hard and ran my tongue over my suddenly dry lips.

Our eyes locked, and from the expression on his face it was clear what was about to happen next. He lowered his head.

"Payton, please . . . ," I begged for his kiss.

"Hey, McLean! Is this a bad time?" A voice broke through the magic of our moment.

Payton stopped in his tracks with his lips less than a quarter of an inch away from mine. He neither let go nor showed the slightest intention of getting up. But he did raise his head a little. His eyes told me, "We're not done yet, you and I."

"What do you want, Ross?" he called out without turning around.

The redheaded boy came closer. He looked angry.

"What do I want? Leave the girl alone, that's what I want! She's none of your concern. She belongs to Duncan."

Payton winked at me, let go of my hands, and stood up. Then he pulled me up and pushed me behind his back, grabbing my upper arm.

"She's traveling with us, so she's under *my* protection. Duncan can take it up with Cathal later to see how they want to deal with the girl, but right now this is none of *your* business."

"Your kind of protection does not seem of the welcome kind to me," Ross said, hinting at the circumstance under which he had found us.

"A lesson, Ross! I was teaching her a lesson. I don't want her to get any more ideas about running away."

"Interesting methods you've got there, really interesting," Ross said while glaring at Payton.

"And what exactly are *you* doing here, Ross?" Payton asked. "Weren't you taking care of provisions?"

Ross took a step back and stared at his shoes. "Provisions, uh, yes. Everything is packed up. The ox and cart are ready, and we're ready to go."

"And yet you're roaming around here in these woods. Surely there must be other things for you to do."

"I . . . I was following a rabbit. Didn't want some lovely, juicy meat to slip through my fingers, that is all," Ross said, wiping his hands on his kilt. "Anyway, now that I'm here, surely the wee one won't try to run away again, so why are we standing still? I'm sure your brothers want to get going as soon as possible."

Payton motioned for Ross to lead the way. With Ross grumpily stomping off and making a lot more noise than when he first got here, Payton finally let go of my arm and bowed slightly.

"After you, dearest. I'll be right behind you. I certainly won't make the mistake again of turning my back to you," he explained, cautiously touching his still-bleeding chin.

My throat tightened. I knew exactly what that wound would look like after it healed. My mind's eye could already see the crescent-shaped scar that made Payton's face so distinct. I could barely even believe that I was the one who'd inflicted it on him.

"Now, get moving, or wasn't I clear enough in my lesson? We can delve into it some more if you decide not to follow my orders."

Was he challenging me? Was that physical desire that I noticed in his eyes? In school I was really more of a wallflower, and boys didn't usually look at me that way. A moment later, I wondered whether I had just imagined the whole thing. Quickly, so that I wouldn't give in to the temptation of throwing myself at him and embarrassing myself in front of ever-vigilant Ross, I started walking.

As we reached the cottage, the men were busy loading any last supplies onto the cart plus a big straw mattress. They gently bedded Fingal down on it. There was a basket of yarrow and ferns at Fingal's feet, and I also spotted a leather skin that, according to Kyle, contained a brew made from the same herbs. Kyle looked at me with an amused expression on his face, then at Payton and his blood-covered chin. Payton mumbled something unintelligible and swiftly helped me up onto the cart. In passing, he slapped his little brother upside his head, but that only seemed to amuse Kyle even more.

I climbed into the middle of the oxcart so that I was sitting more or less on the axis. This was probably the part that would sway the least while moving. As I was doing that, I also kept an eye on Fingal. The bandages still looked pretty tight, and his chest rose and fell evenly. His lips quivered with every breath, and he was softly snoring.

A good sign, I decided. I wiped the white hair from his sweaty forehead and felt his temperature. His skin felt feverishly hot under my fingers, and I anxiously bit my lip. I wasn't sure how to reduce his fever. Sure, I could cool his body or wrap cold, wet cloths around his lower legs. But would that be enough?

The men around me didn't seem too worried. They fulfilled whatever little tasks remained, and finally our posse started moving. Ross sat in the coach box, with the cart being drawn by two skeletally thin oxen. Ross's horse had been tethered to the back of the cart with a tied-up lamb lying right across it. The lamb bleated miserably, and Ross pulled an unhappy face when the lamb relieved itself on the saddle. The dogs barked, jumping up between his horse's legs, and the horse was clearly getting nervous. Finally, Ross gave a sharp whistle, and things went dead quiet. The dogs silently scatted in all directions and turned into invisible companions that followed us through the underbrush. Even though I knew that they would never run too far from their master, I was now unable to spot them. After a while, I stopped straining my eyes for Barra by the side of the road, and instead tried to relax.

There wasn't much I could do for Fingal, except keep washing his wound with the herbal brew every now and then. I regularly checked his breathing and his pulse. The constant drizzling rain that accompanied us didn't bother me all that much, because my dress had been soaking wet ever since my botched attempt to escape. Besides, the rain helped cool Fingal's feverish body, and the men on their horses didn't even seem to notice that it was raining.

But the road kept going from bad to worse with every hour that this awful weather lasted. We'd left the forest, and the foothills of the Highlands now lay before us. This dark, bluish-gray mountain range had already made an impression on me during my first trip to Scotland. The mountaintops were shrouded in dark, heavy clouds. They were hidden from plain sight, while at the same time exuding a dark, somber mood—which only added to their rugged beauty.

I remembered Roy describing this land to me such a long time ago:

"The mystical landscape of the Highlands has made us Scots a very superstitious people, aye? The fog, the bare cliffs, the darkness—it's all part of our heritage and legends. They lead the people here to a deep belief in magic. Dwarves, giants, fairies—stories about such things have been part of our lives for such a long time that we do believe in them. Many people come to this country without ever understanding this. Others only believe what they can prove. My wish for you is that you learn to understand Scotland, its beliefs, its history, and above all, its people. So don't be afraid of your dreams. Maybe dreams show the people their destiny."

And he was completely right. I myself had become part of these myths because I'd left my own era behind, because I had traveled back to the past on a path that *only existed according to legend.*

Destiny? Why was this word suddenly and relentlessly echoing through my head? Images drifted into my mind, tiny fragments of a memory, like colors that had been washed out by the rain, like smoke that I could never wrap my hands around. Images. Bloodred images.

I wiped the rain from my face and took a deep breath.

Calm down, Sam. It's only the Highlands, only the mountains—not spirits and not the strings of fate making you dance like a puppet to a supernatural tune.

I was in charge. I made all the decisions. I answered only to my own conscience, and I determined my own actions. I had free will! Still, I didn't seem able to get rid of this deep chill in my bones or to fully shake the echo of Roy's words.

After a while, we almost came to a halt. The two oxen pulled with all their might but were powerless against the wooden wheels that were now stuck in the deep mud. The road led steeply uphill, making it even harder on the animals. One of the oxen had no strength left. It dug its legs into the muddy ground and refused to take another step.

The cart swayed, and Fingal moaned. Ross cracked his whip and tore on the reins. Sean, who was at the rear end of our posse, hurried over to help.

"It's not working. The cart is too heavy for these old oxen, and the slope is just too steep."

Sean pushed his wet hair from his face and looked at me. Then he nodded.

"She can walk. We're going slow anyway. Your horse will help the oxen. We'll tie it to the front of the cart, and hopefully that will be enough. We still have a long way to go to Kilerac, and I don't think we'll make it there tonight. But we need to cross the pass before we set up camp for the night."

Meanwhile, the other McLeans had come over, and I shyly smiled at Payton when his eyes briefly met mine.

"Father can't spend the night out on the heath," he said. "We need to make it to Kilerac. At least he'll be able to sleep in a cottage."

"Maybe the road will improve a few miles up?" Kyle interjected. But I could tell from all the cranky faces that this was not likely to happen.

"Get off," Sean ordered. He helped me climb down from the cart before busying himself with Ross's horse's reins. In no time at all, they had lengthened the cart's wooden shaft, using a tree branch and some rope so they could hook the horse to the cart in front of the oxen.

With a sense of horror, I stared at the road ahead. It stretched before us—muddy, steep, and seemingly endless. I was supposed to walk on *that*?

Once, in my former life, Payton had talked me into hiking up Ben Nevis mountain. Even though it had been one of the most unforgettable days of my life—it was the day I'd gotten my first kiss—I still remembered my pathetic physical shape. I had shuffled behind him, out of breath the entire time, and reached the limits of my capacities very quickly.

This time it wasn't the highest peak in Scotland that lay before me, but still it didn't exactly look like a walk in the park.

"She can come with me," Payton suggested, stepping beside me. When Sean frowned disapprovingly, Payton quickly cut in, "If she walks, it'll slow us down even further. Besides, she needs to keep up her strength so she can look after Father properly."

Sean didn't say a word—he just glared at Payton. They stood there for a long time, locking horns, without either of them giving in. Finally, Blair decided the matter by nodding in my direction.

"Get on your horses already. I have no intention of letting Father sleep under an open sky. We all need a decent meal and dry beds. Now, get moving."

Sean turned to look me up and down. "With a woman like her in front of you, it will probably make for very uncomfortable riding. Have you thought about that, Payton?"

"*Fan sàmhach,* Sean! Let that be my problem, not yours."

Impatiently, Payton pulled his horse's reins and helped me into the saddle before pulling himself up behind me. I gasped in surprise when he wrapped his lower arm around me, pulling me close against his body. His thighs touched mine when he gently squeezed to make his horse move. And with the horse's first step, my head was thrown back against Payton's chest. For the next few minutes, I sat as stiff as a poker in front of him, trying to ignore that nice feeling of intimacy and familiarity he stirred. Fortunately, everyone else's attention was focused on the cart and the safety of our passage, so nobody seemed to notice my emotional turmoil.

"Relax," Payton whispered into my ear.

"What?" I found it hard to even hear him over the pounding of my heart.

"You can lean against my chest. If you're going to sit like this, all stiff and tensed up, you will feel every single muscle in your body later."

I found it touching that he cared, but I was still holding a grudge for his awful behavior earlier. My feelings were hurt because the kiss I had so longed for back in the woods had been nothing to him but a lesson he wanted to teach me. What a jerk! And even though it was unfair to blame him for what his brother Sean said earlier, I did think it was pretty rude of him not to disagree that my presence would prove "uncomfortable." And so I stiffened up even more and tried—as idiotic as that was—to shift away from him.

He gave a pained groan, and another Gaelic curse escaped his lips.

"All right, do what you want, Sam, but don't say I didn't warn you."

An hour after refusing his peace offering, I was barely able to stay in the saddle. My entire backside was flooded with pain, my shoulders were stiff, and the muscles in the back of my neck were rock solid. Because the road had been getting better for a while, I kind of expected to be loaded back onto the oxcart. I prayed for it to happen as quickly as possible, because I really couldn't make it much longer. I shifted from my left butt cheek to my right, stuck out my chest, and tried to briefly take the pressure off my back. It didn't work.

The sound of wild laughter tore me from my self-pitying thoughts. Sean and Kyle were riding level with us, and both were grinning from ear to ear. I didn't understand what was so funny, but Payton evidently did. He glared at his brothers and hissed at me:

"Keep still already! You're fidgeting like you're sitting on an anthill!"

The expression on his face didn't bode well, so I clenched my teeth and tried to stop squirming. My being here was probably just as uncomfortable as Sean had said. After all, to him I was a Cameron—the enemy. I could not afford to forget that. With my last ounce of pride, I stuck out my chin. Under no circumstances would I show any weakness—no, sirree!

I distracted myself by admiring the artful embroidery on Kyle's saddle. Highland thistles lined up in a row and contrasted with the pale leather.

Kyle had spurred on his horse, but I could still hear him chuckling from up ahead. Sean was not nearly so tactful.

"If this is getting too hard for you, Brother, I would be happy to swap," he said, pointing to the space in front of his saddle.

Vigorously shaking his head, Payton replied through gritted teeth. "*Pog mo thon,* Sean! I can only imagine why you'd want to *sacrifice* yourself. Thanks, but no thanks."

Sean laughed and spurred on his horse. "You're a hard one to trick, aye?" he called over his shoulder while giving me a sly wink.

I almost didn't catch Payton's mumbled "So are you" because he had already stopped his horse and was in the process of dismounting. He busied himself with the saddle strap and nestled on his kilt, before motioning for me to climb down myself.

"What's wrong? Why are we stopping?"

Puzzled, I watched as the rest of our posse disappeared around a bend.

"We will walk for a while. The horse needs a break."

He reached into his bag, brought out a silver bottle, and took a generous sip before handing the bottle to me.

"There, drink! It'll give you energy."

I flinched as I reached for it. My shoulder muscles heavily protested making any sort of movement.

"Ow!"

Payton gave me a triumphant look.

"Didn't I warn you? There, drink, it'll loosen your muscles. Or at the very least it will numb the pain."

I didn't really trust that Scottish cure-all, but I still took a sip of the stuff anyway.

Bah, if I continued like this, I'd be an underage alcoholic by the time I got back to the twenty-first century.

"Thanks."

I enjoyed having Payton all to myself. Finally I was able to collect my thoughts and, because I no longer had to worry that I was bothering him on account of my presence, my anger at him faded into the background.

The sky had turned a dark blue and was on the verge of showing off its nightly star-studded gown. The distant mountain peaks had turned into black shadows that surrounded us like a soot-colored cauldron. Only in the far distance, in the valley before us, could we make out a shimmer of light.

"What is that?" I asked.

"Kilerac. That is where, God willing, we will find lodgings for the night."

"And if not?"

Payton smirked. "If not, we'll have to camp out here on the heath and keep each other warm."

I found the way he talked completely unnerving. At times, he would call me a burden, but then later he would try to provoke and tease me. And I hadn't forgotten that moment earlier when he was *this close* to kissing me.

"Well, I would rather freeze to death than allow *you* to keep me warm," I snapped because I just didn't know how to react. "Besides, I don't want to make this another *uncomfortable* night for you."

I quickened my step and promptly left Payton and his horse behind me. I didn't stop, even when I heard them following me. Jesus, I could no longer make heads or tails of myself. I had loved Payton for a long time, yet it felt like I was just now falling for him.

He was so hard to predict, but at the same time he was incredibly honest and genuine. Payton's dark moodiness that had come about due to bearing a curse for two hundred and seventy years—all that was missing from the man here with me. His laughter was contagious, and a wonderful sense of humor always twinkled in his eyes.

Even now I could hear the suppressed chuckle in his voice as he called after me.

"As God is my witness, Sam, you have no idea *how* uncomfortable that night would be for *me*."

Hurt and furious, I spun around with my fists clenched by my sides.

"You are such an asshole, Payton McLean! What gives? Why would you say such a thing? Isn't it enough that you took me prisoner? Do you really have to put me down, hurt my feelings, and strip me of my dignity? Is that what you're trying to do?"

Payton dropped his horse's reins and stepped closer. He came so close that our bodies almost touched. I felt queasy. Had I gone too far? After all, I didn't know what this man was capable of.

He lifted my chin, and again I could see the desire in his eyes.

"You want to know why I'm saying these things?"

His grip on my chin tightened, and with his other arm he grabbed me by the waist and pulled me closer.

"Because it's the truth. Riding with you was an ordeal. *Hell on Earth.* Sheer torture. Just the thought of keeping you warm at night—of covering your body with mine—has me at the limits of my self-control."

His iron grip was unrelenting. Each of his words came like a lash of the whip, even though he was whispering. "You're a Cameron, I wouldn't trust you as far as I could throw you. But do you want to know what I'm planning to do to you? Let me show you."

His hand slid to the back of my neck, and although I tried to resist, he pressed his lips passionately against mine. He stole a kiss from me that made me forget *where* and *when* I was. Luckily his hands clutched me tightly against his chest, because my legs were completely useless after this sudden rush. I prayed this moment would never end.

Much too soon, Payton let go of me and pushed me away. He took a step back as if he needed to establish a safe distance. Completely distraught, he ran his hands through his hair.

"I am sorry, Sam. I swear you have nothing to fear from me." He turned away and shook his head in disbelief over his own actions.

I found it hard to think straight again after that kiss. At least I now knew that he thought of me as his enemy, but that his discomfort had to do with him being drawn to me rather than with him rejecting me. I almost had to grin when I thought about how he must have felt as we rode together. And this explained Sean and Kyle's strange behavior earlier. They were teasing him because of me!

"Answer me, I beg of you. Can you forgive me for taking advantage of you? I have no idea what got into me. I am so sorry," he assured me.

I raised my hand to my lips, still feeling his kiss.

"Do you do that often?" I asked quietly.

"Do what?"

"You know what I mean! Kiss girls that are supposed to be your enemy?"

I was grateful that night had fallen and that it was almost dark, because this conversation reminded me of another talk I'd had with Payton—a talk in a different space and time. I was sure he could see my turmoil.

"No, never! Normally I am very sensible and conscientious."

"Do you think it sensible to kiss a Cameron?" I said.

His words came almost in a whisper.

"No. It's the least sensible thing I have ever done in my life," he admitted.

I searched for his eyes, but he held his face turned away from me. To loosen our strange mood, I joked: "I don't think you're in any danger from a Cameron right now. You've got my dagger, so it would appear that I'm not going to kill too many people in the very near future."

His laughter sounded lighthearted. "Yes, you're right. Not in the near future, anyway."

This déjà-vu I was having of another walk by Payton's side—and during which we'd had a similar discussion—made me laugh. I grabbed the horse's reins and started walking again. Every single one of my muscles hurt, and I was soaked to the bone from all the rain. I just wanted to arrive at our destination—no matter what might happen to me there. The last few minutes had sparked a realization.

Payton McLean was falling in love with me all over again. The power of this knowledge would carry me through. It would make me forget the strain of this journey and help me find a way to save him. Because something else was becoming obvious. It wouldn't be so easy to return to my own era. Every mile that we walked also brought me closer to Vanora—and her blood. There was only one possibility now. I had to meet her and somehow get some of her blood. Until that time, I would just continue to get to know Payton the way he once was.

"All right, then, I'm not sorry," Payton said after we'd walked awhile in silence. He took the reins from me and stopped. "Come on, get on the horse."

"But I thought it needed a break?"

"I lied. I was the one who needed a break. The temptation of you being so close, and I could just reach out and . . . but let's not talk about that. It's safer with both of us on the horse, trust me."

I put my foot in his interlocked hands and pulled myself into the saddle.

As he took his seat behind me, I thought I heard him mumbling a quick prayer before spurring on his horse. This time I leaned against his chest because I was truly exhausted. I also really enjoyed the warmth of his body.

"I'm not sorry, either," I whispered into the dark. And the fact that his arm at my waist pulled me just a little closer told me that he had probably heard me.

Chapter 19

The faces of the men and women were lit by a brightly burning fire. Benches had been placed in a circle around the blaze, and a barn housed the dining tables decorated with flower garlands. People were laughing and gathering to dance, and the newlywed couple was being showered with the blessings of well-wishers.

Inside the barn, Payton leaned against a beam and stretched out his legs under the table. The serving tray in front of him was clean but for a few leftover crumbs, and the foam of freshly drawn beer was spilled over the side of his mug. He took a drink.

The wedding party in Kilerac had reacted quickly, generously sharing their feast with the surprise visitors and making room for the two oxen and the horses in one of their stables. When the late arrivals—Payton and Sam—had reached the village a little while later, the rest of their posse was already mingling with the wedding guests.

The young couple had been kind enough to leave their bridal chamber to the injured laird, and so Fingal was lying in one of the small cottages on a bed covered with fresh white linens and decorated with flowers.

No sooner had Payton helped Samantha off his horse than she was called away to tend to Fingal.

Payton seriously contemplated following her to the cottage. But not just because he worried about his father. He pulled the beer mug closer. That little Cameron lass now haunted his thoughts. And to make matters worse, Kyle was approaching with a big grin on his face.

"*Slàinte mhath,* Brother. So you finally made it, huh?"

"As you can see," Payton grumbled. He didn't feel like explaining himself to his little brother.

"What took you so long? You didn't get lost, did you? Perhaps under the skirts of a lady?"

"Kyle—shut your dirty trap," was all the youngest received for a reply.

"Or maybe you weren't well? I had the impression that perhaps you were in some pain," Kyle continued unblinkingly.

"Good heavens, would somebody please protect me from you and your big mouth?" Payton said. "You had better be quiet, or you will be sorry."

"Who's going to be sorry?" Sean asked as he found his way into the barn. He put down his half-full mug and sat with the other two.

"Father is fine. He woke up briefly, asked for whiskey, and is now probably sleeping it off until the morning," he reported. "But your little prisoner almost went for my throat when I handed Father the whiskey bottle. He was allowed water or hot soup at the most, she said, but then Fingal's orders to 'get that pigheaded wench out of his hair' made her see the error of her ways."

"She's pretty feisty, that Cameron woman," Kyle agreed.

"She only means well," Payton defended Samantha's behavior. Immediately, he found himself the butt of their jokes again.

"Watch your tongue, Sean. Payton was about to challenge me to a duel before you came—only because I asked about the wee lass. We don't want him having to fight the two of us, now do we." Kyle laughed and pulled Payton's beer mug closer, which he then proceeded to gulp down in one thirsty swig.

Payton stood up, shaking his head. "You half-wits. That Cameron lass has a lovely bottom that was rubbing up against me all day. That's all there is to it. And now you had better stop mocking me. Stuff has been building up today, if you know what I mean!"

Followed by Sean's and Kyle's roaring laughter, Payton escaped from the barn and stomped round the fire toward the stables. Once there, he found himself a quiet spot and slumped onto a heap of straw.

His brothers' taunts hit him hard because they came way too close to his true feelings for the pretty prisoner.

He ran his hands through his hair and cursed. *"Bas mallaichte, she was a Cameron!"* She was probably even in league with the cattle thieves. So why couldn't he get this girl out of his head? In his eyes, she was truly beautiful, even though she was so much skinnier than most other women he knew. But then that dark bruise on her cheek was not exactly attractive. Plus, there were all those scratches she had incurred during her ridiculous attempt to make her escape through the woods. But why then was he seeing her with different eyes? Why had he given in to his desire and kissed her? This could mean trouble for him if his brothers ever found out.

While they found it entertaining to tease him about her, they didn't have an inkling of his true feelings.

"She's a Cameron, goddammit!" he called into the dark, and a horse's snort was the lonely reply. He touched his still-painful chin to remind himself who had caused him the injury.

But her hair had smelled so nice, her lovely bottom had almost driven him out of his mind, and—whenever he thought about their kiss—his body reacted in a way that betrayed his strictly rational side.

Kissing her had been the least sensible thing he had ever done. And that would be that. He would not go near the beautiful prisoner again.

Deeply absorbed in thought, Payton only noticed the giggling, embracing lovers when their shadows entered the faint glimmer of light in the doorway. He immediately jumped to his feet, noisily clearing his throat to avoid any embarrassment.

The couple quickly separated, and Sean protectively stepped in front of the girl.

"What are you doing here?" he asked, startled at seeing his brother.

"I'm resting after a long day. What you two are doing here"—Payton nodded at the girl—"is fairly obvious. You will excuse me."

To give them their privacy, he exited the barn. There were lots of happy, laughing people outside. The fire seemed to have attracted everyone, and dancers spun and swirled breathlessly to the sound of the music. After the day's rain clouds had finally dissipated, this clear and starry night was perfect for love. The newlywed couple had just been talked into giving yet another toast, and everyone was emptying their beer mugs amid wild cheers. As always, Sean never passed up an opportunity when it presented itself, and Payton hoped that the girl's father did not notice she was missing. Sean's self-confidence had to be a big reason that the fair sex was always so kindly disposed toward him. One day, or so Payton worried, Sean wouldn't be able to get out of one of his affairs so easily. But that would not be Payton's problem.

When he discovered his brother Blair by the fire, he sat down beside him. Blair was much quieter than the rest of the McLean brothers and not really interested in excesses. He never overindulged in drinking, nor did he laugh at other people's jokes all that often.

"Good party, isn't it," he greeted Payton, making room for him on the bench.

"Sean said Father woke up?" Payton immediately changed the subject. Blair was a man of few words and only made conversation to be polite.

"Yes. And right away he got terribly upset about that wench. But she is looking after his well-being, don't you think? She does not want to harm him?"

Payton shook his head energetically. "No. Don't worry. She would not harm him."

"But Ross said she gave you that cut on your chin. Is that true?"

Sheepishly, Payton looked down at the ground. For how long had Ross stood observing them in the woods before making himself known?

"It was my fault," he replied, shrugging it off. Then he asked, "What, exactly, was her crime? Why did the Stuarts take her prisoner?"

"I am not really sure, because I didn't follow the whole story. But Cathal seemed really upset. He said that Duncan and Dougal were idiots. They abducted this Cameron woman even though they knew that the peace between the two clans stands on shaky ground. They suspect she knows who is stealing our cattle—or that she is maybe even wrapped up in it herself."

"Oh, but that's nonsense. I've been spending a lot of time with her, and if there is one thing that she is not, it's a cattle thief. She cannot even get up on a horse without help."

Blair nodded. "She certainly does not seem particularly dangerous. But when it comes down to it, that's none of our business. As Cathal requested, we'll be taking her away from the borderlands, and I don't care what his plans are for her afterward."

Payton stared into space. It was always the same story with Blair. He wondered what kind of a laird his brother would become one day. It was always enough for Blair to bend to Cathal's views. Of course, the Stuarts and the McLeans had been allies for a number of years, and they had sworn peace to each other under oath. But Payton worried that one day the fate of the McLeans would be decided by Cathal Stuart alone.

Payton was distracted when the door opened to the cottage where Fingal lodged. Three women stepped out and briefly talked to one another before parting ways. Sam was not one of them.

"May I offer you a mug of beer?"

A young woman with shapely hips, wavy blond hair, and freckles all over her face slid onto the bench next to Payton and handed him the mug. "You look all too serious. This is a celebration of happiness. Don't you want to celebrate with us?"

Payton's eyes wandered over to the cottage. The door remained closed. He turned to the woman by his side brazenly placing a hand on his knee.

"You are worried about your father, is that right? I am Kelsey, and I could take your mind off things for a while—if you like. I have been watching you all night, and I think it is time to see you laugh."

"Kelsey, listen, that's really nice of you, but—"

"No buts! Drink up, and then we will dance! It took all of my courage to come over and speak to you. So you will not get rid of me without at least one little dance."

Her smile beamed brightly and, even though she was blushing, she firmly held Payton's gaze.

"All right, Kelsey. One dance it is," he agreed.

I had thanked the women for their help and was now leaning, exhausted, against the door inside the cottage. Alone at last. I closed my eyes and took a deep breath. Mistress MacQuarrie had been very nice. She had basically taken care of Fingal all by herself and eventually advised me to take off my wet clothes. Because I had nothing else with me, she offered me one of her dresses, which had become too small for her on account of her growing belly.

Full of gratitude, I looked at the simple, dark green dress. It was of much better quality than the one I'd been wearing. The fabric felt smoother and softer, and a braided brown belt gave the whole thing even a touch of elegance.

I poured the last bit of warm water into the washbowl. Because Fingal was fast asleep thanks to the half bottle of whiskey he had polished off earlier, for the first time in days I had something resembling privacy.

I dipped a clean rag into the water and washed my face, my neck, and my arms. Then I unfastened the bow that hung loosely around my waist and listened anxiously for any noise coming from outside. My stomach tightened at the thought of someone entering with me in nothing but my underwear. But I couldn't hear anything except the music and distant laughter of the partygoers. If I wanted to take a chance, it had to be right now. I reached for my hem with a final glance over at Fingal. He was still sound asleep. As quickly as I could, I slipped out of my housedress and reached for the green one. My heartbeat slowed only once I finished adjusting everything. That threat gone, I felt more courageous. I lifted my skirts and washed my legs.

It was great to finally feel clean again. It wasn't exactly a nice hot shower, but I had learned to appreciate the little things.

The dress fit me remarkably well. It was softer and even warmer than my other dress, but the neckline was too low for my taste. Especially here, in the company of these uncivilized Scots, I would have preferred a less flashy garment. It didn't seem to be made for everyday chores but rather for special occasions.

I washed my old dress as best I could and wrung it out with all my strength. With any luck, it would be as good as new in the morning.

My hair, on the other hand, was in terrible shape. It was completely matted and full of knots. I combed it with my fingers as best I could and pleated it into a long, firm braid. Using a thread from the woven belt over my dress, I tied up the end of the braid and was more than happy with the result. I could now pass for a Scottish woman of the eighteenth century.

Thanks to kind Mistress MacQuarrie who had put in a good word for me, I—a prisoner—was now allowed to help myself to the wedding banquet in the barn. If there was anything left of it.

My stomach was very vocal about wanting a good meal, so I opened the door and stepped out into the night. There weren't as many people in the center of the village as when we first arrived. The celebrations were drawing to a close.

I looked around, unsure of myself, but I didn't spot anyone from the McLean gang. I walked over to the barn and was glad to see food left on the tables. Ravenous, I broke off a chunk of bread and bit into a big smoked sausage. It was delicious. Happy and content, I slumped onto the bench and enjoyed finally being able to eat a proper meal.

I had just gorged myself on a third sausage when I got the feeling that someone was watching me. I turned around and smiled at seeing Ross leaning against the barn door.

"Hello, Ross. Have you eaten?"

He strolled over and sat down, holding two cups full of dark red wine. Was that adoration I saw in his eyes?

"I almost didn't recognize you. Did you get all dressed up for me?"

"Why, of course! Just for you," I teased.

He slid one of the cups to me.

"*Slàinte mhath!* To us, the unworthy in our group!" he called out while raising his wine.

"Why do you think you're unworthy?" I asked.

"Bottoms up! You are supposed to toast with me, Samantha. Let's celebrate."

It dawned on me that Ross had probably raised a mug or three already. He was in a strange mood.

"Let's drink! And then we'll dance before the fiddlers play their last song," he proposed, knocking over his cup and spilling the rest of his wine on his shirt.

I tried to get up, but he reached for my hand.

"One thing I swear to you, Samantha. I will not allow this Payton McLean to lay his hands on you ever again. I saw everything. I saw how he threw you down on the ground! That brute! But me, I am not like that!" he exclaimed. "I will protect you!"

I looked at his shirt. His chest was bloodred.

Red from the wine, or red from blood?

I shrieked, then tripped backward over the bench. I landed in the straw and thrashed wildly on the floor. I didn't see the barn roof or Kyle's worried face as he rushed toward us.

I saw something else entirely.

I could feel that the heart underneath my fingers had stopped beating. A single word flashed through my addled brain: betrayal.

I lifted my head and looked into his eyes. A tear, burning hot like melting metal, burned its way down my cheek and fell, unhindered, onto the blood-soaked earth.

Slowly, as if guided by an invisible hand, I pulled the dagger from his chest, unable to take my eyes off his face. Why, Ross? Why? The blood on his lips was his silent response to my sorrowful cry.

My throat burned as I came to. I coughed and spluttered. Tears welled up in my eyes, and I pushed away the bottle someone was holding out to me.

"Stop!" I wheezed, swallowing the rest of the whiskey that had been poured into my mouth.

I found it impossible to get rid of the images of my strange "dream," even though I was no longer dreaming. Kyle's friendly face moved into my field of vision, and I immediately felt better. It seemed in his nature to cheer people up.

"Finally, Lady Cameron is back in the land of the living. You know, you should really stay away from wine if it knocks you out after only a few sips," he suggested with a mischievous grin. Then he helped me to my feet.

Ross was nowhere to be found, and I saw no one else in the barn, either. Shaking, I climbed onto the bench and tried to collect my thoughts.

"Are you well?" Kyle asked with genuine concern.

"Yes, I must have just tripped," I lied. But nothing was well. Everything was wrong! I couldn't deny what I had seen. And if the events of the last few months were anything to go by, then this had most certainly not been a dream. It was a *vision*. And, contrary to the couple of times I'd seen those disturbing images before, I now knew what they meant.

I would kill Ross Galbraith.

But why? To keep from passing out again, I took a deep breath. I breathed in, and I breathed out. Why would I do such a thing? I wasn't a killer. I tried to banish all thoughts from my mind. All that mattered was the air flowing into my lungs. That was what I focused on.

Kyle gently ran his hand up and down my back. As soon as I felt a little better, he helped me get off the bench.

"Come on, lass, let's get you to bed. I'm sure you will feel better tomorrow."

When we reached the door to the cottage where I would sleep by Fingal's bedside, I turned to thank Kyle. What I really wanted to do, though, was tell him how sorry I was that I wouldn't be able to change his fate.

He took my hand and gave it a squeeze.

"Don't worry about it, lassie. You're all right," he said, stopping me from thanking him and saying all those other words that I would have found so hard to say anyway.

I nodded, and then glanced over my shoulder. Payton was dancing with some blond peasant girl right in the middle of the village square. I couldn't believe it. That bitch was throwing herself at him! I could see her shamelessly wrapping her arms around his neck. And Payton seemed to be enjoying it! I quickly looked away and discovered Ross standing behind the two of them under a tree, staring right at me. I shivered when our eyes met. Quickly, I pulled the door shut behind me.

Chapter 20

Compared to the excitement of the previous few days, the next day went off more or less without a hitch. Fingal was awake but in a foul mood because he was hungry. He only stopped whining when I served him a generous portion of oatcakes.

Now that he was wide awake, it became even clearer that Fingal McLean was a born leader. I saw strength, courage, and firm resolve in his eyes, and while I well remembered Duncan and Dougal's sarcasm from earlier, this man's natural authority demanded that he be met with the utmost respect. Compared to Ross's brothers, he was a different caliber of man altogether. The twins might walk around with big chips on their shoulders, but they only won people's respect by threatening violence.

After Fingal had taken a few bites, he gave me a friendly look.

"Thank you, lassie. I swear to you—I am famished."

"You should slow down, sir. Your stomach has been empty for several days, and—"

"Och, nothing!" he replied, munching away happily.

I raised my eyebrows. As far as I was concerned, I couldn't care less. He was old enough to do as he pleased, and it wasn't as if I could stop him. So I left him to his meal and turned my attention to my old housedress. Thanks to the fire going in the cottage, the dress was almost dry. I folded it up so I could take it with me.

"And now tell me who you really are. You have healing hands, but the sadness in your eyes makes me unwell."

He had folded his hands in front of him on the bedcover, and he was looking at me expectantly.

"Milord, I am a prisoner. If you don't like my eyes, then perhaps you should let me go," I suggested.

His roaring laughter made me cringe.

"Delightful! Truly delightful, lassie."

Fingal was a good-looking man, and the laughter making his eyes twinkle was contagious. I couldn't stop a smile from twitching around the edges of my mouth. The way he was calling me "lassie" made it almost sound like a pet name a father would give to his daughter.

"All right, then, *prisoner.* How about you start by telling me your name so I know who to thank for treating my injuries."

"My name is Samantha Camer—"

"Yes, yes. Cameron, I see that. But I wonder why I've never heard of you before. Trust me, Samantha, for years I have made it a habit to know my enemies better than my friends. And, even though going by your face you could be the child of Isobel and Tomas Cameron, you don't seem to be. You are too old. They have not been married that long. Besides, you wouldn't be wearing a simple dress like that if you were the laird's child." He pointed at the neatly folded dress and gave me a questioning look.

I picked at my fingernails, not knowing what to say. This man had only been awake for a few hours, and already he was seeing right through my disguise—or whatever you want to call this makeshift identity I had created for myself.

What should I say? I actually was Isobel and Tomas's direct descendant, but there were at least ten generations between us. Why I would show such a close physical resemblance to my ancestors, I did not know.

Because I didn't respond, Fingal nodded good-naturedly.

"Very well, Samantha Cameron. I will return to this topic a little later since it seems we will be enjoying each other's company for quite some time. And now go check on my useless sons who are no doubt sleeping off their hangovers. Ask them when they intend to take me to Burragh. I am an old man, and I want to die in my home."

"You're not going to die, sir. You're a lot better already. The fever has broken," I reassured him.

He shooed me to the door, grumbling: "Oh, I know, but these little scoundrels don't seem to know that. Let them worry a bit about their old father. Go now. I need to take a piss, and unless you want to watch, you had better do what I tell you."

I slipped out the door and shook my head, thinking about Payton's dad. I liked him. He had a sense of humor, and he was boisterous and alert at the same time. Spending more time with him should prove interesting.

The cold early-morning air blew under my skirts, and I rubbed my arms. Before long, we would get the first night of frost. By that time, I hoped, I'd be back in my own era, watching a movie in my favorite yoga pants while eating microwave popcorn. Anything but the old *Highlander* movies, I thought. If these people here only knew what they were missing . . .

"Madain mhath," Kyle greeted me, wishing me a good morning. "Is he still alive?" he asked, nodding toward the cottage door.

I smiled as always when Kyle looked at me. He was such a breath of fresh air.

"Yes, he's alive, but he wants that to be our little secret. I wouldn't be surprised if he burst out wailing and whining as soon as you enter the cottage."

Kyle chuckled. "Yes, that sounds like him. But don't worry! I will offer him a generous dose of sympathy and try to cheer him up with this." He held up one of the smoked sausages from the previous night and then walked past me toward his father's cottage.

I headed off in the direction of the stables. If the men were preparing for our departure, that was where I would find them. I ran into Sean. Literally. I turned a corner and bumped right into him, banging my knee into his shin.

"Ouch, sorry!" I said, massaging my knee.

"*Thoir an aire!* Careful! Easy does it," he cautioned. "If you want to get up close with me, all you have to do is ask." He gave me a teasing wink, and much to my embarrassment, I blushed. How did he always manage to come up with a clever line to flirt with a girl, no matter the situation? Ryan Baker, my high school's Prince Charming—and a former major crush of mine—still had a lot to learn.

I ignored Sean's remark so I wouldn't embarrass myself again in the same way I had embarrassed myself in the presence of heartbreaker Ryan.

"Your father wants to know when we're leaving."

"We're ready. As soon as Ross is done strapping the oxen to the cart, we will head out. Payton and Blair already left. A villager spotted redcoats in the area, and we should try to avoid them if possible."

"Redcoats? Why?"

I racked my brain, but I had never paid enough attention in history class. What was the story again between the English and the Scots?

Did this have anything to do with the uprising Payton had mentioned on our first day together? Didn't that happen in 1745? But Vanora would speak her curse in 1740, five years prior, banning the McLeans to a life without emotions. I was absolutely certain that this day hadn't come yet.

"Because they're redcoats." Sean winked at me. "Camerons and Sassenachs can all go jump in the lake together, if you know what I mean. I hope you will forgive me."

"The cart is ready, and we can go," said Ross, interrupting this strange moment.

My skin crawled as I looked at him in the early-morning light. He smiled, but it didn't get through to me because all I could see were his eyes as I'd seen them in my dream. Eyes that had lost their spark.

For the life of me, I couldn't imagine what might possibly go wrong enough for me to attack and kill him.

Except for our initial encounter, Ross had been nothing but nice to me. I liked him. I even pitied him a little. The way everyone treated him wasn't right. So why would I do such an awful thing? I could never kill anyone, I was sure of that. But that vision . . .

Completely engrossed in thought, I went through the motions of all the tasks I had been assigned. It was only after we'd been traveling for a good while that I remembered that I no longer carried a weapon. It *was* as Payton had said: I wouldn't kill anyone any time soon.

What a relief. Satisfied, I turned my head toward the coach box, and when Ross smiled at me over his shoulder, I smiled back.

Chapter 21

The castle gates were open. Several people who were out and about on the streets greeted us as we approached on the narrow path leading up to Castle Burragh. That day's sun had not dissipated the thin veil of mist, so with every yard that we advanced, we saw the dark and gloomy stronghold rise, bit by bit, through the fog. The oxcart rattled through the open portcullis whose sharp iron tips loomed menacingly overhead. The horses' hooves clattered over the dry, trampled-down clay ground, and a handful of chickens scattered when the oxen politely offered to stomp right over them.

Ross directed the cart toward the castle keep, which—contrary to the outer walls whose only openings were the narrow arrow loops—offered a number of neat-looking stained-glass windows. Wooden wall-walks encircled the castle two rows deep so the building could easily be defended in every direction.

To my left, I saw a pointed archway leading into another courtyard, where a horse was just being shod. A young apprentice held the horse's foot while an overweight, grunting blacksmith fitted the iron shoe.

Even though I had been to this place before, everything seemed strange and unfamiliar. The castle yard seemed bigger than on the day the taxicab had brought me here. The hustle and bustle took away the dreariness of the gray stone walls and distracted from some corners that, in my present-day life, I would have found unpleasant and fairly run-down.

Still, it was like coming home, probably because we had finally come to the end of this long and rain-soaked journey. And perhaps it also had something to do with the handsome Scot who was just then walking down the stairs.

I had been missing his company all day. Since Payton and Blair hadn't returned to our posse, Sean had taken that to mean that the English redcoats posed no threat. This in turn had meant that we could take the direct route and reach the castle faster.

As Payton walked toward us, I felt like a groupie at a rock concert unable to take my eyes off my idol for even a second. He must have taken a nice long bath, because his hair was wet and his skin was slightly reddened from a shave.

He called for a stable boy, handing him the bridle and ordering him to unyoke and take care of the oxen. Then he walked around to the back of the cart to help me off before offering his father a hand. Fingal was unwilling to show any signs of weakness in front of his people, so he climbed down and walked over to the castle keep by himself, with his head held high and his teeth clenched.

"You seem to have worked miracles with Father. He is as grumpy as he's ever been," Payton noted. He led me to the courtyard and, in the opposite direction, halfway around the castle keep.

"Yes, he's doing much better today. I redressed his wound earlier. The inflammation is going down, and the edges have started closing up," I reported. He led me through several stone arches and down several steps. The smell of garbage and wastewater was getting stronger.

Besides the two of us, nobody else was around in this part of the castle. The outer wall ran very close along the living area and just about blocked out the sky and the sun.

"Where are we going?" I asked. My voice echoed against the walls and sounded ghostly.

Payton didn't say a word, and I assumed that he hadn't heard me, which was why I repeated my question.

"Listen, Sam. This wasn't my decision. I even put in a good word for you, but I couldn't get Blair to change his mind."

He looked at me, visibly embarrassed and obviously unhappy about his task.

"Where are we going?" I whispered, suddenly feeling very cold.

"It's not going to be for long, and I promise you will want for nothing."

"Where are you taking me?" I screamed, backing away from him. He was scaring me, but there was no possibility of escape after he grabbed my lower arm with a vise-like grip.

"To the dungeon, Sam. I'm taking you to the dungeon."

"No!"

Desperately, I tried to tear away from him, to free myself from his grip.

The *dungeon!* The word alone triggered a panic attack. The dread was suffocating me, and I could barely breathe. I lashed out, flailing my arms, with everything that I had.

"Sam! Stop! Calm down, please. I will do what I can so you can get out of here as quickly as possible, but right now you have to obey," he implored. "If the guards see you resisting, they will put you in chains. So please, in the name of God, calm down and trust me!"

He pressed to his chest so there wasn't enough room for me to punch him.

"No! No, I can't! Payton, please," I pleaded. "Please, Payton, I beg of you, let me go. I'm not your enemy! I love you! I'm only here so I can save you! But I can't save your life if you lock me up. This is not making any sense right now, I know, I know, but . . . please, for the love that I feel for you, just let me go. Please, please, don't do this to me."

My words were gushing out of my mouth so fast that I could barely understand them. I sounded choked, tearful. And I was very close to seizing up in a panicked fit. Rats, rusty chains hanging from walls, rigid iron bars, and torture. Those were the things I associated with a dungeon. I was painting them all in vivid detail before my mind's eye.

I already felt the cold, unyielding chains on my wrists, chafing my skin and making me easy prey for all the rats that would come out during the deepest, darkest hours of the night to finish me off. It was a nightmare. The garish images in my mind wouldn't go away, and Payton's reassurances did nothing to lessen my horror.

No light, no air, and no means of escape. I fought relentlessly. Payton would have to knock me out cold to get me to come with him. Nothing could make me go with him, nothing!

"Please, Payton, please! Let go of me, please."

As if he hadn't heard me, he said, "Sam! Stop! You're making no sense, and you're only making it worse!"

He shook me and turned his head, surprised to hear the sound of boots coming nearer.

"Great! You've alerted the guards! There's nothing I can do for you now," he railed, expertly avoiding my attempts to kick him in the shins.

Two men, real giants, filled the narrow passageway almost entirely with their bodies as they stormed toward us. While still holding on to me, Payton pushed me behind his back and lifted a hand in greeting.

"Is that woman troubling you?" the guards asked as they drew closer. They seemed prepared to bend me to their will by force, if necessary. I realized the hopelessness of my situation and gave up. There was only one thing worse than ending up in the dungeon, and that was ending up *injured* in the dungeon.

"No, she's not. I don't need you. Go back to your posts," Payton said.

The sentry with the bulky neck of a bull shook his head and said, "Not possible."

"We have orders to come and get the prisoner," the other explained. His breath stunk, and I inched closer to Payton. The dungeon almost lost its horror as I tried to imagine the kinds of awful surprises that might await me in the presence of those two monsters.

"Says who?" Payton barked.

"McLean. He wants to see her in his study," Mr. Stinky-Mouth replied.

I raised my head and got up on tiptoes to get a better look.

"McLean? Who, Fingal? I mean, the laird?" I asked.

The men didn't seem in the habit of answering to a woman, and they stared at me in disbelief. Even Payton turned around to me, eyebrows flared.

"Of course my father. Who else do you think would be authorized to revoke Blair's orders?"

"I don't give a hoot who has what authorization, and why. As long as you take me away from here as quickly as possible," I replied, wresting my arm free.

The sentries pulled out their broadswords.

"Leave it, men. I am the laird's son, and I will deliver her personally."

The guards gave a doubtful nod, but they obediently put away their swords and turned back. Payton waited only for a short while after their footsteps faded away before turning to me and snarling. "You stupid, stupid woman! Are you out of your mind? Don't you know what men such as these do to prisoners who resist? They won't ask a lot of questions before kicking your teeth in! Is that what you want? I'm sure your smile won't be half as bewitching without those pretty teeth of yours."

His words made me flinch. He was truly furious. I couldn't tell whether it was because of my behavior or because he had been worried about me. My money was on the latter, though. In a pacifying gesture, I reached for his hand.

"That's not what I wanted. But I can't go to the dungeon. I just can't. Please, you can't allow it."

"It's not up to me," he replied brusquely.

"Payton, please. Be honest with yourself. You kissed me, you took me with you on your horse, and you just defended me in front of those guys. You care about me, I can see that. So please, don't allow them to lock me up in the dungeon."

He took a step back.

"You are mistaken about the things you seem to believe. Besides, it doesn't matter anyway. On my honor, Sam, I swore an oath to my father when I was twelve years old, to follow him and to accept his word as the law. Nobody cares about what I want when it comes to important issues. So you see, you can stop your false declarations of love, because I really can't help you."

And with that, he started walking, pushing me ahead of him. We went back the same way we had come and back into the castle yard. Past the blacksmith whose anvil was now deserted, and back into the castle keep. We traversed a dark hallway and made straight for a set of double doors. The standoffish expression on Payton's face stopped me from saying anything. Because he wasn't in the mood to hear the only thing that I could have said. No, I wasn't wrong. He had felt *something*!

We knocked, Fingal's voice asked us to come in, and we entered his chambers.

"Father, you sent for the prisoner?"

Fingal was leaning against the open stained-glass windows, looking down into the castle yard. Slowly, he turned around to face us.

"That's right, *mo bailaich.* Blair wanted to make provisions, but he's not acquainted with what I want. So before I decide what"—he nodded in my direction—"we're going to do with you before Cathal's arrival, I wish to find out a bit more. I find ye intriguing, lassie. Which is why I suggest we all wash the travel dust off our bodies, sit down to a nice meal in the Great Hall, and afterward you will take a look at my injury together with Nanny MacMillan."

Fingal walked over to his desk, reached for a thick, leather-bound book, and slid it into an empty space on the bookshelf behind his desk. "Two healers are better than one. It is thanks to you that I'm on the path to recovery. Which is why I might not allow you to walk around unattended. But I will treat you as a—shall we say—*special guest.* You will take care of my injury, and in return I will allow you to move around freely."

He studied my face. "Do you accept?"

I could barely believe what he had proposed. Quickly, so as to not give him enough time to reconsider, I nodded.

"Yes, sure, I—"

"Very well," he said, and walked around the desk toward us. "Payton, leave us alone for a moment, if you would."

With that, he shooed his son from the study and closed the door behind him before turning his full attention to me.

"What—?"

"Silence! I have just made it very clear that everyone here is to treat you like a guest in my home. This means much more than merely my protection. In return you will swear an oath to me, because I do not want a traitor living under my roof."

He planted himself in front of me, as tall as his sons and towering above me. I only reached up to his chin, and so I was forced to tilt my head back so I could look him in the eye. He grabbed my hand.

"Will you swear this oath to me?"

I swallowed hard. An oath? What exactly was that, an oath? Like a promise? A contract? Whatever it was, I was ready to swear it just so I wouldn't have to turn on my heel and return to the dungeon.

"What kind of an oath?" I croaked, because it's all fun and games until you have to *sell your soul.*

"You swear by your blood to not raise a weapon against me and mine. You swear to not betray me and mine, and to not bring malice onto my house. You swear on your life to follow my orders for as long as this agreement shall be in effect," he demanded. And it felt like he could see all the way to the bottom of my soul.

I was afraid he would see how little importance I attached to this oath and how quickly I might be ready to break such a vow and defy his orders just so I could get back to my own century. I closed my eyes to keep my deep, dark secrets to myself, and licked my lips so the lie would pass with greater ease.

"I swear," I whispered, only to cringe half a moment later. I pulled back my arm and stared at the blood collecting in the palm of my hand. A straight cut ran from there to my wrist.

In horror I stared at the dagger in Fingal's hand. He dipped the blood-smeared tip into a goblet of wine. He pulled the knife out clean and stuck it back in his belt. Then he took a sip from the goblet.

"To blood, sweet and red as this wine. *Slàinte mhath.*"

He handed the goblet to me with a white linen cloth that reminded me of the napkin in Alison's kitchen. Carefully, he draped the cloth over the throbbing slash on my hand. Tiny, delicate flowers were embroidered on the napkin's edges. And just like at the Learys' home, I couldn't stop myself from running my finger over the embroidery. My finger followed the most conspicuous thread. It was a bold and vibrant red and the highlight of the entire image, outshining the prettiest of all the flowers with its intense radiance. I blinked and gasped when I spotted it: a faulty stitch. I almost dropped the cloth.

Fingal looked at me expectantly. Quickly, I closed my fist around the linen cloth, reached for the silver goblet with a trembling hand, and raised it to my lips.

A short while later, I came to on the way to my newly assigned bedchamber. Payton was talking, but I wasn't really listening. Why wouldn't that metallic taste of blood in my mouth go away? It was as if I were holding a penny under my tongue with its coppery taste overpowering all other senses. My hand burned, even though the cut had stopped bleeding by now.

"You were just frightened. But at least I don't have to take you down to the dungeon with you screaming bloody murder. Instead, I can take you to a nice bedchamber. Now that was worth a little bit of blood, wasn't it?"

I had to agree. The cut wasn't all that deep. Also, ever since I had started taking care of Fingal's injury, nobody would dare to refer to me as someone with a delicate disposition who got squeamish at the sight of blood. My reaction to this whole situation, therefore, seemed somewhat unreasonable. My nerves were raw, that was all. But I could finally breathe easy. I was under Fingal McLean's protection. All I needed now was the help and support of his son. And so it suited me just fine that the latter was opening the door to my new bedchamber.

"So, what do you think?" he asked as he stepped aside to let me enter first.

The room was spacious and bright, and the simple bed with its blue canopy and blue coverlet went very well with the dark blue tapestries. To the left and right of the door, hunting trophies—antlers—adorned the walls, and the large wardrobe was painted with hunting scenes.

Payton entered behind me, closed the door, and traversed the room. He opened the window wide to allow fresh air to stream in.

"Beautiful, truly beautiful. Please give my thanks to your father."

I ran my hand over the coverlet and sat down on the edge of the bed. I could not allow myself to get into another situation like earlier, that much I knew. I needed to enlist Payton's help.

"Sam? Why did you say that thing earlier?"

He was leaning against the windowsill and gave me a piercing look.

"What do you mean?"

"You said you loved me. What made you say that?"

"Payton, I have to tell you something. It is really, really important. But when I tell you, you're not going to believe me. You will turn away, you will probably think I'm crazy, and . . ."

In a panic, I got up and started pacing the bedroom—because I didn't dare get too close to him.

"Why don't you try me. I am here now, and I am listening. No more, no less."

"It's not that easy. What I have to tell you is something you can't even imagine in your wildest dreams. It's so . . . crazy. You noticed yourself that I'm different. This whole time I've been trying to find the right words to explain this to you. Would you believe me if I told you that one day you're going to love me?"

He didn't reply but kept looking at me with interest.

"Would you believe me if I told you that I know the future? That your life in that future is in danger, and that it is my job to save you?"

With each word, my voice got louder. I realized how muddled and confused I sounded. I had no hope that this down-to-earth Highlander would ever believe me. Which was why my next few words came only as a whisper: "I love you, but I can only save you if you trust me, Payton."

Payton walked over to me. As he had done so many times, he grabbed my chin so I could look him in the eyes. He was so close, I was shaking all over.

"My life is in danger? And you are the only one who can save me, Sam?"

I nodded weakly.

"The Fates are not exactly in our favor if they're sending an oaf such as you to save me," he said airily. "And besides, you are mistaken. There will not come a day that I fall in love with you."

I closed my eyes, unable to bear looking at him when he said things like that. I couldn't stand that he dragged me and my feelings and my overwhelming fear for his life through the mud with a few careless words.

"Sam, look at me!" he demanded, grabbing my chin tighter. "That day, Sam, that you mentioned, is already here.

I've been trying to fight it. I have told myself that I didn't feel what I feel, but it was all for naught. And now tell me, *mo luaidh,* do you truly love me?"

His lips grazed mine—a silent question that I was more than happy to answer. I lifted myself up on tiptoes to return his soft and gentle kiss, and allowed myself to sink into his arms. I allowed my emotions to take me away, abandoning myself completely to his kiss. Too glorious was that feeling of being exactly where I belonged, of being where I had always wanted to be, and in all that bliss I completely forgot about being worried for his life and the fact that his time was slowly running out.

Chapter 22

Cemetery by Auld a´chruinn, Present-Day October

Payton opened his eyes and adjusted the back of his sport seat back into an upright position. He'd been getting worse these last few days. He was sleeping a lot, frequently needing to leave the cold, wet cemetery to warm himself up in the car. His body was no longer strong enough to do it by itself. The fever was eating him up from the inside, and the cramps in his muscles made him scream in pain at times.

He was glad whenever he could find some sleep, because that was when he saw Sam. He saw her in his newly created memories. He could feel her presence as if she were right beside him. But the images were faint. Only moments of particular intensity seemed more tangible. He longed for those moments when yet another wave of excruciating pain washed over him, as it was doing right now.

"Stay strong, Brother. He'll be here soon. Maybe he can help us," Sean implored. He'd been watching the dirt road in the rearview mirror and heard the sound of a car approaching.

"That'll be him." Sean exited the car, waiting for the dark green Land Rover Defender to come to a stop a few yards behind them. The driver got out.

"Roy Leary?" Sean asked, even though he was pretty sure that it was the right man. The description—a redheaded giant—was to the point.

"Aye, and you are Sean? We spoke on the phone. I came as fast as I could," he explained. "What you told me is inconceivable. Are you absolutely sure? Truth be told, it would be a sensation!" He sounded both excited and agitated.

Sean nodded and pointed toward the cemetery that lay peacefully deserted before them. Nothing at all hinted at the incredible story that had happened there.

"A sensation? A disaster, more like it. Samantha is in grave danger. There must be a way we can help her."

They passed Payton's car and Roy glanced through the window, greeting the young man he found hard to recognize.

"We shall see, aye? But what's wrong with him? Wouldn't he be better off in a hospital?"

"He's refusing to leave this place."

Roy raised a curious eyebrow.

Sean tried to explain.

"If I thought they could help him in a hospital, I would have no trouble taking him there. But he doesn't have the common cold, now, does he. No medicine on Earth could possibly take on a curse. And so I'm letting him have his way."

Roy nodded and walked toward the cemetery with Sean following behind.

"So she's really found the portal through time, aye? I would never have dared to believe that it actually exists," Roy admitted.

Sean pointed at the memorial stone bearing the name of the five sisters. Roy pulled his glasses from a shirt pocket and crouched down.

"This is where it must have happened," Sean explained. "We can't say for sure, because we only noticed the stone the next day. It looks just like all the other gravestones, which is why it didn't spark our attention at first."

Roy checked the names that were chiseled into the stone.

"Fantastic. The legend of the five sisters is one of the most beautiful tales ever. Their haunting story makes even a full-grown man such as myself well up. I can barely believe that there should be some truth to it. Just look at those mountain peaks. Do you seriously believe that those were young women once?"

"I don't know. But Samantha has disappeared, and she keeps popping up in our memories as if she's rewriting our past. We are afraid she might be caught between two fronts. Besides, we have to think about Payton, too. He urgently needs help."

Roy examined the stone as closely and thoroughly as an archaeologist, letting the earth run between his fingers, and inspecting its surroundings.

"What was she doing right before she disappeared?" he asked quietly.

"We don't know. We've tried everything, but nothing's happening," Sean explained helplessly.

Roy got up and wiped his hands on his pants.

"Is it possible that it only works for women? After all, the father was clearing the way for his daughters," Roy contemplated.

Sean had thought of that before, and he shrugged helplessly. Payton didn't have much time left, and Samantha was in mortal danger. As he reflected on the time before Vanora's curse, all he could remember were lies and betrayal, deceit and dishonor. The blood feud between the Stuarts and the Camerons had cost many lives and brought pain and misery to all involved.

There had to be a way of taking Sam out of harm's way. He was a warrior! He had fought many battles and had always won. And now he was feeling like a helpless child, unable to get this situation under control. They had to save Sam, if only for his brother's sake. Payton couldn't die without knowing that Sam was safe. That was why Roy was here. He was their last hope.

Chapter 23

Castle Burragh, October 1740

Our hearts beat as one. We looked deep into each other's eyes and knew that our feelings were mutual. I had to tell Payton, and it had to be now. I couldn't keep this secret to myself any longer. But just as I was about to open my mouth, he shook his head and took a step back.

"Sam, whatever I'm feeling for you, it's not right. We can't be together. I don't want to get you into any more trouble than you're already in."

"You won't. Please, Payton, don't say things like that."

He pushed me from him as I tried to get closer again.

"*Bas maillaichte!* Everyone here in this castle is going to be against us, don't you see? You are a Cameron. If this fact shakes me to the core—*me!*—then how do you think everyone else is going to react? They are not going to see *you,* the girl with the beautiful eyes who stole my heart. They will see only one thing—the clan colors of the Camerons. That's all they will see, I swear to you."

"But—"

"No, Sam. We can't see each other anymore. I will ask Father to assign someone else to guard you. Trust me, it is safer for you."

He was about to turn around and go, but I held him back.

"Please, Payton, stay! Don't leave before I have told you the whole story." I could see the agony in his eyes: He didn't want to leave. He wanted to be with me, but it was against his loyalty and honor to follow his heart. I couldn't even imagine what it would be like to be caught on such an emotional roller coaster.

"What I said before, about the future . . ." I tried to help him recall our talk earlier. "I don't know how to explain this to you, but your life really is in danger. Not now, but later on. You have to believe me."

I was terribly distraught and hated hearing my pathetic attempts at telling him the truth while trying not to put the responsibility and blame—about everything that would happen and needed to happen—on him. It was pitiful. Even I wouldn't have believed myself.

"Are you blessed with the powers of the *second sight?*" Payton asked, looking at me attentively.

Second sight?

I'd heard that term before. Clairvoyants were said to possess *second sight.* But nobody could say for sure whether it was a blessing or a curse, I thought.

I recalled the fate of Cassandra, probably the most famous seer in Greek mythology. Apollo, the Greek god, had offered her the gift of prophecy so she would give in to his advances, but she rebuffed him nevertheless. As a consequence, he cursed her gift so that nobody would ever again believe in her prophecies.

I suddenly wondered whether I wouldn't be burned alive at the stake. Was the *second sight* to the Scots perhaps as unpopular as witches were?

"Uh, well, something like that," I stammered. I was still contemplating whether time travel was less threatening than the gift of prophecy.

Payton nodded. He seemed alert and interested, as if he thought magical blue vapors might suddenly surround me as I pulled white rabbits from my sleeves.

"Do you believe me?" I asked doubtfully. I wasn't sure whether I should continue talking if he didn't.

A loud knock made us both jump. I backed a good distance away from Payton while he opened the door. Ross stood outside, holding a bundle under his arm.

"What are you doing here, Ross?" Payton asked.

Ross looked up and down the hallway, then back at Payton, who was still standing in the doorway and blocking him from entering the room. He tried to catch a glimpse of me, behind Payton.

"I have something. Samantha left it on the cart, and . . . uh, I mean, I wanted . . . I'm sure she'd want it back," he explained, lifting the package under his arm.

I recognized the beige-colored bundle as my old housedress, and even though this was the most ill-timed moment he could possibly have picked, I was relieved to have it back. Walking past Payton, I stepped into the hallway.

"Thanks, Ross. How nice of you to bring it back."

I smiled, but he barely paid any attention to me. His eyes bored holes into Payton's chest; his clenched fists gave away his anger.

"I didn't know you had company. He's not bothering you, is he?" he asked loudly enough for Payton to hear.

And Payton heard him just fine, judging by his contemptuous snort.

"No, Ross. I'm fine. Thank you for the dress. And please don't worry about me. I'm under the laird's protection now. Nothing is going to happen to me."

"I see. . . . Well, in that case . . . I won't disturb you—I'll just return this."

He thrust the dress into my hands and took a step back.

"*Slan leat,* Ross!" Payton dismissed the young man. He stepped aside so I could return to the room.

But Ross wasn't easily fobbed off. "Sam," he said, "do they allow you to take your meals in the Great Hall?"

I shot Payton a questioning glance, and he nodded. His lower jaw twitched, something I'd seen many times when he was annoyed, so I lowered my gaze. Ross noticed the nod, too, and slapped on a confident smile.

"I will see you there, then. I assume you will sit with the servants, and I look forward to your company."

With that, he bowed politely and turned on his heel. I couldn't make heads or tails of his actions. Before I could exchange a word about this with Payton, two housemaids came walking up the hallway. They brought everything I needed so that I could—as Fingal had ordered—wash the "travel dust" off me. They waltzed into my room, and Payton was forced out into the hallway. I ran after him and grabbed his arm.

"Payton? Don't leave. Tell me first whether you believe me," I asked quietly.

He looked past me, down the hallway.

"I don't know," he admitted begrudgingly. "I have fallen for you, so I guess I should believe you. On the other hand . . . you are also a Cameron . . . which is why I probably shouldn't." He wiped some dirt from my cheek.

"Go wash up. I need to think about it, Sam. I will come and get you for supper."

With that, he left me to my handmaidens who must have been given orders to keep an eye on me. I heard them happily giggling and chattering away while I washed myself.

An hour later, I was nervously pacing my room. I was clean and dressed in fresh clothes, and one of the girls had brushed my hair and pleated it into a simple braided crown. The dark brown dress had a fitted waist and almost touched the ground. A cream-colored *arisaid,* a cloaklike garment, covered the wide rectangular neckline—which in turn revealed the thin, light-colored linen chemise I wore underneath.

I felt strange wearing this dress, but I realized that I had been given very high-end, expensive clothes.

The handmaiden who'd brought me the garments offered the laird's thanks for my efforts in taking care of him. Apparently there was a fine line between distrust, which required my constant surveillance, and gratitude, which had yielded this wonderful gown.

What would it be like to turn up in the Great Hall wearing this outfit? Almost as if I were one of them?

A vigorous knock on the door jolted me from my daydreams, and I nervously pushed a loose strand of hair, which had been artfully arranged by the handmaiden, from my face. I opened the door and found myself face-to-face with Payton. His jaw dropped as he looked at me.

"Milady, I have to admit I am speechless. You look magnificent. Rest assured that the aversion of several McLeans against the Camerons will decrease significantly once they lay their eyes on you. On the other hand, there is a possibility that it will be the ladies' turn to incite a war because you will be, without a doubt, the most beautiful woman in the entire hall."

His silly compliment made me blush, and I tried to curtsy before pulling the door closed behind me.

"Can I count on you to protect me should that case arise?"

Payton stared at me as if seriously considering raising his sword against his own people in order to protect a Cameron. Then he winked, reaching for the strand of hair that had again fallen into my face and pushing it behind my ear.

"Don't fret, milady. With me by your side, you are in no danger. The worst thing that could happen to you is this."

He tilted his head and kissed me. It was a gentle kiss, almost only a brush with his lips. A touch as light as a ray of the summer sun, and just as soft and warm.

"Ready?" he asked, placing my hand on his arm so he could escort me like a real lady.

"Have you thought about it?" I whispered as soon as we were walking along the hallway and our footsteps drowned out our voices.

"Thought about what?"

"Whether you believe me? Payton, I'm serious. Time's running out," I implored.

"The more time I spend near you, the easier I find it to trust you. But let's talk about that tomorrow. There is one important thing I urgently need to take care of. After that, I am all yours, I promise."

I had no time to argue, because we were entering the Great Hall. The tapestry-covered walls and high, wood-beamed ceiling looked exactly as they did in my own era. Other than that, the room was barely recognizable. A suckling pig was roasting over the open fire inside the massive fireplace, with two young, sweaty boys rotating it. There were a lot of people sitting at the long wooden banquet table. I saw men in full Highland regalia as well as simple men in their work clothes.

I recognized the overweight blacksmith and his skinny helpers sitting at the lower end of the table. I spotted several women wearing similar dresses to mine, but also maidservants whose simple robes in pale earth colors were made of rough wool and gave away their lower rank. A beer maid brought a mug of beer to the table and gave me a hostile look in passing.

Suddenly dogs were bolting through the hall, and one of them made directly for me. It was Barra, who leapt toward me with her tail wagging, full of joy at seeing me again. A sharp blow of the whistle stopped her from throwing me down into the straw spread all over the floor.

In the sudden silence that followed, several curious heads turned in my direction. Some were staring at me, while others put their heads together and whispered quietly. Still others spat on the floor as the name *Cameron* was carried from person to person.

I felt sick to my stomach at seeing the blatant hostility toward me. Only Payton's hand, which firmly held mine, gave me a sense of assuredness. But even his eyes hardened. He stared across the hall toward Ross, who looked surprised—and not altogether pleased.

"Come on," Payton whispered, leading me to the head of the banquet table. Fingal, Blair, Sean, and Kyle had already taken their seats.

Everyone's eyes were on us.

Fingal got up, and I tried a clumsy attempt at a curtsy again, until the laird reached for my hand and allowed me to stand up straight.

"Mistress Cameron, I am glad you have followed my invitation. Would you please raise the goblet with me in front of all my people so we can drink to your oath."

He handed me his goblet, which was lavishly decorated and encrusted with precious stones. His piercing eyes prompted me to do exactly as he had commanded, and so I lifted the cup to my lips, and drank. A satisfied nod was his sign to me that I could now lower the cup and return it to him.

"*Mòran taing,* milord!" I thanked him, glad to have memorized those few Gaelic words Payton had taught me.

He raised his goblet into the air with a satisfied smile, and he turned to the people in the hall.

"Please welcome Mistress Cameron as a guest in our midst—and drink!" he demanded. He motioned for the beer maids to refill everyone's vessels before emptying his; then he offered me a place by his side. Payton pulled out the chair and handed me a full goblet before taking his seat opposite me.

I found myself sitting across from Fingal's sons, on the women's side of the table, and I greeted the lady beside me with a shy smile. Her long, jet-black hair hung down her back. Several strands of hair to the left and right of her temples had been pleated into braids, which had then been wrapped around her head in a crown. Her skin was lily-white and in stark contrast to her shiny dark hair and emerald eyes, which looked at me with open hostility. I almost knocked over my mug of ale when I realized whom I was sitting beside: Nathaira Stuart.

I could tell by looking at this mysterious beauty that she would have preferred crushing me under her heel like an insect to having to share a table with me.

I reached for my beer to hide the uncontrollable shaking of my hands. I prayed nobody would notice that I had broken out in a cold sweat. This woman was the source of all evil. She was a witch and a murderer, a liar who would kill her own mother in the very near future. If her confessions at the motel back in the present were anything to go by, years must have passed since she'd poisoned her stepmother.

And even though I knew that she was with Blair, somehow I hadn't counted on meeting her here.

I wiped my forehead with the flat of my hand and didn't dare lift my eyes from the table. I feared having to look into this woman's face one more time.

How many lives could I save if I killed her?

Somebody kicked my shin under the table, and I raised my head. I saw Payton's questioning look, and I attempted a smile.

"Can I offer you a piece of meat?" he asked, pointing at the steaming piece of suckling pig a servant was holding out to him.

Suddenly, I didn't feel hungry at all. I didn't think I could swallow a single bite of food with Nathaira sitting beside me. The thought of poison brought a bitter taste to my mouth, and the hostile look in her eyes made my blood curdle. But it would have been impolite to refuse Fingal's meal, so I nodded and pushed my empty wooden plate over to Payton.

He loaded it with a slice of meat, turnips, and a chunk of bread before returning it to me. Then he offered me his dagger so I could cut up the meat—other than that, we only had wooden spoons for utensils. I observed the other guests to see how they skewered chunks of meat with the tips of their knives and lifted them to their mouths. Trying to remain as inconspicuous as possible, I started to eat.

My nerves were raw, and all sorts of sensations washed over me simultaneously. The racket of the voices in the hall, the smell of the food, and the heat emanating from the great fireplace all blurred to one fuzzy image overloading my senses. Only Payton's upset voice suddenly made me prick my ears. He and Sean were arguing.

"You think what about me?" Sean said. He sounded livid.

"That you're chasing every single skirt you see. And don't even try to deny it."

"*Amadáin!* I just wanted to talk with her," Sean defended himself.

"Talk, Brother? That's why you had to sneak into the barn? Don't play me for a fool, *mo bràthair*!"

"You can believe whatever you want to believe! But if you're interested in what Aline told me in confidence, then shut up and listen."

Sean's eyes met mine, and he tried to lower his voice so I couldn't hear him anymore over all the noise in the hall. Besides, something else was grabbing my attention at the head of the table.

A plump woman with gray hair arranged in neat waves was the cause of the ruckus. She'd yanked the goblet from clan chief Fingal's hand and was working herself into a very spirited frenzy.

"And believe that just because you're a big man nothing can stop you! But I'm telling you this only once: Keep up with the booze, and I will not stitch you up again when you tear open your wound in a state of drunken stupor," she threatened, shaking her fist at him.

I leaned over the table and whispered at Payton, who was also following the spectacle.

"Who is that? Is she crazy?"

Payton grinned. "That's the honorable Nanny MacMillan. You could say she's the heart and soul of this castle."

"The *heart and soul*? She sounds like a gangsta rapper!"

"Gangsta . . . *what?* Don't let her hear you say that," Payton warned me, massaging the back of his head. "Otherwise she'll teach you some manners and give you a good ol' slap across the head."

I was confused. Fingal now actually got up from his chair and allowed himself to be led away from the table by the old lady, like a schoolboy ordered to the front of the class.

"What? I don't understand. . . ."

"Nanny MacMillan was our wet nurse when we were children. She's also a healer, a midwife, and a teacher. She manages our household, even though that's not her job at all. Father is only too happy to let her do this, because we've been lacking the female touch ever since Mother died. Nanny MacMillan fills that void."

Laird and Nanny were almost out the door, when Fingal suddenly stopped and turned around. He called one of the manservants to him and pointed in my direction. The boy immediately came over to me.

It was obvious that he had never talked to a Cameron before. I could see a mix of fear and disdain in his eyes when he stopped to inform me that I was expected in the clan chief's chambers right away.

"In his chambers?" I turned to Payton. "I'm not sure I can find my way back there."

"I'll take you. You can go back to work, Michael."

The young servant didn't need to be told twice and quickly disappeared amid the other servants. One look into Payton's sparkling eyes, and I had to admit that I preferred his company a thousand times over. Endlessly relieved that I had survived dining next to Nathaira, I allowed my sweet Highlander to escort me from the Great Hall.

We could hear Nanny MacMillan's voice out in the hallway. She sounded irritated still, but the worried, tender undertone in her voice was unmistakable.

After a brief knock, Payton opened the door, and we entered. A young, delicate-looking girl stood close to the door inside. She wore a tidy apron around her waist and a bonnet over her blond braids, and she looked like she was trying to be invisible. She was probably usually on the receiving end of such angry outbursts, which made her feel guilty and in the wrong even when Nanny MacMillan was scolding someone else.

The tough old lady had undressed the clan chief as much as necessary to remove the bandages. She was now carefully touching and checking the wound, and when Fingal flinched under her touch, she was off again.

"Right you are. Pretend to be a little whippersnapper who knows no pain down in the Great Hall, but then cringe at the slightest touch when you're in your private chambers!"

"Be quiet, woman! Your constant nagging is impossible to bear!" Fingal exclaimed, motioning for me to step closer. "By the way, this is Mistress Cameron. She took out the arrow."

I curtsied to the older woman. She briefly looked me up and down before giving a nod and stepping aside so that I could join her at Fingal's bedside.

"It looks really good," she praised me, continuing to check the wound with her fingers. "I couldn't have done it better, but I'm worried about the inflammation."

Even my untrained eye told me that the wound was inflamed, and I didn't know what to do about it.

"I tried to keep the wound as clean as possible, and I boiled the rags first," I explained.

"We need some witch hazel and a little garlic, some yarrow, and a little help from our Lord, and he'll be just fine." She shooed away the blond girl to collect the herbs and then busied herself grabbing strips of linen from the basket by her feet.

"You were very lucky that the arrow didn't kill you," she explained to the laird. "If it had hit your chest just slightly higher, then we would only be left with your cold, damp grave to cry over. In the future, you should leave such things to your sons," she suggested.

Fingal snorted. "In the future, I hope *such things* will not happen. I am tired of fighting. The older I get, the more I long for peace."

He smiled at me. "What about you, lassie? Are you the peaceful kind, or do you have war and battle in your blood?"

Even though he had said those words seemingly offhandedly, the back of my neck tingled.

"I can fight, sir, for things that are important to me. But I am not interested in eternal blood feuds."

"That's sensible, child," Nanny MacMillan interjected while thrusting a small bowl of brownish ointment into my hands. "There, apply this to the edges of the wound," she ordered, and then made Fingal take a sip from a bottle. It caused him to retch and gasp for air.

"Are you trying to poison me, woman?" he bellowed, wiping his mouth and angrily glaring at the old lady.

"What do you think? And now lie still so the child may apply the ointment properly."

Nothing much else happened for the next few hours. We prepared a brew from the ingredients the servant girl had brought, soaked the strips of linen cloth in it, and redressed Fingal's wound. Nanny MacMillan would remove the herbal poultice and reapply the bandages later on that night. She thanked me for my help and handed me over to Payton, who had been waiting patiently for us to finish our work.

Payton now led me back through the darkened hallways, and a pale sliver of moonlight occasionally lit our path.

My days spent in this era didn't really leave me with enough time to think. There was so much going through my mind right now. Payton, who was waiting for me back home; Payton, who was walking by my side. Fingal and his recovery, and the future that lay ahead of them all.

I was especially stressed about that thing with Kyle because I had grown to like him more every day. And then there was the horrible vision in which I had witnessed myself killing Ross. All of this and more was going through my mind, so I didn't give it another thought when Payton entered my room before me. But as soon as he closed the door behind us, he touched my arm and turned me around to face him. One look into his hungry eyes, and I knew what was on his mind.

"Sam, I . . . May I kiss you?"

I felt how difficult it was for him to hold back, and couldn't say a word. Instead, I raised my face up to him. I could tell that he really wanted to pull me into his arms, but he kept his passions under control and kissed me very gently and then gingerly placed his hands around my waist.

"It's . . . ," he mumbled very close to my lips, "this gown. You look positively enchanting. I've wanted to kiss you ever since I saw you in this dress, and I've thought about nothing else all evening."

His touch almost burned my skin, and I trembled under the onslaught of his kisses. Letting go of all fear, I allowed my hands to wander underneath his shirt. Lord, he felt better than I could ever have imagined. I was elated. His kisses were medicine for my aching soul, which had been so anxious and restless with worry. But in this moment, only he and I existed. Only our love: stronger than time, stronger than the hatred the clans held for each other. *Stronger than reason.*

The moment of peaceful bliss only lasted a short while. When my hand caressed his chest, coaxing a soft groan from him, I noticed the missing bandage and the missing scar that I was so used to feeling on him. Suddenly I felt bad to the core. As if I were cheating on Future Payton with Past Payton. Was I putting Future Payton's life at risk because I was throwing myself into Past Payton's arms?

God, I was utterly confused. Either way he was Payton, right? So were my feelings for him right or wrong? I shrunk back and wiped the stray hairs from my face that had come loose during our stormy caresses.

"Payton, wait." I pushed him away. "We have to stop. I can't do this."

He ran his hands over his face, nodding quietly. "You're right. It's insane, and it's dangerous. I have never felt like this before, never had such a sense of trust with anyone else."

"We are meant for each other, Payton. You have to believe that. It's no coincidence that I'm here, but I can't stay with you. I will have to leave you again soon. There's no other way if I want to save you. Payton, when everything is all over, you will forget about me. You will forget about me, but you will be alive. Just trust me on this."

Payton leaned against the door and didn't say a word. Finally, he took a deep breath as if faced with a difficult task.

"Come here, *mo luaidh,* please."

I did. I laid my head against his heart and snuggled into his chest. His hands ran up and down my back.

"Whatever you say, Sam—I will trust you, so help me God! I don't know why I do, but I trust you, even though I don't understand a single word you're telling me."

I closed my eyes and only heard the beating of his heart. This heart was everything I ever wanted. No matter the era. I couldn't allow it to stop.

"Then help me, please," I pleaded.

He pressed me against his chest and kissed the top of my head.

"How?"

"I have to find Vanora. Vanora, the witch. And then I have to get back to the little stone cottage where Ross and his brothers first found me."

"Cottage? What cottage?" he asked, suddenly sounding irritated.

I broke away from his embrace because his body, his all-too-familiar scent, was too unnerving.

"You know, the cottage by Loch Duich. I don't know where exactly it is, but it's near the shoreline and at the foot of the Five Sisters. I have to find it."

"That's impossible." He shook his head. "What you're saying makes no sense, Sam."

"What do you mean?"

"Well, because whatever building you are referring to—they most certainly did not take you prisoner at Loch Duich."

"They did! I'm sure of it!" I disagreed emphatically.

"It's impossible, *mo luaidh.* The mountains you are talking about are on Cameron territory. No Stuart would ever dare to advance that far into Cameron land."

"Stuart? I'm talking about Ross and his brothers," I explained, feeling unsettled.

Had my journey through time taken me not only to a different era but to a different place entirely? Was that even possible? After all, I had not seen any traces of the cemetery when I arrived. But the water: I had seen water. I recalled the fog that was, as I had assumed then, rising from the lakeshore. I put my palm to my forehead, trying to remember.

"Ross and his brothers *are* Stuarts. Why else would they have taken you prisoner?"

If I was confused before, now I was completely lost. I sat down on the edge of the bed, and Payton poured some whiskey into a cup and handed it to me.

"Ross told me his name was Galbraith," I said flatly, cautiously nipping at my drink.

Payton had poured a cup for himself, too.

"That's right. But Duncan and Dougal are Stuarts. They have the same mother, but their father is Grant Stuart. The clan chief. Shortly after Duncan and Dougal's birth, he recognized them as his own, gave them his name, and sent for them so they would live with him and be raised inside his castle."

"But . . ."

I didn't know what to believe anymore. Where exactly had these men picked me up? I would need help from Ross if I wanted to find the portal leading back to my own century.

"Sam, it's been a hard day for you. You should go to bed and close your pretty eyes. Let's keep saving my life for tomorrow, because I worry you might collapse on me from exhaustion."

The whiskey had indeed made me tired. I suppressed a yawn and tried to object, but my headstrong Highlander put his finger on my lips.

"Shhh, *mo luaidh.* I swear to you that I will love you for all time, even if you don't manage to save my life."

He pulled the *sgian dhu* from his belt.

"I swear to you," he said, making a cut across his hand, "that I will forgive you if you don't succeed in saving me. I will love you forever nonetheless, and I will die in the hope of having been worthy of your love."

Payton dipped the bloody dagger in his whiskey, then carelessly dropped it to the floor as he raised his cup to my trembling lips.

"Payton, I . . ."

I wanted to reassure him that I would save him, that I didn't need his oath. I had no intention of failing.

"No, my sweet Sam. Drink—and then kiss me one last time before I disappear into the cold, dark night," he demanded.

And like a puppet on destiny's strings, I obeyed.

Chapter 24

A knock on the door startled me from my sleep. The air in my room was icy, and I was worried my toes would freeze to the floor as I tiptoed to the door wrapped in thick blankets. I opened the door a crack and was surprised to find a maid waiting with a breakfast tray.

"*Madain mhath.* With compliments from the laird. He inquires whether there is anything else you might need?"

I accepted the tray containing oatcakes, honey, a pot of steaming hot tea, and a candied apple.

"No, thank you. Please give him my thanks and assure him that I have everything I need."

The girl curtsied and left me to my tray of delicacies.

I was surprised at Fingal's generosity. He didn't treat me like a prisoner at all. On the contrary, I felt like a welcome guest in his house—not taking into account the constant supervision by Payton, which of course I didn't mind too much.

I was wearing a clean nightgown; there was a washbasin with a pitcher containing fresh water; and there was even a small piece of soap with the fresh scent of pine needles. Plus, I had all the soft, thick blankets; this beautiful room; and a breakfast fit for a queen. . . .

I was sure that all of this would be considered lavish waste by most people in this era. So—why was he granting me these luxuries?

If I thought back to the type of accommodation Blair had planned for me, the whole setup surprised me even more. Prisoners were sent to the dungeon and were certainly not invited to dine in the Great Hall. I had wondered about this yesterday when I felt the residents of Castle Burragh giving me the evil eye.

But my worried thoughts were dispelled as soon as I tasted the delicious oatcakes smothered in honey. The caramel apple and hot tea drove the cold from my bones.

Once I finished my breakfast and put on Mistress MacQuarrie's green dress, I felt like a new person. I picked it because it was the warmest of the few clothes I had. Still, I would have given anything to slip into a comfy pair of jeans and a hoodie. When would those be invented?

I opened the window. The cold, clear morning air poured into my room and announced a sunny day ahead. There was not a single cloud in the sky. Typical, just typical. Now that I no longer had to spend my days on horseback, the rain had stopped. I felt joy at seeing the first few rays of sunshine paint the horizon with bright orange brushstrokes. The peaks of the Grampian Mountains glowed red in the early-morning sun, an indescribably beautiful sight. It was one of those magical moments that I had only ever experienced in Scotland.

But this was only the beginning of my day, and I didn't want to picture what else it held in store for me. Payton trusted me, sure—even though my story sounded less than plausible to him—but I was not one inch closer to saving him, because I didn't know where exactly Ross had found me. Learning that was my first priority of the day.

To my surprise, the Fates were smiling upon me for a change, because a moment later they brought Ross to my door.

He looked less warrior-ish, as he wasn't wearing his sword and leather chest piece this morning. This made him look even younger than I had taken him for. He almost seemed my age.

This realization only increased my respect for the young Scot. I had seen him fight men twice as strong and twice as old as he was. He must have been fighting since a very young age if he was that good and that experienced. When I looked into his eyes, I even thought I saw Ross Galbraith fighting every single day of his life. Suddenly, it seemed really important to find out as much about him as possible—and to figure out why I was seemingly destined to kill him.

Such a horrible act seemed unimaginable, especially now that he was looking at me with such kind eyes. I invited him in because he was carrying pieces of fabric over his arm.

"What's all this?" I asked, following him. On the bed he spread out two beige-colored bodices, a beige skirt, a green apron, and a woolen shawl.

"Your new wardrobe. The laird must be particularly happy with your *services*."

I disliked his tone as much as I disliked the look on his face. He scanned the room assertively, stopping on the two cups still sitting on the table from my talk with Payton the previous night. As if this had just confirmed his worst assumptions, he nodded and pointed at the cups.

"What the heck, Ross? What are you trying to tell me?"

"Nothing, my dear. I'm not blaming you. If all I had to do was spread my legs to get a nice little bedchamber and all this trumpery, then I wouldn't think twice about it, either."

I was acting on raw impulse when I raised my hand and slapped him so hard that the pain traveled from my fingers all the way up to my shoulder.

"How dare you talk to me like that!" I snapped, my voice vibrating with anger. "How dare you even think that about me? I'll tell you this once, Ross, and you'd be wise to remember it: I'm not 'spreading my legs' for anyone around here. Do you get me?"

Ross squirmed under my furious glare as he massaged the bright red handprint on his cheek.

"I am . . . sorry, Samantha, but I thought . . . ," he said, making a pathetic attempt to apologize. "This special attention you've been getting . . . you were dining at the clan chief's table. . . . I thought . . . ," he broke off.

"I know what you thought, Ross!" I said, still seething.

"All I mean is, I would have understood. You are dependent on their mercy. You are afraid of what might happen when my brothers return and take you away. Being under the great McLean's protection is nothing to be sneezed at."

"Shut up already! Of course I'm worried about not knowing of what might become of me. But I would never . . ."

"All right, all right, I apologize. It's just that I wish I could protect you. But instead, all I'm doing is hurting you with my rash and thoughtless words."

"Forget about it. I don't want to talk about this anymore. I'd rather you tell me what the plan is for me today. Do you know?"

Relieved to be back in shallow waters, Ross straightened up. "Yes, they asked me to take you into the woods. We are to gather juniper berries and keep an eye out for goldenrod. Nanny MacMillan wants to brew one of her magic potions."

I still felt miffed from our discussion, but I reached for the shawl and wrapped it around my shoulders. After all, I had questions that I hoped Ross knew the answer to. Maybe I could sound him out during our expedition to the forest.

"All right, then, let's go," I egged him on.

I wanted to get him out of my room as quickly as possible, because I had noticed something flashing on the floor. It was the silver tip of the *sgian dhu* that Payton had used to swear his oath to me. It was peeping out from under the blue bed curtains. In passing, I pushed the knife deeper under the curtain so that it was no longer visible. I didn't know what lay ahead, and I wasn't planning on having that knife taken away from me a second time. But most importantly, I didn't want to carry the dagger with me whenever Ross was near. His moment of death was ingrained in my memory all too vividly. Ignoring my goose bumps, I pulled the door closed and followed him into the castle yard.

Payton was standing atop the battlement with the wind blowing in his face. He enjoyed feeling the sunshine on his skin. He'd been up here on guard duty for hours, and he'd admired the unique play of colors during the sunrise.

He knew he needed to reflect on all that was happening. But he was too preoccupied to think straight. He could still feel Sam's kiss good-bye from the night before. Instead of the grave situation Mistress Cameron had shared with him, all he could do was think about her eyes burning deep into his soul. What was the matter with him?

He had never thought of himself as someone particularly passionate. He had never guessed that he could fall head over heels for a girl. At sixteen, he'd had a brief love affair with the daughter of a traveling showman whose theater troupe performed at the castle. After the performance, during which the girl had juggled burning torches and offered herself as a target for the knife thrower, she had lured Payton behind the troupe's wagon and seduced him. He had succumbed to her feminine charms, but he had quickly realized that many young men had gone before him in her life. She was skilled in the art of seduction, and she clearly enjoyed the pleasures of their carnal union. The theater troupe moved on only two days later. Payton had no regrets and didn't shed a tear for this girl. After all, he didn't really know her, never mind love her.

But then, out of the blue, Sam entered his life and turned everything upside down.

Was it because he'd had a moment of weakness when he noticed her at first? Or was it true what Sam had said—that they were meant for each other? Was that even possible? He did some soul-searching, conjuring up that feeling that had washed all over him when she had stumbled into his arms at McRae's cottage.

It wasn't just passion; it went much deeper than that. He wanted to protect her. He didn't want to ever let her go, because holding her in his arms seemed so right. It was as though she belonged there.

It felt so natural to him to share with her his worries about his father, even though he never normally showed that level of vulnerability to anyone. And despite the stress he was under, she always managed to make him laugh. It had never occurred to him to treat her as his enemy. Instead, his heart must have known right from that very first moment that she was the one he would love. He could barely believe that it had only been a few days; his feelings for her were deep and true.

He leaned against the battlement, closed his eyes, and conjured up her image.

She was so delicate, so slender, like only a few women were. But her courage made her seem big. She had put up a good fight yesterday in the Great Hall, considering how hostile everyone had been toward her. He wished he could have spared her the experience, but his father was convinced that it was the right thing to do, showcasing her like that.

"That way everyone will see that she's under my special protection," Fingal had explained. "Also, because she's a Cameron, they will keep their eyes on her. Thus, I don't have to constantly worry about her sneaking away."

No, *sneak* away she would not. But she had told him openly that she needed to leave him soon. That she had to do it in order to save his life.

He still didn't completely understand what she was talking about. All he knew was that he believed her. Unquestionably. But could he assist her and take her away against his father's will?

He had sworn an oath not only to his father but also to Blair, who would be Fingal's successor one day. He'd sworn to accept their word as the law and never act against their will. Could he break that oath?

Once more his thoughts returned to their kiss. Could a kiss be more important than an oath he had sealed with his blood? If he listened to his heart, he already knew the answer—even though his mind was still reluctant to accept this truth. For him it would mean pain and loss to give himself to Sam fully and in all its consequence, but it was the only way to prove himself worthy of her love.

His temples were throbbing painfully, so intensely was his mind working. He looked down into the courtyard.

Sam was accompanied by Ross, strolling through the main gate and carrying a wicker basket. Payton squinted and mumbled a curse. He didn't like seeing that boy near her all the time.

The forest barely looked like one. Only a few trees rose up into the sky, because a huge woodland area had been cleared, with hundreds of tree trunks piled up and awaiting further processing.

"This is supposed to be your forest? What happened to all the trees? Why have they all been cut down?"

"We're making room for pastures. Our borders to the other clans aren't safe, and we need our cattle to be grazing closer to the castle. So, the woods have to go," Ross enlightened me.

I wasn't convinced that this approach made any sense, but I continued walking, and I bent down to collect my first batch of juniper berries. At least it wouldn't take us long to find our berries in this so-called forest. And precisely because it wouldn't take long, I needed to get to the point.

"Tell me, Ross, what exactly is the story with these cattle thieves? Why do you think it's the Camerons who are stealing your cattle? Have you caught them in the act? Is that why you advanced that deep into their territory?"

Ross jerked his head up and stared at me with suspicion.

"It *was* the Camerons, that's for *sure.* That clan has been nothing but trouble for us since forever."

"Is that why you knocked me down at the stone cottage? Is that the reason you abducted me? Just because *we Camerons* have been causing you trouble since forever?"

Ross scratched his neck and self-consciously tugged on his shirt collar. "I wouldn't have taken you with us, and I honestly don't know what Duncan's plans are for you. But then again, it is none of my business. He made that clear."

He looked at me, and I saw brief anger flare up in his eyes.

"What do you mean?" I asked.

"Nothing, don't worry about it. It wasn't exactly the first time that they beat me up."

"They beat you up? Who?"

"Sam! Mind your own business. Just collect your damn berries."

I stepped closer to him and put my hand on his shoulder because he had turned his back to me.

"Ross? Why do you allow them to treat you that way? They're your brothers—why would they do such a thing?"

Ross gave a wretched laugh but looked me square in the eye. Many years of anger and hurt were clearly written on his face.

"Brothers? Aye, they might be my brothers, but they're also the devil's spawn! And just like the devil, they enjoy hurting people. Don't ever forget that, Sam. They enjoy the feeling of humiliating you, kicking you, and then seeing you writhe in the mud before them."

Cold shivers ran down my back. I could tell that they had done all of this to him, and probably more. Misery and suffering were bursting out of him. I couldn't say anything, didn't know what words to use to comfort him. But he seemed to appreciate my silence. He bent down to gather some berries and put them in the basket before facing me once more.

"My mother was still very young. She had just been married to my father. He was a shepherd working for the Stuarts, just as I am now. Those were great big flocks of sheep, and Father was gone a lot. One day, Grant Stuart, the son of the old laird, came to our cottage. He wanted to pick up two lambs that my father had killed for him."

Ross turned away from me and continued gathering berries. It seemed he had lived through—a thousand times over—the story he was about to tell me.

"Mother was alone. She was unable to fight him off. Nobody stopped him from taking whatever he desired. And he must have enjoyed her pain, too, because he kept coming back for more—over and over. Father confronted Grant and threatened to take it to the old laird should he ever dare to come near his wife again. But that dirty, evil man just laughed and commanded his men to cut Father's throat should he cause any more trouble. Then he defiled Mother right before Father's very eyes. He planted his evil seed in Mother's womb. When he was done, he had his men beat Father almost to death. Since that day, Father has been blind in one eye. If only they had taken both of his eyes, he wouldn't have had to witness the devil's seed growing inside his wife's belly. She gave birth to twins, Duncan and Dougal. Without regard for the disgrace and dishonor he brought upon his wife, Una, who had given birth to his legitimate son and heir only months before, Grant sent for the boys, had them brought to Galthair, and recognized them as his own."

The skin on his hands was stained from the dark juice of the juniper berries he was dropping in the basket.

"It took almost ten years for my mother to tolerate the touch of a man again. So I guess I should be grateful that I was even born at all."

He picked up the basket and went deeper into the thorny underbrush. I followed, lifting the hem of my dress so it wouldn't get caught in the brambles. This story—his story—was truly awful. I could not believe that people were capable of such brutality.

"Why would you even stay with them, work with them? Don't you have every reason in the world to hate them?" I called after him.

Ross stopped and turned around. The anger and hurt on his face had turned into grim determination. He came closer and stopped only a few inches short of me.

"Hate them? Maybe—but I hate my father more!" he hissed through gritted teeth. His breath, so close to my ear, made my skin crawl.

"I will not be the kind of man who accepts a dagger at his throat while his woman is being violated. I will never stand idly by while my son is being beaten to a pulp and writhing in pain. One day, Samantha, I'm going to stand on the other side. On the winners' side!"

I took a step back and pulled the shawl closer around my body. I felt cold, despite the sunny day.

"I wonder what side your mother would prefer to see you on?" I snapped, and received a snarky grin in reply.

"My mother's dead. She killed herself when I was only seven days old. Do you want to know why?"

No, I did not. I wanted to leave him and his horrible story behind, but he gruffly grabbed my arm.

"She killed herself because Grant Stuart sent her a birthday gift for me. In it was the dagger that they had held to my father's throat so many years before, and a letter. He wrote that he would stop by soon to congratulate her in person. And before Father could take the dagger away from her, she used it to end her own life."

He pulled the dagger from his belt and held it under my nose.

I felt dizzy. I recognized the intricacies of its ornaments, knew it from my hallucinations. This was not only the dagger that had taken his mother's life, but it would bring death to Ross, too. I tore away from him, stumbling backward.

"Leave me!" I shrieked. I had to put some distance between him and me, as I was afraid I would plunge the knife's blade deep into his chest like I had seen in my vision. "Put the knife away, Ross!" I begged.

As quickly as he had pulled it out, he made the dagger disappear inside its leather sheath and raised his hands.

"Aye, *tha mi duilich,*" he apologized. "I didn't want to frighten you. Well, I think we have gathered enough berries. Let's return to the castle and see if we can exchange the berries for some cold meats," he suggested in an obvious effort to smooth over the unpleasant conversation we'd just had.

"Wait! I've got one more question, Ross," I said. Although now that I was aware of his terrible past, I instinctively knew that he wouldn't answer any of my actual questions. Whatever he knew, he wouldn't share it with me. He looked at me without saying a word.

"Do you really think that the person who once squirmed in the mud before them can be the one *holding* the dagger? Isn't that person forever damned to be the one on his knees?"

"If you're smart, Sam, you will use the dagger that is pressed against your throat to gain the upper hand. The moment of surprise is your biggest advantage."

Chapter 25

The gray tower of Castle Galthair welcomed him from afar. Cathal Stuart felt relieved to be back home, even though he could report only limited success. They had neither hunted down the cattle thieves nor found the missing animals. It was surprisingly quiet in the borderlands, aside from more and more cows going missing every day.

They cantered into the castle yard, and Cathal jumped from the saddle before his horse came to a stop.

"*Fàilte,* milord!" the stable boys greeted him and took over the reins.

"Where is Nathaira? Why isn't she here to welcome me home?" he demanded.

"Her ladyship is residing at Burragh. A messenger brought tidings that the laird had been injured, and she left right away. She thought him on his deathbed and wanted to look in on him personally," one of the boys informed them.

Cathal nodded. Even though he urgently needed to speak with his sister, he was glad to know she was with Blair, who was without a doubt also by his father's bedside. He was especially glad since Alasdair Buchanan, the Norseman, was now dismounting beside him.

"Cathal, a word, please?" Alasdair called, asking him to approach.

"What is it, *mo charaid*?"

"I wanted to talk with you concerning a very important and personal matter," Alasdair explained, stroking his beard.

Cathal suppressed the urge to blurt out a curse word and instead nodded casually. He prompted the blond warrior to accompany him as he traversed the courtyard and walked toward the Great Hall. He had a pretty good idea of what his liegeman wanted to talk to him about. After all, it wasn't an accident that he had assigned him to securing the borderlands in the farthest corners of his land.

Cathal Stuart knew about the love affair between Alasdair and his beautiful sister, but no matter how much he loved Nathaira, he could not allow himself to take her romantic feelings into account where the well-being of his clan was concerned. His clan needed a strong bond with the McLeans to ensure lasting peace.

It was for this reason that she would face her responsibilities and wed his best friend and important ally, Blair McLean, in the very near future. As far as he was concerned, it was best for Alasdair to not see his sister beforehand.

"So, what is it, Buchanan?" Cathal asked when they were walking side by side.

"Well, it's something of the gravest importance to me, and I would prefer not to discuss it in passing. I would like to present myself to you formally—if you will allow me," Alasdair explained.

"Of course. I suggest you come to my study tomorrow, and we'll share a cup of beer. Then you can present me this matter in detail."

Cathal was glad to delay the meeting, for he had more pressing business to attend to. He needed to gather the most influential men of his clan so he could reassure and appease them before the voices of those questioning his leadership grew ever louder.

"Alasdair, you could do me a service and keep your eyes and ears open for me. I need to know how many of my men are still loyal to me—and who might stab me in the back," he asked of his Nordic liegeman. He couldn't be sure that Alasdair himself wouldn't turn against him if he denied him Nathaira's hand in marriage, but for as long as Alasdair was unaware of this, Cathal could count on his loyalty.

"Aye, I understand. I will keep an ear to the ground."

With that, Cathal exited the Great Hall and walked up the stairs to his chambers, passing his ancestors' portraits on the wall. He could feel the Norseman's eyes on his back the entire time.

He slammed the door shut behind him and, exhausted, slumped down into one of his armchairs. These last few days had been hard and weren't exactly crowned with success. As he had done so many times before, he cursed his late father for lacking vision and foresight. How could Grant not have known how much pressure he was putting on his son? Hadn't he known that Cathal's authority would stand on shaky ground?

Everything would be just fine if it hadn't been for those cattle raids. It was as if the Camerons knew exactly what damage they were inflicting upon him. This pack of lowlifes couldn't think of a more desirable outcome than for their long-term enemies to tear themselves to shreds from within.

Cathal slipped off his boots. Today, instead of setting out for Burragh, he would drown his anger in whiskey. And tomorrow he would arrange for his sister's engagement. Only it wouldn't be to the man who'd be proposing to her.

Alasdair was content: Tomorrow he would propose to Nathaira. He had been wanting to ask for her hand in marriage ever since his first assignment in the borderlands, but he hadn't been able to get near her. He had been told she was ill and unable to leave her chambers. And not long afterward, Cathal had sent him far away on an urgent mission. Since that time, his desire for this raven-haired beauty had grown every day. To the outside world, she always acted like a tough, strong-minded lady who was used to giving orders. But he knew her to be very different. When she lay in his loving, protecting arms, she allowed herself to be vulnerable.

His eyes wandered across the castle yard, full of yearning while searching for his beloved's face behind every window. He had no luck. All he noticed was Dougal standing with a squad of sentries. Alasdair strolled over to them. Perhaps they could tell him where he might find his beloved.

"Cannot trust his protection any longer. There are men who are better suited. . . ." He caught Dougal's last words just as he joined the group.

The sentries saluted, and Dougal nodded in Alasdair's direction. "Be that as it may, go think about what I told you." He finished his speech and stepped up to the Norseman.

"Alasdair, *mo charaid.* It's great to be home after all this time, is it not?" he asked.

Both men towered over the rest of the men by almost a head. They had fought many a mock fight against each other with their broadswords, and they knew about each other's skills and physical strength.

Alasdair nodded.

"Three months is a long time," he agreed.

"Especially since it was such a *wasted* time." Dougal poked the fire. "Not a single Cameron was caught in the act, and yet many more cows were lost. It is only thanks to my brother that we have at least some information as to the cattle."

"We have information? What kind of information?" Alasdair asked in surprise.

Dougal looked over his shoulder at the sentries who were still standing together and sharing a tankard of beer. He put his hand on his shoulder and led him a short distance away.

"Oh, you know, this Cameron woman. Maybe you didn't notice her when you met up with us at the campsite. After all, night had already fallen, and your wineskin was keeping us well entertained. Anyway, Cathal sent her away with Blair the next morning. She was to help take care of Fingal. If you ask me, I would rather die a painful death than allow a wench like her to look after me."

Alasdair vaguely remembered a woman he had seen that morning.

"We would have our cattle back by now if Cathal had only allowed Duncan to question her," Dougal declared.

Alasdair nodded. He had once witnessed the twins "questioning" a man. Not a pretty sight, as far as he recalled, but it had been effective.

"Just imagine—we could have returned home with all our stolen cattle! It would have been a day of celebration for the Stuart clan. But no, instead we're returning empty-handed, and my brother's prisoner is now at Burragh."

"Why don't you just go get her and question her now?"

"We will. As far as I'm aware, several men are setting out for Burragh tomorrow. Ross already rode with Blair, and it seems that Lady Nathaira was so worried about Fingal's well-being that she also left for Castle Burragh yesterday."

Alasdair pricked his ears. "Oh, is that so?" he asked.

"Aye. Do you want to join in? The McLeans have no shortage of pretty girls on offer. And after three months in the saddle, I'm sure you wouldn't mind some fun of the female kind. What do you say, my friend?"

"Why wait until tomorrow? I've already got one in mind," Alasdair mumbled, picturing how easy it would be at Castle Burragh to slip into Nathaira's bed. Much easier than doing that here, where they would have to hide from the entire Stuart clan—until, at least, he had formally spoken to Cathal.

Chapter 26

After my woodland excursion, I spent the rest of the day with Nanny MacMillan, preparing ointments, hanging herbs to dry, and stocking up on bandages. Every now and then we looked in on Fingal and his wound, but the old laird was well enough to not take the old nanny's scolding and lecturing anymore.

Right now, he was slamming shut the door to his chambers and bolting it from the inside. He had threatened to have Nanny put in chains if she kept insisting on allowing him only chicken broth and oatmeal. And that was when Nanny MacMillan fled his room, skirts billowing behind her, causing Fingal to jump from his bed and brace himself against the old lady's return. And so, the door was closed. When he turned around, he noticed me and gave me a conspiratorial wink.

"Lassie, I almost forgot about you. That woman clearly needs a man who can tan her hide from time to time. Honestly, I think she saves all her screams and shouts for me."

I kept my eyes firmly on the ground because the mighty clan chief stood before me wearing nothing but a shirt. Luckily his shirttails were long enough to hide all of the important parts.

"I'm sorry to disagree, milord, but I spent almost the entire day with her, and I can assure you from personal experience that she's letting everybody else have it exactly the same way."

"Really? Well, I always assumed it must be a sign of affection if she's giving me a good talking to."

I chuckled.

"I don't think so, milord. She's been scolding me all day today—and she doesn't even know me," I said, trying to disprove his affection theory.

"Or"—he raised his index finger high up in the air—"I'm right. After all, it's not really that hard to be fond of you."

Was he trying to tell me that he liked me?

He grinned when he saw my baffled expression.

"Samantha, dear. Don't look at me like that. I know our families don't exactly get along, but there are bad people everywhere." He put on his plaid and rummaged for his belt. I grabbed it from the back of his chair and handed it to him, waiting for him to continue.

"So are good people."

He locked eyes with me.

"Did you know the arrow probably came from a mercenary? A soldier for hire? Who do you think pays for men to destabilize our borders? Our enemies? Or perhaps the English who are afraid of another Jacobite uprising? I'm telling you like it is: I'm tired of fighting. This feud between the Stuarts and the Camerons has been a thorn in my side for a long time. An alliance among our three families would be to the benefit of everyone, don't you think?"

My knees went soft, and my mind went into overdrive. Was this possible? Was it possible that history was being written right here and now? Payton had never breathed much about the time before Vanora's curse, but I knew that the terrible massacre on the clan of my Cameron ancestors had something to do with an old blood feud between them and the Stuarts.

I needed air, and so I stepped over to the window and opened it. I took a deep breath, palms sweaty. This was so screwed up! I cursed my own lack of insight. Why had Payton never talked about what happened before Vanora spoke her curse?

He probably felt guilty, blamed himself, and didn't want to hurt me by telling me that he had killed in his previous life. That he had murdered my ancestors. And now? Now it was too late. I couldn't ask him. I didn't know what to do, what I *could* do to save him and all those he loved. Was it even possible to save them all? How had everything started? Like this? With Fingal wanting peace?

"Lassie, are you not well?" he asked, and walked over to me. "You look pale. Here, take a sip." He pressed his cup against my lips, and I obeyed. I was slowly getting used to the taste and the warming, soothing effect of whiskey. Age limits didn't seem to matter much in the eighteenth century. Fingal tied the white hair on the back of his neck together and pinned the brooch to his plaid before facing me again.

"I will attain this peace—and you are going to help me," he explained matter-of-factly, holding his hand out to me.

"Me? What . . . How can I possibly help you?"

He led me to the door and released me into the hallway, where Payton was already waiting for me.

"Well, Samantha, I'm going to tell you very soon. But first I need to discuss a matter with Blair," he explained, saying good-bye.

Payton grabbed my hand as the door closed behind us.

"What does he need to discuss with Blair?" he asked, pulling me after him.

"What are we doing? Where are we going?"

He wasn't taking me back to my room, that much I could tell.

"You'll see. So, what does he need to discuss with Blair?"

"No idea. He thinks I can help him ensure peace between the clans. Besides, you were right. The arrows really—"

"Came from mercenaries, I know. Sean found out from a maidservant in Kilerac who is very fond of him. She told him that a group of men were drinking and celebrating in her father's village inn, and they drunkenly bragged about getting paid for stealing. She could have sworn that their arrows were outfitted with metal tips."

A narrow, winding staircase lay before us, and Payton grabbed me firmer by the hand so that I wouldn't trip and fall on the uneven steps. A hatch led up to the flat roof of the castle keep, and the roof itself was surrounded by high battlements. It was the highest point in the castle, and the view was breathtaking.

"I was hoping I could show you the sunset," Payton admitted with regret in his voice because the sun had already disappeared behind the horizon.

It was stunning all the same. The clear night sky with its millions of stars was glorious above our heads.

"It's fantastic," I assured him. Suddenly feeling awkward in his company, I realized how much we had in common but how little we really knew about each other. I looked up at the stars. We had found each other once before and fallen in love against all odds.

I stepped closer to the parapet, feeling his body near me even though I had my back to him. This was exactly how it had always been. Something, someone was weaving the fabric of destiny, folding my thread and Payton's into a pattern.

"This is my favorite spot in the castle. It's where I can think and be alone. Not many people come up here."

I turned around self-consciously.

"Is this why you brought me here? To be . . . alone with me?"

Payton gave a sheepish grin as if I'd just caught him with his hand in the cookie jar.

"That, too," he admitted and came closer. "But what I really wanted was to give you a gift. Problem is, I don't really own much a girl would enjoy. Which is why I wanted to share my favorite spot with you. As I said . . . I was hoping . . . the sun . . . you know?"

I got up on tiptoes and kissed him. "It's a wonderful gift. Thank you."

He kissed my nose and turned me around so he could wrap his arms around me from behind.

"We might be undisturbed up here, but we're not invisible. I don't want to start a war just because I'm kissing the most beautiful girl in all of Scotland."

"Dougal said I had nothing that could please a real man," I corrected him.

He kissed the back of my neck and whispered into my ear. "Dougal is stupid. And blind on top of it."

His hands ran across my stomach as he pulled me closer. I could feel his heart beat faster when his tongue traced the outline of my ear.

When I gasped for breath, he let out a throaty laugh that melted my insides. Then he pointed at the horizon.

"Over there, that bright spot, that's Castle Galthair. And that shimmering line, that's a small river indicating the border between the land of the Stuarts and the McLeans."

"And that?" I pointed far to the north, where I noticed the dark outline of a stronghold against the starlit sky.

"Don't you recognize it? That's Castle Coulin—Cameron territory. Your people."

Of course he'd expect me to recognize the castle of the Camerons—I was one of them, after all.

"Payton, I have to tell you something. I can't stop what is about to happen from happening, but I still have to warn you." I looked at him imploringly. I had to somehow get him to believe me. "There's going to be an awful, awful battle. A battle that will cost many lives. I don't know when it's going to happen, or if I'm still going to be here."

"A battle? What do you mean?"

"I can't tell you, Payton. I'm afraid of what might happen. . . ."

"Afraid? Of what?"

"My world . . . I . . . the future . . . I might jeopardize everything, and I can't risk it. I don't belong here, but if my world stops to exist in the future because . . . ," I said, starting to stammer again, "well, if I intervene and stop things from happening . . . then how can I ever get back? How can I ever save you?"

"Calm down, Sam. I don't understand what you're telling me, but I do trust you."

Payton was trying to comfort me, but he only increased my feelings of shame and guilt. I knew what was about to happen to him and his family, and yet I was doing nothing to stop it. He shouldn't trust me! I was such a coward and liar! But although I knew, I just could not act against my conviction. I turned around.

"Promise me something," I said, hoping to lessen those awful feelings of guilt and help him accept his fate. "Promise me that you'll take care of yourself, that you won't blame yourself for things that cannot be changed. I can tell you this much: You will achieve forgiveness in the future when you least expect it, and you will get your chance to make amends. Promise me that you won't lose hope." I ran my fingers over his cheek and the fresh scar on his chin. "It will change you, it will take away your smile, it will make your soul freeze . . . but it won't break you, Payton. *I* will save you. Don't ever forget that."

I touched his lips and kissed him very gently. His kiss tasted salty. "I love the man you will become, Payton, but I wish I had the courage and strength to spare you this fate." I sobbed against his chest, and he stroked my back as my tears flowed freely onto his shirt.

"Sam. I'm not afraid of my fate. It has led you to me, and—whatever it may have in store for me—I accept it willingly as the price to pay for your love."

"I just hope you won't wake up one day and think that the price was too high," I whispered.

The warmth of his body soothed my aching soul, and his scent stirred in me an urgent desire to be close, to be intimate.

"Let's go inside. It's getting cold, and you're shivering," Payton determined, and pointed at the hatch. He let me go first and helped me on the way down. Then he escorted me back to the section of the castle where all the bedchambers were. We turned a corner, and Payton peered around before opening a door and quickly pulling me into the dark room with him.

"Your chambers," I said without hesitation. I didn't need to ask because I recognized the room even in the pale moonlight, with its green tapestries barely contrasting against the backdrop of the bare stone walls. I had already spent a night in here. In a different century, sure, but with the same man by my side.

"Yes . . . but how . . . ?"

"A wild guess," I replied, because I felt that any further explanation would be too hard to take in. "Why did you bring me here?" My heart beat faster, and I couldn't help but glance over at the ebony-colored bed, the heavy brown bed curtains, the wide, straw-filled mattress . . .

Payton looked past me, seemingly nervous.

"I've spent all day thinking about you."

He looked at me, no longer trying to hide the fire in his eyes. "I've been trying to picture what it would be like . . ."

He walked over to the table and lit a candle. Then another, and another. I held my breath. Slowly he walked toward me, coming closer, closer. I retreated until I felt the door against my back. His hands took mine and lifted them above my head. He held them prisoner while caressing my ears with his lips.

"What it would be like to do this." He leaned down and gently kissed me. "Or maybe this." He ran his hands down my arms, then along my neck and down to the top of my breasts, which were vaguely discernable under my low neckline. Then he wrapped an arm around my waist and loosened the thin leather belt that held my dress.

I came undone, unable to pull away from his tender, seductive moves. But then again, I didn't want to. I wanted his hands against my skin, to experience his presence with all of my senses and fall into the safety of his love.

"Is this what you had in mind?"

I caressed his chest and unpinned the brooch holding his plaid together. I looked up at him, happy, smiling—an invitation for another kiss. I didn't need to ask twice, and while he was very gentle, I felt his hunger, his rising desire.

"Sam?" he asked against my lips, eyes tightly pressed together. "Are you sure?"

Every flexed muscle told of his self-control as he awaited my reply.

"I love you, Payton. Please, don't stop now." I let my hands slide under his shirt, enjoying the pleasurable goose bumps.

"*Mo luaidh,* you're driving me crazy," he whispered hoarsely, then lifted me up into his arms and carried me to the bed.

When he carelessly threw his shirt to the floor, I very briefly wondered who was driving whom crazy.

Later that night we held each other in a tight embrace,

and Payton played with my hair. He wrapped a strand of it around his finger while looking at me with so much love.

"I never thought it could be that wonderful with such a skinny woman," he said, caressing the back of my neck.

"What?" I sat up and pulled the cover to my chin.

"Nothing, my sweet Sam. You are beautiful."

He pulled the cover off me and gently forced me back onto the mattress. Then he rolled himself on top of me. "I feel so strong when I'm with you. You're so delicate, so fragile. You make me want to protect you—and feed you."

He kissed me, and I couldn't help a smile. Yep, size zero was just a modern fad. In the eighteenth century, *more* really was more.

"Victoria Beckham would be appalled to hear you say that." I giggled, playfully biting his lip.

"Victoria who? Should I get us something to eat?" he asked, and was about to get up.

"No, please stay. Don't leave me tonight."

He looked me in the eye and stretched out beside me.

"As you wish, *mo luaidh*."

He caressed my shoulder, continued down to my collarbone, and kept going down. My skin burned wherever he touched me, and a pleasant tingling sensation started spreading in my belly.

"Sam? How much time do we have?"

I was barely able to follow, because his fingers were now tickling my belly button.

"Too little, Payton—far too little time to do and say everything I want to do and say."

"But we've got this night, aye?"

I nodded, even though my world was melting away under Payton's touch.

"Right," I stammered, and wrapped my legs around him. "Then we should make the most of it."

Chapter 27

When Alasdair reached Castle Burragh and entered through the portcullis of the outer wall, he was unable to suppress a smile. It was dark, but up there on the roof of the castle keep, he could just about make out a pair of lovers lying in each other's arms.

"My, my, what have we there. I didn't think young McLean had it in him," he mumbled.

When the sentries, who were standing close together in the courtyard, recognized him, they raised a hand in greeting and let him pass. He dismounted and led his horse to the stables where he hoped to shelter it for the night.

"Master Buchanan," the stable boy welcomed him. "Shall I look after it, or will you be leaving again shortly?"

Alasdair handed him the reins and shook his head.

"I'm staying. Thank you, Iain."

Then, with a spring in his step, he set out to find Nathaira. Burragh was an expansive stronghold, but there weren't many possibilities for a woman like her: Her accommodations were no doubt located in the three-story castle keep. He therefore entered via the main castle keep door and hurried into the Great Hall. And there she was. She immediately caught his eye. All other humans paled in comparison. She had the beauty and the grace of a queen, and he felt irresistibly drawn to her, like a bee to the honey jar.

She was sitting with her back turned to him, a cup of wine in front of her. Taking a deep breath, he tiptoed closer, grabbed the armrests of her chair, and bent down to her ear.

"How dare these philistines leave such a beautiful woman to dine all by herself. Allow me to correct this shameful oversight and offer my humble presence."

Nathaira stiffened, slowly turning her head. Her eyes widened.

"Alasdair." His name sounded like a prayer on her lips, and Alasdair realized that she struggled to keep her composure.

"My beloved," he said, kissing the back of her hand a moment longer than politeness demanded—yet not long enough for any observers to grow suspicious.

"What are you doing here? When did you get back?"

The shock about his unexpected arrival brought back painful memories of the weeks past. They were memories she'd wanted to leave behind in the same way she had rid herself of her problem: the child growing in her belly—Alasdair's child.

A thousand questions had been running through her mind back then: What would Cathal, her brother, do to her should he find out about her condition? Would he cast her out? Would he kill Alasdair? She had been sure of only one thing: Cathal would never have agreed to a union between her and Alasdair.

Frozen in fear, she had done the only thing possible: She had crept away. She rode north for two days, hoping to find the Wise Woman who lived in the hills. Nathaira couldn't say for sure what happened then. Only one thing was painfully certain: She loved Alasdair Buchanan, and she had killed his child.

"I returned to Galthair with your brother today, hoping to see you. When they told me you had gone to Castle Burragh, all I could think about was catching up with you."

Nathaira scanned the Great Hall, wrinkling her forehead.

"Is Cathal with you? I don't see him."

"No. I came alone because I didn't want to be without you a single moment longer." He returned the greeting of some man who was traversing the hall, and turned back to her. "Come, my beautiful, let us find a spot where we can be undisturbed."

Nathaira seemed nervous as she slowly rose from her chair and allowed him to escort her from the hall.

"Do you keep chambers here?" he asked hoarsely, growing more and more impatient with every minute he spent in her tantalizing presence. Seemingly indecisive, she stopped, gazing up the stairs where the guest chambers were located, when a dog slipped through the main door, barking and racing toward them. In the pale, flickering light of the handful of wall torches, the shaggy wolfhound seemed even more menacing than during the day.

Ross's bright red shock of hair appeared behind a second wolfhound, and he immediately called the two dogs to order. With surprise on his face, he approached.

"Nathaira." He bowed before her. "Alasdair. Are you here to come and get Samantha?" he asked.

Nathaira snorted in discontent, and her companion did not seem too pleased about the disturbance, either.

"Samantha? Samantha who?"

"The prisoner, of course! Aren't Duncan and Dougal with you?"

"No, I came alone. Everyone else is coming tomorrow." He wanted to leave the boy and take his beloved up to her chambers to show her how much he had missed her. But Ross wasn't easily dissuaded.

"Did you see them, perhaps?"

"See who? Duncan and Dougal?" Alasdair snapped.

"Samantha! Did you see *her* or Payton somewhere? I really have to talk to her."

A smile crept onto Alasdair's face. That McLean! He was even more audacious than he had given him credit for. The woman he saw Payton kissing up on the battlement must be Cathal's prisoner and not, as he had assumed, some maidservant.

"Now I remember, yes, I did see them! But I suggest you wait until the morning. That woman seemed *very busy* to me," he responded, shooting Ross a meaningful glance.

"Busy with what?"

"You know, having her way with her guardsman," he growled, because *having his way* was exactly what he had in mind for himself. At that point, Ross's jaw dropped, and Alasdair seized the moment to leave the castle keep, pulling Nathaira with him. They would never make it to her chambers undetected, so he was now pursuing a different idea.

"Alasdair, wait!" Nathaira called out, fighting against being dragged along. "We have to talk!"

The cold of the night made Alasdair even more aware of the heat in his belly, of his burning desire, and he pulled Nathaira against the castle wall. There, in the shadows, he was finally able to cover her body with his, hiding her from the world and hungrily stealing a kiss. Heavens, how much he'd missed her.

"Stop it!" she screamed, and pushed him away. "We mustn't! We can't continue like this." She struggled to regain her composure. "I must wed, Alasdair!"

"I will wed you. Tomorrow I will ask Cathal for your hand in marriage."

He caressed the shoulders that her robe left bare, enjoying the feel of her velvety-soft skin against his hands. He also felt her tightening up against him.

"No, Alasdair, you won't! Don't you understand what I'm telling you?" She withdrew from his touch, placing her palms flat against his chest to keep him at a safe distance. "It was a mistake to give in to my feelings for you." There was regret in her voice, but also resolve.

"Cathal would never accept you as my husband. You are nothing but his liegeman. His liegeman! And what Cathal needs are allies. He needs to think of the clan. The deal is already done—I'm going to marry Blair McLean."

Alasdair faltered under the weight of her words. What was that she was talking about? Cathal had said nothing of the sort. And what was the point of this, anyway? He loved Nathaira, and he wouldn't just give her up!

"You can't do that. You lay with me—didn't that mean anything to you? Have you already forgotten about that?"

"How could I forget? After all, you left me alone with a child in my womb, while you chased cattle thieves out in the borderlands!" she screamed.

Alasdair shook his head, thinking he had misheard her.

"A child? What do you mean? You are with child?"

Nathaira wiped away her tears, as she didn't want him to see her pain. Quietly, almost as if not wanting him to hear, she replied: "No, Alasdair, I am not with child. You left me, and I had to make a choice. I chose my brother—and I chose against you and the child."

Alasdair grabbed the same shoulders he had caressed only a moment ago, and he shook her violently.

"What are you saying? I've never left you! I followed your brother's orders! And now, woman, you are going to tell me what you have done, or I swear to God I will forget myself!"

Nathaira found it easy to see in him the fury and anger of his ancestors: murdering, pillaging, plundering Vikings. She was scared of him. At the same time, she loved him so much that it hurt, and she hated herself for having to do this to him.

"Leave me! Take your filthy hands off me! I did what was necessary to not bring the bastard child of a nobody into this world! You presume a great deal, Viking, when you think that a place in my bed would secure you a place in my heart. All my love and all my loyalty belong to only one man: my brother."

Overtaken with pain and rage, Alasdair reached for Nathaira's throat and pressed hard. He didn't want to hear another of her spiteful words. She was destroying his future and had ripped his heart out.

He pressed down harder, enjoying her resistance, enjoying her pain.

Oh, she had it coming. With her eyes wide open in terror, her arms hanging limp by her side—she had never seemed more beautiful to him. He leaned in for one final kiss before releasing her throat and whispering against her tear-soaked cheek:

"I hope your brother will cast you out when his ally realizes on his wedding night that his beautiful bride is no longer a virgin."

Then he pushed her hard, and Nathaira slumped down against the wall, gasping for air.

She held her throat, retching and coughing, and drew delicious fresh air into her burning lungs. Hatred and loathing flared in her eyes, and a blinding flash of lightning tore across the sky. She defied fate! It no longer mattered whether or not he killed her—she had died the day her unborn child had died.

"Not that my wedding night is any of your concern, but when I left Blair's bedchamber earlier, he wasn't complaining. By the way, when it comes to matters of the flesh, he has greater skills than you do."

Triumphantly, she presented her cheek to him, enjoying the angry punch she knew he would throw. The pain would wear off and prove that life beyond pain was possible.

Through a veil of tears, she saw the love of her life disappear into the darkness. She prayed that something resembling a life without pain and suffering waited for her. A life devoid of feelings—now wouldn't that make things easier.

Chapter 28

Fingal had sent for his oldest son, Blair. It was early in the day, but a fire was already burning in the fireplace, and a cup of sweet, heavy wine was warming him up. He didn't like to admit it, but his wound and the subsequent fever had cost him a great deal of strength. On top of that, he'd had a bad fever of the lungs several months back. That had also almost killed him, and he had not been able to fully recover since then.

For the first time in his life, he felt his age, and it made him restless. There was so much left to do before his time would come. He owed that to his sons, and to his clan. He had taken a first step already when he expected not to live through that fever. Back then, he had called on his sons to recognize their eldest brother, Blair, as his successor and future clan chief. They swore Blair loyalty and allegiance, just as he had demanded. While that took care of his succession, the constant feuds and cattle raids along the borders worried him more every day.

When Blair entered, Fingal hoped that his son would recognize the importance of long-lasting peace and submit to his wishes.

"Blair, *mo bailaich,* come in and sit with me. I have to discuss a matter of the utmost urgency with you."

Blair took a seat in his favorite spot by the chessboard. As befitted the game of kings, two magnificent chairs invited players to sit down for a game.

Fingal joined him, taking a fragile pawn and opening the game by moving the piece forward two squares. He set down his cup of wine and took his seat opposite Blair. They had played so many games against each other that Fingal already anticipated Blair's first countermove: pushing his own pawn two spaces up against his. He smiled when his son did not disappoint.

"I have asked you here today because I've been thinking about something," he started their conversation. He moved a knight onto the board.

Blair countered with his own black knight and looked his father square in the eye.

"What I want for you is a life without conflict and strife. These constant unrests need to be resolved once and for all. We must make peace between the clans."

"Aye, Father. But what do you want us to do? We cannot put up with these cattle raids."

"This is why we need to establish and strengthen alliances, my son. Not just by an oath but by arrangements that are longer lasting. We must unite our families and establish blood ties."

Blair's hand floated above his chess pieces.

"I agree with you, *m'athair.*"

"A marriage would unite our clans far better than any oath," Fingal continued.

"An arranged marriage? And you will allow me to choose my own wife, Father, will you not?"

"Of course I'm not going to force you, but I'm sure you will do what is necessary."

"I will, but I prefer to choose my own bride. However, I will gladly take your suggestions into account."

Fingal was relieved. He had expected to be met with greater resistance.

"And if children were to come of such a union," Fingal enthused, "then we would gain long-lasting, enduring peace."

He rose from his chair feeling satisfied. Placing a hand on his son's shoulder, he said, "I am very proud of your understanding and sense of responsibility. You are going to lead our clan into peaceful times."

"Father, don't talk like that. You are on the road to recovery and will regain your health and strength in no time. You will be managing our clan's affairs for many years to come," Blair countered, making his next move on the chessboard.

A knock on the door interrupted their conversation, but for now Fingal was content. Blair would know what was right, and he would act accordingly. Kyle stuck his head through the half-open door.

"Father, we have visitors. Duncan Stuart and some of his men are in the Great Hall. I had roast meats and beer taken to them. Would you like to join them, or do you want me to ask Payton to keep them company?"

"Where is Sean? I want him to fill in for me for a while. Blair and I are just not finished with our talk."

Kyle shrugged. "I don't know. I haven't seen Sean all day. He wasn't even in the hall at breakfast time. Nor was Payton."

Fingal was visibly displeased. He pressed his lips into a thin line and turned to Blair.

"Since your brother Sean has apparently decided to chase after skirts right now, we will have to continue our conversation at a later time. But we're in agreement on the important things, which I find reassuring. Would you go greet our guests whilst I'm having my bandages changed? This damn poultice is soaked through and running down my side."

Blair was already back on his feet.

"As you wish. I will give them your regards." With that, he made for the hall with Kyle wanting to join him—but Fingal had a task for his youngest.

"Wait. Go look for Payton. I need someone to keep an eye on that Cameron girl while we have the Stuarts in the house. And I need her here in my chambers. Nanny MacMillan is still a little scornful because I might have been grumpy toward her yesterday."

Kyle chuckled because he knew that she could hold a grudge for a long time, despite being an otherwise kind soul.

"Aye, Father, I will see what I can do," he said on his way out.

Fingal McLean stayed behind and emptied his goblet of wine. All that was left for him to do was to inform an unsuspecting Sam of his plan of marrying her to Blair. The McLeans, after all, had been friends with the Stuarts for a long time, and this marriage would add peace and an alliance between the McLeans and the Camerons. The long-standing blood feud between the Stuarts and the Camerons, on the other hand, was none of his concern.

It was high time for Payton to take me back to my own room. I was nervous about someone finding me in his chambers. We had slept way in, and we hadn't even wanted to fall asleep to begin with. But being together and feeling safe and secure in each other's arms had obviously made us drift off.

I tried my hardest to smooth down the creases on my dress, which had been carelessly tossed to the floor the previous night.

Payton seemed relatively unfazed. At least he wasn't in a great hurry to button up his shirt or comb his disheveled hair.

"What if someone is looking for me? What if your father needs my help?" I pointed out.

"Father has Nanny MacMillan. He would ask for her first."

An urgent knock on the door startled us and made Payton frown. Now he suddenly got really busy with his horn buttons. Quickly he slid over to the door but only opened it a crack.

"What do you want?" he growled.

I pricked my ears.

"What's going on? What's keeping you? We were supposed to help mend the pasture fence behind the stables. Did you already forget?" Kyle asked, and pushed past Payton. He stopped when he noticed me. Reflecting his astonished disbelief, his gaze wandered from me to Payton, down to Payton's wrongly buttoned shirt, and back to me.

"What the . . . ?"

"Hello, Kyle," I said sheepishly, frantically racking my brain for a plausible explanation for my being in Payton's room. It turned out that I didn't need one.

"I was picking up Sam in her chambers," said Payton, "and we were on our way to the hall, when one of Ross's stupid dogs jumped up on me and wiped its filthy paws on my shirt. I had to go and get changed."

I nodded eagerly, and—even though it was obvious from Kyle's face that he didn't believe a single word—Kyle gave a quick nod and folded his arms across his chest.

"Aye, I understand, *mo bràthair.* Well, as soon as you've changed into a *clean* shirt that you *absolutely* need for working on those fences, you are to take Samantha to Father's chambers and then get your ass over to the hall. The fences will have to wait. We've got visitors."

With that, he shot me a grin and, walking backward on his way out, he playfully punched Payton's shoulder.

"He knows, right?" I asked.

"Aye, he knows. Luckily, it's Kyle. He will keep his mouth shut."

"How can you be so sure?"

"We've always been very close. Blair and Sean stick together because they're the oldest. Kyle and I are united in the feeling of only ever bothering the *grown-ups.* We look out for each other, ken, and we help each other. It has always been that way."

I swallowed hard. Payton's simple explanation, the casual ease with which he assumed his brother's loyalty, and the brotherly love that resonated in each of his words were almost more than I could take.

How could I send Kyle to his death—Kyle, that ray of sunshine with his entire life still ahead of him? How could I possibly allow it? But I didn't have a choice, did I. I couldn't risk changing the future so significantly. His death would lead to a whole avalanche of events, and I didn't dare interfere with the course of history, couldn't risk changing it—perhaps cutting off my own roots and my own lifeline in the process.

But even though there was nothing I could do to change these brothers' fates, I had to do *something*. I couldn't let Payton lug this guilt around with him for the next two hundred and seventy years. I had to help him find hope and forgiveness before we met again in the twenty-first century.

"You coming?" His question jolted me from my thoughts.

"Huh?"

"Are you coming? We should hurry so we don't arouse any more suspicion."

I nodded, but only because I didn't trust my voice. I felt like breaking down and crying. Where had my inner strength gone?

We walked beside each other like strangers, Payton McLean with his prisoner, Samantha Cameron, each trying not to touch the other, or even look at the other. Nobody could know how close we had been the night before.

Once we arrived at Fingal's door, Payton gave me a quick wink and promised to come and get me for supper. Then he handed me off to his father and left.

"Samantha, come in. I took the liberty of removing the poultice myself. If you could just help me apply fresh bandages."

I walked over to the washstand and took a clean linen strip from the basket that Nanny MacMillan had left behind when she stormed out of the room the day before. In silence and still deeply engrossed in my own somber thoughts, I wrapped the piece of cloth firmly around Fingal's chest. The wound was healing well. Sometime in the future, a small scar would take its place and prove to the world that I had in fact existed here—in this era.

"Lassie, you look glum. Are you frightened of something?"

To share with Fingal what I was going through would surely go well beyond his imagination. Being scared would have to do, and so I nodded.

"You don't need to worry. I have placed you under my protection." He slipped into his shirt and looked me straight in the eye. "And not only that—but as I mentioned before, you are going to help me leave a legacy of long-lasting peace for my sons. I just talked with Blair. He understands his duties and obligations to the clan, and I'm sure that you, too, will come to see your benefit in this." He stopped talking to study my face, and then he nodded. "You two are a good fit."

I didn't understand. What the heck was he talking about?

"Once you are married, Cathal might actually change his mind and put an end to this old feud between the Stuarts and the Camerons."

"Married? Me?" I looked at him wide-eyed and completely befuddled. I was sure that I had misheard him.

"Calm down, my dear. Consider the alternative: Cathal takes you with him, uses you for his own desires and purposes—whatever they may be. Who knows what kind of a future you would have with him. On the other hand, you could choose a marriage to Blair, a peace-loving, responsible man whom I raised well and who will treat his wife well and with respect."

Oh my God! I had not misheard him! Crazy laughter rose from my throat. This was insane! I didn't even belong here!

"Samantha, think about my proposal before you reject it flat out. I will await your reply tonight."

"Milord, really, I don't need to think about it. It is completely impossible to enforce peace between your clans by marrying me to your son. I'm not as close to the Cameron clan as you perhaps imagine. In fact, I'm pretty sure that nobody at Castle Coulin actually misses me."

I almost burst out laughing again, because the fine folks at Castle Coulin would be really surprised to learn of my existence.

"Oh, nonsense. This has nothing to do with your standing in the clan and everything to do with your having Cameron blood in your veins. Which will be perfectly sufficient as a sign of peace and goodwill."

I didn't know how to respond: It all sounded utterly absurd.

I was saved by a knock on the door, and I breathed a sigh of relief when Fingal walked over to open it.

"Is there no peace in this house, ever?" he thundered, outraged at yet another interruption. After yanking open the door and exchanging a few words with my nameless savior, he asked me to wait inside.

"I'll be right back," he promised.

The door closed behind him with a thud, releasing me from my paralysis. I had to get out of here! I had wasted way too much time already, and Fingal's plan very clearly showed this. No matter how much it would hurt me to leave Payton, I really had no other choice.

I hurried over to the window, jerked it open, and realized that I would break every single bone in my body if I were to try to take that route. Climbing down the castle wall was risky even if I had enough time to tie together Fingal's bed curtains and use them for a rope.

"Shit, friggin' shit!" I exclaimed, looking for a different way out. My eyes wandered across the room and landed on the narrow secretary desk, complete with sheets of paper and a quill pen.

Jesus, a quill! And where would one find a regular pen or pencil? Seriously, everything in the past just sucked! My hands were shaking as I pulled the stopper from the small inkwell and dipped the tip of the quill in it. What should I write? What words could give Payton comfort over the next few hundred years or so? How could I tell him what I needed to tell him in the short amount of time I had left?

A giant inkblot dripped onto the page.

"Dammit!" I put the tip of the quill to paper, clumsily scratching over the page. Blots, smudges, illegible handwriting . . . but I eventually managed to get the words of forgiveness out and onto paper. With every minute that passed, I grew more anxious that Fingal might return and catch me red-handed at his desk. So I signed the letter and, while waiting for the ink to dry, I tried to rearrange everything in the exact way I had found it. When I heard steps outside, I quickly folded the page and pushed it into my corselet at the same instant the door opened.

My attempt at leaning against the windowsill in as low-key a manner as possible failed miserably when I realized who was standing in the doorway. My pulse quickened, and the little hairs on the back of my neck stood up.

CHAPTER 29

When the others passed the stone bridge in front of her, Nathaira finally had a moment to study the prisoner out of the corner of her eye. The girl seemed baffled and not exactly overjoyed about leaving McLean territory. The sharp winds had brought a good color to her cheeks, but Nathaira found her to be quite plain. Still, if Alasdair had spoken the truth the night before, then one of the McLean men must have taken a liking to her.

Or perhaps it was Ross, the young upstart, for he had been trying to make a name for himself for the longest time, always trying to keep up with his older half brothers. At any rate, as he sat on his horse with the Cameron wench in front of him, the smug and satisfied expression on his face seemed to imply as much.

Even Duncan and Dougal, the twin brothers, certainly seemed pleased with themselves, and only Blair riding beside her acted as detached and aloof as he always did. Nathaira wondered what was so special about this Cameron woman that she was that important to the twins. What were they up to? One thing for sure was that she would need to keep an eye on that lass.

Dark storm clouds gathered above the mountains to the east. The wind picked up and blew strands of shiny black hair from her face. Nathaira took a deep breath. She loved the wind. It was brash and wild and free, just like she always wanted to be. It also had enormous unseen strengths at its disposal.

Nathaira let go of the reins and opened her arms. Her cloak billowed behind her, almost seeming like it wanted to raise her up and give her wings.

Again she looked at the mysterious woman who was pulling her shawl tighter in the icy breeze.

Earlier, Nathaira had fetched the prisoner on Fingal's orders. She was to give her a chance to collect her belongings before leaving.

Fingal had been livid about having to give in to the twin brothers' demands regarding the Cameron woman, but she was still the Stuarts' prisoner and not the McLeans'.

Still, or so Fingal had said, he was eager to discuss his claim to the girl with Cathal. Except Cathal hadn't been able to make today's journey due to new incidents at the border, and Fingal had had to admit a temporary defeat.

Nathaira scowled. Had the old man taken a liking to that wisp of a girl? Her suspicions were fueled when he had insisted that Blair accompany the prisoner and ensure her safety until he could come to an agreement with Cathal.

Nathaira stuck out her chin and straightened when she caught up to the men. She was sick of worrying about that skinny, unimportant wallflower. Instead, she wanted to find out more about the situation on the Stuarts' front lines. She had overheard some voices wanting to see Cathal replaced as clan chief, with Duncan taking his place. And those voices needed to be silenced! Only Cathal was the rightful clan chief and heir. All of her love and affection was for him.

Never in her life had there been another person she had respected and trusted—and to whom she meant something.

Her stepmother, Una, had hated her and made sure she was aware of this every day of her life, until she was left with no choice but to poison that wicked woman who'd never been a mother to her. Not a single day went by that Nathaira regretted what she had done.

And her father, the mighty Grant Stuart, a despicable demon who had violated so many women: her own mother, countless maidservants, and of course Duncan and Dougal's mother. She hadn't dared kill him, but she was glad when he died.

Only Cathal, her brother—who to this day did not know that they did not share the same mother—had always stood by her. He had saved her many a time from the bitter Una's blows. And for that, she loved him. Which was why it was imperative for him to stay clan chief: She couldn't bear to submit to someone else's powers and abuse ever again. She would sacrifice anything and everything for Cathal.

Her thoughts wandered to Alasdair, the love of her life, whose love and child she had already sacrificed. Now she had nothing left to lose.

Night had fallen when Payton and Kyle returned after a long day of working on the pasture fence. They had been standing in mud and dirt up to their knees while digging holes for new fence posts and then hammering them in. Several miles of fence remained to be built around the newly cleared woodlands, so that they could drive the cattle here from their summer pasture before the fall of winter. They had never needed fences before, but it seemed the most sensible thing to do after all the trouble they'd experienced in previous years.

Kyle was whining as they entered the castle yard through the main gate.

"My hands are all blisters! I won't be able to hold as much as a spoon tomorrow."

Payton looked down at the calluses on his own hands, and he had to agree. Driving the rough-cut wooden stakes into the earth had been hard work. He blushed ever so slightly when he pictured how he would bring Sam to affectionately care for him and his aching hands.

"Say, have the Stuarts left?" Kyle's question startled him out of his daydreams.

"What did you say?"

"I've been looking forward to a nice big feast at the end of a long day, but it would appear that the Stuarts have left. Which means that Father will only spring for some fried herring for supper," Kyle grumbled.

Payton took a good look around. Indeed, he didn't even see the wolfhounds that had been monopolizing the castle yard these past few days.

Their boots left muddy prints on the stone floor as they entered the Great Hall. Everything was quiet in here, too. Only two male servants and the blacksmith's young apprentice were sitting together and playing a game of cards. They looked up briefly when the two brothers entered but, after greeting them, turned back to their game.

Payton and Kyle had missed supper, so it was no surprise that all the guests would have by now withdrawn to their chambers for the night. The hall was cold and drafty, and even Payton shivered from the cold, wet mud still sticking to his lower legs.

He said a regretful good-bye to the idea of letting Sam massage him to sleep. While he briefly considered paying her a visit in her bedchambers, he decided against it. In his current sorry state of filth, he wouldn't make much of a favorable impression on any woman. Not even if he brought her the gift he had arranged for her in his chambers.

"Well, there's no way I'm going to bed hungry!" Kyle griped as he headed for the arch door leading to the kitchen. Shrugging, Payton followed his younger brother.

The kitchen was warm and cozy, and Kyle helped himself from the loaf of bread, the butter churn, and the honey jar. Then he lifted every lid of every pot in search of extra delicacies. When he reached the beef and vegetable stew, he nodded, ladling a generous helping into a wooden bowl. He handed it over to Payton, who in the meantime had found a warm, comfortable spot on the wooden bench in the corner.

Dish upon dish started piling up on Kyle's plate, until he looked sufficiently satisfied and sat down with his brother. Payton raised his eyebrows and grinned at all the food.

"What? I'm still growing," Kyle defended himself, dipping a chunk of bread into his stew.

"Kyle, you've already outgrown Father by several inches. If you keep eating like this, you're only going to grow sideways."

"Amadáin!" Kyle's only reply was the curse word and a well-aimed kick against Payton's shin under the table.

They ate their stew in silence, and it was only when Payton got up to get a cup of beer that Kyle asked, "Why did you consort with Samantha?"

Payton let the dark ale flow from the barrel directly into his cup.

"What do you mean?" He tried to evade the question.

"Don't pretend you don't know what I'm talking about. I've got eyes, you know."

"Well, then you don't need to ask."

Payton regretted having poured himself all that beer, because now he would have to stay and answer all of Kyle's questions until the cup was empty. He took a big gulp.

"She's a pretty girl," Kyle noted simply.

"Aye."

"And she smells nice," Kyle went on.

Payton lifted his head. "How do you know?"

Kyle smirked. "Wrong answer. 'I wouldn't know' would have been the correct answer. Besides, you should have made more of an effort to disguise the jealousy in your voice."

Payton didn't respond. He couldn't lie to Kyle. But he also had no intention of discussing his innermost feelings with his brother like an old blabbermouth.

"I see, *mo bràthair.* Well, Sam seems very nice. If she weren't a Cameron, I might actually take a liking to her myself."

Payton squinted, suddenly angry. "Are my feelings wrong only because she's a Cameron? Should I deny my feelings on account of that? Love her any less for such a ridiculous reason?"

Kyle's eyes widened. "You *love* her?"

Payton buried his face in his hands.

"Well, what do you think?" he stammered without looking up.

Kyle slammed the flat of his hand down on the table.

"Then you'll have to tell Father. I'm sure he wouldn't want to bring misery upon you by sending her away with Cathal. Did you know Duncan was planning on *questioning* her? Luckily, she's safe here with us."

The sheer thought made Payton shudder. Cathal's half brothers were vicious bullies who lacked any sense of honor and decency. Committing Sam to their care would surely send her to a violent death. He knew how delicate and fragile she was. A well-aimed blow to the head would easily strike her down.

"You're right. I have to talk with Father. But it's not that easy. Sam is . . . well, I don't know how to explain it. She's different."

The incredulous expression on Kyle's face prompted Payton to continue.

"She's got the gift of second sight. She sees things. She says the Fates have sent her here to save my life."

He knew how crazy that must sound, but there was no doubt in his heart that it was exactly as he had explained—exactly as she had told him. He had seen proof, even if that proof raised many more questions than it answered.

Kyle massaged his chin. A deep vertical line popped up on his forehead.

"You believe her. You trust her." It wasn't a question but a statement of fact.

"Aye, I believe her. She says something terrible is about to happen," Payton admitted quietly.

Once again, Kyle frowned. "And you believe that, too?"

"Aye, Brother. I believe that, too."

I didn't get much of a chance to take a closer look at Castle Galthair. Right after we passed the gate, Ross had taken me to a room that I suspected was the guardroom. At any rate, there were four tough and sturdy-looking warriors sitting together on simple wooden benches. They looked up as I was being brought in. The stench of BO was overwhelming, and I confined myself to breathing as shallowly as possible.

Ross greeted the men and exchanged a few words in Gaelic with them before leading me to one of the free tables and setting down my travel pouch beside me.

"Stay here. As soon as I've taken care of the horses, I will come to get you." He motioned at the googly-eyed brutes in the room. "They will keep an eye on you, so no funny business."

What was happening? He wasn't going to leave me alone with those savages, was he? I clung to his arm, begging him to take me with him. "But I can assist you," I offered, but Ross shrugged off my hand.

"I told you I was coming to get you! Now go sit down and let me do my work."

With that, he walked out of the guardroom. He briefly turned around in the doorway. He clicked his tongue, and Barra the dog trotted in casually. When she reached my side, she turned around twice in a circle before lying down at my feet. She looked tired, but she was alert—and she carefully watched the four men.

I gave Ross a grateful smile as he disappeared. I was sure he had left the dog here for my protection.

I pulled the pouch into my lap and was greatly relieved to feel the handle of the dagger I had once again tied to my thigh. The brief moment that Nathaira had granted me to use the chamber pot behind the folding screen had been enough to hide the knife under my dress. I was glad about this tiny safety line, especially now that the guards' unwanted attention made my skin crawl. But the more time passed, the less notice they took of me.

I sidled up against the wall, exhausted and with my meager belongings clutched to my chest. My pathetic attempt at using the shawl to keep warm was doomed to failure when they changed guards, keeping the door open seemingly endlessly while they stood outside chatting and laughing.

My instincts told me it was already the middle of the night, but I was too anxious to think about sleep. Not so the men who had just finished their shift. They drank a few more mugs of beer before stretching out on the wooden benches. They all fell asleep, snoring.

I was under no illusion that I'd be able to sneak out undetected. Those guys would probably reach for their weapons and pounce on me at the slightest sound. I pulled my knees up to my chest and rested my head on them. That way at least I'd stay warm. The night trudged on sluggishly and seemed endless. When the first faint morning light made its appearance as a bluish sliver under the door, I had chewed off almost all of my fingernails.

Barra yelped, and her yellow eyes shone brightly when she lifted her head. I yawned, sitting up and petting her long, shaggy fur. Again she yelped, excitedly wagging her tail when the door opened. She jumped up, embracing Ross with her big front paws, but he quietly pushed her aside and motioned for me to follow him. The dog trotted off with her nose close to the ground.

My toes almost froze off as I followed Ross across the courtyard, wearing nothing but flimsy sandals. In the pale morning light, the uneven ground turned into an obstacle course. In some areas, I lifted my feet up unnecessarily high, and still I hit my toes on several protruding rocks.

I was so preoccupied with my feet that I only started wondering about where he was taking me when we stepped onto the road with the main castle gate behind us. The path down to Galthair Village, which surrounded the entire castle like an outer circle of defense, was not far, and Ross hurried on with giant strides.

"Ross, wait up!" I called after him, already out of breath. "Where are we going?"

Something rustled in the shrubs to my right, and it made me flinch. What kind of beasts might be waiting here for us? I thought of wolves who were perhaps trying to get at leftovers from the kitchens or slaughterhouse, or maybe rats drawn here by the stench of the wastewater ditch. That damn Scot just kept ignoring me.

"Ross!" I would not take another step unless he replied immediately. I stopped with my arms crossed across my chest.

"Come on! You don't make Duncan wait," he explained.

"Duncan? Why would I go and see him?"

I reached for my throat and suddenly found it hard to breathe.

"Samantha, don't pretend like you're stupid. You know what he wants. Answers. He has gathered his men, and they all want to know where their goddamn cows and sheep are."

Why was he suddenly being so hostile? What was going on? We had exchanged only a couple of words since they had put me on his horse, and he had completely avoided any conversation with me. And now he wanted to hand me off to his brothers? I didn't know anything; I couldn't answer any of their questions.

"But I don't know anything about your stupid cattle!" I screamed nervously. I had to bring him to believe me. I had to appeal to the kindness of his heart. "Ross, please, I don't know what to do. Can't you help me?"

He came closer, and I saw a flash of anger in his eyes.

"I don't believe you! Tell them where the cattle are, and they will let you go. Tell them quickly, or they're going to beat it out of you."

"For God's sake, Ross! I swear I've got nothing to do with it!"

I looked around for a chance to escape, but there was nowhere to go. In front of me were the village and the men; behind me were the castle with its guards; and beside me was Ross, who just had to yell for help.

He grabbed my upper arm and hissed into my face:

"I could have taken you away and protected you. But what did you do? You sold yourself to Payton! You womenfolk are all the same. You're all dirty little whores! Would you open your legs for me if I promised to save you from Duncan? Would you?"

He forced his lips onto mine in a rough, hateful kiss. I reached for my skirt, trying to lift it just enough so I could grab my dagger, when he suddenly thrust his tongue deep into my throat.

In trying to push him away, I noticed something. I bit his tongue and snatched his own knife from his belt. Breathing heavily, I aimed that dagger right at him, forcing him to keep his distance. My hand was shaking, and images flickered into my mind—images I really didn't need right now.

"Don't you *ever* touch me again!" I screamed with tears streaming down my face. It wasn't just the shock about his unexpected attack. I was also acutely aware that someone like me could not keep a warrior like Ross at arm's length for long.

And I was proven right not a moment later. Ross grabbed me and pulled my arm behind my back, twisting my hand upward. I was sure he had every intention of breaking it. Screaming in pain, I let go of his dagger. Ross pushed me to the ground, kicking the knife away and planting himself dangerously close over me.

"You little bitch! I loved you once!"

I scrambled backward, but he kept coming at me.

"Loved me? Ha! When you love someone, you don't treat them like that!"

"I said, I loved you *once.* I didn't say that I still do!"

"Oh, whatever! How deep could your love have been? After all, you don't seem to have a problem handing me off to your brothers!"

"I do! I do have a problem with it! Which is why I don't want you to be late and be beaten to death because of it. And which is also why I'm giving you this word of advice: Answer all of their questions and don't give them any reason to get angry at you."

"How many times do I have to tell you? *I don't know anything!*"

"Then tell them what they want to hear! If you tell them in front of everyone that the cows are at Auld a´chruinn, then they have no reason to harm you!" Ross had finally taken pity on me.

Auld a´chruinn? My mind was working overtime. That place sounded so familiar. Now I remembered the City Limits sign. It was crooked, as if someone had hit it with their car. We had crossed the small town of Auld a´chruinn on our way to the cemetery where Payton and Sean expected to find the portal of time. Payton had explained that the town was right at the center of Cameron land. So if the Camerons really were responsible for stealing the cattle, then it would make sense for them to drive them as far inland as possible—although Payton had doubted it. But how could Ross know where the cattle were hidden? I needed to find out more; I had to take this risk.

"The stone cottage. That's why you punched me to the ground that time, right? Did you think I had something to do with the cattle thefts? Tell me, what exactly were you doing so far away from your clan borders?"

Ross flinched, straightened his back, and waved an angry finger in my face.

"None of your business! I've made a mistake trying to help you!"

He yanked me to my feet, grabbed me by the back of my neck, and in that same manner pushed and steered me toward the village. I kept trying to get at *my* dagger, but it was useless. My skirts were too long and in the way.

"You had no good reason to be there, right?" I asked through gritted teeth.

"Yes, I did," Ross replied listlessly, and I knew that whatever feelings he might still have for me didn't matter now.

"Right! So you were there looking for approval from your brothers. Am I wrong? You allowed them to use you!" It was a shot in the dark, but considering everything I knew about him, this was the only possible explanation.

"Shut your mouth!"

My knees gave way under his iron grip.

"I don't allow anyone to use me! But once Duncan is made the new clan chief, I won't have to herd sheep or castrate bulls ever again. A life of comfort! No more going hungry and going without!"

"Why would Duncan be made clan chief? The Stuarts already have a laird: It's Cathal," I pointed out, just in case he had overlooked this minor detail.

Ross dismissed me with a contemptuous laugh, and his eyes narrowed to slits as he countered my argument. "And what a laird he is! A laird who allows almost half of his cattle herds to disappear in the space of only a few months. One who has proven himself incapable of stopping the attacks. I ask you, what kind of a clan chief is that? His men will turn their backs on him once Duncan brings back the missing herds and finds the Camerons guilty of cattle theft. Your testimony this morning is going to prove that."

"But it wasn't the Camerons, now, was it? We were just part of a bigger plan!"

"Who else would it be if not the Camerons?" he snapped.

"You! That's what you were doing when I fell into your hands. You weren't chasing cattle thieves. You *are* the cattle thieves!"

"Cathal would never believe it. We have spent many a night drinking together, only to learn about new raids the next morning. It couldn't have been us," he explained, very sure of himself, but I knew the truth because I had pulled it from Fingal's bleeding chest.

"Mercenaries!" I cried.

The word floated like a lit fuse in the air between us. We both knew of the imminent blast, but neither one of us had the power to stop it. I saw in his eyes that I had gambled and lost.

Still half crouching under his iron grip, I lunged back with all of my strength, turned, landed on my palms and knees, and scrambled to my feet. I managed to take exactly one step before he caught up with me and grabbed me by the collar. But I got away with another quick spin. I was sprinting back toward the castle, but there was no other way. I ran as fast as I could, with Ross immediately behind me.

I don't know if I ever stood a chance of outrunning him, or if it was my destiny all along to trip and stumble right in this spot. At any rate, my foot caught on a rock. It was a bad fall, and it squeezed all the air from my lungs. I thought my rib cage would burst under the impact. My hands were dirty and scraped, and I was bleeding from the elbow.

My eyes caught sight of something shiny in the grass in front of me. The early-morning light led the way: All I had to do was reach out.

When I was yanked up from the ground, I shut my eyes tightly in anticipation of a violent punch to my face.

"You? What are you doing here?" Ross asked angrily, obviously standing several yards behind me and talking to someone else. I turned around and froze.

"I will not allow any harm to come to Cathal."

I heard the sound of rolling thunder.

"Go back to your bedchamber, woman, and leave me alone!" Ross bellowed, and his bitterness and resentment turned his skin the same bright red as his hair. Nathaira was not the least bit impressed. She looked me up and down, and I could see the contempt in her eyes.

"So I see it takes a Cameron to spot the enemy from within," she stated matter-of-factly before turning her stony eyes back to Ross. The two circled each other, sizing each other up. I had seen that expression on Nathaira's face before—in Delaware, when she had tried to kill me. And, even though her hatred was not aimed at me this time, I held on tighter to that dagger I had found in the grass.

"I will say this only one more time before I forget myself and raise my hand against a defenseless woman," Ross warned her, coming closer. "Go! Away!"

The wind was picking up, and a flash of lightning tore across the sky.

Nathaira spat in his direction. "I have not given up everything in my life just to have my plans thwarted by the likes of you!"

"You can't stop Duncan. He has already rounded up all the men he needs for taking power."

Ross seemed confident and very sure of himself when he reached for my arm.

The wind tore at my clothes, and I shrunk back in panic, clutching the knife tighter.

"You dim-witted toad! You are messing with the wrong person." Nathaira laughed, raising her arms. "I *know* what I'm doing. Traitooor!"

With all her strength, she pushed Ross toward me, and a blinding flash of lightning crashed into the ground.

I threw up my arms in horror, raising the dagger in the same instant that my vision caught up with me.

Everything went black, and I started screaming.

Pain spread like wildfire through my arm all the way to my fingertips, which were completely numb. I gasped for air. The smell of copper filled my nose and mouth, making me sick to my stomach. Then slowly, as feeling returned to my fingers, I opened my eyes and stared down at my hands. Blood, hot and slimy, gushed onto the dagger—and onto me. I clutched the knife in my hand. I had thrust it in so deep that my fist touched the man's lifeless chest, and I could tell that the heart beneath my fingers had stopped beating. A single word flashed through my addled brain: betrayal.

I lifted my head and looked into his eyes. A tear, hot like melting metal, burned its way down my cheek and fell, unhindered, onto the blood-soaked earth.

Slowly, as if guided by an invisible hand, I pulled the dagger from his chest, unable to take my eyes off his face. Why, Ross? Why? The blood on his lips was his silent response to my sorrowful cry.

"I loved you once!" His words still echoed through my mind.

"No! Ross!" I shrieked.

My entire body shook. I had caused his death. My terrifying vision had come true! But, even though there was blood on my hands, it wasn't my fault. It wasn't my fault! It was hers! Nathaira had guided the *sgian dhu* with her mind! All I had done was respond, react, defend myself, protect myself! She had done exactly what Ross had told me in the forest: She had used the moment of surprise to her advantage.

I got up, holding the blood-smeared dagger as far away from me as possible. At that moment I noticed Nathaira calling for help.

I was completely rattled. It was impossible for Nathaira Stuart to be scared of me, so why would she . . . ?

Slowly, I turned around and noticed the shocked faces of the guardsmen up by the battlements. I knew exactly what they were thinking.

The prisoner—a Cameron—had killed one of theirs!

"Run," Nathaira whispered, and I stared at her in befuddlement.

"Run," she repeated. "Today I am letting you go, but this is far from over!"

I shook my head because I knew what was about to happen. I knew about the avalanche of events that had just been set off—set off by me.

This wasn't the end. This was the beginning of the end.

Chapter 30

Cemetery by Auld a´chruinn, Present-Day November

The days of fall were colder and rainier than they had been in previous years, and the trees had already lost most of their leaves. As fast and unrelentingly as the leaves were losing color and floating to the ground, Payton's strengths were also fading. Luckily, the days where he would throw up anything he ate were behind him. But only because he had stopped eating altogether. Instead, he would now bleed from the nose every time he sat up or moved in any other way. His skin was sallow, and his eyes were glassy with delirium.

Still, he smiled every time a new memory flooded into this mind. A memory of Sam. It didn't surprise him how hard he had fallen for her from the first moment on—because she was his fate, his destiny.

Sean, on the other hand, seemed to only have very faint memories of Sam. He sincerely hoped that his weren't just figments of his imagination, created in his mind only because he so desperately wanted to find her.

So many days had passed and she hadn't returned yet. Was that even possible? Would she be able to come back? Roy hadn't found a way to help Sam, either. The memorial stone wasn't doing anything mysterious, nor was there any other hint as to Sam's disappearance. Which was why Roy, the great scholar, had returned home to Aviemore empty-handed. But he gave his word to go through his records once more with a fine-toothed comb. He promised to be in touch should he think of anything else.

Payton didn't take any of this in. He just leaned against the Five Sisters stone and found his escape in his memories.

Nonetheless, he did know that time was running out in the same way that the leaves around him were falling mercilessly.

Chapter 31

Castle Burragh, November 1740

"How could you allow this to happen?"

Payton's angry voice resounded throughout the castle. He ran his fingers through his hair, anxiously pacing back and forth. "Don't you know what they're going to do to her?"

"Calm down, Payton!" his father said. "I had no right to keep her here. I tried, I really did, but Dougal insisted. He was entitled to keep the girl. What could I possibly have done?"

"You could have told them to go to hell!"

"Enough!"

Fingal seemed to struggle with a guilty conscience for letting Samantha go. But at the same time, he felt no need to justify his actions before his son.

"I did what I could. Blair is at Galthair, too. He would not allow anything bad to happen to Samantha. I've instructed him to request that she be treated kindly. Also, as soon as my health allows, I will personally travel to Galthair and talk with Cathal. He's our ally, and he will not refuse my request to leave the girl to my care."

Payton was unconvinced. If only he had gone to see her the previous day, he could have noticed Sam's disappearance and been able to follow her.

"That won't do, Father! I can't wait that long. I will go myself and make sure she's all right," he declared.

"No, you will not! This girl is a sore subject, and you will stay out of it. I assure you that I'm the last person who would want anything bad to happen to Samantha, but I cannot risk a rift with Cathal Stuart and his entire clan. I will wait for an opportune moment and then make my request. Cathal has different issues to worry about right now. Don't fret. Everything will be just fine."

Payton stared at his father in disbelief, but Fingal wouldn't budge from his stance.

"The girl is smart and has her wits about her. She can well take care of herself."

Payton snorted. His concern for Sam drove him to pace up and down nervously. His palms—never sweaty during battle—were clammy now, and he felt the overwhelming urge to punch something.

"Go to the Great Hall and calm yourself. I will follow in a moment and discuss my further plans with you. I could do with a mug of beer."

With that, the matter was obviously settled for Fingal, and the discussion was over.

Payton briefly considered disobeying his father and making his way to Galthair on his own, but in the end he came to accept that he probably wouldn't succeed in such an endeavor. They'd never even let him near Sam.

With a heavy heart, he trudged into the hall and poured himself a tankard of beer.

Kyle, who was sitting at the table with his head in his hands, didn't look up when Payton sat down beside him.

"What's the matter with you, then?" Payton grunted.

"I'm a *man,* so she shouldn't be permitted to slap me so hard that my ears ring," Kyle exclaimed. And it was clear from his loud voice that his ears really were buzzing.

"Who slapped you?"

"Anna, the cook!"

"And why?"

"Ach! Only because I was play-fighting with Lou . . . and maybe I spilled some milk," he finally admitted sheepishly.

Fingal, who was just entering, laughed at his youngest's story.

"A *man* would not be play-fighting with the dog, so I think your punishment was most fitting."

Payton felt the need to come to Kyle's defense. "Father, I beg you, a tussle with Lou is like taking on an entire pack of those four-legged demons! You have no idea how strong that dog is. It's fight training of a different kind!"

"Well, in that case I'm sure you'll be able to stop all these cattle thefts," said Fingal, turning the conversation back to what he had wanted to discuss with his sons before bringing it up with Cathal.

"Another two cows missing," he reported, slowly running his fingers through his shoulder-length white hair.

"I've been thinking about a long-term solution to this problem for quite some time now. And I would like to hear your opinion on it."

Payton nodded. He was ready to find out what his father's intentions were with Sam.

"Many years ago, we joined forces with the Stuarts, because only together are we strong enough to fight attacks from other clans. This alliance has stood the test of time. After the old Stuart passed away, Cathal and I renewed our oath and our commitment. I'm sure your brother Blair as my heir and future clan chief will be as invested in our peace with Cathal as I have always been."

Everything up to that point made sense. Payton and Kyle already knew all of this.

"Some people might say that this old fool is becoming sentimental in his old age, but all I really want is to leave my sons with a more peaceful world than I have ever known. This blood feud between the Stuarts and the Camerons has been a thorn in my side for a while. It often spells trouble for us, even though we McLeans don't contribute to it in any way. It is for this reason that I have decided to enter into an alliance with the Camerons."

Payton looked from his father to Kyle and back to his father. Setting aside the differences between the clans in such a way meant new hope for his love for Sam. On the other hand, he could easily imagine that the Stuarts wouldn't be all too happy about the idea.

"Father, how did you picture such an alliance? Do you want us to forget about the constant cattle raids and no longer ward off any attacks?" he asked. That was exactly the outcome he was hoping for.

Fingal shook his head. "No, of course not. We have to stop stealing each other's cattle and instead start protecting each other's herds. This would allow us to double the number of cattle we raise on our territories, because the borderlands would be safe."

"Sounds good. But how?"

"An alliance that is stronger than an oath!"

Fingal looked into his sons' expectant faces. "A marital alliance. I have already talked with Blair—although he didn't seem too excited about my suggestion."

Kyle chuckled behind his tankard of beer. "And I'm sure Nathaira Stuart won't be in favor of that idea, either."

Fingal nodded. "Yes, you might be right, but since when do we allow women to have a say in such important decisions? No, Blair will do what is asked of him. He knows where his duties to his clan lie."

"Father, if Blair should refuse to marry a Cameron, then I don't mind doing it," Kyle offered generously, kicking his brother under the table.

"You?" Payton laughed because he knew perfectly well what Kyle meant with his kick.

"Yes, me! Did you take a good look at those Cameron women? Each prettier than the next. I wouldn't say no to that!"

He kept teasing Payton with a conspiratorial wink, and Fingal—who was completely oblivious to it—slapped his thigh, laughing.

"Oh, I see, so that's the way the wind blows."

They were interrupted when the door opened, and everyone's head turned in the direction of the new arrivals.

In her new—albeit not yet official—status as Blair's bride-to-be, Nathaira had joined her soon-to-be husband and her brother Cathal, entering the Great Hall behind them. It hadn't taken much for Blair to agree to take her hand in marriage, and all that was left to do was to ask the old laird for his blessing. While Cathal wanted to take care of this as soon as possible, it was a different issue that had brought them here today.

Fingal rose to welcome the visitors. Only Cathal took a seat, while Nathaira preferred to remain standing by Blair's side.

"Cathal, *ciamar a tha thu?*" Fingal asked.

"I am not well. There have been more raids. This time one of my shepherds was killed," Cathal said angrily.

Nathaira's instincts told her that Ross's death had affected her brother deeply. He really had no idea that the dirty little traitor had been plotting against him—together with his bastard half brothers, Dougal and Duncan.

"I can't tolerate these thefts any longer. Tonight I am going to the Camerons. We will see whether they have our cattle standing in their stable."

Cathal had to assume as much now that the prisoner had escaped without submitting herself to their questions. He believed she had killed Ross because he'd witnessed her escape and tried to stop her. Even the most loyal of his men now demanded retaliation. Cathal would need to prove to those men that he was prepared to stand up and fight for his clan before they would stand shoulder to shoulder with him again. This was the reason Nathaira hadn't come clean with him, even if it meant that Duncan and Dougal were getting away with their treacherous plan for now. But now that Ross was dead, she had no way of proving what she had found out.

"Aye, I understand, but unfortunately you will need to forego our support this time," Fingal explained in a firm and steady voice.

"Athair!" Blair interjected in stunned disbelief. "Father, what are you talking about? Of course we will lend our support to our friends and allies."

"No, we will not!" Fingal thundered.

"Father, you can't be serious! I will no longer bow to your orders! Cathal needs our help!"

Nathaira was irritated at Fingal's rejection. It didn't matter that Blair was expressing his support and taking their side: The stubborn old laird was still the one holding all the strings.

"Fingal, for everything that is sacred! You cannot refuse your support! We both swore an oath in blood!" Cathal said vehemently.

The old clan chief of the McLeans rose slowly, steadying himself on the table, and spoke with more resolve than Nathaira would have given him credit for. "Cathal, *mo charaid,* I understand why you're angry, but there are other ways than direct confrontation. At my age, all one desires is to safeguard and preserve one's legacy. I will not be the cause of an uprising on my land, nor am I willing to lose good strong men in battle or submit my people to random acts of revenge. No, this is a path we will never walk again. An alliance is the only way to bring you and us long-lasting peace."

The men glared at Fingal in silence. Nobody uttered a word. Nathaira wished for the old fool to be struck down by lightning. Unable to restrain herself, she went for him.

"You wretched old coward! Just because you don't have the balls anymore. Our entire clan will refuse to follow Cathal if he cannot ensure their safety!"

She planted herself in front of Fingal, glaring at him furiously, when suddenly Kyle grabbed her by the arm, yanked her away from his father, and slapped her across the face.

"How dare you, woman! Don't meddle with men's business," he snarled, pushing her toward the exit.

He also gave Blair a reproachful look. "Maybe you should choose a Cameron for a wife, because you'll have nothing but trouble with this one!"

Blair's impulsive attempt at defending himself ended with him, Kyle, and Payton in a heated scuffle. It was only when Fingal's fist came down hard on the table that the brothers came to their senses.

"*Seas!* Stop this at once!"

Nathaira noticed the warning glare that Fingal shot her before he continued. "Cathal, take your sister and go! You know my response. As for you, Blair, you will stay here. I have a few things to discuss with you in my study!" With that, he left the hall, and Nathaira stared after him with fury in her eyes.

"Calm down, milady!" Payton tried to defuse the situation, but Nathaira wouldn't allow herself to be put in her place by him.

"Blair, what does Kyle mean when he says to choose a Cameron? You are going to marry me, you hear? You promised when we . . . you know!"

"Yes, I know! There's nothing for you to be upset about!" Blair reassured her, running his hands over his face.

"You idiot! How can you put this *nighean na galladh* above your own clan?" Kyle yelled when Blair turned back to Nathaira to comfort her.

"Nobody—and especially not an almost-child like you—calls my sister the daughter of a dog! Get the hell away from me before I forget myself!" Cathal responded to this insult through gritted teeth, swinging his fist in Kyle's direction.

"All I'm saying is that if I were clan chieftain, I would realize how important a marital union with the Camerons could be for my clan. I would think with my brain instead of my pecker!"

At the very last second Kyle fled from the hall—because Blair really looked about to go for his youngest brother's throat.

"Blair, you are going to be clan chieftain soon. I'm calling for your help. Otherwise, I, too, will deprive you of my support and protection." Cathal's words echoed menacingly through the Great Hall.

"Of course, *mo charaid.* You can count on me. Sean, Payton, and I will accompany you," Nathaira's meek groom-to-be replied to his bride's brother, and pressed a kiss on Nathaira's cheek before following Fingal to his chambers. Nathaira had already seen that while he shied away from confrontation, he certainly wouldn't risk either Cathal's friendship or her affection, not even for his own father.

Tonight, Cathal would be able to prove that he and only he was laird, and that nobody else would take his place. He would ensure peace once and for all.

She knew where the stolen cattle were being kept. She just needed to pretend she had learned it from a Cameron. And once the cows were back, those vile bastard twins wouldn't be able to lift a finger without giving themselves away as active participants in an elaborate plot. Not that she planned to let them get away with it. As soon as Cathal's position within the clan was secured, she would make sure Duncan and Dougal would never again rise up against her brother. Maybe she could employ the services of some mercenaries, she pondered. The thought made her smile.

Full of anticipation, she stormed from the Great Hall, right by her brother's side. Cathal was livid and would call on his men now. Blood would be shed tonight.

It was a night that would change everything, of that she was sure.

Chapter 32

Hysterical. I was completely hysterical! My lungs wouldn't work the way they normally did: I was gasping horribly for breath but felt like I was choking on air at the same time. That coppery taste in my mouth was just a figment of my imagination, I knew that much, but the blood on my hands and my clothes was not. It was real.

I was gagging. There was the sharp, acidic taste of bile in my mouth, and I almost welcomed its bitterness because it was better than tasting actual blood.

Right now I was crouching in a crevice somewhere in the rock, hiding from the world because my legs refused to function. In reality, I couldn't afford to take a break. The guards were for sure after me. But the realization of what I had done was so shocking, so distressing, that I'd found it hard enough to get even this far.

And so I was huddling in my cold, hard corner, trying to make myself small so anyone potentially following wouldn't spot me. I was also trying to make sense of what had happened.

A long time ago, Payton had told me that the death of a shepherd had been the last drop. A shepherd! This whole time, even after arriving in eighteenth-century Scotland, I had always assumed that the shepherd was killed during one of the cattle raids. But that wasn't what happened!

I had killed Ross, the shepherd. Even though it wasn't my own doing, the guards had witnessed the whole thing and assumed that I had acted on my own accord. Which was the last drop in making the cup of rising hatred against the Camerons run over. It forced Cathal's hand and made him take his revenge—a bloody revenge resulting in a massacre that brought that awful curse on everyone involved, including Payton, the man I loved.

Again my stomach convulsed, and I held my breath to suppress the urge to throw up.

It was impossible! I could not be the cause of all of this—I didn't even belong here! Or did I?

After all, my vision in Roy's kitchen had predicted exactly what I was going to do, or rather what I would do in this past. So was I predestined to be here? In the past? Perhaps destiny and fate really did exist. Truth be told, it shouldn't surprise me after everything I had experienced. Was everything happening because I was here (and really shouldn't be), or was I here because everything was predestined anyway? What if everything I had ever done in my life had led me to this exact place today? Led me to holding the dagger destined to kill Ross?

This wasn't helping! So, if *I* was the cause of this awful, awful day from the get-go, then it was also within *my* powers to allow for Vanora's curse to happen—or not—wasn't it?

This whole time I had tried to blend in and not get involved, but the result was that I was now responsible for everything that would ever happen. Me! How could I ever live with myself? How could I look Payton in the eye again?

Strictly speaking, *I* was Payton's curse! I was responsible for what was about to happen this coming night. I was responsible for Vanora's curse.

No longer able to ignore this overwhelming nausea, I threw up all over the fern growing next to me by the crevice. It grossed me out, and I wiped my mouth and stepped out into the open. My arms and legs were shaking, and the bright daylight hurt my eyes. I spat on the ground and staggered a few steps forward.

"Friggity shit!" I mumbled, feeling better immediately. "Crap, crap, crap!"

Oh yes, using foul language definitely helped.

"You can all kiss my ass! I'm done playing your goddamn shitty game!" I hollered, pulling Payton's dagger from its hiding place on my upper thigh.

Destiny was trying to screw me over! *Face your destiny?* Bah! It was high time to show destiny the middle finger and get on with making my own decisions!

I looked around and tried to figure out my alternatives.

I couldn't go back to the Stuarts, because they would throw me in the dungeon without batting an eyelid. There I would probably rot for eternity, and nobody would ever believe a single word I said.

Back to Payton? Not a great idea, either, because the risk was too great of falling into the hands of the Stuarts, who were just thirsting for revenge.

That left only one other possibility: I had to somehow make it to Cameron territory to stop the massacre and the curse from happening. And if that meant that Payton in the present day wouldn't stare death in the eye because he would have been dead for several hundred years—well, then so be it! This would be my attempt at achieving forgiveness.

I turned in the direction toward where I expected to find Castle Coulin, and I started walking.

Vanora stood by the battlements atop Castle Coulin, her gaze fixed on the horizon. An angry wind lashed at her face, spreading a sense of foreboding and whispering the future into her ear.

And Vanora listened. She had always listened to the voice of the wind, and throughout her life she'd learned to trust it. Today was the day she had long ago seen in one of her visions, the day when they would meet again. A smile spread over her face. Today she would see her daughter—for the first time since Grant Stuart had cast her out of Castle Galthair after she had given birth to the child. She pushed her memories back into the recesses of her mind and turned back to the voice of the wind.

A girl runs, fights, cries . . .
as, within her, guilt and innocence unite.

Vanora heaved a deep sigh and closed her eyes. The fate of this unknown girl was her fate, too. They both carried the burden of having seen the future, and yet they seemed unable to use that insight.

Vanora raised her arms and with her hands directed the wind, making it turn so it was in the unknown girl's back, driving her, supporting her, instead of blocking her way. She had to make haste, or else it would all be for naught.

It was in this girl's hands alone to seal everyone's fate and complete the circle. Only then would love triumph over hatred.

The Highlands, Vanora's self-chosen prison, had become her home over all these years, her exile: a substitute for the family she had been denied.

Yes, today hatred would win. But hope would live on in Muireall Cameron, a child of love.

Vanora turned around, ignoring the beauty of the mountains around her, and focused on fulfilling her task.

Muireall Cameron had to live. She would make sure of that, for she carried within her the roots of love itself.

"Cuimhnich air na daoine o'n d'thanig thu, Muireall," she whispered into the wind, asking Muireall to remember those from whom she was descended.

Kyle, who had run from the Great Hall after that heated argument, had regained his composure in the meantime, but the cacophony roaring from his father's chambers and echoing through the castle worried him greatly. He had never seen Blair lose his temper like that, which was why he returned to the hall to find out what Payton and Sean thought of the whole sorry affair. To whom were they more loyal? Their father, who was still the laird, or Blair, to whom they had also sworn their oath of allegiance?

"Don't sit here like you have nothing better to do! Get yourselves ready—we'll leave with Cathal in an hour!" Blair hollered, angrily traversing the hall and making a beeline for his youngest brother. Kyle couldn't get out of the way in time.

"And as for you, get lost!" Blair barked, shoving him aside.

"Is Kyle not coming with us?" Sean asked. He was just returning from his early-morning weapons test and had missed the dispute entirely.

Kyle noticed the scornful look in Blair's eyes when the latter replied, "No, we have no use for insolent children!"

With that, Blair hurried out into the courtyard, and Kyle rose, feeling irritated. He returned to the table, where Sean was in the process of emptying the tankard of beer he'd left behind.

"What do we do now?" he asked.

He was met by blank faces. Payton was visibly worried about Samantha, and Sean just shrugged in resignation.

"I will ride with Blair," Payton finally decided, running his fingers through his hair. "I need to speak with Cathal about Sam as soon as possible. Father won't be in good standing with him for a while, but he might listen to me if I ride with him."

"I'm coming, too. For one, because Blair ordered us to; and for another, because someone has to try to smooth things out between him and Father. He will listen to me if he knows that we trust his judgment," Sean said.

"And what about me? What should I do? Do I really stay here?" Kyle asked in disbelief.

His brothers nodded in unison, and Sean placed a hand on his shoulder.

"You need to learn to hold your tongue, for you have sworn your allegiance to him. You should try to put this dispute to rest by the time we get back. I heard that all he wanted was to inform Father of his engagement to Nathaira. You need to come to terms with your future sister-in-law."

With that, Sean got up and left Kyle alone with Payton to ready himself for the upcoming conflict with the Cameron clan.

"He must be out of his mind! And so is Blair if he is intent on marrying that wretched woman!" Kyle grumbled.

"Listen, Kyle, even if Blair has no use for you right now, there is something important you could do for me."

Payton got up and started pacing. "I will try to talk with Cathal, but I really would feel better if I knew that Sam was safe. Could you ride to Castle Galthair and keep an eye on her?"

Kyle was less than amused to obey Blair's orders and stay at home like a naughty child while his brothers were allowed to go to war. But he realized how important it was for Payton to know that the girl was well taken care of. And so he caved in, even though he had no intention of making nice with Nathaira.

"Aye, Payton. I will take care of Sam."

Payton thanked him with a great sigh of relief, and then hurried to get ready for the ride ahead.

Kyle stayed behind by himself, raising his tankard of beer to his lips and snorting in disappointment when he saw that all that was left of it was the frothy foam. Not wanting to cross paths with Blair again, he decided to allow himself another drink before getting his horse ready. He grinned as he thought back to Payton's baffled face earlier when he, Kyle, had declared that he would marry a Cameron. There was no doubt in his mind that Payton, once all of this was over, would receive their father's blessing, and that there would be a nice little wedding ceremony for them all to enjoy.

Kyle had almost finished his fresh draft of beer, when Payton stuck a frenzied head through the door one more time. He looked relieved.

"Oh good, I thought you'd already left. I just remembered something important. This morning, when I went to get Sam for breakfast, I had a package for her on me. It is now in her bedchamber, and it is very important to me that she get it. Could you take it with you?"

Kyle smirked. "A token of your love?"

"Oh, shut up. Just do it, all right?"

"Of course, Brother. And now go—the others are leaving," he said as he heard hoofbeats out in the castle yard.

"Thank you, Kyle," Payton mumbled. It was obviously important to him to know that Sam was safe and protected.

"My life for you, my brother," Kyle replied with the motto they had been using since they were children. They'd said it whenever they pulled a prank on their older brothers or shared a secret.

When Kyle entered the bedchamber that Samantha had been using for the last few days, he immediately spotted the small package Payton had mentioned. It was lying on the table by the bed. It was soft, and wrapped in pale leather and held together by a leather band. He was tempted to lift a corner of the wrapping, but then he thought better of it. The gift was Samantha's and none of his business. He would merely pass it on to her, whatever it might be. Stuffing it into his *sporran* caused a distinct bulge, but he just about managed to close it.

Then he turned around and smiled as his eyes fell on the many hunting trophies on the wall. Sean had slain most of those beasts when he was younger, with only a single one killed by Kyle himself. Kyle's trophy was the tiniest pair of antlers, and back in the day it had caused hysterical laughing fits in his older brothers. Even today he found it hard to stop grinning when he compared it to the rest of the trophies, but his father and Payton had insisted that it was just as nice to look at as the rest, and that it absolutely deserved its special place on the wall—a special place in the bedchamber that was reserved for special guests.

He was somewhat surprised that his father would offer this room to a prisoner. Fingal must have been mulling over an allegiance with the Camerons for a good while, perhaps while they were still traveling. His eyes wandered, and he wondered what kind of room the Stuarts had offered Sam. He didn't think it likely that she would sleep in a fancy bed like this.

Something caught his eye. What was that? He stepped closer and folded back the bed covers, surprised to find a note. He unfolded it.

Beloved Payton,

If you're holding this note, then I'm probably no longer here. But I will always be with you—and, yes, waiting for you. Our time together isn't over; our love for each other isn't over. Not by a long shot! I'm going to save you in the same way that I will now try to stop you from blaming yourself for everything. You need to understand that you could not have stopped the massacre. Please don't try to find an explanation. There isn't one.

If you want to blame someone, then please blame me. I knew what would happen and I still couldn't stop it, couldn't warn you.

Perhaps you still experience some feeling when you're reading this. If so, then I beg of you: Please don't hate me! Forgive me for not having stopped it.

Hold on to the feeling of bliss you had with me, because for an endlessly long time it will be the last thing you're allowed to feel. Yes, I know about the curse—and I didn't stop it, didn't find the courage to challenge fate. How could I? I just couldn't risk never meeting you. I couldn't bear the thought of living a life without ever knowing that you exist, without ever feeling your love. And with the same selfishness with which I'm allowing everything else to happen, I'm now asking for your forgiveness. I ask you to love me beyond all time. Don't forget about me when your heart turns to stone and your soul is dragged into darkness.

Payton, mo luaidh, *I'm going to save you. And then I will be forever by your side.*

Sam

Kyle's fingers trembled as he read the letter over and over, trying to make sense of it.

"She's got the gift of second sight. She sees things. She says the Fates have sent her here to save my life," he said, remembering Payton's words. His brother had trusted her, even when she had foretold disaster. *"Aye, I believe her."*

Payton had said this without a shadow of a doubt in his voice. Which was why he, too, had to trust her and not hesitate. Payton had to read these few lines, and fast.

As Kyle pushed the note into his fur pouch, the skin on his arms prickled. Sam had written about a massacre. If she told the truth, he could not stand idly by as his brothers rushed headlong to their doom—or, as she referred to it, a curse. He had to stop it.

Only when he reached the stables did he realize he was still carrying the package for Sam in his *sporran.* He wouldn't see her at Galthair but would instead follow his brothers as quickly as he could. He would therefore just return the package to Payton. No sooner had he stuffed everything into his saddlebags and reached for his weapons than the stable boy handed him the reins. With one final glance up to the darkening, cloud-heavy sky, Kyle drove his horse out of the gate.

Chapter 33

My foot was bleeding. I had stepped on some sharp wooden stick, which had pierced the sole of my flimsy sandals. Every step I took was painful, and I almost didn't have the strength to keep going. I had been hiking since the morning and didn't expect the road to Castle Coulin to be that long. Night had fallen, and I needed to be careful not to lose my way. I caught a glimpse of Castle Coulin after I had finally reached the mountaintop—from which I was now descending again. *Just don't lose it now that you're in the home stretch,* I kept reminding myself.

I pressed my hand against my side, but it didn't help. My body ached all over, and I needed a quick break.

"Goddamn Highlands!" I wailed, slapping my cheek when I felt yet another midge bite. Those tiny, wretched flies had been following me all day, and I felt as though I must be covered in hundreds of bites.

I was so close to Coulin that I didn't want to give up now, and so I put one foot in front of the other, trying to ignore the pain, the itchiness from the midge bites, and my physical exhaustion, just so I would get there in time.

A small noise nearby made me spin around and whip out the dagger.

"Shit!" I whispered, remembering the bandits. I ducked and tried to be perfectly still while anxiously scanning my surroundings. In this darkness everything looked like a bush or rock to me.

Then I finally made sense of a black shape nearby and hunkered down even lower. I suppressed another cussword, even though I had several good ones lined up on the tip of my tongue. Cautiously, I glanced around. I was sure that there had to be someone—a person—because a fully saddled horse wouldn't be wandering around the Highlands all by itself. But that was exactly what it looked like: The horse was alone, roaming here and there and just chewing on grass.

I watched it for a while longer to make sure that I wouldn't run into its owner, wherever he or she might be. But I was in a hurry, and a horse suited me and my aching foot just fine—even though I had no idea how I would even get up on it.

I stood up and started quietly speaking to it. When it turned its head in my direction, I carefully held out the palm of my hand. It didn't seem shy at all and came closer while I blabbered on and on, hoping to gain its trust. Eventually I was able to run my hand slowly down its neck, trying to find the reins.

Startled, I withdrew my hand when I felt something wet and sticky underneath my fingers. I couldn't see it in the darkness, but I knew right away that it was blood. My hands were covered in blood, and I recoiled, trying to fight my panic.

Dammit! I couldn't lose my cool now. That horse was my ticket out of here, and I wiped the blood from my fingers in disgust before firmly and determinedly reaching for the pommel. In doing that, my hand accidentally grazed the embroidery on the saddle. I could just about make it out in the fading light: Highland thistles, all lined up in a row around the seat, all the way down to the saddlebags.

"No," I stammered in terrified disbelief, shaking my head and denying the obvious truth. "No, please, don't let it be true," I begged, running my hand over the enormous bloodstain.

It couldn't be! Again I saw the Scotch thistles before me and remembered how Kyle had ridden off into the sunset in this very saddle, laughing. I needed to be sure. In a frenzy, I tore open the saddlebags, rummaging through them in search of some kind of proof. Was this really Kyle's horse? Was this Kyle's blood on my hands?

There had to be a different explanation. But deep in my heart I knew that Kyle's destiny had already been fulfilled. And all because I hadn't had the courage to warn him.

Desperately, I rifled through the bags. Through my veil of tears, I barely saw what I was pulling out: a long leather band, a fishing line plus hook, a package wrapped in soft leather, and a piece of paper. There was nothing that I could specifically ascribe to Kyle, and so I unfolded the piece of paper and froze. The note slipped from my numb fingers, and I watched it, shocked to the very core of my being, as it slowly drifted to the ground.

How did the letter I had left behind for Payton get into Kyle's saddlebags? And what was Kyle doing here, anyway?

Payton's words popped up painfully in my memory. Words of explanation and apology for what he had done—what he would do—this very night:

~

"And surely everything would have turned out differently if Kyle hadn't died! He was the youngest of the alliance. He wasn't supposed to be there at all that night, but he rode after the others, secretly following them."

~

He was following the others! Why?

The letter rose from the ground, spun around, and rose higher and higher until it was swallowed by the darkness, as if the wind wanted to carry my words up into the sky so everyone would know of my guilt and shame. Had Kyle followed his brothers because of me?

"No! Oh God, please . . . no!"

I wept uncontrollably. I had been so sure that I didn't have a choice, but now the feelings of guilt overpowered me. As I recalled Payton's words, they were like a knife thrust into my heart:

~

"Cathal had spotted him in the distance and immediately sent someone back to take Kyle home. But it was already too late. Kyle had

been attacked—stabbed from behind with a short dagger. He had drowned in his own blood.

That cowardly and deceitful attack changed everything. Now everyone called for revenge. Kyle had been one of them, and everyone wanted to avenge his death. Within a few minutes, they had charged the enemy's castle. It was the middle of the night, and most of the inhabitants were asleep."

And *I* was the only one who knew that it wasn't the Camerons who had killed Kyle! Nathaira Stuart had invented the ambush to hide her own treacherous act!

"If Kyle hadn't died that night, the McLeans wouldn't have joined our fight. They would never have taken part in the massacre of the Camerons without a personal reason to join in. I killed Kyle for us!" Nathaira had admitted to Cathal back at the motel, shortly before dying herself.

When she told this story back in present-day Delaware, I had felt the pain and anger about this betrayal very deeply. But now that I was living through it all myself, experiencing it firsthand—being responsible for it, on top of it all—I crumpled to the ground in a pathetic, helpless heap and sobbed uncontrollably. Dark storm clouds shifted, covering the moon and throwing the world into a black abyss. A blinding streak of lightning twitched across the night sky and burned itself into the darkness.

"Murderers! Cowards! They're going to pay for this!" the men roared.

"Damn them all to hell!"

"Their castle must burn!"

The voices screamed for revenge, and then the one female in their midst pulled her sword and reared her handsome black stallion. "Let us put an end to this feud once and for all! Nobody will dare attack us ever again! Death! Death to the Camerons!"

She dug her heels hard into her horse's flanks, breaking into a gallop toward the enemy's castle. Her raven hair blew behind her like a fateful beacon of warning, beckoning the men to follow her. Payton looked over to his oldest brother, the man he had sworn an oath of allegiance to, the man whose orders he would follow no matter what.

The news of Kyle's murder had hit Blair hard. The last words he had spoken to the boy had been in anger, and Payton knew that Blair regretted this deeply. Hatred burned in Blair's eyes when he pulled his sword and commanded, "Revenge for our brother!"

Nobody stayed behind. Everyone scrambled for their weapons—not a single man hesitated. They all wanted to repay murder with murder.

Payton, too, wanted to numb this boiling pain with blood. He wanted to kill the person who had done this with his own two hands, and so he turned and raced his horse toward the castle, pulling his broadsword in full gallop.

It hadn't taken them long to storm the poorly defended parapet and open the castle gates from within. Now they hacked and slashed their way into the heart of the castle keep, with the Camerons taken by complete surprise and falling easy victims to their burning, bloodthirsty hatred. Men, women, and children perished under the angry blades of their attackers.

Payton's grief and raging pain guided his hand, and over and over made him raise his sword against an onslaught of enemy warriors.

By his side was the youngest of the alliance: Cathal's little brother, Kenzie, whose very first battle this was. Blinded by his thirst for revenge, he was charging an enemy much superior in experience and strength, and Payton had no choice but to cover the young hothead's back.

He followed him into the castle keep, almost stumbling over the limp, lifeless body of a slain maidservant. Still behind Kenzie, he saw him charge up the stairwell and hurried after him, listening for the clinking of swords and angry shouts of men as he started climbing the tower. The winding staircase was dark, with only a faint shimmer of moonlight coming through the tiny arrow loops.

The blackness made Payton stop for a moment, mercifully numbing the bloodred noise swirling inside his head. With his chest heaving, he pressed his forehead against the cold stone wall. Tears streamed down his face as he detected the metallic scent of blood on his clothes and felt the heavy steel blade in his hand.

The image of his slain brother burned into his raging mind, and his throat felt so tight that he thought he would suffocate right here in the stairwell.

Kyle had been what they called a child of the sun. Wherever he was, there was joy. He would never have wanted all these people to die. He didn't approve of violence and had never even enjoyed hunting.

Payton stumbled on. He kept going with the sudden realization that he'd made a terrible mistake. The freezing air on the battlements awakened his numb mind. Disoriented, he spotted Kenzie facing a man who'd barely had enough time to get dressed before grabbing his weapon. Even without shoes or a vest, the man swung his axe with deadly precision.

To end this brutal massacre, Payton couldn't allow Cathal's brother to get hurt. He needed to come to Kenzie's aid, even if he had no intention of ending another life, enemy or not. For whatever was happening right now, it was terribly wrong. There was no other word for it but *murder.*

He had to bring the others to their senses if he ever wanted to redeem his mortal soul. Was it too late for that?

There was Cameron blood on his hands, and it had soaked through his shirt. A name flashed through his mind: Sam. And, as if the mere thought of his beloved conjured her image, she appeared right before his very eyes.

The wind lashed at her hair, pressing the white nightgown tightly against her body. Seeing the terror on her face, Payton instinctively stepped toward her. She held out her arms as if trying to push him away, looking over her shoulder in a frenzy. Two of Cathal's men blocked her exit and moved in with a cold and calculating precision.

Sam? Why was she here? Was she really here? Payton shook his head to get rid of the apparition—but nothing happened; she was still there. The horror in her eyes, the desperation . . .

"Tomas!" she screamed at the man with the axe. One of the warriors grabbed her arm. "Tom—"

The blow to her head made her stumble, and she broke away in Payton's direction. He was struggling to tell reality and delusion apart.

The half-dressed warrior noticed the woman and went berserk.

"Isobel!" he yelled, knocking the shield from Kenzie's hand and bringing his axe down on the boy in a blind rage.

Payton heard his heartbeat and felt the blood rush through his body. He smelled the ozone of a lightning flash that was setting the sky ablaze. He saw the firm resolve in the woman's eyes as she climbed the battlements, pressing her trembling hands against her mouth, sobbing. She would rather throw herself to her death than submit to those men—Payton was sure of it. She leaned against the wind, eyes locked with those of the man she had called Tomas. But she had no time to issue a warning cry before one of Cathal's men plunged a dagger into Tomas's back. He stumbled forward and saw the blood slowly spread on his shirt.

Payton was too far away to come to Kenzie's rescue when Tomas Cameron raised his axe in a final move. He brought it down on young Kenzie without ever taking his eyes off Isobel, his wife.

To Payton, she seemed like an angel, climbing the battlements and shining bright against the dark night sky.

"Sam!" he roared with a sudden flash of recognition. Had he really just seen her? Payton wasn't sure. He only knew one thing: She was innocent! She couldn't die!

Payton saw her sway. She staggered backward. He was paralyzed, trying to move to come to her aid, but his body wouldn't respond. He reached her too late, clutching desperately at her falling body. At the very last second, he grabbed her arm. Her scream pierced the very core of his being, and he saw the terror in her wide-open eyes—the same pair of eyes that had looked at him with such love and lust only a few hours ago. With every breath that he took, he could feel her fingers slowly slipping from his hands. He realized that he didn't have the strength to pull her back over the battlements. Little by little, she slipped closer to the abyss. From his throat rose a panicked scream as the woman lost her grip and fell to her death.

He closed his eyes so he wouldn't have to see her body hit the sharp rocks below, and instead he let himself slide back down on the floor. He was shaking. He didn't need to turn to know that both Kenzie and Tomas had not made it through this cursed night.

Something soft was touching his cheek. A strip of white linen against his skin, it had a caressing, comforting feel, like the loving touch of a mother. Carefully he released the piece of fabric from the edge of the battlement. Isobel's nightgown was embroidered with soft, delicate stars.

Without feeling anything inside, he clawed his way back to the two slain men whose glassy eyes were turned up to the sky. He closed Tomas's eyes with the flat of his hand, then pried open the man's hand and gently laid the strip of fabric across his palm. Then he crawled over to Kenzie and lifted the boy into his arms. Before climbing down the stairs, he looked around the top of the tower one last time. He, too, had died up here tonight. When he climbed down the stairwell, he had become a stranger to himself. He turned his back on this battle, the men, and revenge.

One single thought kept him going: *I need you, Sam! Save me! Forgive me, please, and save me!*

Chapter 34

Cemetery by Auld a´chruinn, Present-Day Fall

"I need you, Sam!" Payton gasped, weakly wiping the blood from the corner of his mouth. His gaze wandered over to the bare, leafless branches of the trees around him. They looked like skeletons, holding their gnarly branches out toward him. The once-colorful leaves of red and yellow and ochre were now nothing more than a carpet of black, dead leaves, burying all life beneath them.

His time was up. Every breath he took cost him energy and strength and sent shivers of excruciating pain through his aching body.

He wanted to die. He didn't want to bear this pain any longer. Only the thought of Sam kept him alive. If he could only tell her one last time how much he loved her, that her love was worth every bit of the pain he was being made to suffer, then he could close his eyes and submit his mortal soul to fate—and perhaps at long last find peace.

Peace: What a pretty word. Slowly, it spread inside him. It helped him release the memory of Sam he'd been clinging to and forced itself into his blood, finally flooding his brain.

Peace. He breathed out, watching the last brightly colored autumn leaf float down and come to a final rest on his chest.

Peace. Endlessly tired, he closed his eyes.

Chapter 35

Time and space lost all meaning. There was only this guilt that weighed heavily on me, and it alone justified my pathetic existence. Absolutely nothing had turned out the way Payton or I had expected. All my efforts of *not* meddling with the past had caused the opposite: Everything happened in exactly the same way Payton told me in his original story.

I had brought disaster upon Payton and his family. I alone had caused the death of Ross, the shepherd. I had helped Nathaira in making Cathal see the threat coming from within his own ranks. And with my letter to Payton, I'd delivered Kyle to Nathaira's blade. All of this culminated in the curse that I would now bear witness to, because the next streak of lightning flashed across the sky and bathed the Highlands before me in a bright light.

Castle Coulin stood majestically in the valley below me, and I saw the flames rising up from the tower and into the sky. The straw-thatched roof only fed the blaze, and the wind carried it on and on.

I struggled to my feet, grabbing the horse's reins and desperately holding on to them.

What had I done?

Frozen in place, I noticed a man on horseback leaving the castle at a fast gallop. Payton! I immediately recognized him, despite only a dim light coming from the fire. He rode off without turning back, his plaid blowing in the wind behind him as he drove his horse faster and faster across the plains.

Faster and faster away from me.

And then, with all my senses on overload, there was only this bright, blinding light that seemed to come from the woman standing atop the hill in front of me, her hands raised high into the night sky.

A final flash of lightning crashed down; then the wind died down, and the clouds disappeared as fast as they had gathered earlier.

Motionless, the old woman stood atop the mountain peak and looked, like me, down at the castle. It was Vanora, the woman I had seen in my visions. She was the witch of Fair Isle who was writing history this very night.

Two shapes on horseback galloped toward her: Cathal and Nathaira. Vanora stood her ground even as they came closer. She actually turned away from the approaching danger and appeared to be scanning the dark hills behind her.

Our eyes met as if there were neither darkness nor distance between us. There was nothing but her and me. She had been waiting for me. I saw that from the expression of hope and inner peace on her face, and once again she spoke to me without moving her lips.

"*Face your destiny. Remember the love you carry deep in your heart. Fear not. The blood will protect you. You are without guilt, yet you are guilty. Complete the circle.*" I heard her voice inside my head.

Frozen in horror, I watched Vanora open her arms without fear and welcome her daughter's dagger as it pierced her heart.

The high-pitched cry of agony that escaped my throat was carried away by the wind and went unheard.

No! Vanora couldn't die—not now! I needed her blood to save Payton! But the triumphant expression on Nathaira's and Cathal's faces left no doubt that Vanora was dead. With no signs of regret, they left the old woman's body where it was. And with fists raised high, they returned to what was left of Castle Coulin and its warriors.

I sank to my knees, unable to stand any longer. I had fought with all that I had. I had tried to do everything right—and still I had failed.

I stared into the night to the spot where I had seen Payton only moments ago. He was gone. The curse had been spoken, and it had damned him to a life without feeling. My letter that could have saved him was gone with the wind. My promise to save him was worthless. All because I had come too late. Vanora was dead. I had failed!

I wept, burying my face in my hands and submitting to the convulsions that almost suffocated me.

Only when strong arms lifted me up and pressed me hard against a warm chest did I find a way back to myself. The Gaelic endearments that Payton whispered into my ear; his quick, soothing pecks on my neck; and his strong, tender hands that massaged away my pain—it all created only one reaction on my part.

I looked into his eyes and saw the same feelings of worry, guilt, and despair that I was experiencing myself. I knew what he had done. I knew that he'd had a hand in murdering my ancestors, because he would confess to it so many years later.

But none of this mattered now that he was about to fess up to his murderous crimes. We had betrayed each other by doing a terrible wrong, and in the process we had damned our mortal souls to hell.

Regardless, only he could comfort me now. I put my finger on his lips to prevent him from talking. I didn't know what he had done or how he had found me. The only thing that mattered was to be near him. And with the only thing we were left with—our mutual love—we granted each other forgiveness. I got lost in his eyes when I raised my lips to his, and with a long kiss, we begged for mercy.

Payton didn't ask why I was here or demand to know what had happened. He didn't even ask how much I was to blame for the events of this fateful night. I didn't say a word. I couldn't find the courage to own up to everything.

An eternity seemed to have passed when Payton finally backed away from me.

"What is it?" I asked. He was rubbing his arm as if he'd been injured.

"My arm hurts. I think I burned myself," he said, pushing up his sleeve to take a closer look.

There was nothing there. But I quickly realized what was going on and was shocked at the speed with which the curse was gaining steam.

Payton glared at me.

"You know what is going on here, don't you. Is it what you predicted? Something is happening to me—I can feel it."

How I would have loved to tell him that he was wrong. How I would have loved to break the tension with one of Kim's flippant one-liners. But in this life I was no longer an eighteen-year-old high school student quoting her best friend. I couldn't even remember what it was like to fear nothing more than getting a D minus in history class. I deserved an F for this stunning feat I had produced here. For sure!

Instead, I told Payton, "It's a curse. Everyone who went to the Camerons tonight has been cursed."

Payton shook his head.

"We were cursed before we set out today. Hatred and battle have guided our lives. Blood feuds have been our daily bread. No curse could be worse than that."

I saw that he meant it. I could tell how much he hated himself, and I didn't know how to help him.

"You told me you would save me. Is that true?" he asked quietly, brushing my hair behind my ear.

This tender gesture made my eyes well up.

"Yes, Payton, my beloved. I swear to you that our love will break this curse, but not today. I don't belong here—I should never have come."

Guilt and shame washed over me, but Payton lifted my chin and kissed my trembling lips.

"Can you tell me what is going to happen? What kind of a curse?" he asked.

I closed my eyes and repeated the very words he had once said to me: "The worst kind. Each and every one of you is now cursed to living a life without feeling—without love, warmth, anger, or pain. Only emptiness. And you will suffer for all eternity because you are never going to die."

Payton didn't say anything for a long time. Then he pulled me close and kissed me with all the love and tenderness he was able to muster. I could tell he was trying to memorize this feeling, to commit it to memory so he could draw from it later.

"Is that why you're going to leave me?" he asked after a while. "Because I don't feel anymore?"

"I never wanted to leave you, but I really thought I could save your life." My voice broke, and I cursed myself for being so weak, for being incapable of doing anything right. "But I can't because I'm too late. Vanora is dead! Her blood would have saved you."

"The blood of the witch?" he asked.

We looked at the hilltop where Vanora had spoken her curse. Her white gown was still visible even in this darkness. Payton pulled me to my feet.

"What are you doing?" I asked as he helped me up on his horse and got up behind me. He had tied Kyle's horse to his with a long rope.

"I want to live, Sam. I want to live right by your side. Which is why I am helping you."

"You don't understand. She's dead—her blood has been spilled!" I called out as he brought us closer and closer to the hilltop.

"Listen, Sam. You just told me what's lying ahead. It all sounds like an awful fate if you ask me. So if the witch who did this to me can also save my life, then I have to give it a try! Don't you understand that I never want to stop loving you? That I'm afraid of not having feelings ever again? And that maybe I find it easier to bear if I know there is hope?"

I understood him well. I admired him for how calmly he accepted his fate, and I couldn't blame him for wanting to try. Who was I to take this hope away from him without giving it my best shot.

"All right, then, let's go!" I yelled, holding on tight so he could spur on the horse. It didn't take us long to reach the hilltop.

The old woman's body lay on the barren rock that had become her deathbed. Her face was peaceful and pale. Her wide-open eyes looked up at the stars, and her mouth was frozen in a smile. Payton steadied his horse, got off, and helped me down without saying a word. Slowly, and full of respect, we walked over to her.

Together we knelt by her side, not knowing what to do next.

I could barely take my eyes off the dagger protruding from Vanora's chest. A dark red stain had spread from the dagger and across her gown. The embroidered flowers on the fabric were soaked in blood, but they were beautiful. It almost seemed as if the white thread had been waiting to be dipped in color.

My eyes followed the red thread that was no longer a thread but a stream of blood.

The handle of Nathaira's dagger was wrapped in black leather, and it disturbed the perfection of the red-and-white pattern on Vanora's chest in a brutal, almost perverse way—as if envious of its beauty.

I suddenly felt very hot, and the world around me started spinning. I wiped the sweat from my forehead before touching the knife, trembling. The black leather was cold and cruel to the touch as I closed my fist around the handle and slowly, inch by inch, started pulling. From very far away I saw fresh blood gushing from the wound, saw how the red flowers unfolded and revealed their full beauty. When I finally held the entire knife in my hand, it was as though the sun itself had offered the flower her radiance, as if the color red had never been so perfect before. Bloodred.

The dagger dropped to the ground as the world around me spun and darkness finally swallowed me.

Birds were chirping when I woke up. My head was resting against Payton's chest, and his breath tickled my cheek. Slowly, painfully, I opened my eyes. I squinted against the bright light coming from the sun high up in the sky.

Only now did I notice that we were on his horse. My limbs felt heavy, and my whole body ached as though I had been run over by a bus. Multiple times!

"Where are we?" I croaked.

"I'm taking you to the cottage you told me about. The cottage by Loch Duich," he explained.

"The cottage?" I found it hard to follow. It would easily take two days to get to the stone cottage by Loch Duich. How long had I been out? And what had happened with Vanora?

Before I could ask Payton about it, he started talking.

"I was right," he informed me.

"What? Right about what?" I really wasn't in the mood for half-spoken sentences and guessing games.

"You are a strange girl. When you were sitting by the witch's side, you didn't seem to notice me or anything else around you. But the idea with the dagger was a good one. The blade is still covered in Vanora's blood. I wrapped it up and took it with us."

He tapped against the saddlebag before continuing. "And now I'm taking you home because I can feel the change inside me. It's getting stronger, and it's time for you to leave me."

I wanted nothing more than to speak up, to reassure him that I would never leave him. Because I didn't want to go. I didn't want to leave him during the darkest years—centuries!—of his life. But I had to, because I wouldn't be alive in two hundred seventy years. I wouldn't be able to stay by his side forever. The only thing I could hope for was to see him again in my own time—provided that Nathaira's curse hadn't killed him by then.

"I love you, Payton," I reassured him. "I always will, and if there were a way for me to stay with you, I . . ."

"Sam, *mo luaidh,* be still. You said it yourself: You don't belong here. Tomorrow at this hour we will reach the cottage, and until that moment I want to be with you. I want to feel your skin and your warmth, and to taste your kisses. I want to remember how shiny your hair is and how lovely your voice sounds. The heavens have sent you to me so that I may accept my fate. Let's not look back. Let's not waste what precious time we have left."

"But Payton, if only you knew what I've done . . ."

"No, Sam! Not another word! It doesn't matter what you or I have done. Guilt and shame and hatred cannot overshadow the only thing I am left with. I haven't been able to forget about you, not ever since I watched you by the lake," he admitted.

I swallowed my tears, fighting against the tightness in my throat that threatened to suffocate. Then his words sank in.

"You watched me?" I asked angrily. "I asked you to turn around and look away!"

Payton laughed, and the sound made my heart beat faster.

"Oh, Sam! How could I not have watched the most beautiful girl in the world bathing in the moonlight? Besides, you were huffing and puffing like an old lady, and I was worried you'd drown."

"Well, I guess that justifies everything!" I exclaimed with feigned outrage.

"Yes, love justifies everything," he said, kissing me.

We made good time on our way north. There were no obstacles blocking our way or slowing us down, only this time I wouldn't have minded a small delay. The closer we got, the more I dreaded that damn marker stone—and whatever was waiting for me on the other end. Was a way back even possible? Was Payton still alive, or would I be too late?

I found it hard to appreciate the beauty of the landscape passing us by, and it was only Payton's presence that managed to distract me from these dark, terrible thoughts. It hurt me to know how much the centuries would change him. His eyes were still open and kind, and his laughter was sincere, but the curse would take all that away from him. I savored the feeling of allowing Past Payton into my heart and no longer felt like I was betraying Future Payton. It was pretty simple, really: Payton McLean held my heart in his hands—forever and across all time.

When we made camp after night had fallen, we held each other close in the knowledge that this would be our last time. The tears I silently shed that night were my secret to keep. I was afraid of leaving Payton, because I couldn't be sure that word of his passing wouldn't be waiting for me in the future.

Couldn't I just risk it, and stay here forever?

Morning broke with a glorious sunrise. The sky was ablaze with the most vibrant colors that sprinkled the clouds in gold and sent the first warm rays of sunshine down to Earth.

"Payton, look! Isn't it amazing?" I whispered into his ear, making him squint open his eyes and follow my gaze.

Then he looked down, flicking a blade of grass from his kilt, and held out his hand.

"Yes, I guess it is," he mumbled before turning around to get the horses.

I felt terribly guilty. The curse was getting stronger. It had already taken the joy from his eyes, had made him oblivious to the beauty of the rising sun. I shivered in the sudden cold that I hadn't noticed while I was lying in his warm embrace. We rode the rest of the way in silence, and I didn't fail to notice that Payton was closing himself off more and more.

It was noon when we reached the mountaintop and saw the dark waters of Loch Duich nestled into the hollow below. The Five Sisters framed this dramatic, breathtaking panorama beautifully: The autumn landscape was vibrant with bright fall colors, plunging the mountains in copper and bronze tones and welcoming us home. Only Payton became more and more apathetic with every minute that passed.

"That's us," he said as he guided us the final yards down to the lakeshore. Now, in broad daylight and without that spooky fog that had confused me when I first arrived, everything looked very different. I could barely even comprehend why I had been so disoriented.

It was clear that the stone cottage had long been abandoned. The roof had caved in and would offer no protection from the elements; and the door was hanging crooked in its frame, flapping in the wind.

From there, my eyes wandered over the heath, searching for the spot where I had regained consciousness. The cemetery did not yet exist, but the marker stone was there, clearly visible between the rolling hills.

Payton silently helped me down from the saddle and grabbed my hand. He seemed to flinch, but the stoic expression on his face didn't give anything away.

"What now, then?" he asked.

Yeah, what now? That was a great question, because once again I was missing some kind of billboard loudly announcing the way back to the twenty-first century.

I trotted over to the stone and carefully walked around it. How exactly would this work? Even though I had experienced firsthand that time travel was possible, now that I was standing in front of this simple stone, I found it impossible to imagine how this thing would ever take me back to my real life. Slowly I held out a trembling arm, ready to pull back at any moment should anything strange happen. I ran my fingers over the cold, rough surface, and finally placed my hand on the smooth top.

Payton watched Samantha as she slowly approached the stone. Whenever he looked at her, he didn't know who or what she was—but he trusted his heart enough to know that she was the love of his life, even as his feelings were getting weaker and weaker. She was a mystery to him, and he could see that she felt guilty. Whatever it was that she blamed herself for, he didn't want to know. He wasn't sure that he was strong enough to forgive her. And so it was better to believe in the love they felt for each other and never find out why she had come into his life. For one thing was certain: She had never wanted to harm anyone.

His own mortal soul, on the other hand, was soaked in Cameron blood. Never, or so he hoped, would he have to own up to what he'd done. But such thoughts were nothing compared to the idea of having to let Sam go. As weak as that feeling was, he realized that it was fear. Still, they had no choice.

The chill spread through him. Colors lost their luster, and even Sam's smile didn't touch him as much as it had only a few hours ago. He didn't want to live in a world where her kiss meant nothing to him, only because he was damned to a life without feelings, emotions, love. No, she needed to leave him and let him walk alone into the dark.

"What are you doing?" he asked as Sam traced the inscription on the stone with her fingers.

"I'm looking for the way. This stupid stone brought me here. I don't know how it happened, but if I ever want to return home, I'd better find out."

Payton knew that only a few hours ago he had been fighting against letting Sam go with every fiber of his being. But now he didn't feel the horror and despair that had grabbed ahold of him then. Yet the faintest echo of those feelings made him now reach out and grab her hand.

"Wait," he said, because he wasn't ready to have her disappear from his life. "The dagger. You'll need the dagger."

Grateful for having found a reason to pull Sam back and over to the horses, he managed to force himself to smile.

He opened the saddlebags and unearthed the leather-wrapped dagger.

"I've got something else for you," he said hoarsely. It had been a shock to him to find the small package when he had searched Kyle's saddlebags earlier for something to drink. Kyle was dead because he had given up his own safety for him. Payton was almost glad that the curse was growing stronger and stronger, wiping out his feelings of guilt about his brother's death—along with all his other emotions.

Payton realized that his mind was wandering when Sam touched him gently on the elbow.

"Do you want me to take it or not?" she asked, pointing at the dagger.

"Sure. There, don't cut yourself. Maybe it's safer to carry it in the leather pouch."

He watched as Sam stuck the dagger into the pouch and placed it under her arm. Then he turned back to the package. Trying to keep his weakening feelings hidden, he thrust the soft, leather-bound package into her hands.

"There, it's a gift. You . . . I mean . . . I'm sure you know what to do with it," he finally managed, but when Sam smiled and slid a curious finger under the leather band to open it, he placed his hands on hers even though the excruciating pain almost made him want to pull away.

"No, *mo luaidh.* Only open it after you get home," he insisted.

"All right, fine. Although I hate being kept in suspense," Sam said, touched by his words. She placed the soft bundle in her bag. Then she brushed his lips with hers, but Payton could no longer feel it. Darkness was moving in.

"You need to go!" he said urgently.

This emptiness inside was impossible to bear! Somewhere in the recesses of his mind he knew what a kiss was, that he should feel something—so why couldn't he feel it anymore? But even the despair that was grabbing ahold of him was a shadow of its normal self. He just didn't *feel* it anymore.

"Go now! It is time!"

Sam's eyes filled with tears as he led her back to the marker stone.

"Do you remember what you did to get here?" he asked.

Sam knitted her brow. She touched the stone and squatted down.

"I wa . . . uh . . . so I bent down in front of the stone because I had dropped something and was looking for it," she explained, trying to retrace her every move. "Then I noticed the names, and I wondered if they maybe had anything to do with the legend of the five sisters."

"The legend? It's not a legend. Over there, the cottage: That's where a druid once lived with his daughters. This is a magical place," Payton explained, reaching for one of the roses growing by the stone. Its smell no longer brought him joy, but he wanted to offer it to Sam.

"That's it! Yes, that could be it!" she called, grabbing his hand before he could prick his finger on the thorns.

Then she looked up with bright and knowing eyes as if she had just solved a mystery. "That must be it!" she cried, now running her own fingers over the soft petals. "I remember that I hurt myself on the roses. I pricked my finger, and it was bleeding. Do you think that could mean something?"

"We'll find out in a moment," Payton said, reaching for his dagger—but the leather sheath by his side was empty. "Where's my dagger?"

"I've got it." She pulled the dagger out from under her dress and solemnly handed it over. "You left it in my room."

He looked deep into Sam's expectant face, forced her up against the stone so that she was touching it with her body, and pulled the sharp blade across the palm of his hand.

"My life for you, *mo luaidh*!" He used the motto he and Kyle had shared all of their lives to say good-bye to the love of his life, and with closed eyes he pressed the flat of his hand against the cold stone.

He kept his eyes shut for fear of finding himself alone.

"Hmm, I don't think it's working!"

Sam's voice snapped him out of his paralyzed state. Relieved, if without feeling joy, he realized that she was still there. A selfish hope grew inside him. Perhaps she was now forced to stay with him forever.

"You're not bleeding," Sam said in astonishment, and Payton looked down at his hands. This was impossible! He had pulled the blade across his palm with all his strength. He'd felt the pain and the burning of the sharp metal, but his skin was completely unscathed.

Sam shrunk back, all color draining from her face, and Payton knew that she was thinking about the curse.

"Payton! I . . . I will stay with you, I can't leave you like this! You need me. Look what she's done to you!"

However much he had wanted to hear her say this *before* the curse, he could not allow it to happen now. With cruel honesty, he started to describe his dying feelings:

"Sam, I'm sorry, but you can't help me. I don't need your love because it no longer keeps me warm. Your kisses no longer reach my heart, and your very touch hurts my skin. I don't remember the feelings I once had for you, not even in the far reaches of my mind. I forgot what it was like to lie in your arms, and I don't remember how I fell in love with you. The man I was is no longer, but I do know that he'd want you to be safe. So go, please, because I cannot bear to be this close to you."

He spoke the truth, and I could tell from his eyes—he was begging me to let him go. I watched his face carefully, trying to memorize his beautiful features, wanting to kiss him one last time. But instead I quickly grabbed his hand that was still holding the dagger. I pulled the blade across the ball of my thumb in the same way I had seen him do and, hand bleeding, I reached for the marker stone.

"My love for you, *mo luaidh*!" I said, tweaking his motto just before pain started to flood my brain.

Bright!

Again I saw the familiar, all-consuming blaze of light.

I felt emptiness.

Except for this explosion of light burning through me, turning my skin white-hot, filling my heart with liquid fire, and pumping rays of dazzling light throughout my body. It plunged my mind into a brilliant, blinding pool of light.

I was falling. I felt my soul break away from my body. I felt both my soul and body aimlessly stumbling, and wandering. And then there was nothingness—no past, and no future. A pair of giant, burning wings carried me into a light-flooded abyss. And an icy fist tore me into individual strands of light.

I tried with all my might to think of the love that had brought me here, but my mind no longer existed.

Everything was so bright and radiant. No thought could penetrate this tidal wave of light, and no feeling was able to get through. Still, I tried to hold on to love, tried to align my burning self to it before the blinding brightness could shatter me to pieces. Finally, I burst under the light that exploded out of my body.

Chapter 36

Cemetery by Auld a´chruinn, Present-Day Fall

"*Bas maillaichte!*"

Sean was covered in cold sweat. He ripped open Payton's shirt, staring at his naked chest. As he placed the heel of his hand on Payton's breastbone in a desperate attempt to resuscitate him, he cursed Nathaira's name.

"I'll be damned if I allow you to take another brother away from me, you black-hearted witch!" he roared.

His tears fell on Payton's motionless chest as he tried to keep his brother's heart beating.

"If you leave me now, Payton, I'll—"

"You'll do what?" asked a shaky voice behind him.

Sean froze in his tracks, turned around slowly, and sank back on his heels. His voice was hoarse and shaky when he replied: "Well, Sam, then I swear I will kill him!"

Sean's face was wet with tears, and his red-rimmed eyes and Payton's lifeless body sucked the rest of my energy out of me. I sank into the wet, dead leaves on the cemetery ground.

I was alive! But even though I had found my way back, I had never felt so lost.

Sobbing, I threw myself into Sean's arms, but he pushed me away.

"Sam!" he yelled, wiping the tears from my face. "Tell me, Sam, can we save him? I know you were there, but did you also find a way to get Vanora's blood?"

I nodded and handed him the bag.

He yanked it out of my hands, frantically emptying its contents. When he reached for the leather-wrapped package, I stopped him.

"No, that's not it! There, that's the dagger Nathaira used to kill her mother. It is soaked in Vanora's blood," I explained, clutching the soft package against my chest.

He wrenched the dagger from its wrapping and gave me a puzzled look.

"This is it? What the—?"

"Yes, Sean! This is it! What do you think it was like, pulling that dagger from the witch's chest? Do you think it was pure pleasure? Would you have had a better idea? Vanora's blood: There it is! I repaid my debt. I've kept my goddamn promise!" I screamed, scrambling to my feet. "It's up to you now to save him! Make it count!"

It was all a bit much for me. I couldn't stay here a second longer. Nothing was as it should be, and my whole goddamn life was in shambles.

My guilt weighed heavily on me. So heavily that I couldn't face the music. Besides, the pain of leaving Past Payton was fresh and deep, and my heart was breaking. And Future Payton was perhaps dead. Why did love always have to hurt so much?

I walked farther and farther away from the two brothers while Sean pulled Nathaira's knife across Payton's chest. I saw that the cut wasn't deep, but the fresh blood gushing out still made me nauseated. With a final glance at the face that I loved so much, I turned around and broke into a run.

My breathing got easier with every step that took me farther away from the cemetery. Slowly, the terror and shock of time travel subsided. I no longer shivered from my dreadful journey back but because it was a cold, damp fall evening.

Thick fog swirled around the rocks by Loch Duich, and I walked right up to the lakeshore. When I was a child, I had always found it comforting to stick my feet in the water of the lake by our house. And so I slipped out of my well-worn sandals and dipped my toes in the ice-cold water.

Straight away, my mind cleared.

I loved Payton. Leaving him was the hardest thing I had ever done in my life. Still, I couldn't bring myself to go back to him, back to Future Payton. Because if Sean should manage to save his life, then I would have to own up to what I'd done and wouldn't be able to keep this terrible guilt to myself.

If I had only dared to tell him the truth sooner, I would have spared him a lot of pain and suffering. I would not make that mistake again, even if it meant losing his love.

And so apparently Nathaira had kept the upper hand. Our love had destroyed her plans. And now she was destroying us. Did she know this would happen when she let me go after that incident with Ross?

There was no answer to my questions, and so I just stared up at the sky whose dark evening blue was slowly turning to a soothing night black. Every star up on the firmament was in exactly the right spot. Why couldn't I find the right spot for me? Why did I always have to wander, never knowing where I belonged?

My feet were numb from the cold, and I sat up, folding my legs under me so they would warm up again. In doing so, I realized I still had that small package that was now sitting in my lap.

Tenderly, I touched the leather wrapping, following the leather band with my fingers. With a big fat lump in my throat I tore the band off the package and unfolded the wrapping.

My heart stopped. Just one look, and I couldn't believe it. Laughing and crying all at the same time, I unfolded the little note that accompanied the gift.

> *Sam,* mo luaidh,
>
> *You stumbled into my heart that night, and I realized how special you were before I ever found this. You don't belong here, you said—but nothing could be farther from the truth. You belong with me, no matter what happens. Don't leave me, for I'd rather die than be without you. Don't leave me, for I love you.*
>
> *But if you do, then do it because you love me, and then hold on to this. Because whatever you do, you are a part of me.*
>
> Mo luaidh, tha gràdh agam ort.
>
> *Payton*

With trembling fingers I held up his gift and pressed the soft fabric against my chest.

"It doesn't matter what you have done, or what I have done. Guilt and shame and hatred cannot overshadow the only thing I am left with. I haven't been able to forget about you, not ever since I watched you by the lake." I recalled his words silently in my mind.

Suddenly I knew where the right spot was for me, where I belonged. I bundled up the Black Eyed Peas T-shirt that he had returned to me, and ran barefoot back the way I had come. Tiny, pointy rocks dug into the soles of my feet, and with every little prick I found the way back to myself. The truth of who I really was washed all over me, and the strangeness of my experiences in the past faded into the background.

"Payton!" I yelled, praying that I wasn't too late, that I still had a chance.

Love flooded my entire being when I saw him sitting up, his face distorted in pain but with a smile on his lips. Without regard for Sean, who was offering him a cup of water, I fell to my knees by Payton's side and pushed Sean out of the way. I wanted to throw myself into his arms, but he looked so weak and sickly that I stopped.

"Thank God you're alive. The blood is helping! I was so stupid! I was so confused. Can you forgive me?" I sobbed incoherently.

"Sam, *mo luaidh!* It's not enough that I have had to wait for you for almost three hundred years and still almost died under Nathaira's wicked curse. And now this? You will have to get used to sitting by my side every time I cheat death, like a good wife! And now get over here!"

Tears streamed down my face as he pulled me into his arms and kissed me.

When he finally sank back, weak and exhausted, I grinned from ear to ear and ran my finger over the scar on his chin.

"Sorry about that," I whispered.

"Oh, this? No need to be sorry. This is nothing compared to the two hundred and seventy years I had to go without you! Now that I remember things, I realize how lost I really was during that time. I've missed you so much. Please, don't ever leave me again," he begged, and I could see the pain in his eyes.

I grabbed the dagger lying beside him, wrapped my fingers tightly around the blade, and looked him deep in the eye.

"Payton McLean, by my blood, I swear this oath to you: I will never leave you ever again. My life is yours."

Sean grinned a wide grin as he handed me the cup that was part of his thermos bottle. There was no wine in it, so water would have to do. I dipped the blood-covered tip of the *sgian dhu* in it and handed the cup to Payton. Then I wrapped my hand in the embroidered linen cloth Fingal had given to me two hundred seventy years prior. It was a family heirloom in a way.

"My life for you, milady," Payton replied, laughing, and he took a sip before pulling me close to his chest and kissing me deeply.

Characters

The McLean Clan:

Payton McLean: 19-year-old in love with Samantha Watts

Sean McLean: Payton's 25-year-old brother

Blair McLean: Payton's 27-year-old brother, McLean chieftain, Nathaira's fiancé

Kyle McLean: Payton's 16-year-old brother, who died in the Cameron massacre

Fingal McLean: Father of Payton, Blair, Sean, and Kyle

Nanny MacMillan: Wet nurse and healer

Kelsey: Girl in Kilerac attending the wedding celebration

Mistress MacQuarrie: Woman who helps Samantha take care of Fingal

Aline: Girl attending the wedding celebration, who tells Sean about the mercenaries

The Stuart Clan:

Cathal Stuart: 29-year-old chieftain of the Stuarts

Nathaira Stuart: Cathal's 27-year-old sister; Blair McLean's fiancée

Kenzie Stuart: Cathal and Nathaira's 17-year-old brother, who died in the Cameron massacre

Dougal Stuart: Cathal's half brother, Grant's son, Duncan's twin brother

Duncan Stuart: Cathal's half brother, Grant's son, Dougal's twin brother

Grant Stuart: Father of Cathal, Nathaira, Dougal, and Duncan

Ross Galbraith: Dougal and Duncan's half brother; not Grant's son

Alasdair Buchanan: Cathal's follower

The Cameron Clan:

Tomas Cameron: Isobel's husband; Muireall's father, who died in the massacre

Isobel Cameron: Muireall's mother; Payton was unable to save her

Muireall Cameron: Sole Cameron survivor of the massacre

The Watts Family:

Samantha Watts: 18-year-old high school student from Delaware, in love with Payton McLean

Lorraine Watts: Samantha Watts's mother
Kenneth Watts: Samantha Watts's father

Ashley Bennett: Samantha Watts's cousin from Illinois

Other Characters in the United States:

Dr. Lippert: One of Payton McLean's doctors
Dr. Frank Tillman: One of Payton McLean's doctors

Kim Fryer: Samantha Watts's best friend

Justin Summers: Kim Fryer's boyfriend

Ryan Baker: Heartthrob at Samantha Watts's high school

Lisa: Popular girl

Other Characters:

Alison and Roy Leary: Samantha's host parents in Aviemore, Scotland

Vanora: Powerful Fair Isle witch, Nathaira's mother

Brèagha-muir: Wise Woman on Fair Isle

Gaelic Glossary

A Dhia, thois cpbhair!
God be with us!

Amadáin!
Idiot! Moron!

An e 'n fhirinn a th' aquad?
Are you telling me the truth?

arisaid
a cloaklike garment worn to provide warmth, the large piece of square fabric being belted at the waist and fashioned over the shoulder or over the head as a hood

Bas maillaichte!
Bloody hell!

black bun
Scottish fruitcake

Ciamar a tha thu?
How are you?

Ciod tha uait?

What's wrong with you?

Cuimhnich air na daoine o'n d' thanig thu.

Remember those you are a descendant of.

Daingead!

Damn!

Fàilte.

Welcome.

Fan sàmhach!

Be quiet!

Ifrinn!

Devil! / Hell!

lass, lassie

Scottish for girl or young woman

Madain mhath.

Good morning.

m'athair / Athair!

my father / Father!

mince and tatties

Scottish dish made with ground beef and mashed potatoes

mo bailaich
my boy

mo bràthair
my brother

mo charaid
my friend

Mo còig nigheanan
Mora, Fia, Gillian, Robena, Alba
Gabh mo leisgeul
Tha gabh mi gradhaich a thu
My five daughters
Mora, Fia, Gillian, Robena, Alba
Forgive me
All my love for you

mo luaidh / Mo luaidh, tha gràdh agam ort.
my love, my darling / My darling, I love you.

Mòran taing!
Thank you!

Nighean na galladh!
Daughter of a dog!

Pog mo thon!
Kiss my ass!

Seas!
Halt! Stop!

sgian dhu
a small dagger, typically carried in the sock

Sguir!
Stop! Stop it!

Sguir, mo nighean. Tha gràdh ort.
Stop, my daughter. I love you.

Slàinte mhath!
Cheers! Good health!

Slan leat.
Good-bye.

sporran
fur pouch that was typically carried on the belt and on a chain

Tha mi duilich.
I am sorry.

Thoir an aire!
Take care!

About the Author

Photo: Guido Karp for www.p41d.com

Emily Bold, born in 1980, has already published a number of best-selling eBooks in Germany. She writes historical romance, and her novels are full of love, passion, and adventure. Emily also writes young adult fiction. The Curse series is her first to be translated into English, a big dream come true for Emily. Soon her historical novels will be available for English readers, too. Emily loves to get in touch with her fans. Leave your feedback on her blog or visit her on Facebook. And don't forget to check out her book trailer!

Find out more about The Curse at:
http://thecurse.de
https://www.facebook.com/TheCurseSeries

Find out more about the author at:
http://emilybold.de
http://www.facebook.com/emilybold.de
http://twitter.com/emily_bold
http://www.youtube.com/user/EmilyBoldTV

About the Translator

Katja Bell was born in Germany and has spent most of her life living, working, or studying in Europe and the United States. She recently completed the Applied Linguistics graduate program at Old Dominion University, Norfolk, Virginia, and now works as a freelance translator in small-town Germany, where she lives with her husband and assorted pets. Katja has been translating professionally since the age of twenty. Before *The Curse: Breath of Yesterday,* she translated several YA novels.